The
French Occupation
Trilogy:

The Sixth Man
The Woman on the Train
The White Venus

Rupert Colley

Rupert Colley was born one Christmas Day and grew up in Devon. A history graduate, he worked as a librarian in London before starting 'History In An Hour' – a series of non-fiction history ebooks that can be read in just sixty minutes, acquired by Harper Collins in 2011. He has also penned several works of historical fiction. Now a full time writer, speaker and the author of historical novels, he lives in Waltham Forest, London with his wife, two children and dog.

Works by Rupert Colley:

Fiction:

My Brother the Enemy   The Black Maria
The Sixth Man   Anastasia
The Unforgiving Sea   The White Venus
This Time Tomorrow   The Woman on the Train
The Red Oak

History In An Hour series:

1914: History In An Hour
Black History: History In An Hour
D-Day: History In An Hour
Hitler: History In An Hour
Mussolini: History In An Hour
Nazi Germany: History In An Hour
Stalin: History In An Hour
The Afghan Wars: History In An Hour
The Cold War: History In An Hour
The Russian Revolution: History In An Hour
The Siege of Leningrad: History In An Hour
World War One: History In An Hour
World War Two: History In An Hour

Other non-fiction:

The Savage Years: Tales From the 20th Century
A History of the World Cup: An Introduction
The Battle of the Somme: World War One's Bloodiest Battle
The Hungarian Revolution, 1956

Historical Note

On 10 May 1940, the armed forces of Nazi Germany invaded France, entering undefended Paris on 14 June. The Battle of France was effectively already won. Two days later, the 84-year-old Philippe Pétain was appointed prime minister. His first act was to seek an armistice with the Germans, which was duly signed on 22 June.

France was split into two; the north and west occupied by the Germans, while the south and east remained unoccupied. The unoccupied region was run by Pétain, now state president, who, together with his government, was based in the town of Vichy in central France. This situation lasted until 12 November 1942, when Hitler ordered the occupation of the whole country.

French people had to decide – whether to resist German occupation, collaborate, or in most cases, tolerate it and try to ignore it. Resistance included milder activities, such as pasting anti-German stickers on lampposts. The number of active resisters was minimal, although their numbers grew as the war progressed. Their work was co-ordinated, where possible, by General Charles de Gaulle, first from London, then from his base in Algiers.

On 6 June 1944, D-Day, Allied forces launched their invasion of Normandy and, from there, slowly pushed the Germans back. Paris was liberated on 25 August. By the end of September 1944, following four years under the yoke of Nazism, most of France was free.

The witch-hunt for those who had served the Vichy regime and their German masters began immediately.

The following three novels all mention the fictional town of Saint-Romain, a couple hours north-west of Paris.

The
Sixth Man

Historyinanhour.com

Rupertcolley.com

Table of Contents

Chapter 1:
July 1943

Lieutenant Lowitz unlocked the heavy door, pushing it open. 'Make yourself at home,' he said in perfect French, stepping to one side, grinning.

The six Frenchmen stepped into the room, each one gazing round, taking in their surroundings. The dank, rectangular room was large and low-ceilinged with an uneven cobblestone floor strewn with a thin layer of straw. Following them and the lieutenant, a German corporal, Schmidt, a rifle slung round his shoulder.

'Well, beats the bloody cells,' said one of the Frenchmen, a former soldier, his hands deep in his trouser pockets.

'It s-stinks,' said another, the former postman, a man with bovine eyes, stuttering, as he often did, on the 's'.

'A rose by any other name…' said the teacher, pushing his glasses up his nose.

The ex-policeman coughed. 'There's a small window at least,' he said. Outside, through the barred window, it was dark.

'I see we've got a mattress each,' observed the former doctor, stroking his moustache. 'Thank heavens for small mercies.'

'Well done, Sherlock,' said the soldier.

'Yeah, but... but look at 'em,' said the postman, pointing. 'They look like an elephant's s-slept on them.'

'Ah,' said the teacher. 'I knew an Indian prince once; owned so many elephants—'

'Wouldn't let me horse sleep on that,' said the soldier.

'*Et requiem capiti meo laboravi,*' muttered the doctor.

'What the hell's that meant to mean?' barked the soldier.

'It's Latin. *I rest my weary head.* My dear chap, you wouldn't understand.'

'Gentlemen, please,' said the lieutenant. 'Like I said, it's only for one night. There's a bucket in the corner for you. Someone will bring you water in a while.'

The German corporal stood guard at the door while the lieutenant, adjusting his cap, addressed his prisoners. 'So, tomorrow morning you will be released. Please make sure you're ready to leave at six sharp.' He glanced at his watch. 'It's now half eleven. So you have precisely six and a half hours.'

'What's to get ready?' asked the doctor. 'Can I have my tie back?'

'Can I have a shave before we go, Lieutenant?' asked the former policeman. 'I'd also like to look smart on my first day out.'

'What day is it?' asked the postman.

'Monday, you idiot,' said the soldier.

'God, I need a drink,' said the teacher. 'I knew an

admiral once; drank like a fish–'

'If I may continue,' said Lieutenant Lowitz. 'Your papers and any belongings you had will be returned to you. We'll be catching the seven o'clock train back to Saint-Romain. Your fares will have been paid. Never accuse the German authorities of not being generous.' He laughed but, noticing no one was laughing with him, felt slightly foolish. Clearing his throat, he continued, 'Yes, well... Once back in Saint-Romain, you'll be free to return to your homes. Hopefully, having spent six months here, you will realise that any attempt to undermine our authority is futile. We will not tolerate it.'

'Your *authority* means bugger all to us,' said the soldier to himself.

'You have something to say, Private?' asked the German.

'No, no,' said the priest quickly. 'He has nothing to say.'

'Hm. Well, keep your noses clean and we need never meet again. Any questions?'

'Will we get breakfast?' asked the teacher. 'After all, a man is half a man without breakfast.'

'Yes,' said the German. 'You will have breakfast.'

'Sausages and tomatoes for me,' said the soldier.

'And perhaps a little wine,' said the teacher. 'Can we place orders?'

'If you want, but you'll still get the usual bread and water.'

Father Claudel asked, 'Will you be escorting us on the train back, Lieutenant Lowitz?'

'Yes, I will be.' He nodded at the men. 'Well, if that's it, I shall leave you to it. I have things to attend to.' Corporal Schmidt, clicking his heels, held the door open for him.

'Goodnight, gentlemen. See you in the morning.'

The Frenchmen watched the two Germans leave, closing the heavy wooden door behind them, and listened as the key turned in its lock.

'It'll be nice not to have to hear that every night,' said the policeman. 'I'm used to locking people up, not the other way round. My Emily used to say–' Slapping his chest, he coughed, unable to finish his sentence.

'Let's not worry about that now, eh, Inspector?' said the doctor. 'There's a good man.'

The men shuffled around, each claiming one of the straw mattresses. There were three along one side, three opposite. Except for Béart, the soldier, they sat down, sighing, leaning against the grey-bricked walls. The soldier made use of the bucket in the corner, the sound of his piss echoing as it hit the metal.

'Just think,' said Béart, shouting over his shoulder, 'this time tomorrow we'll be free men, sleeping in our own bloody beds.'

Garnier, the teacher, snorted. 'As free as you can ever be with a curfew and the wretched Boche tripping you up and asking for your papers every five minutes. I knew a man once–'

'That's better,' said Béart, buttoning up his fly and taking his place on the last mattress.

After six months of incarceration, all six men were only vaguely aware of how filthy and stinking they were – their clothes and shoes, skin, fingernails – everything layered in grime. None had looked at himself in the mirror in all that time. Frankly, it was a blessing because they would have been shocked by what they saw: their hair, long and matted, like men marooned on a desert island, their complexions the colour of wax from the lack of fresh air. Their breaths smelt of decay. They'd all grown beards, although a couple had had ones previously. And naturally they had all lost weight, and having had their belts confiscated, their clothes now hung from them.

Each of them had, over the months, wondered how the Germans had known about their meeting. Someone somewhere had snitched on them, someone they'd trusted. But who? Their little resistance cell had to be the most spectacular failure since the start of the occupation. They had met just the once, drunk wine and gossiped. They hadn't even had the chance to *plan* anything, let alone *achieve* anything.

Father Claudel spoke, 'I think we should each say the first thing we're going to do on getting home.'

'Now, that's an idea,' said Garnier, the teacher. The men fell silent for a few moments, each considering their options. 'Why don't you start, Father?'

'You want me to go first? OK. Let me think…' Tall and stooped, with long, bony fingers, Father Jean-Paul Claudel had, until recently, maintained a degree of vanity, a trait left over from his younger, pre-church days. His hair, although now receding, had preserved its tawny brown colour and he was once considered a fine-looking man. But vanity, like so much else within the prison, had become a long-forgotten luxury. He'd been permitted to wear his cassock in prison, but of course, after six months, it looked worse for wear. He was a man frustrated with life. Had been for years. Just turned sixty years old, he'd been a priest for the best part of forty years and had once desperately wanted to become a bishop. He had been prepared to up sticks and move, if need be. But things hadn't worked out. They rarely do. All that dreadful business ten years back with that ruffian had undone all his plans and ambition. That dreadful boy. He shivered, preferring not to think about it.

'I know it's rather obvious for a man in my position but I will go to church and pray, to thank the Lord for our safe deliverance. I rather miss my church. For me, it's like a home; it's where I feel safe. I miss my congregation and I'd like to think they miss me.' He smiled at the thought. 'And I certainly miss God in this Godless place.'

'I thought God was everywhere,' said the soldier.

'He is, Private, he most certainly is. But still… What about you, Professor?'

'Me?' Gustave Garnier was a humble teacher but known ironically as 'Professor'; by his own admission not a particularly good one. French literature was his main subject, a connoisseur of nineteenth century French poetry plus a bit of Shakespeare. He wore an ash-brown jacket with elbow patches, now filthy after six month's wear, the patches lined with grease, and thick-rimmed brown glasses. He too was a man dissatisfied with his lot despite being young enough to do something about it. But, lacking ambition, he lacked motivation. Instead, until his incarceration, he was content to plod along, moaning about his job, his colleagues, the town and life generally, existing with the slight nagging feeling that at the age of thirty-two, life had already sucked him dry. If there was one thing he craved, beyond a drink that is, it was respect. His pupils liked him because he was a pushover and his colleagues thought him a fool. And of course, he'd recently lost his last vestiges of respect to a bloody art teacher, of all people. Removing his glasses, he shuddered at the memory. Sometimes, he rather fancied himself as a hero of the resistance – but he knew he hadn't the gumption. 'I shall go to my own sort of church,' he said with a smirk. 'One that serves beer. I've been dying for a drink from the moment I stepped into this awful place. One large, ice-cold beer, all frothy at the top. Condensation running down the glass.' He sighed. 'That's all I want. I'd give up all my fame for a pint of ale. That's from Hamlet, you know.'

'I'm too hungry to drink.' This was André Le Vau, the town's doctor until a few years back when he took early retirement. Well, he didn't really take early retirement; more a case of having been obliged to do so. Forced into it. He'd been quite the dashing doctor about town, admired and sought after. A long, prosperous career beckoned. A silver-haired man in his mid-fifties, he spoke with a gentle lilting Parisian accent and wore too many rings on his fingers than was considered right for a man. Known for never being seen without a collar and tie (although the former had gone almost black with dirt and the latter, along with the rings, had been another item confiscated by the Germans), he used to pride himself on having the smartest suit and the shiniest briefcase. A woman had been his downfall. Women are at the root of all man's failings. It was all his own fault, he knew that. He should've known better at his age. No fool like an old fool, as his mother used to say. 'I shall eat like a king – I've got the menu all planned out in my head.' He proceeded to describe his perfect meal, a variety of dishes that involved veal, mushrooms and dauphinoise potatoes, all the time fiddling with a ring that wasn't there any more. 'I shall be dressed as a gentleman, served by a buxom maid and finished off with strawberries and meringue and a dollop of fresh cream. *Quod esse perfectum*. That would be perfect.'

'Not asking for much then, Doctor,' said Roger Béart, the former soldier. 'I'd forgo the meal for the buxom maid bit. I shall go home, grab my missus by the hand, take her upstairs, throw her on the bed and…'

'Yes, yes, thank you, Private Béart,' said Father Claudel. 'Spare us the details.'

'Yeah, right. I need a woman, I do. Six months in this shithole, I'm getting desperate, I'm telling you.' Roger Béart, mid-forties, had fought with the French cavalry during the Great War, serving in the Palestinian desert. He still missed it, in a way. Not the heat and sun and sand but the camaraderie that only men in combat understand in its purest form. He missed the horses too. He knew others found him a bit rough round the edges but he cared not one jolt for what men said. Horses were his love. Always had been. He'd reminisce about horses he'd known and loved as others might pine a lost love. And that had been his downfall – putting the life of a horse ahead of a man's. He'd been a young man at war, barely twenty. He felt as if his whole life since was but an anti-climax. Such a long time ago but one didn't forget these things, try as one might. He'd worked in bars, on the farms and as a labourer, never able to settle to anything. He'd married young to a girl attracted by the uniform but little else. Once the uniform was gone, not much remained. But still, twenty-five years on, they were still together – just. Rubbing his crotch, he sniggered. 'A man has his needs, don't he?'

'Perhaps, but he doesn't always need to voice them,' said the priest.

'You wanted to know.'

Turning to his left, the priest asked, 'What about you, Inspector?'

The former policeman, Nicholas Leconte, a gaunt man with a handlebar moustache, smiled wistfully. 'I'd want my wife but since that's impossible, I want my garden.'

'Your garden?' said Doctor Le Vau. 'Strange thing to hanker for.'

'Since I retired and after Emily died, I spend all my time in my garden, well, I did until… you know, the Boche put my life on hold.' He drummed his fingers on his kneecap. Leconte, respected and appreciated, had also fought in the war but in 1917 his involvement had been cut short by the effects of a gas attack. Instead, he swapped uniforms and joined the police. A quarter of a century on, he still occasionally coughed his guts up and still occasionally had nightmares of flailing in the fog of poisonous gas, waking up with his hand over his mouth, wanting to vomit. He married, had three children, who, one by one, had left home. His eldest son, Robert, had been killed three years back, fighting the Germans. His wife had died of a broken heart soon after. People assumed he'd retired because of his grief. It had nothing to do with his wife's death. No, it was that Jew, damn him. When he went to bed at night, it wasn't his wife he thought of, it was the Jew.

'And what would you want to do in your garden, Inspector?' asked the priest.

'After all this time? It'll need a good clear up, a whole lot of weeding and cutting back. Plenty to keep me busy.'

'That leaves just me,' said the man nearest the door, Henri Moreau, a young postman, a short, once stocky man. Half a year in prison had finally rid him of his excess weight. He had also lost his wife and child, although he couldn't be sure they were *both* dead. His Jewish wife, Liliane, and their daughter had been rounded-up and deported. He'd done everything to save them. Everything. There was nothing else he could have done. He just hoped if he said it often enough he'd come to believe it.

'Go on, then, tell us,' urged the policeman.

'All I want is to go home, have a deep, deep bath and s-shave, and get rid of this layer of filth and the s-smell. We forget how much we s-stink – all of us. I hate feeling this dirty. Then I would worry about everything else. But I can't do anything until I feel clean again.'

'Well, gentlemen,' said the priest, 'we all have our different desires, some a little more basic than others, and in just a few hours we may all get to fulfil them. That is what I shall pray for,' he added, crossing himself.

'Yes, assuming the Boche don't double cross us in some way,' said the doctor, jerking his thumb towards the door.

The policeman raised his eyebrows. 'In what way, Doctor?'

'Never trust a German, old man, that's what I always say.'

The soldier nodded in agreement. 'The only bloody German you can trust is a dead one.'

'And you'd know,' said the doctor.

'What's that meant to mean?'

'Nothing, dear man, nothing, Keep your hair on. Just saying, because I know you were in the war.'

'Wrong enemy, you know that. I fought the bloody Turks.'

10

'Oh, not the bloody Germans, then?' said the doctor with a grin.

'No, I told you. The Turks. Bloody slippery lot, I can tell you.'

The six men leant back against the walls. They were tired. Doing nothing all day, every day, was a tiresome business. The policeman began humming a little tune, tapping his fingers against his knee as if playing the piano, the teacher watching him, his thoughts far away. The priest and the soldier closed their eyes. The doctor, sitting upright, picked at a scab on his ankle while the postman twisted a piece of straw round his finger.

Six months. To each of them it had felt like six years. They wondered what the world would be like outside – whether life had become more tolerable living under German occupation, whether they'd be welcomed back as heroes or failures. The idea of feeling the wind in their hair, of feeling the warmth of the sun for more than just a few minutes per day, seemed blissful. The forgotten pleasure of life – of seeing people going about their everyday business, of seeing kids playing in the village square, of hearing birds singing in the trees, of hearing dogs barking, the smell of freshly-baked bread, the smell of the hedgerows, of all the small, routine things one took for granted. For the first time in six months they felt able to relax. Yes, the low-ceilinged room was dank and dark, the place stank, the mattresses dirty, there were bugs and insects, and a bucket of piss in the corner, but there was light now at the end of their tunnel, an end in sight. Just a few hours to endure. Six small hours between now and freedom.

Chapter 2

The time was approaching midnight. A German private had brought them their water. The six Frenchmen had settled on their mattresses, ignoring the scratchy, rough surface, ignoring various insects and rodents scuttling around, and fallen asleep. They slept well, still in their clothes, comfortable in the knowledge that they were only hours from freedom. The air inside was muggy, the low ceiling and the warmth of the night outside making for a claustrophobic environment. The piss bucket in the corner was already half-full.

Having discussed the first thing they'd do on release, they fell asleep imagining their various scenarios. Father Jean-Paul Claudel, dreaming of his church, fell asleep, as he did every night, with a prayer and hoped that the boy, not such a ruffian, would hear him and find it in himself to forgive him. Gustave Garnier, the teacher, conscious of the dryness in his throat, imagined a pretty young woman pouring him his first icy cold beer. He would toast the art teacher, who, on reflection, wasn't such a bastard, and wish him well. Dr André Le Vau's mouth salivated as he savoured the thought of cutting into a mushroom roulade, even though he knew such delicacies were nigh-on impossible to find during wartime. Surely, he thought, even lovelorn fools were allowed the occasional luxury. Roger Béart, the former soldier, went to sleep with an erection, dreaming of making his wife scream. But, instead of hearing his wife, his head was filled with the sound of a horse screaming in terrible pain. Nicholas Leconte, the ex-policeman, dreamt of taking his dead wife's hand and presenting her with a bunch of roses, freshly plucked from his well-managed garden. Instead, he found himself handing them to the Jew, his head bowed with contrition. Henri Moreau, the postman, dreamt of wallowing in a deep, hot bath with bubbles everywhere. But no amount of hot water and soap would scrub away the ingrained sense of shame that had scoured his soul.

France, their once proud and great nation, had been living under German occupation for over three years now. Even before their incarceration, the six men knew things were changing. The Germans of three years ago had gone. Looking back on those early years, the Boche had been polite, keen to show who was in charge but in such a way as to win over the French. Apart from dealing with the occasional and usually ineffectual act of sabotage, these men realised they had an easy ticket, a holiday posting. But once Hitler had invaded Russia, the Germans here knew they were on borrowed time and they all lived in terror lest they be posted to the Eastern Front. And sure enough, division by division, they were. And those that took their place had seen action in Poland or Russia or North Africa. These were hardened men, hardened to the realities of war at its most relentless, hardened to killing and dying. Now, in mid-summer forty-three, the war was going against them – and they knew it. The Germans had suffered and lost at Stalingrad, the Red Army was fighting back; the useless Italians were caving in. All this served only to make the Germans uppity and nervous.

The priest, the teacher, the doctor, the soldier, the policeman and the postman. All were fast asleep. None heard the approach of footsteps on the stone floor in the corridor outside. None heard the turning of the key in the heavy wooden door. None heard the door creak open, nor the soft tread of leather boots entering the room. None saw the dim shaft of light from the corridor. It was perhaps the priest who first half-opened his eyes, vaguely aware of a dark figure nearby, the reality merging with his dreams. Grimacing, he covered his eyes. 'No, no, do not enter this house,' he mumbled. 'Satan, back to hell with you.'

The Devil-like figure tapped a well-polished shoe.

'What… what's going on?' This was the postman, aware of the priest muttering next to him.

'Who's that?' called out the doctor, immediately awake.

The teacher adjusted his glasses.

Soon all six were awake, rubbing their eyes, sitting up, their backs pressed against the wall behind them, eyeing the figure standing near the door.

'Who… who are you?' asked the postman, unable to disguise the tremor of apprehension in his voice.

The men blinked as their eyes focussed.

'Good evening, gentlemen,' said the figure. The man in front of them was a German officer, wearing the grey-green uniform of the Wehrmacht, a large cap, braided over the peak, the German eagle on its front, oak leaves on his collar, a gold swastika on his top button, a row of medal ribbons, black leather gloves.

Looking at each of them in turn, he removed his cap, exposing a full head of neatly-combed strawberry-blond hair. 'My name is Colonel Geist,' he said in French with a deep, measured German accent. He was about fifty years old, clean-shaven, with defined cheekbones, distinguished by a raw scar shaped like a bolt of lightning across the right side of his jaw. He had bright, piercing sapphire-blue eyes that made the priest shudder. He'd never seen eyes like that before.

'I am sorry for disturbing your night's sleep but I have come to tell you there has been a change of plan.'

'Change of plan?' repeated the doctor, trying to get to his feet. 'What on earth…'

Colonel Geist put his hand out. 'Please, Dr Le Vau, stay seated. I won't take up too much of your time.'

The doctor sat back down and watched as the colonel slowly paced to the far end of the cell, his gloved hands holding his cap behind his back. On reaching the end, he turned. If he noticed the stench from the piss bucket, he made no sign of it. He paced back to the door, turned again and faced the men.

'I spoke to Lieutenant Lowitz. He informed me you six men are here in what he calls the holding cell, and that at six tomorrow morning, you are to be escorted to the station to catch a train back to your town. You have completed your sentence, and he trusts that you will present no further problem for the German authorities here. However, I come as the bearer of bad news.'

'Bad news?' asked the teacher, his eyes almost popping

out of his head.

'What do you mean, Colonel?' asked the priest.

'There has been a development, Father Claudel.'

Leconte, the policeman coughed, the imaginary taste of chlorine gas on his tongue. 'A development?' he spluttered, unable to hide the note of incredulity in his voice.

With a raised finger, the colonel continued. 'I will explain, Inspector Leconte. At seven twenty-two this morning, a German train passing through on the line to Saint-Romain was blown-up. It was, alas, a highly efficient operation. The train was derailed, the line buckled beyond use. Many troops were hurt. Five were killed. Five!' He paused, looking intently at each of the men in turn, his features hardening. 'Also, an equal number of Frenchmen were killed. They were caught in the blast; they would have died instantly. Plus many more injured – one of them lost both his legs.'

The priest's hand went to his mouth. '*Both* his legs? Oh my, poor fellow, both his legs.'

'He may live; he may not. It depends.'

The others watched as the priest crossed himself. 'Colonel Geist, would you know the names of the five Frenchmen who died?'

'No, and I have no interest in them whatsoever. They are of no consequence.'

'But, Colonel…'

'Silence. I'm more concerned about the five young men doing their duty for the Führer, five sons of the Fatherland.'

The soldier laughed. 'Ha, better to die here than somewhere like bloody Stalingrad–'

'I said silence! You will not trivialise the barbaric killing of five of my most able men, Private Béart.' He paced forward again, before turning and resuming. 'We will find the culprits and they will pay. Mark my words.'

The priest cleared his throat.

'Yes, what is it, Father?'

'We're sorry to hear of your misfortune, Colonel Geist. But… if I may ask, what has this to do with us?'

'Indeed,' said the policeman. 'You can hardly suspect us. We've all got the perfect alibi.' He laughed feebly.

'Five young men were killed,' said the colonel, now speaking quickly. 'The news has got round already. There'll be much celebration amongst the baser elements of your community. The culprits will have made their escape. They will be caught but it might take a while. Meanwhile, it is essential that no one is encouraged to mimic their deeds, even in the most minor way. There must be no repetition. Everyone must see that such actions will be dealt with in the harshest way possible.'

'You mean… r-reprisals?' asked the postman nervously.

'Yes, exactly, Monsieur Moreau; there must be reprisals. Severe reprisals. Otherwise, how will you people learn? And this, gentlemen, is where you come in. Five German soldiers were killed. Five of you will die as a result.'

All six men stared at the colonel in stunned silence as the enormity of his words sunk in.

The colonel waited while the six men absorbed what he said. They were all on their feet now, panic etched on their drawn, dirty faces.

The priest stepped forward.

'Stay back, please, Father.'

The priest did as told, stepping back. 'Five of us?'

'I know,' said the colonel. 'The usual practice is to

17

execute ten of yours for each one of ours, so I know you'll be grateful for this relative show of mercy.'

'Isn't the death of those Frenchmen enough?' asked the policeman.

'Certainly not, Inspector. Their deaths were unforeseen; they will not act as deterrents. Therefore, five of you will be executed by firing squad tomorrow morning at six fifteen.'

The six Frenchmen looked at each other. Again, it was the priest who spoke for them all. 'There are six of us, Colonel. You have to tell us – which one of us will be granted his life?'

The colonel took a deep breath. 'You decide.'

'Me?' said the priest, jabbing himself in the chest.

'No, not you individually, but all of you.'

'All of us?'

'Between you, you have to decide which one of you should live – and which five should die.'

'But… but…'

'That's bloody ridiculous,' said the soldier. 'How do we do that?'

'I do not know,' said the colonel. 'It is not my concern. How you decide is entirely up to you.'

'But, Colonel…'

'Yes, Dr Le Vau?'

'I must protest; this is monstrous. You cannot possibly imagine that we will decide on such a thing.'

The teacher slapped his hands together. 'He's right. We won't do it. We refuse.'

The colonel sighed, running his finger along his scar. 'It's your choice, Monsieur Garnier. You have to decide. If you won't, or are unable to, then you will all be executed.

At least this way, one of you will live.' Fishing inside his tunic, he pulled out a silver watch chain. 'It's quite simple. I shall leave you to it.'

'Bu... but wait...' stuttered the postman.

'Yes, Monsieur Moreau? Is there anything else?'

'I... I mean, we can't... How long have we got?'

'As I said, the executions will be carried out at precisely six fifteen. The five men due to be executed will be collected at exactly six. They will be accompanied by a priest. The other will be escorted home. It is now midnight. Here... listen.'

The men listened but to what they didn't know. The teacher opened his mouth. The colonel, seeing he was about to speak, put up his hand. The teacher closed his mouth.

From outside they heard a church clock strike the hour. They remained silent as the last peal faded into the night.

'You have exactly six hours.'

'But surely, Colonel Geist...'

'I'm sorry, Father, but there is nothing else to add. This is the way it has to be; nothing you say can change this.'

The priest shook his head.

Replacing his cap, the colonel said, 'I bid you well in your deliberations, gentlemen. Good night.'

The six Frenchmen watched silently as he opened and closed the door behind him, plunging them back into near darkness, only the faint moonlight shining through the barred window. They listened as he turned the key in the door, listened as his footsteps disappeared down the corridor outside.

Only then did they turn to face each other.

Chapter 3

'This cannot… It cannot be true.' The postman paced to the far end of the room and back.

'Well, I'll tell you one thing for now,' said the soldier. 'I'm not bloody dying in front of no German firing squad.'

'Oh, so that's what you've decided then,' said the doctor. 'Well, that's good to know. *Quod est*. That is that. Pleased we got that over and done with; we can all go back to bed now.'

'Gentlemen, we must maintain our composure,' said the priest.

'Composure?' screeched the postman. 'We've all got a five in s-six chance of being dead in a few hours and he talks about composure. I've got to get out of here, for Christ's s-sake, I've got to find my wife and me daughter.'

'Yes,' said the policeman, thumping his chest to prevent a coughing fit. 'And I have to tend my dear Emily's grave. It'll be so overgrown by now.'

The teacher leapt towards the door. 'We'll break out,' he screamed, pushing against the door. 'If we all push together…'

'Don't be daft,' said the soldier. 'The door's solid. Look at that lock. You'd need a bloody stick of dynamite for that.'

'So what do we do?' said the teacher, removing his glasses. 'What do we do, for Christ's sake?'

'Calm yourself down, for one thing,' said the policeman, sitting back down on his mattress.

'I wonder who the five Frenchmen were,' said the postman. 'We probably know them. I deliver to everyone.'

'Or the poor soul who lost both his legs,' added the priest.

'It's too awful,' said the doctor. 'Too awful.'

'This is what we'll do, men,' said the policeman.

The others realised he was holding in his hand a clutch of straws.

'You can't mean that,' said the postman. 'You want to decide our fate by drawing s-straws?'

Returning to his feet, the doctor said, 'He's right though. What else do you suggest, dear chap? Musical chairs?'

The soldier sniggered. 'Musical mattresses.'

'It's the only way,' said the policeman. 'It's fair, it's simple and it's quick.'

'Too quick – that's the problem,' said the teacher. 'We can't decide our fates by something so basic. I knew a judge once–'

'So what do you suggest, Professor?'

'I… I don't know,' he said, pushing his glasses up his nose.

'I know,' said the postman. 'We'll draw the s-straws – but not now. All of those who lose will have hours to ponder their fate. Best do it at the last minute.'

'By G-god, P-postie's right,' said the soldier, mimicking the postman's stutter. 'Two minutes to six.'

'That sounds good to me,' said the doctor. 'Are we all agreed?'

There were nods all round.

'So what do we do now?' asked the teacher.

'Go back to sleep,' said the policeman.

'Go back to s-sleep? Probably our last night on earth, and you s-say go back to sleep.'

'What else would you have us do, dear chap?' asked the doctor. 'Play "I Spy"?'

'No, but… I don't know.'

In silence, the men paced up and down, their eyes fixed on the ground, kicking at clumps of straw and loose bits of stone. Only the priest sat down on his mattress, leaning against the wall, his head in his hands. For five minutes the others continued their pacing. They stopped on hearing the church clock strike once. They looked up at the window as if they could see the church spire from there.

'Is that one o'clock, or half twelve?' asked the teacher.

'Half twelve, I think,' said the doctor.

'Christ almighty, another five and a half hours to go,' said the soldier.

The men resumed their pacing. The policeman, his hands on his chest, coughed. The soldier spat onto the straw while the postman pulled on his beard.

It was the priest, still sitting on his straw mattress, who finally broke the silence. 'I have an idea, gentlemen.'

The men stopped as one. 'You do?' asked the postman and the policeman in unison.

With some difficulty, the priest rose to his feet, aided

by the doctor. 'Thank you, André,' he said, wiping the dust from his cassock. 'You will know, I'm sure, the story of Saint Peter at the Gates of Heaven. Jesus, according to the Gospel of Saint Matthew, tells Peter, "I shall give you the keys of the Kingdom of Heaven, and whatever you bind on Earth shall be bound in Heaven, and whatever you loose on Earth shall be loosed in Heaven".'

'What's that supposed to mean then?' asked the soldier.

'You idiot,' said the policeman. 'It means once you're up there, Saint Peter looks at your record, and if you've been good on Earth, you'll get into Heaven, and if you ain't…'

'You go down there,' added the postman, pointing at the floor. 'Down, down, down.'

'So what I propose,' said the priest, 'is our own version.'

'What?'

'Hear me out, Professor.' Clearing his throat, he continued. 'We each have done good things in our lives, we have each contributed to the wellbeing of our fellow citizens, to the community. We won't want to talk about the bad things because, men being men, we might not be entirely truthful. This is understandable. Yet I propose we each confess our greatest sin. In the eyes of God, this being each man's last confession, forgiveness will be granted only to the ones who speak the truth – regardless how painful that may be. When done, he who has committed the lesser sin shall live.'

'Why should we be honest, then?' asked the teacher.

'It'll be your last confession, Professor. God will be listening and you will need His forgiveness before you meet Him, be that in six hours or six years.'

It took a while before anyone spoke as the five men exchanged glances. Finally, clearing his throat, the policeman asked, 'And how do we judge, Father?'

'God will judge. Having listened to everyone, we will each cast a vote on who we think deserves to live, and God will guide us in our deliberations. The five people with the least votes, well… There you have it.'

'Bloody ridiculous,' said the soldier. 'Excuse my language, Father, but that's… it doesn't seem right.'

'And drawing straws at two minutes to six is?' asked the doctor.

'He's right, it's not a bad idea,' said the teacher.

'No, but… but hang on a minute,' said the soldier. 'It was my job to kill; to be ruthless.'

'In a good cause, Private Béart,' said the priest.

'Exactly,' said the teacher. '*Sine qua non.*'

'Meaning?'

'Meaning, old man, it was essential to your job.'

'As long as you all recognise that.'

'What does everyone think?' asked the priest.

The men fell silent for a few moments. Some resumed their pacing.

'I'd rather draw s-straws,' said the postman quietly.

'Dear chap, you won't be saying that after you've drawn a short one,' said the doctor.

'And talking will help pass the time away,' added the policeman. 'We're all as good as dead anyway, so why not?'

The soldier shrugged his shoulders. 'Fine by me.'

'We'll put it to the vote,' said the doctor. 'Blessed Germans may have stolen our democracy but it doesn't mean we can't use it ourselves.'

The six men looked at each other. One by one they

nodded their agreement.

'Right,' said the doctor. 'Those in favour of Father Claudel's suggestion, say "aye".'

All but one said "aye".

'Looks like you're outvoted, Roger,' said the teacher.

The soldier spun away. 'It's unfair.'

The doctor patted him on the back. 'Come on, Roger, my dear man. You can do it. You have as much chance as anyone else.'

'So, who should go first, Father?' asked the teacher.

'Ah, for that, perhaps we should use the straw,' said Father Claudel.

The priest scooped up six strands of straw from the stone floor and snapped one in half. Circled round the priest's mattress, they one by one took a straw, each one relieved that their lives did not depend on so simple an act.

It was André Le Vau, the doctor, who drew the first short straw.

Chapter 4:
The Doctor's Story

'What, you want me to stand?' asked the doctor.

'Why not?' said the teacher.

'I'm not performing.'

'In some ways you are,' said the priest. 'We all are – performing for our lives.'

'All right, old man, if I must.' The doctor rose wearily to his feet. 'So,' he said, facing his audience, 'you want me to justify my existence by confessing the worst thing I've ever done, that sort of thing and hope it's not as bad as anyone's else.'

'Something like that,' said the policeman.

'Let's put it more bluntly,' said the priest. 'Why is *your* life more worthy than ours?'

As a doctor, André Le Vau had difficulty recounting tales of his misdeeds, after all, his job was to heal and do good. He confessed to the occasional misdiagnosis, a mix-up of prescriptions, nothing too damning. He'd worked in a small practice in town – just him and Dr Lenoir, his partner. Then, in the autumn of 1939, just after the war had broken out, he'd taken early retirement. It was, he admitted, rather sudden and left Dr Lenoir in a bit of a fix until he managed to find a replacement. Lenoir, furious with him, hadn't spoken to him since. And that was his final confession.

'It isn't quite though, is it, Doctor?' said Garnier, the teacher.

The doctor, his face flushed, spun round. 'What? What did you say?'

'You retired, you say? I heard something different.'

'What did you hear? It's not true.'

Garnier sighed. 'My sister was a patient of your Dr Lenoir. She put in a complaint 'cos she could never get an appointment. Dr Lenoir explained himself and apologised. He told her straight – it was because, he said, he had to find a new partner. He was angry, my sister said, I mean really angry. Dr Lenoir said his ex-partner had let him down. He was upset so he told her everything. Something about a woman. What was her name? Claudia. That was it – Claudia something.'

The doctor felt rather weak all of a sudden. Needing to sit, he lurched over to his mattress.

Claudia Aubert. He never thought he'd hear that name again.

'Doctor?' said the soldier. 'Got something else you need to tell us?'

'No.'

The priest spoke, 'Remember, André, God is listening. You have to confess all.'

Unwittingly, the doctor glanced upwards. Rubbing his eyes, he said, 'OK, OK, have it your way.'

* * *

Dr Andre Le Vau and his lawyer friend, Jean Cassel, were enjoying a drink in the Wild Boar bar. They were both of a similar age, in their mid-forties, and both successful in their respective fields. They liked to meet every couple of months or so, always the Wild Boar, and drink and congratulate themselves on their success. The tavern with its subdued lighting, its wooden beams and log fire and record player playing American swing was warm and welcoming. They sat at the bar, nestled on high stools, each with a drink, Le Vau with his cigarette, Cassel drawing on his cigar. Tonight, approaching Christmas 1936, they talked mainly about women, as they often did. Like Le Vau, Cassel had never married, and the doctor found him a little too obvious in his eyeing up of the opposite sex but never said anything.

'So, come on, André, what about it?' said Cassel, peering at his cigar. 'You're not a bad-looking chap, you're solvent, reasonably intelligent–'

'Thanks very much.'

'Seriously, there must be someone on the horizon.'

'No. I wish I could say to the contrary, but no. I've left it too late, I know that.'

'Pah, it's never too late.'

Cassel himself was undeniably good-looking, a leonine figure, tall and thin with long sideburns and greased-back hair, never seen without a three-piece suit; he was quite the dapper lawyer around town. 'Listen, what are you doing for Christmas? I insist you come round to my parents' with me. My mother, bless her, is already preparing. We've got the tree, the presents, and even the goose is on order. It'll be just great.'

Le Vau nodded. 'Sounds divine, but I wouldn't want to impose.'

'"Wouldn't want to impose." Listen to yourself, André! That's your problem, never wanting to impose, never wanting to be any trouble. Life's not gonna wait for you to stand by, being all proper and polite, while every other bugger steals a march on you. Go out there, grab life by the balls, mate. You and I, we're not getting any younger, you know.'

'I know, Jean, I know. You're right, I know you are.'

'Hey, Marie,' shouted Cassel over the bar to the young barmaid with heavily rouged lips. 'I was just saying to my doctor friend here, you've got to grab life by the balls. That's right, isn't it?'

Polishing a glass, she giggled. 'That's my philosophy exactly,' she said with a wink.

An hour later, the two men stepped outside, ready to go home. 'My word, it's snowing,' said Cassel, doing up the top button on his gabardine coat. 'Could be a white Christmas.'

The two men walked down the street, still lots of people about, a thin coating of snow forming on the ground. The light from the street lamps added to the festive atmosphere. They were approaching the fork in the street where the two men separated to go their own ways. 'Well, it's been great catching up with you again,' said Cassel.

Le Vau was dimly aware of two women walking past, arm-in-arm, dressed in long black coats with hoods, but, talking to Cassel, took no more notice. 'And you, Jean.'

'Let me know about Christmas. It'll be fun, lots to eat, lots to drink, usual stuff.'

'Yes, I'll – hey, that woman's dropped something.'

'Where? You'd better catch up with her.'

It was an envelope, damp already from snowflakes. Scooping it up from the ground, Le Vau ran after the two women. 'Excuse me! Excuse me, ladies.' The women turned round. 'I think one of you may have dropped this.'

The woman on the right, the taller one, put her hand in her coat pocket. 'Oh my, it's mine.' She reached forward to take the envelope and in doing so stepped into the light of a street lamp. It was then, holding out the envelope, that Le Vau saw her face. It took his breath away – she was beautiful. Pale, flawless skin, sparkling blue eyes, petite nose, perfect lips; wisps of blonde hair peeking out from beneath her hood. 'How silly of me. Thank you,' she said in a voice as gentle as lilies floating on a lake.

'It's a… a pleasure.' He realised that in his trance he hadn't let go of the envelope. 'S-sorry,' he blurted.

She smiled and something within him melted.

'Thank you,' she said again. 'Merry Christmas to you.'

And then, re-joining her friend, linking arms, she walked away, their footsteps visible in the slushy snow.

He returned to Cassel, his heart fluttering like that of a teenager, feeling as if his feet were floating above the ground. He found Cassel lighting a cigar. He almost said something but stopped himself just in time. His friend would only say something lewd, and he didn't want to hear that. He'd fallen in love with a woman he'd seen for but a few moments and would never see again. But in love he was and he didn't want the moment to be tarnished in any way.

*

It was about five months later, a Tuesday morning in May 1937. Doctor Le Vau was, as usual, in his surgery, seeing to an endless number of patients with their usual ailments and complaints. Late morning, while the surgery closed for a few hours, the doctor and his partner, Dr Lenoir, would split the home visits between them and set forth. On this particular day, Dr Le Vau had a list of five appointments drawn up for him by the surgery's receptionist. If he was quick, and he usually was, he'd be done in time to enjoy a hearty lunch at the café over the road from the practice. His last call was one Madame Aubert, an unfamiliar name – certainly not one of his regulars, who lived in the most salubrious part of the area, a short tram ride away. Walking down the avenue, lined with trees, well-built houses either side, he breathed in the spring air and reckoned if he was no more than five minutes, he could have a full hour for lunch before surgery re-opened for the afternoon shift. The Auberts lived in a fine limestone townhouse, three stories high, a balcony, lanterns either side of the front door. He jogged up the front steps and pulled on the brass ringer. Immediately, he heard quick footsteps from within. The door opened.

'Hello, I'm Doctor... Oh, my...' His mouth gaped open – it was her, the woman he'd seen in the street.

'It's my mother, Doctor. We've been expecting you.' She was even more beautiful than he remembered – long, flowing blonde hair, those eyes. She wore a flowery summer dress, tight round the waist, accentuating her figure. 'Well, do come in.'

'Yes, of course, I'm sorry.'

He followed her in, into the marbled-floor hallway with a potted plant in one corner next to a telephone table and landscape paintings hanging from the walls. The place was undoubtedly luxurious, thought the doctor, if slightly soulless. Certainly no children ever stepped foot within this house. He followed her up a winding staircase, breathing in her scent. 'She took to her bed last night feeling quite unwell, and… well, I don't understand what's wrong with her, but I'm worried, Doctor. I simply had to call you. I hope you don't mind…'

'No, no, of course not.'

She led him into a bedroom, the sunlight piercing the muslin curtains, a bright red rug on a wooden floor. And there, lying in the middle of a four-poster double bed, was the mother, a grey-haired woman, probably in her late sixties, with a thin, tight face, her eyes half-closed. The room smelt stale.

'Maman?' said the daughter, taking her hand. 'Maman, the doctor's here.' Propped up on a number of pillows, Madame Aubert wore a nightdress buttoned to the top.

'Has she had anything to eat?' he asked, knowing straight away that the woman had suffered a minor stroke.

'No, and only a sip of water to drink.' She stepped away, allowing the doctor access to his patient. 'I had to help her to the lavatory. I hope I never have to do that again,' she added quietly.

'Madame Aubert,' he said, addressing the mother. 'My name is Dr Le Vau. I understand you're not feeling yourself today?'

'Not good.' Her words were slurred; one side of her face seemed to have dropped.

He did the usual checks – pulse, blood pressure and temperature, aware of the daughter's presence a few feet behind. 'What day is it, Madame?'

She placed her rheumatic fingers on her neck. 'Monday?' came the slurred response. 'No, Thursday. I don't know.' Yes, she was confused. Further questions confirmed it.

'My mother doesn't usually talk like this,' said the daughter quietly. 'She's usually rather… how should I put this… cantankerous.' She said the word in a whisper.

'I see.' Turning to her, he asked, 'I'm sorry, I didn't catch your name…'

She smiled briefly. 'Claudia,' she said, offering her hand.

He took it, feeling the warm softness of her touch. 'Claudia, your mother has had…' God, she was beautiful.

'Yes, Doctor?'

Concentrate, he thought, concentrate.

'Has had what we call a cerebral vascular accident, more commonly known as a stroke but…'

'Really?' she said. For a fraction of a second, she looked elated. No, he thought, he'd imagined it, he must have. 'That's… that's bad news, isn't it, Doctor?'

Suppressing his slight sense of unease, he put on his reassuring face, head tilted to one side. 'It can be but not in your mother's case – it's a very minor stroke.'

'I see. Should… should she go to hospital?'

'Usually, yes. But it's so minor that it won't be necessary. I can prescribe a course of medicine – something to help thin the blood. She'll need lots of water and of course a lot of rest.' Turning back to the mother, he added. 'You'll need to stay in bed for a few days, Madame

Aubert. But we'll soon have you up and about again. In no time, you'll be right as rain; you'll see.'

The woman mouthed a thank you.

Sitting down at a writing table tucked in the corner, he wrote out a prescription.

'I'll come back this time tomorrow to check on her,' he said, as Claudia showed him out. 'Would that be convenient?'

'Yes, of course. I'll be here.'

Stroking his moustache, he wanted to ask whether there was anyone else in the house, her husband, for example, but not wanting to sound impertinent, stopped himself in time.

The afternoon passed in a haze. She was as wondrous and beautiful as he'd remembered. After bumping into her in the street, back at Christmas, he'd thought of her often, saddened by the thought of never seeing her again. And now, five months later, he was to be very much part of her life – if only for a few days. She remained in his thoughts constantly as he saw to his afternoon patients, full of happy anticipation of being able to see her again. That evening, he fell asleep in his armchair dreaming of her, inventing little scenarios in which he asked her out – an evening at the theatre, a walk in the woods, a boating trip on a hot summer's day. Claudia. He repeated her name time and again, rolling it around his tongue, as if tasting something exciting and new. Claudia Aubert, Claudia Le Vau...

The first thing he did the following day, the Wednesday, was to tell the receptionist of his plan to visit Madame Aubert. He found himself dismissing his morning patients as quickly as possible, conscious of the need to remain civil and professional but without his usual relaxed manner. Lunchtime couldn't come soon enough. He was out of the door as fast as he could, back on the tram and pounding the pavements back to the Aubert house.

She opened the door to him. 'Claudia, hello.' God, she looked heavenly, he thought, wearing a rose pink dress decorated with little white spots.

'Doctor, thank you for coming over again.'

'Please, mademoiselle, you must call me André.'

'Oh, I don't feel… If you insist.'

She didn't correct his use of 'mademoiselle'. That was good. 'So, how is the patient today?'

He found Madame Aubert in bed again but looking much healthier. The colour had already returned to her cheeks, she'd eaten a small bowl of soup, her daughter told him, and taken her liquids.

'That medicine is doing the trick, Doctor,' said the old lady.

'Good, good,' he said, feigning interest. 'Now, just let me take your temperature, et cetera.'

As Claudia accompanied him back down the stairs, she offered him a cup of coffee. He almost skipped in delight.

He sat in the drawing room, while she disappeared to the kitchen. The drawing room felt welcoming, bathed in sunlight, heavy red curtains, bookshelves everywhere, a chandelier, but it had an older person's stamp all over it; he could see no trace of Claudia. She returned carrying a tray of coffee, crockery and a plate of biscuits. 'Here, let me…' he said, getting to his feet.

'Thank you, it's fine.'

He watched as she poured. Her skin, so pure, not a blemish; her hands, so delicate and feminine. 'You know we've met before,' he said.

'Have we, Doctor? I don't recall.'

She still called him 'Doctor', not a good sign, and not the response he was hoping for, but he proceeded to tell her about the envelope she'd dropped.

'Of course, that letter. It wasn't so important. Nonetheless...' she added, perhaps aware of having been a little dismissive.

In the following twenty minutes, he found out that she lived alone with her mother, her father having died a couple years before, and that she was an only child. No mention of a man in her life. She spoke with a soft country accent, with clear singer-like diction. He had to ask her out. She worked occasionally, she said, in a theatre as a make-up artist. He got the impression she worked for the social interaction rather than any financial need. Her father had left his wife and daughter comfortably off. 'My mother, she's half German, you know.'

'Is she? Oh. I speak a little schoolboy German, a bit rusty now. *Guten tag.*'

She laughed. 'I think her father came from Dortmund originally. My parents met... let me see...' She told him about her German heritage, how her parents came to be in this small town in northern France. He listened and thought he could listen to her all day; that he could die listening to her beautiful voice. Eventually, though, she stopped talking. Now, he thought, now was the moment.

'They say the weather will be fine this weekend. I wondered, Claudia, whether, I mean, if you weren't–'

A little bell rang. 'Oh, Doctor, excuse me. That's my mother. She is in need of something.' Under her breath, she added, 'She's always in need of something.'

'Yes, of course.' He saw the time on the mantelpiece clock. He was already running late. Swallowing his disappointment, he declared he had to go.

'I'll pop in tomorrow,' he said quickly. 'Make sure–'

'It's very kind of you but Mama is so much better already, you needn't–'

'No trouble at all. It'd be for the best. You never know with strokes.'

For the rest of day and that whole evening, he replayed their conversation again and again, deciphering every look, every gesture, trying to find something that he could interpret as an interest. There was nothing, he concluded sadly. But it would come, he told himself, it would come, and one day, he would make the beautiful Claudia Aubert his wife. OK, there was a bit of an age-gap but still he'd never been so sure.

The third day, the Thursday, he found Madame Aubert out of bed, sitting in the drawing room, reading a newspaper, a walking stick propped up on the *chaise longue* next to her. Dressed and wearing a hint of lipstick, she looked a different woman. He told her so. She thanked him. 'It's so nice to feel oneself again, to read the news and catch up with what's happening in the world.'

Claudia, having let him in, had, much to his chagrin, disappeared again. He tried to listen to the old woman as she talked about what she was reading, hoping Claudia would return. She did not. But his disappointment was truly compensated when, as he was leaving, Madame

Aubert invited him to join her and Claudia on a picnic the coming Saturday week – 'By way of a thank you, Doctor.'

'Well, that's most kind of you, Madame Aubert. I'd be delighted. I'd be delighted also to meet Claudia's boyfriend.'

She looked aghast. 'Boyfriend? My daughter? How I wish.'

He tried to suppress his grin.

'I'll be frank with you, Doctor. I've told her – if she wants my money when I'm gone, she needs to be married. I'm utterly serious. Otherwise she'd end up spending it all on silliness. Does she listen? Does she, my foot.'

'My, oh my.' Slapping his knees, he rose to his feet. 'Would you like me to come back tomorrow – just to–'

'No. It's most kind of you but there is no need.'

'I'll see you Saturday week then. I look forward to it.'

Yes, he thought, he really was looking forward to it. It couldn't come soon enough.

The doctor fretted about what to wear, about his shoes, whether he should bring a contribution, a bottle of wine, perhaps. The morning finally came. In the end, he chose his corduroy trousers and a pale, linen jacket and red tie, and took nothing. The sun had failed to show; the day, although still warm, was overcast. Still, no matter, he thought, he left the house with a spring in his step, anticipating a memorable, enjoyable day ahead.

He wasn't sure what to expect but he hadn't anticipated such a large gathering – perhaps twenty or more adults with numerous children running round the place. A number of blankets had been laid out on the grass not too far from a large cedar tree with long, overhanging branches, each blanket piled with baskets and hampers of food and drink. A few dogs chased each other, darting between the guests. He spied Claudia talking to a couple girls her age. His heart flipped. Madame Aubert greeted him with a huge smile, a glass of wine in her hand and a kiss on each cheek. '*Guten morgen, Herr Doctor*, how lovely of you to have made it.' She smelt of expensive perfume. 'Here, have a drink; you must need one after your week's work.' She poured him a large glass of white wine. '*Prost*,' she said, clinking glasses. 'Now, I simply must introduce you to everyone. I shall be testing you later,' she said with a wink. 'So pay attention to everyone's names.' While he drank back the wine, Madame Aubert introduced him to everyone as her lifesaver, telling all her friends that should they ever find themselves poorly, then Doctor André here was the man to call. 'Such a lovely manner about him,' she said several times.

The doctor shook many hands and promptly forgot everyone's names until Madame Aubert called for her daughter.

Claudia came to greet him, also kissing him on the cheek. 'Doctor, it's lovely to see you again,' she said in a purring voice. His heart fluttered. She'd put on lipstick, and a little dash of colour around the eyes.

'You look absolutely lovely,' he said. 'Stunning, in fact.'

Ignoring his compliment, she said, 'Come meet a couple of my friends.'

The doctor soon found himself surrounded by young, attractive women, an enviable situation one might have thought. But not so. He only wanted Claudia, not these silly girls and their inane chatter about films and film stars and silly questions about being a doctor. 'You must've seen so many dead people,' said one. He could have screamed. Claudia thrust a plateful of food in his hand and refilled his glass, as did almost anyone who passed. Not an hour had gone when the doctor realised he was feeling decidedly tipsy. Eventually, breaking away from a young man who worked as an accountant, he managed to buttonhole her.

'Doctor,' she said, 'I wanted to thank you again for looking after my mother. You've been an absolute angel. As you can see, she's right as rain. More's the pity. Your practice must keep you awfully busy.'

'Oh yes, but never so much as to keep me away from my special patients. Anytime your mother is poorly or you, Claudia, you know whom to call.'

She laughed politely. 'So, I told you all about myself, tell me about you. How long have you been a doctor?'

This, he thought, was perfect – her undivided attention. He gulped back his wine. And so he started telling her about his life. So enraptured by the occasion, he failed to notice her glancing over his shoulder, failed to read her body language, failed to see the evident relief in her face when some swine interrupted them, saying Claudia's mother was looking for her. He excused her and, smiling with satisfaction, watched her saunter away, admiring the swing in her hips and her slender, gracious legs.

Another hour passed during which time the doctor found himself embroiled in a game with several overexcited children and dogs, playing 'the monster is coming to get you'.

Feeling jubilant, irrepressibly buoyant, rather drunk and a little sweaty, he approached Claudia.

'You seem to be enjoying yourself,' she remarked with a smile.

'Very much so.' Taking her gently by the elbow, he manoeuvred her away from the others. 'Claudia, could I have a word with you?'

'Of course. Is there something wrong?'

'No, no,' he said, as he led her up the slight incline to the other side of the cedar tree. 'I just wanted to ask…'

'Is it to do with my mother?'

He glanced back at the party. They were far enough away now. In a few minutes, they would return to the gathering with some rather special news. 'Claudia, I know we've only just met but I feel as if I know you so well already.'

'Thank you, Doctor.'

'André. Please call me André.' He felt a confidence he'd never experienced before. He expected to stutter, to make a fool of himself, but no, not now, not any more. 'I know I should wait and do this properly and have bought a ring, et cetera—'

'A ring?'

'But I can't contain myself a moment longer. Claudia, will you do me the honour of being my wife?'

*

When, that night and the weeks, even months, to follow, Doctor Le Vau thought back to that moment it always made him wince with a mixture of shame, humiliation and anger. The image of her mouth shaped like an 'O', and the wide look of shock in her eyes, he knew immediately he'd made a terrible mistake. But what really hurt and would rankle forever more was the laugh that followed – a sort of bemused chuckle at first, then an outright laugh as if he'd just said the funniest joke she'd ever heard. He felt himself reeling back down the incline, dropping his glass, past the tree, his head in an utter daze. He should have skirted round the party but instead he walked right through it, pushing someone to the side, spilling their drink, bringing conversations to an abrupt halt. He heard Madame Aubert's voice, 'Doctor, what on earth...' And still, in the background, he could hear her faint laughter, mocking his stupidity. He could hear it still as he staggered out of the park and back into the street. And it was still there, ringing in his ears, as he boarded a tram heading home. In an instant, out there on the heath, just beyond a cedar tree, love had turned into hate – hate for her, of course, and hate for himself. How could he have been so brainless, so deluded to think that a young, beautiful girl as she should show the remotest interest in a middle-aged, portly man as he, a provincial doctor of limited means and limited ambition. How could he have so misread the situation? What a fool; an utter, utter fool.

*

The weeks passed; spring turned into summer, summer into autumn. Doctor Le Vau continued at work, his mind closed off to everything and everyone bar what was immediately in front of him. The pain and humiliation of that moment on the heath never receded – not properly. He learnt to live with it but not an hour passed by when the memory didn't come, unbidden, to the fore. Every night at bedtime he would lie awake rethinking the whole course of their relationship during those few spring days, trying to remember every word of every conversation, trying to work out where he'd gone so spectacularly wrong. The memory obsessed him. He ate poorly, would go days without shaving, didn't venture out, refusing even his usual three-monthly meet-up with Cassel.

Claudia Aubert. The name and the memory attached themselves to him like a tumour. He began to loathe her with an intensity that surpassed even the love he'd felt for her. He wanted to avenge himself, to hurt her in some way, to frighten her even. But he was, in essence, a good man, a man who had never done wrong. He knew he had neither the imagination nor the capacity to do something bad. His only consolation was work. He worked harder than ever before, earning the gratitude and admiration of his many patients.

It was some two years later, on a cold, blustery November morning in 1938 that his receptionist put through a telephone call from a patient requesting Dr Le Vau by name. His heart hammered on hearing Madame Aubert's voice. 'Doctor, I don't know what's wrong with me except I feel terrible. I can't move, I'm sick all the time, my limbs feel like dead weights. Can you come?' She sounded dreadful.

'I'll send Dr Lenoir.'

'No, please, Doctor, it has to be you. You can let yourself in; the front door will be open.'

'Is your daughter at home?'

'She's out until lunchtime. She thinks I put it on, Doctor. That girl is becoming more wicked by the day.'

'I'll come now then,' he said, slamming down the receiver.

He approached the house in a state of high nervousness, his palms damp with sweat. Would Madame Aubert know that he'd asked her daughter to marry him? Would she know of his moment of humiliation? Would

Claudia really be out? He walked up the steps to the front door, his legs trembling beneath him. The door, as promised, was unlocked. Inside, nothing had changed, the potted plant in the corner no bigger, the pictures hanging from the walls the same. How strange, he thought, how awful it was to be back inside this house. Its opulence which had so appealed now appeared ostentatious. He had visited only the three times yet everything seemed horribly familiar. He knocked on the bedroom door and entered on hearing a groan from inside. The room smelt stale, faintly unpleasant. Again, nothing had changed except Madame Aubert herself. Whereas before she looked poorly, now she looked truly sick, her face deeply grey, her skin dry as parchment. Her grey tongue showed between her thin, bloodless lips.

Her breathing seemed laboured. 'Madame Aubert, it's me, Dr Le Vau.'

'I've got my piano lesson. Doctor, help me get to my lesson or Mademoiselle Dubois will be awfully cross with me.'

'You seem confused, Madame.' He immediately took her blood pressure – it was low; while her heartbeat was alarmingly fast, more than ninety per minute.

'Madame Aubert, we need to get you to a hospital. Do you have a telephone?' Of course, there was one in the hallway.

He phoned through for an ambulance, then, having fetched a glass of water from the kitchen, returned to Madame Aubert. She seemed more composed now. She drank down her water, thanking him. 'Madame, I believe you have sepsis,' he said, taking her temperature. 'We need to get you to a hospital as quickly as possible. I've phoned for an ambulance.'

'Thank you,' she said in a rasping voice. 'Thank you, Doctor.'

'Have you been ill recently? An infection perhaps?'

'Yes, I've had a terrible kidney infection.'

He waited next to her bed as she dozed off, her grey hair spread across the pillow.

Looking down at her, he suddenly felt rather sorry for the woman, alone and widowed in this grand but soulless house. Sepsis was serious stuff which could easily result in septic shock – and not many, especially of her age, came back from that. As much as he wished to avoid Claudia, he felt annoyed that she wasn't here, next to her mother, looking after her. Was she out with her accountant friend, or her giggly friend, or applying her silly make-up backstage somewhere? He shook his head at the shame of it all.

Fifteen minutes later, the ambulance arrived. Madame Aubert woke up as the medics hoisted her onto a stretcher. 'Doctor, please come with me,' she said, reaching out for his hand as she was manoeuvred through the house.

Taking it, he replied he couldn't. 'I have to see my afternoon patients; please forgive me.'

'Visit me then. Come tomorrow. Please, Doctor, I beg you.'

He nodded. 'Of course, Madame; it'd be a privilege.'

Having watched the ambulance whisk Madame Aubert away, he quickly returned to the house. Finding a notepad and pen on the hallway desk, he wrote a short note to Claudia, telling her that her mother had been taken to the hospital. He wondered how to sign it. In the end, he opted for Dr Le Vau. Leaving, he quietly closed the front door behind him. Looking up and down the street, he could see no sign of her – still too busy enjoying herself to return home.

He spent the evening thinking about Madame Aubert, and the more he thought about it, the more convinced he was that she didn't deserve a daughter as uncaring and thoughtless as Claudia. He'd half expected Claudia to ring the surgery to ask after her mother. But she hadn't. For over two years he'd wanted to avenge the deep-felt humiliation that still ate into his very being day after day. And now, for the first time, he realised the opportunity had come. He couldn't wait…

The following day, having palmed off his afternoon surgery on Doctor Lenoir, he went to visit Madame Aubert in hospital. As directed, he found her on a large ward full of elderly women like herself. Passing through the rows of beds with their miserable occupants, he found her at the end, near a window overlooking the town. A weak sun filtered through the clouds. They'd attached an intravenous drip to her, dehydration being a symptom of sepsis. But, he thought to himself, she looked no better. Apart from a glass of water, there was nothing on her bedside table – no fruit or flowers, nothing to show that her daughter had been to visit. All the better, he thought, to help ease his conscience into doing the work of a devious man.

'Madame Aubert,' he said quietly, sitting down next to her bed. 'It's me, André, Dr Le Vau.'

She opened her eyes and he knew she had no idea whether it was day or night or where she was. She muttered about her piano lessons again and he realised she was referring to herself as a young girl. Delirium had set in. It would come and go, often briskly. He just had to wait.

After a while, she dozed off again only to awaken ten minutes later. He could see from her eyes that the delirium had gone. Good, he thought, the time had come.

'How are you feeling, Madame?'

'Oh, Doctor, how lovely to see you,' she said weakly. 'Where am I?'

'You're in hospital, Madame Aubert. You're not well, I'm afraid to say.' He tried to explain while trying not to distress her but he could tell she was unable to take it in.

'I feel most strange. My husband – where is he?'

'Your husband, Madame Aubert? He died a few years ago.'

Looking puzzled, she asked, 'Did he? Are you sure? I swear I…'

'Yes, Madame?'

She shook her head. 'I heard his voice; I'm… I'm sure I did.'

She struggled to sit up in her bed. The doctor, taking an arm, helped.

She lay back on her pillow, eyes closed.

After a few minutes, she opened her eyes, beamed at the doctor and patted his hand. 'It's reassuring to have someone to trust. I've missed that since Georges died.'

'Your husband?'

'Yes.' She smiled at the memory. 'God rest his soul.'

'Your daughter – has she been in to see you?'

'Claudia? Not that I recall.'

'Should she not be here with you now?'

'Pah! Too busy with her own life.' The mention of her daughter seemed to concentrate her mind.

He pulled his chair in a little. 'Did she ever marry?'

Knotting her eyebrows, she said slowly, 'No, and it's not for the lack of offers. D'you know, Doctor, I think she prefers…' She glanced round the ward. '…women.'

'No! How utterly strange. Most unnatural.'

'My words exactly, and I've said it to her face.'

'You once told me…' He cleared his throat. Lowering his voice, he continued, 'You once told me that if she didn't marry you'd… well, you said you would disinherit her.'

Her eyes narrowed. 'Unless she bucks her ideas up, I fully intend to. She thinks she has me wrapped around her finger but I'll show her; I intend to have the last laugh. I've been looking for a charity.'

'Oh, really? Well, if you don't mind me suggesting something… there's a very good charity for doctors and nurses who have fallen on hard times. In fact, I happen to be the director. Part time, of course.'

She tilted her head to one side. 'Is that so? Tell me about it.'

He did. People always think doctors and nurses never fall ill, he said, but, of course, coming into contact with so many sickly people, they are very susceptible. And the pay they get, especially those poor nurses, isn't great, you know. He furnished her with a couple of examples of stricken medics and how reliant they were on him and his charity. He described his role as director and the difficult decisions he sometimes had to make – because there were always too many cases and not enough funding. He spoke for some time, talking off the cuff. By the time he'd finished, he'd almost convinced himself. 'It is not something I talk about often,' he said by way of conclusion. 'It's all terribly confidential, so if you would be so kind to keep this in the strictest confidence, Madame…'

'I won't tell a soul.' She considered him with, he thought, a degree of tenderness. 'You are an angel on earth,' she said. 'An angel.'

She looked tired again, he thought. Wishing her well and promising he'd visit again, he bade her farewell.

And so, he reflected as he returned home, he'd laid the seed. It was simply a matter of nurturing it – day by day, bit by bit.

Each day for a week, Dr Le Vau went to visit Madame Aubert, much to Dr Lenoir's increasing annoyance. Each time, fearing he might bump into Claudia, he would pause at the ward doors, peering through the little round window. His luck held out. She'd been, that he could tell, but he tried to avoid using her name in front of her mother. Once, as he walked down the street leading away from the hospital, he saw her from afar, approaching. With his heart thumping, he darted down an alleyway, managing to avoid her. She still looked beautiful but it was now, for Dr Le Vau, a tarnished beauty.

The old lady's health was improving but she was still weak. The drugs and the occasional bouts of delirium, together with the shock the illness had wrought upon her, had left her vulnerable and confused. She would survive this, but no matter – he was in no hurry; he'd be happy to wait years. Each day, he would give another example or two of the charity's work, tales he'd prepared the night before. He even brought in a couple of 'thank you' cards from appreciative beneficiaries. He told her they were still a small organisation, so small, in fact, that they didn't even have their own bank account yet. Everything had to go through his personal account. But, rest assured, as he told Madame Aubert, he was a man of conscience and absolute integrity. Madame Aubert didn't doubt it.

On the sixth day, reading her medical notes on a clipboard at the end of the bed, he feared he was running out of time; he had to conclude this before she returned home. 'You look so much better, Madame.'

'Your visits, Doctor, they have restored my faith in mankind.'

'And how is your daughter?'

'Now, Doctor, I've been thinking...'

He plucked off an invisible speck of dirt from his lapel. 'Hmm? Sorry, Madame Aubert, you were saying?'

'About my will. I've been thinking...'

He listened intently, soaking up every word. Once she'd finished, he put his palms in the air. 'Madame Aubert, I'm touched, truly I am.' He wiped away a tear. 'Your generosity, Madame Aubert, it's... in this world of darkness, it's like a light shone by the good Lord Himself.'

She liked that; he could tell.

Picking his words carefully, he said, 'I have a lawyer friend. He's very good, very discreet. He did my will, not that I have anything to leave but what little I have I shall leave to the charity. He's always so busy but I know he could pop in, if it wasn't too much of an imposition.'

*

The Wild Boar bar was quiet, the rain keeping most people away. Marie was behind the bar, wiping glasses, batting away innuendos and lewd proposals from the bar's less refined customers. 'That girl knows how to look after herself,' said Cassel. 'She's been here too long though; she needs a better job. So, you're telling me, she's leaving the house and garden to you, the whole house and everything in it.'

'Indeed, my friend. But the daughter gets the cash.'

'How much?'

'No idea. Whatever it is, it's more than she deserves, I tell you.'

Cassel gulped down his drink. 'I congratulate you, my friend. If this house is as grand as you say, you'll have the ladies queuing up.'

'You know I'll pay you handsomely for this, Jean.'

'Should hope so!' He lit a cigar. 'So, this is above board?' he asked, puffing hard.

'I didn't think that sort of thing worried you.'

'André, listen, I may sail close to the wind sometimes but, you know, even I have my limits. And you want me to draw up this will straightaway – while she's still in hospital?'

'I know it seems a little irregular, but it's that daughter – she can't be trusted.'

His friend blew out a long plume of smoke. 'Consider it done, my friend.'

* * *

'But it never was, was it?' said Gustave Garnier, the teacher.

The doctor, his face flushed, shook his head.

'It was never done. Your lawyer friend, Cassel, he lost his nerve.'

'I don't know. I… Well, I… If you must know, I never saw him again.'

'Perhaps you don't know then,' said Garnier. 'But I do.'

All eyes turned on him. 'You do, Professor?' asked the priest. 'Do tell us, pray.'

Twiddling a piece of straw between his fingers, the teacher said, 'My sister told me. Dr Lenoir had told her. Le Vau didn't retire from the profession, he was struck off.'

The doctor felt himself diminish as a chorus of gasps circled round the cell.

'Your lawyer went to the hospital. There, he bumped into the daughter, a real looker apparently, and he fell head over heels in love – right there and then. He couldn't do it. The daughter wanted to know what he was doing there. Once she'd got it out of him, she lodged a complaint. And that was it – Le Vau was struck off. Weren't you, Le Vau?'

Le Vau nodded. 'I wasn't to know…'

'Actions have consequences, Doctor,' said the teacher.

The priest, shaking his head, said, 'Oh dear, oh dear, Doctor. You broke your Hippocratic oath.'

'I know,' he said quietly. 'It's something I have had to live with. I was stupid; I know that. I don't know what came over me.'

'What happened to Cassel?' asked Béart, the soldier.

'I don't know.'

'I know,' said Garnier. 'You won't like it but… well, he got married.'

'Oh no,' said Le Vau. 'Not her; please tell me it wasn't her?'

Garnier, unable to suppress a grin, nodded.

Chapter 5:
The Postman's Story

The men heard the church clock strike one o'clock. They had five hours to go. Having drawn the second short straw, Henri Moreau took his turn next. Standing where the doctor had stood, he started.

He thought he'd be honest, and tell them about the day everything changed. And they would see, God would see, that it wasn't his fault; he'd only been trying to do what he thought was right. And so he began…

* * *

16 July 1942. Henri Moreau, as was his routine at eight in the morning, was on his bicycle delivering the post. He'd already been working for an hour and a half. It was a bright summer's morning, the sky sapphire blue. People waved at him. The sight of the postman doing his daily round was a reassuring presence. They thought his job an easy one; a pleasant, sociable way of earning one's living. A

job that could be done and dusted by lunchtime each day. They didn't appreciate that Moreau had to be up and out of bed at half five every morning, six days a week, fifty-two weeks a year. It wasn't so bad this time of year, but all those cold, early starts during winter were tiresome indeed. They didn't see him cycling round in the dark, often in the rain, cold and wet, while they were still tucked up in bed or enjoying a warm breakfast in front of the fire. They didn't realise the heaviness of his post sack and the physical strain it put on his aging shoulders. And the job came with a responsibility. People, businesses, shops – they didn't appreciate how dependent they were on him doing his job and doing it well. The one time, the one single time, he dropped a letter, it was found by some snot-nosed schoolkid and handed in to the post office. And then there was hell to pay. But what really irked was when people accused him of being a collaborator because he had to deliver the German post. Post was post as far as he was concerned.

On the whole, though, Henri Moreau was pleased with life. The German occupation, painful though it was to see, was bearable, and life at home was cosy. But he was concerned, deeply concerned, because his wife was Jewish, and therefore, by default, so was his daughter, the six-year-old Marguerite. They'd been married ten years, he and Liliane (Lilly), and, if truth be told, it was only Marguerite that kept them together. Until recently, his wife's Jewishness was not something that had worried him. Nor anyone else. She was just a Frenchwoman; Marguerite just a French kid. Then came the Germans. Yet the Germans in this neck of woods had been more relaxed than their urban cousins, so although conscious of the Jewess he'd married, it wasn't a problem. But things had changed. Six months previously, the edict had come from the government – all Jews were compelled to wear a yellow star upon their clothing, with the word *Juif* clearly written upon it. Those who didn't and were caught out faced harsh punishment. Now, people who had been pleasant enough to Lilly, turned their backs on her, walked to the other side of the street with their noses in the air, as if offended by an unpleasant smell; Marguerite was shunned at school, made to sit at the back, avoided at playtime. He was no anti-Semitic, he told himself, but nonetheless… nonetheless he couldn't help feel *ashamed* somehow. Ashamed that he had married a Jew.

On this particular warm July morning, Moreau, wearing a pair of shorts and a collared shirt unbuttoned at the top and his postman's cap, cycled the one kilometre from home to the post office, picked up his post sack, exchanging pleasantries, as always, with the postmistress, then made a start on his deliveries. Just like any other morning these last twelve years. Only this morning was slightly different. Today was the first day of the school holidays. Marguerite was beside herself with excitement – no more school for a whole two months, no more going to bed early, a whole summer to play with her friends in the streets, at least the ones she could still consider her friends. But the start of the summer holidays wasn't the only reason why this morning was to be different. This morning would see Henri Moreau's life, as he knew it, come to an end.

It was still only eight o'clock; Moreau was about a quarter through his deliveries. There was something odd in the air; he could feel it, and whatever it was he didn't like it. Turning into a wide residential street, still in the shade, he heard noises – it sounded like screaming. There was a bus, a green and cream coloured bus, parked on the side of the street, and some policemen – no, not some, but lots of them. So many police. Braking to a halt, Moreau wondered what sort of criminal lived in the town to warrant such a huge number of policemen. He saw a man in a black jacket pushed to the ground, his beret flying off, shouting. With his hands over his head, the man cowered as a cop hit him on the back with his truncheon. Moreau let slip the sack from his shoulder where it fell onto the road with a heavy, dull thud. A moment later, a woman appeared from the house, a policeman either side, screaming, her face full of terror. Passers-by rushed away. A couple stopped next to Moreau – near enough to see what was happening but at a safe distance. Another policeman, this one carrying a bawling child, appeared. The woman screamed for her child. A cop hit her in the stomach, doubling her over. Moreau and the others flinched.

'What's happening?' asked Moreau, more to himself.

A man to his left said, 'Haven't you heard? They're arresting all the Jews.'

Then Moreau saw it – the familiar yellow star bright on the man's black jacket. There were other cops at the entrance of the bus. The man, woman and child, all three crying, were dragged towards the bus and one by one physically forced up the steps and pushed inside.

'They're arresting the Jews?' asked Moreau, his heart thumping, thinking of his daughter. 'Even the children? Why? What have they done?'

'I know, it's despicable, isn't it?'

In a shrill voice, a woman to his right said, 'It serves

them right, if you ask me; bloody parasites.'

Moreau turned to look at her. She was a respectable, well-dressed woman; the sort of person who, before the war, would never have thought, let alone say, such a thing.

Back at the end of 1940, the French authorities had made all Jews register themselves. Moreau had dutifully gone along on the appointed day and registered his wife and daughter. He was regretting it now.

The cops were running, their feet heavy on the cobbles, disappearing down a narrow side street.

'Where are they going now?' asked Moreau, although he knew the answer.

'They know where all the Jews live,' said the man.

'Good,' said the woman. 'They should've done this years ago.'

'Oh my God.' He felt quite dizzy for a moment. The world seemed to move out of focus.

'Are you OK, buddy?' asked the man.

'What?' Marguerite. Something invisible seemed to be choking him, squeezing his throat. 'I've got to go…' he said breathlessly. Clumsily, he turned his bicycle around, facing the way he'd just come. He had to get home. Before it was too late.

Cycling off, he heard the man shout after him. 'Oi, wait, you forgot your post.'

'He can't just leave it here,' came the woman's shrill voice.

Henri Moreau had been on his bicycle every day, bar Sundays, for years and years. Yet he had never, until this moment, ridden it with any speed. But by God, he did now. Standing up on the pedals, he speeded down the streets, round corners and sharp bends, the wrong way down a one-way street, past the shops, overtaking slow-moving cars, a horse and cart, and other cyclists. He passed another family of Jews, screaming, hysterical, being hauled out of their homes by a different set of policemen. He kept going, the breeze causing his eyes to water, his heart pounding with exertion and fear. He could hear sirens, more shouting, a car screeching to a halt, a motorbike and sidecar. Everything was happening around him, but still he pressed on. No one noticed the postman racing past them on his bicycle.

Eventually, he came to his street. No police here – yet. Thank God for that. He lived not far from the centre of town in a third-storey two-bedroom apartment that overlooked a cobbled courtyard. He took the corner into the courtyard at full speed, under an archway, skidding dramatically to a halt. Leaving his bike prostrate on the ground, its front wheel still spinning, he leapt off and ran inside. Panting heavily, he ran into the lobby, past the rows of metal post boxes, sidestepping Madame Blanchet, the concierge, her sleeves rolled-up, a bucket of water cradled in the crook of her arm. 'Everything OK, Monsieur Moreau?' she asked in her sharp tone. Ignoring her, the postman bounded up the darkened stairs, taking two steps at a time, reaching the third floor.

Fumbling for his keys, aware of the sweat dripping from his every pore, he pushed open the front door. Slamming it closed behind him, he called out. 'Lilly! Marguerite!' No answer. The apartment seemed strangely quiet. No one in the kitchen; no one in the sitting room – Marguerite's toys scattered everywhere, as always, a doll here, a teddy there. His heart stopped – oh Lord, they've been taken. 'Please, no.' He called their names again, hearing the panic within in his voice. Trying to catch his breath, he darted back to the kitchen, as if he might have missed them first time, back to the sitting room, both bedrooms. Everything seemed in place; no sign of a struggle; Marguerite's favourite teddy bear, Lanky, flopped on her pillow where she left it everyday; the breakfast things stacked away, all in order. He tried to think – where could they be at this time of morning? Madame Giono – he'd ask his neighbour. Leaving the front door ajar, he darted out into the corridor, and knocked furiously on next door. Madame Giono, the young Italian widow, whom he'd always had a soft spot for, answered, concerned by Moreau's frantic knock. 'Good God, Henri, is there a fire?' She held a placid black cat to her bosom.

'Lilly, Marguerite. Have you s-seen them?' he asked in a rush, conscious of his breathlessness but still, even at this moment, aware that, as always, she looked divine in her silk dressing gown.

'No, should I have? Is everything OK, Henri?' She ran a finger down the lapel of his postman's jacket.

God, she was sexy. 'Has anyone called for us? Did you hear anything?'

'No. Why, should–'

'Thanks,' he said. 'Sorry, Madame Giono, must rush. You look lovely by the way.'

'Why, thank you, Henri,' she said, stroking the cat.

He'd go out, look for them. No, what if they returned in the meantime? He had to stay, had to wait for them. Where in hell were they? Where could they have gone? He felt weak with dread, so much energy, but nothing he could do. From one room to another, he paced up and down feeling like a caged animal, trapped and afraid, very afraid.

From outside, he heard the sound of an engine. Looking out the kitchen window, his heart jumped on seeing the motorbike and sidecar pull up within the courtyard. Parking up in the street, beyond the archway, he saw the green and cream bus, a number of French police disembarking. He pulled away from the window, his breath coming in quick bursts. Then, at the same moment, he heard the key in the door – they were back. Lilly came running into the apartment, her coat flapping, dropping a bag of groceries in the hallway, Marguerite behind her. 'Henri,' she cried. 'What do we do?'

'I… I don't know.'

'They're outside. There's no escape.'

'Lock the door. Double lock it.'

'Papa, what's happening?'

'I'm not sure, s-sweetheart. It's probably nothing to worry about.'

'So why's Maman crying?'

'I'm not crying, love,' said Lilly, trying to hide the fear in her voice. 'Come, let's go sit down. Maybe a bit later we can make a start on that jigsaw puzzle of yours.'

Henri watched her remove her coat, saw her grimace at the hated star. Stuffing it in the little cupboard in the hallway, she turned to him, her face red with tears. 'There's nothing we can do, is there? We're trapped like rats.'

He didn't know how to answer. Then they heard it – the footsteps on the stairs, dozens and dozens of them, so it seemed, footsteps on the landing, coming to a halt outside their door. A moment of silence. Then the loud rap against the door. 'Police. Open up,' came the voice from outside.

Marguerite reached for her mother's hand. Henri put his finger to his lips. Another knock, even louder. 'Open up. All Jews are subject to arrest.'

'What's arrest mean, Maman?' whispered Marguerite.

'They… they just want to talk to us.'

The knocking on the door continued, on and on, a constant pounding.

'Make them stop,' said Lilly, her hands over her ears.

'I don't know what to do. I'm s-sorry.'

Grabbing him by his shirt, she said, 'Don't desert us, Henri Moreau. Do whatever you have to do, just save us. And if you can't…' Wiping away her tears, she continued, 'if you can't save me, save… save her.'

He tried to speak but managed only to nod, biting his lip, desperately trying not to cry in front of their daughter.

The knocking suddenly stopped. Moreau held his breath, knowing they were still on the landing.

'What's that noise?' asked Marguerite, hiding behind her mother, clutching her skirt, her voice barely audible.

It took him a few seconds to work it out. 'They're unlocking the door.'

Lilly clenched shut her eyes. 'Madame Blanchet – she's given them the key. The bitch.'

And then they were there; the door bursting open, a man in a trench coat in their hallway, two uniformed men behind him in their peaked hats and capes. 'Monsieur Moreau?' asked the officer, holding up a piece of paper.

Moreau couldn't speak.

Marguerite gripped onto her mother's skirt. Lilly reached back, taking her daughter's hand. 'What is it you want?' she asked, unable to hide the quiver in her voice.

'Madame Moreau? You are all under arrest.'

'Not the child,' said Moreau. 'S-surely not the child.'

'All three of you.'

The two men in uniforms sidled behind them, dark faces under their peaked hats, set mouths.

'You,' said the officer, pointing at Lilly. 'Pack a small case for all three of you. Essentials only. You have two minutes.'

She hesitated, as if she didn't understand the instruction.

'Go on, now!' he shouted.

Spurred into action, she took Marguerite by the hand and raced to the bedroom, the uniforms following her.

Left alone with the officer, Moreau had to speak. Glancing behind at the bedroom, he turned and whispered, 'You can't arrest me. My wife's Jewish but I'm not.'

The officer frowned. 'You're not?'

'Look, my coat.' Retrieving his coat from the cupboard, he twisted and turned it in order to show the officer the breast pocket where the yellow star *would* have been.

'Doesn't prove much. Anyway, you're on my list so there's nothing I can do. You can speak to someone later down the line; try and sort it out.'

'What about them?'

'No way out of that. But you – for sure. Where are your papers?'

He would've showed the man but just at that point Lilly and Marguerite returned, a small black suitcase in Lilly's hand; Lanky, the teddy bear, in Marguerite's.

'Here, let me,' said Moreau, reaching for the case.

With their coats on, the six of them marched down the stairs, the officer in front, the two uniforms at the rear.

Between the first floor and the ground, they overtook Madame Giono descending the stairs. She pinned her back to the wall, her mouth gaping open, as the Moreaus and their escort passed by. No one spoke but Moreau's felt his face flush red; he hadn't wanted her to see his moment of humiliation. At the bottom of the stairs, watching them descend, was Madame Blanchet, wiping her hands on her apron, an impish smile plastered on her pinched face.

Outside, the Moreaus were pushed towards the waiting bus.

Glancing behind, Henri Moreau saw his bicycle lying on the cobble courtyard. So many people won't get their letters today, he thought; I've let them all down.

*

The bus was packed with Jews, most carrying bags or small cases. Young and old, grandparents, the decrepit, babes in arms, Jews together, crying, pointlessly pleading to each other, not knowing their fate.

Their town passed them by – the familiar streets, the shops, the apartment blocks, the cafés, the post office, the library, people going about their everyday business unaware that the bus driving by was full of desperate, frightened people. Moreau wondered if he'd ever see his town or his home again. The ride on the bus was brief, no more Jews to pick up – the Moreaus were the last. Ten minutes after leaving the Moreaus, they were at the train station. The station car park was full of green and cream buses, hundreds of Jews disembarking, all with their yellow stars, all but Henri Moreau, a heavy police presence surrounding them. A train awaited, the sun glinting off its engine, already emitting bellows of steam in preparation for departure.

Henri Moreau never realised there were so many Jews living in his town, until he heard someone say there were from another town about ten kilometres north. So, that explains it, he thought; the police had cast their net far and wide. Everyone, each and every one of them, looked small and diminished. There was crying, for sure, pitiful weeping, but no one was protesting, as if they all knew to do so was futile. The police merely had to herd them onto the trains, no one had to be forced, no coercion was needed. Lambs to the slaughter.

Marguerite held onto her mother's hand, Lilly to his. He would have tried to reassure them, but it was pointless. What could he, even as a Gentile, do in the face of this barbaric efficiency? He wanted to scream, 'I'm not a Jew! I'm not a bloody Jew!' Back at the apartment the officer had said he should speak to someone. But there was no one to speak to, no one in charge. Perhaps if he could get inside the station, the ticket hall or somewhere, he'd find someone to speak to, someone with authority. As he took the steps onto the train, his hand momentarily let go of hers. 'Henri, please,' she cried, her hand reaching out for his.

'I'm s-sorry,' he muttered. He knew with a sudden, prophetic certainty that as long as they stuck together he was as good as dead. He'd once loved her, and perhaps, in some way, he still did, but not enough to forfeit his life. Not enough. He had to do something to lose her.

Marguerite suddenly let out an ear-piercing scream. 'Lanky! I've lost Lanky.'

'Henri,' urged Lilly. 'You have to find Lanky.'

'What?' Marguerite burst into tears. 'Yes, of course.'

Pushing someone aside, he jumped off the steps.

He could see the bear on the ground, trampled in the dirt, but a policeman was on him in an instant. 'Oi, what're you doing?'

'My daughter, she's dropped…'

'Get back on,' said the cop reaching for his holster.

'Papa…'

'It's just there…'

'Henri, hurry…'

'It'll only take a minute.' Sidestepping the policeman, he managed to grab the bear. Turning back, he didn't see it coming, aware only of staggering back, falling to his knees, of the shooting pain over his eye.

Groaning, his hand over his eye socket, Moreau got up, clutching onto the bear.

People let him pass as he climbed up the train steps to join Lilly and Marguerite at the top, Lilly stroking her daughter's hair. 'Here,' he said, his eye throbbing with pain. 'Take it.'

'Thank you, Papa.'

'Thank you, Henri.'

They were among the first on board; the first into an empty carriage. Having put their suitcase and their coats on the overhead rack, they sat down. Within seconds, every other seat was taken, and Marguerite, holding onto Lanky, had to sit on her mother's lap in order to allow an elderly woman a seat. A man in a brown suit, sitting opposite, passed Moreau his handkerchief while Lilly used hers to wipe away Marguerite's tears and blow her nose. Moreau thanked him, daubing his swollen eye.

By the time the train left, some twenty minutes later, every seat in every compartment was taken; people were standing squashed in the gangways, the smell of sweat and fear everywhere. And so much noise – babies, children and adults crying, whimpering, people asking each other, 'Where are we going, where are they taking us?' Some commotion was taking place in the next door carriage – some man trying to jump out of the window. No chance, thought Moreau, you couldn't squeeze a rabbit through that. Idiot.

Marguerite had fallen asleep on her mother's lap, sucking her thumb, a habit she'd broken a good year back. Moreau kissed his daughter's head, breathed in her smell. He knew what he was trying to do, he wanted to change his own mind, to persuade himself that whatever her fate, this little girl, he should share it. He stroked her cheek. She smiled in her sleep.

Leaning towards him, Lilly whispered in his ear. 'Henri, there must be something we can do. I married a Gentile; that must count for something. Find someone; get us out of here.'

He nodded.

Rising from his seat, he took his coat from the rack.

Lilly pulled a face, as if to say, 'why do you need that?'

Pretending not to understand, he said 'excuse me' numerous times as he pushed his way out of the carriage and down the corridor. 'The toilets are blocked, chum,' said someone.

'I'll give it a go,' he said in return. 'Excuse me. Sorry. Excuse me.'

Finally, he found a policeman standing guard between two carriages.

'Excuse me.'

'Get back.'

'Listen, there's been a mistake.' Lowering his voice, he said, 'I'm not a Jew.'

'So?'

'Look,' he said, showing the man his coat. 'No s-star.'

'Nothing I can do. Now get back.'

'Can't I…'

'No. I'm not going to tell you again.'

Back in his carriage, a woman in a headscarf had taken his place. Lilly shrugged her shoulders in a "what could I do" gesture. 'Well…?' she mouthed.

He shook his head.

She sighed and turned her attention to the countryside rushing past outside, squeezing Marguerite closer to her bosom.

*

An hour later, the train finally slowed down and came to a halt. The words 'where are we?' were on everyone's lips.

'Out, out, out!' shouted the policemen. 'Hurry up, out, out, out.'

Collecting their belongings, they were herded off the train and marched down a bleak, deserted street with few buildings, the pavement full of potholes. The smell of cut grass wafted through the air. What a lovely smell, thought the postman, the smell of normality, of freedom. The silence of so many people, thought Moreau, is an oppressive noise, just the shuffle, shuffle, shuffle of so many feet. The name of the street, he noticed, was Rue de la Liberté. Carrying the suitcase, he felt hot wearing his coat on so warm a day. Eventually, they came to what looked like a huge residential multi-storey complex, a very modern if ugly piece of architecture. The same word filtered down the unending line of Jews making people shake with alarm – *Drancy*. Drancy. The word was enough to strike fear in the stoutest of hearts. This was the government's biggest concentration camp for Jews, north-east of Paris. Rumours about the place had circulated for years – about trains coming to take them away from here, taking them to faraway places from which no one ever returned. People slowed down. 'Hurry, hurry,' shouted the policemen, pushing the odd Jew along. 'Get on there.'

Lilly squeezed Moreau's hand. 'Henri, I'm frightened.'

'I know. S-so am I.'

'Don't be frightened, Maman. I'll look after you.'

Despite herself, Lilly managed a laugh mixed in with her tears. 'Oh, my little love, I know you will.'

Approaching, the main gates loomed large; beyond the gates, a large, mud-packed yard, surrounded on three sides by these futuristic-looking apartment blocks. And everywhere, French police in their capes, swinging their truncheons. There was noise now, the screaming of the adults, the wailing of the children, the shouting of policemen. They crowded into the yard, hundreds of them, Jews with their stars on their coats, pushed together like so many sheep, the sun beating down on their heads. Many were tired after the journey and the constant state of nervousness, especially the elderly, but the police wouldn't let them sit, forcing them to their feet, kicking them. 'Please let me sit,' said one woman, no more than twenty, 'I'm pregnant.' The policeman grabbed her by her hair, yanking her up. Her face crumpled into tears, as she supported the weight of her bulging belly. An older woman put her arm around her. The pregnant girl sobbed into her shoulder.

Marguerite also was crying. Lilly picked her up, kissed her wet face. 'We'll stick together.' She looked at her husband. 'Won't we, Henri?'

It was as if she knew.

The booming voice through the loud hailer caught everyone's attention. They were about to be told something. 'Messieurs, Mesdames.' Moreau couldn't see where the voice was coming from but he could hear it all right. 'Messieurs, Mesdames, listen carefully, please. You are now at the Drancy detention centre. As Israelites, you are here under the direct orders of the Vichy authorities. The length of your stay here is yet to be determined. Each one of you has been allocated a space within the centre. The running of this camp is heavily regimented and you will be expected to obey all rules, which will be relayed to you presently. The slightest infringement of any rule will be dealt with most severely. You have been warned. There are separate accommodation blocks for men and for women and… for children.'

It was almost as if this dismembered voice was expecting it – the pause before saying the words 'for children'. The spontaneous scream shattered the silence as mothers, wetting themselves, knowing their worst fear had come, clung onto their children. And then it started. Police came charging in wielding their batons, pulling mothers from children. The women, seized by primeval reflexes, impervious to the punches and brutality of the police, desperately trying to hold onto their children. Lilly, her face white, beside herself, clung onto Marguerite, squeezing the life out of the screeching child. Henri tried to shield them, knowing it a pointless task. Fists flew, batons swung, children thrown onto the dirt, mothers on their knees, their skirts covered in dried mud, hysterical; the air filled with screaming, a wall of screaming. A figure in black punched Lilly in the mouth. She fell back, losing her grip on Marguerite. The policeman made a grab for the girl. With eyes like those of the devil, Lilly leapt forward, lunging at him, pulling at his hair, knocking his hat off, scratching his face, drawing blood. Trying to scoop Marguerite up with one hand, he fought Lilly off, ripping the buttons from her dress. Moreau, shouting 'No!', pulled manically at his arm, trying to free Marguerite from his grasp. A sudden, unexpected blast of water threw them apart. Moreau found himself face down in the sodden dirt. Staggering to his feet, he searched for them among the wailing desperate women, the water knocking people down like bowling pins. He saw her, saw Lilly, on the ground, her hair soaked, her face and chest caked in mud, her arms seizing the policeman's legs. He called out her name, his voice lost amidst the screaming. Something smashed onto the back of his head. His eyes glazed. The intensity of the primordial noise clouded over. Swaying, he could see the blurred outline of his wife on her feet, hitting the back of the policeman as the man gripped his daughter by her midriff; Marguerite, kicking her legs, bellowing for help, reaching out for her.

And then everything went black.

*

Henri Moreau opened his eyes. What was that filthy smell? It took a few seconds for his eyes to focus but the memory of what had happened came to him in an instant. Lilly and Marguerite – where were they? He lifted his head but fell back again as the piercing pain shot through his head, his eye still hurt from where the revolver had smashed into him. Checking his pockets, he still had the handkerchief the man on the train had given him. He was in a bed covered by a thin, scratchy blanket. Sitting at the end of the bed a gaunt man in spectacles, his beard turned yellow, biting his nails. They seemed to be in a dormitory of some sort, hundreds of men, the sound of a hundred quiet conversations. His throat felt dry, he realised just how thirsty he was. Clutching his head, gagging on the smell of decay and desperation, he swung his legs off the bed.

'Good morning,' said the bearded man. 'I'm afraid you missed breakfast.'

'Breakfast?'

'Oh yes, my friend.' The man counted the items on his fingers. 'We had sausages, a boiled egg, croissant, fresh ones, mind you, mushrooms, they were to die for, tomatoes and black coffee, very sweet.'

'What?'

'OK, I exaggerate – it was a small piece of rock-hard bread and black tea. Hello, my name is Mirabeau, Gabriel Mirabeau,' he said offering his hand. 'Your eye's a mess.'

The man wore small, rounded spectacles, had bushy eyebrows and had, thought Moreau, a reassuring smile. 'Henri Moreau. I'm a postman – at least I was until yesterday. So, it wasn't all a dream then.'

'Sadly not. It really happened. The French really have turned on their own people, doing the Germans' dirty work for them. To think I used to be proud to call myself a Frenchman. Not any more.'

'They took the women and children.'

'Yes, we're all being kept separately.'

'Did they s-say anything else? How long they intend to

keep us here.'

Mirabeau laughed. 'Henri – may I call you Henri? I've been here six months and I know nothing, except…'

'Except?'

'You've just arrived. Maybe it'd be too much to tell you.'

'Tell me.' It was obvious he wanted to.

'They send people off on trains. Where no one knows. But rumoured to be east, way out somewhere in Poland. And I don't reckon… They say they kill them there with gas.'

'Gas? That's… that's ridiculous.'

'You would've thought so.'

They sat in silence for a while, Moreau massaging his head, pressing the handkerchief to his eye. Already he was becoming accustomed to the stench of so many dirty men thrown in together. It seemed strange to think Lilly and Marguerite were close by but so far out of reach. He needed a drink, water, anything, something to eat. He wanted a bath, a shave; he needed to feel clean. He realised Lilly had made a mistake packing all their things into one case – for now he had nothing, no clean pair of pants, no toothbrush, no soap, nothing. Good God, they keep pigs in better conditions than this. The minutes ticked by, the hours. He wandered around a bit, so many men, so many stripped of their individuality, reduced to filthy, hungry animals, their every thought consumed by nothing but the most basic needs. Returning to his space, he asked Mirabeau what people did all day.

'Nothing,' came the reply. 'Nothing to do but worry. Oh, we have roll call first thing and they let us out for a bit of fresh air in the afternoons. They worry in case we all get

TB or dysentery or something.'

'I'm not even a Jew,' said Moreau.

Mirabeau's large eyebrows knotted in puzzlement. 'You're not a Jew?' he said slowly. 'I don't understand, so what are you doing here?'

'I don't know. An administrative oversight, I guess.' He didn't mention Lilly.

'My God, man, then you're saved,' said Mirabeau, slapping him on his knee. 'Have you spoken to someone about this?'

'I've tried but I keep getting palmed off.'

'Do you have your papers?'

'Of course,' he said, checking his inside pocket.

'All you have to do…. No, that might not work. Now that you're in here, they might be happy to let you rot. We have to think.'

After a while, Mirabeau put his finger up. 'Got it,' he said. 'Tell them you've got TB. Like I said, they're terrified of it – you'll be out of here in a jiffy.'

'Tuberculosis? What do you mean? Surely, if it's that easy, why doesn't everyone do it; why don't you do it?'

'Because we're Jews. A Jew with TB? Best thing is a bullet. But you'd get away with it. Oh, Henri, I'm so happy to have met you. You've got to get out of here. If I can go to my death knowing I've saved a man, just one man, I'd be very happy.'

Moreau thought of Lilly. *Don't desert us. Do whatever you have to do, just save us. And if you can't save me, save her.* He shook his head, trying to rid himself of the memory.

'Henri? Henri, listen to me. Rub your face hard with your hands – again and again until your skin is bright red. Then bite your tongue until it bleeds. It'll be hard but you have to do it. Then holler for a guard. Trust me, you'll be out of here by nightfall.'

Mirabeau was right – the biting of one's tongue was hard. But with his new friend's urging, he finally managed it. Mixed with his spittle, Moreau was surprised at the amount of blood he'd managed to produce.

'Well done,' said Mirabeau. He shook his hand. 'You're as red as a beetroot. I'm sorry to be losing you already but out you go, my friend. I wish you all the luck in the world. Are you married?'

'No.' He said it without hesitation.

'Excellent. Get out of here, live, and make love to as many women as you can.'

'Thank you,' said Moreau, putting on his coat. 'I'll never forget you.'

The man smiled, exposing his rotting teeth. 'Go now. Call for a guard.'

Moreau staggered through the dormitory, his hand at his mouth, crying in pain. He never knew he could act so well. He pounded at the wrought iron gates at the end of the dormitory. 'Guard, guard. Help!'

A man appeared, short and plump, not a policeman but still a Frenchman in prison officer uniform. 'Get back. What is it? What's all this noise?'

'I'm ill, truly,' said Moreau breathlessly. 'TB.'

The guard stared at him for a moment, his eyes widening on seeing Moreau's red face, his bloodied eye and his bleeding mouth. 'Shit.' Calling over his shoulder, he shouted, 'Faure, I need some help here.'

The man called Faure appeared. 'Look at him,' said the first guard, pointing at Moreau. 'TB.'

'You're joking,' said Faure. 'Get him out quick. Go call

the superintendent.'

It didn't take long. Moreau was led outside, away from everyone, back onto the central yard. How lovely, he thought, to breathe in the fresh air. It was a dull day, heavy clouds sweeping across the sky. Everything grey. With a jolt, he saw snaking towards him, a long line of children wearing their coats and hats, some with small cases or parcels, escorted by numerous guards. The main gates were open, a few policemen standing by. Were they going east, to Poland, as Mirabeau had said?

The superintendent arrived, a gaunt man with a pencil moustache. 'How long have you had it?' he barked.

'I s-saw my doctor last week.'

He eyed Moreau, squinting. 'Looks bad. You better not have passed it on. Why didn't you say anything?'

'I tried but no one listened.'

'Where's your star?' he asked, pointing at Moreau's coat.

'That's it, I'm not a Jew.'

'You're not? Your papers,' he said, snapping his fingers. The man took them, holding them gingerly, as if fearful of contracting the disease. 'Why, you really are not a Jew.'

'I tried to tell them that too.'

The man eyed him while Moreau held his handkerchief to his mouth. For good effect, he coughed.

The superintendent returned him his papers. 'Get out of here. Faure, give him a few francs for the train fare.'

'Eh? Me?'

The superintendent walked off. Moreau stopped himself from thanking him. Reluctantly, Faure handed him the money.

'Thank you.'

He stood there, coughed again, unsure what to do.

'Well, what are you waiting for?' asked Faure. 'A taxi? The gates are open. Fuck off out of here.'

'Oh, right.' Moreau couldn't quite believe it could be that easy. Mirabeau had been right. 'Right, yes. Thank you.'

As he turned to leave, his heart hammering with delight, he heard the scream. '*Papa!*'

Shit, it was Marguerite. Turning he saw her amongst all those children, holding Lanky to her chest. 'Papa, Papa!'

'Oh my God,' he muttered. His daughter, his gorgeous daughter. 'Marguerite,' he called. Calling her name was a mistake. Marguerite, on hearing her father's voice, broke away from the pack and, still clutching Lanky, started running towards him, sidestepping a guard.

'Stop,' cried the guard.

'Papa.'

'Marguerite.'

'Halt.'

'Papa.'

A gunshot ran out.

His heart hammered. 'No, Marguerite, get back; for Christ's sake, get back.'

'Papa!' Still she ran towards him, her coat flapping open.

'Halt.'

'Stop, Marguerite.'

A second gunshot. She seemed to fly through the air before landing in a crumpled heap on the mud-packed ground, her fingers still gripping onto Lanky.

'Noooo! Marguerite, Marguerite, Margueriiiiiite!'

* * *

The postman seemed on the verge of fainting. 'Are you OK, Moreau?' asked the Gustave Garnier, the teacher.

"There was nothing I could do for them while I was there,' said Moreau, aware of all eyes on him. 'If I escaped I could have helped them. That was my idea; to help them.'

A voice from behind asked, 'And how is your lovely neighbour, Madame Giono?'

Moreau looked round – who'd said that? 'Who?'

Roger Béart, the soldier, stepped forward. 'I hear she's not your neighbour any more, hmm?'

'What? How do you know that?'

'I know her sister-in-law, she does me missus's hair. She told me wife about the postman who walked out of Drancy. Rumour has it you didn't even go home, that you went straight to hers, your Italian bird.'

'No, it wasn't like that.'

'The sister-in-law reckons you and her were carrying on even before her brother died, Madame Giono's husband.'

'No–'

'She moved in pretty quick after your release, so you probably weren't in that much of a hurry to get your wife out of Drancy.'

'Stop! Just stop.'

'Is this true, Henri?' asked the priest.

Moreau cast his eyes down. 'Yes,' he said quietly.

'I know I couldn't have done it,' said Leconte, the policeman. 'If I knew my wife and child were there, I would've stayed. Just in case. I couldn't, in all good conscience, walk out like that.'

'Yeah, but he wanted to shack up with his sexy neighbour, didn't he?' said Béart. 'Couldn't wait.'

'Cowardly in the extreme, if you ask me,' said Garnier.

'He had no intention of saving his wife,' said Leconte.

'If you hadn't been there, Moreau, making good your escape,' said Le Vau, the doctor, 'your daughter wouldn't have been shot.'

'Yeah, but where would s-she be now?' said Moreau. 'I told you what Gabriel Mirabeau told me.'

'The gassing? Maybe it's true, maybe it isn't,' said Béart. 'But even the bloody Germans wouldn't murder the kids.'

'You're the priest, Father,' said Garnier. 'What do you think?'

'You've suffered,' said Father Claudel to Moreau. 'That much is obvious, but it's also true your cowardly behaviour was motivated purely by self-preservation.'

The postman, slouched on his mattress, put his head in his hands.

The men eyed him for a while, feeling a mixture of contempt and pity. No man should see their child killed like that. No man.

Outside, the church clock struck two a.m. Eventually, Nicholas Leconte spoke, breaking the uneasy silence, 'Do you want me to go next?' he said in an almost jolly tone.

'Shouldn't we stick to drawing straws?' asked Béart.

'No, if he wants to go next, let him,' said Garnier, the teacher.

Chapter 6:
The Policeman's Story

'Lord, this is more difficult than I thought.' Running his fingers through his hair, Nicholas Leconte, the former policeman, coughed and muttered something to himself. 'OK, as you probably know, I fought in the war, the last one that is. I was there for three years, three very long and difficult years out in the Palestinian desert. I fought at Gaza, October 1917.'

'Like me,' said Roger Béart, the soldier.

'I know. I'm sure, like you, Béart, I saw things I sometimes still have nightmares about. After Gaza, I got transferred to the Western Front and got gassed. That was my ticket out. I'd done my bit for this nation. I went off to war singing; I returned in silence. Then, after the war, I swapped one uniform for another and I became a policeman, rising to the rank of inspector. I retired when my wife, Emily, fell ill after the death… the death of our son. I looked after her for as long as I could until… until it became too much. I tried. I… I d-don't know what else to say. I killed a man once, in combat, I'll tell you about that, if you like.' He coughed again to the point his eyes started watering.

'What about that case you were on, Leconte?' This was Le Vau, the doctor. 'That murder case; the young girl strangled.'

'Nathalie de Chardin,' he said, wiping his eyes. 'Back in thirty-seven. What about it?'

'Tell us about it.'

'I'd… I'd rather not.'

'You didn't retire after your wife fell ill; you retired years before; soon after that case, didn't you, old man? Why was that?'

Leconte looked flustered, beads of sweat broke out on his brow. 'I don't know. I was tired.'

'Nothing to do with the case itself, then?' asked Le Vau.

The teacher interrupted. 'What are you getting at, Doctor?'

'Tell us, Leconte. Tell us about Nathalie de Chardin.'

* * *

Nathalie de Chardin's body, snug amongst the straw bales, stared up at them, her eyes bulging from her head, still open, the expression of terror still etched within. Florès, the police doctor, wearing a long, cream trench coat despite the July heat, had just finished his initial inspection of the body. 'Strangulation,' he said in his usual booming voice before disappearing. Numerous policemen wandered round the place, including Halimi, the forensics man, looking for clues, turning things over, taking notes.

'Who found her?' asked Leconte, fanning himself with his felt hat.

The old woman in the headscarf, Madame Toubon, the Chardin's housekeeper, plonked her basket of clean washing behind her, dried, ready to take indoors. Glancing at it, Leconte saw the piles of shirts and blouses and, resting on top, various bits of feminine underwear. He glanced back at the body. 'Maurice, her brother, he found her.'

Perrin, his assistant, standing at Leconte's side, also took notes, scribbling in his notepad.

'What time was this?'

'About two hour ago, round noon.'

The inspector tried to avert his gaze from the woman's jagged teeth, the colour of mustard. 'How old is the brother?'

'He be twenty-six, sir.'

The girl, apparently, was twenty-one years old. Her blonde hair, the colour of the straw surrounding her, was held in place by a hairband. She wore a pretty white, floral frock with a red waistband. It didn't appear to be torn in any way. The purple bruises of the murderer's hands were visible around the poor girl's neck.

'Where were you this morning then?'

'Me?' said the woman. 'In the house, polishing. It's what I do ev'ry Thursday morning.'

'And her parents?'

'Monsieur was out at a meeting and Madame was having coffee down town with some lady friends.'

'And Maurice de Chardin?'

'He were out too but I wouldn't know where, sir. He came back half eleven.'

'And who else was around? Did you see anyone else in or around the house this morning?'

'No, sir.'

'Think carefully, woman. It could be important.'

'Well, there were Albert. But he's always here. Part of the furniture is Albert.'

Perrin asked, 'What does this Albert do?'

'He's the odd-job man, sir. Gardening, fencing, cutting, mending. Jack of all trades, if you like. He's from Nantes originally.'

'Is he?' asked Perrin, scribbling this down in his notebook. 'How long he's been here?'

Madame Toubon considered her answer for a moment. 'Two year, maybe. Maybe three.'

'Did you see Albert this morning?' asked Leconte.

'Aye, sir.'

'Whereabouts? What was he doing? Did you see him in here, the barn?'

'No, not exactly, sir. But he would have come in here. Does every morning. Come gets the straw to feed the horses. Stands to reason he was here.'

'Yes, of course.'

The three of them, Leconte, Perrin and the old woman, continued to stand over the body. Her lipstick, Leconte noticed, was smudged. Had she been kissed?

'I suppose you've known her all her life.'

'That I have, sir. Since she were a babe-in-arms. Lovely girl. Had a temper on her, though. It's terrible, this. Who'd do such a thing, eh, Inspector?'

'Did she have a boyfriend?' asked Perrin.

'I wouldn't know that. I'm not one to pry into people's personal doings, sir.'

'Did she always wear lipstick?' asked Leconte. 'Even this time of day?'

The woman thought for a few moments. 'Maybe. Can't say I noticed, sir. Why? Is that important?'

'Probably not. OK, thank you, Madame Toubon; you've been most helpful.'

The woman remained beside him, still gazing down on the body.

'I said thank you, Madame.'

'Oh, begging yours, sir. I'll be off then.'

Leconte and Perrin watched her scoop up her basket of washing and scuttle away.

Satisfied she was out of earshot, the inspector turned to his assistant. 'So, what did Halimi reckon?'

'He reckoned she knew her assailant. Not much evidence of a struggle, so it wasn't like she was dragged into here. She came of her own accord. He checked for footprints but, as you know, sir, there's not been a spot of rain for weeks. Ground's rock hard.'

'Any sign of a sexual assault?'

'None apparently.'

The undertakers had arrived, ready to remove Nathalie de Chardin's body.

Putting his hat back on, Leconte said, 'Come on, we'd better go see the parents. Get it over and done with.'

*

Inspector Leconte knew a little about Bertrand de Chardin and his family. De Chardin was comfortably off; his family had lived in the same house for centuries, a grand affair a good couple of kilometres outside the town itself. They owned some local land, most of which they rented out at what was considered a highly reasonable rate. De Chardin himself was seen as a generous man – helpful to the needy, presents for all his tenants at Christmastime. He ran his estate competently and expertly, with the full assistance of his son, Maurice. And now his daughter was dead – murdered in the barn.

Leconte and Perrin emerged from the de Chardin kitchen twenty minutes later, feeling battered and full of pity. Two police officers were already there, their job to offer succour for the grieving mother. All they did was stand in the corner of the kitchen looking like spare parts. Sitting at the kitchen table, Madame de Chardin, unable to speak for tears, collapsed on her husband. Maurice, still in shock from having discovered his strangled sister, paced up and down the kitchen, smoking one cigarette after another. A couple of tabby cats tiptoed in, their tails erect. Leconte asked the family about Nathalie's love life, an awkward but necessary line of questioning. There had been boyfriends, they said, boys her own age but nothing serious. Leconte asked if he and Perrin could see her bedroom. They weren't keen, he could tell, especially Madame de Chardin, but reluctantly she agreed.

Maurice de Chardin insisted on accompanying the two men. He waited at the door, his hands in his jacket pockets, watching them intently, making them feel ill at ease. Nathalie de Chardin's bedroom was spacious, infused with natural light, overlooking the barn, the fields and the woodland beyond. It was, mused Leconte, a heavenly view. Wooden floor with a Persian rug, dark green wallpaper, a double bed, a framed print of a painting by Renoir. It was the room of a young girl, a girl, as her mother had said, full of dreams, in a hurry to start living. She had a mahogany writing desk, with a leather top and numerous drawers and little compartments. Leconte pulled a drawer open – filled with pens, bits of paper, a writing pad and a pocket-sized bible. A copy of Proust lay on her bedside table. Leconte spotted a sheet of paper folded in half within the leaves of the book. He swiped the paper and pocketed it. Maurice narrowed his eyes but said nothing.

Monsieur de Chardin, having given Leconte a photograph of his daughter, showed the two men to the door. Taking Leconte's hand in both his, he said, 'Inspector, find the man who did this. I beg you – find him. Whoever did this doesn't deserve to live. We won't rest until we see him on the gallows.'

'Yes, sir. We will find him.'

Standing outside, the sun blazing over the fields in the distance, Leconte, adjusted his hat. Turning to his assistant, he said. 'Ours is a difficult job, Perrin. Let's get out of here.'

'Shouldn't we speak to the odd-job man, sir?'

He sighed. 'If we must.'

Having asked Madame Toubon, they found Albert in his cottage, a converted, thatched-roof outbuilding on the outskirts of the estate. He opened the door to them, wearing a pair of stained dungarees, a handmade cigarette in one hand, a mug of coffee in the other. Both Leconte and Perrin had to duck to enter the front door. Albert, a short man, showed them through to his living room, a dark, cramped space, but cosy in its way. A wooden table dominated the room, a bowl of fruit; a large stove in the corner, on it a framed photograph of a middle-aged woman.

'You're going to offer us a coffee then?' asked Leconte.

'Does this look like a café?' The man had a faint odour of horse manure about him.

Sitting down, Perrin opposite him, Leconte swallowed his disappointment. He was desperate for a coffee. The Chardins hadn't offered him one and it hadn't been the time to ask.

Leconte and Perrin asked Albert the usual questions – he'd been in the fields, he said, strengthening the fences, and no, he hadn't seen or heard anyone or anything.

'Did you like Nathalie de Chardin?' asked Leconte.

'You asking me?' He shrugged. 'Didn't really think about it. If truth be told, she was a stuck-up little madam; spoilt rotten, she was. Feel sorry for her though. She didn't deserve that. No one does.'

'How did she treat you?'

He took a long drag on his cigarette. 'Put it this way – she made sure I knew my place.' The heavy stench of tobacco smoke hung around them. 'She'd click her fingers: "Do this, Albert; do that, Albert". Nice arse though.'

Perrin leapt out of his seat, 'Oi, you bastard, the girl's not even in her grave yet. Show some respect.'

Albert put his hands up. 'Alright, alright. I'm sorry. No offence.'

He did look genuinely remorseful, thought Leconte. 'What's your full name?' he asked.

'Albert Kahn.'

'You Jewish?' asked Perrin.

'Yeah, what of it?'

'So,' said Leconte, waving away the smoke, 'you come from Nantes.'

'What about it?'

'What did you do there?'

'Worked in a factory. Tractor parts. Then as a gardener.'

'What happened?' asked Perrin. 'Why did you come here?'

'Fancied a change.'

'That's it?'

He pulled a face. 'What do you want me to say?'

'How long have you worked for the Chardins?' asked Leconte.

Looking skywards, as if mentally counting off time, he said, 'About two years. So, what's this got to do with that girl?'

'We like to get a full picture of anyone associated with the deceased.'

'You don't think—'

'No, not at all; rest assured. Were you married?'

Unwittingly, Albert glanced at the photo on the stove. 'You're sharp, you are. Wasn't married but had a woman for a while. Few years.'

'What was her name?'

'Mirabelle.'

'What happened?'

'You sure ask a lot, don't you? She left me; buggered off with the factory manager.'

'Children?'

'Nah.' He stubbed his cigarette out in an empty ashtray. 'That's why she left me.'

'What do you mean?' asked Perrin.

The man looked down. After a while, he said, 'She couldn't have kids but she blamed me.' He looked at Leconte. 'Don't you go repeating that, right?'

'And who would we be repeating it to?'

*

Driving back to the town, Perrin at the wheel, Leconte studied the photograph of the dead girl. She had bright blue, piercing eyes, plucked eyebrows, an air of confidence and vitality. 'She was some looker.'

'Let's see,' said Perrin.

'No, you fool, keep your eyes on the road.'

He retrieved the sheet of paper he'd taken from Nathalie's bedroom, aware of Perrin watching him from the corner of his eye.

'My God,' he said, puffing his cheeks. 'She had an affair with Bloch.'

'Bloch? Gaspard Bloch? You're joking, right?'

'I'm afraid not. Isn't he due to run for town mayor? You'd think a man in his position… This is a letter he wrote to her.'

'Hell, what does it say?' asked Perrin, swerving the car.

'Blast it, man, mind where you're going.'

'Sorry, boss.'

'The letter, it says *Find someone your own age, my darling. You're a beautiful young girl, Nathalie, you must have a hundred suitors queuing up at your door. Someone who will love you with all his heart. But please, we cannot go on, you must realise this. Won't you reconsider our situation? Think of your future. I'm a family man. I'm too old for you. In my position, we'd never be free. I know you're a sensible girl and you wouldn't want a fuss. I'm sure you understand.*' At first, he thought the writer had made a mistake writing 'cannot' but then realised that the letter pad on the typewriter had made the 'c' look a little like an 'o'.

'Risky,' said Perrin. 'Writing a letter like that.'

'He thinks she won't make a fuss. But just in case, listen to this… *Nathalie, if you're ever short of anything, or if you need a helping hand, don't be afraid to ask.*'

'He's asking to be blackmailed. Does he sign it?'

'No. We don't even know it's from him, and it's typed. But there's a scribbled note, presumably from Nathalie, saying *I hate you, Gaspara Bloch*. I think tomorrow we'll go see Councillor Bloch. Perrin, for God's sake, were you born blind? You almost ran that woman over.'

*

That night, Leconte tried to make love to his wife. But he couldn't. The image of the purple bruises around Nathalie de Chardin's throat kept haunting him.

*

First thing the following morning, Leconte phoned Councillor Bloch. Reluctantly, Bloch agreed to see the policeman – but not at home, he said, at his office in the town hall.

Leconte made no mention of the councillor during his early morning meeting with the chief inspector, Villiers. Stuffing himself with a couple of croissants, washed down, despite the early hour, with a glass of wine, Villiers, a portly man with yellow teeth, listened as Leconte briefed him on Nathalie de Chardin's murder. 'Looks like you might have your man right there,' said Villiers.

'Who?'

'The Jew. This Alfred Kahn.'

'Albert.'

'Whatever. Get the lowdown on him,' he said, spluttering flakes of croissant. 'Ring the boys in Nantes, see whether they got anything on him.'

Exactly as Leconte had planned to do. 'Yes, sir.'

'You sure there was no sexual element to this? She was a pretty girl,' he said, looking again at the photograph.

'No sign at all.'

'That's one thing, I suppose. Look, Bertrand de Chardin is an influential man. My brother-in-law is one of his tenants. He's a big supporter of the police. Everyone's talking about this. I mean, Christ, this is only the second murder we've had for twenty years. We'll be judged on this, so we need an arrest – and quick. Shouldn't be difficult. She knew her killer by all accounts. So get out there, Leconte, and do your job. You've got all day.'

He coughed. 'Day?'

An hour later, Leconte was sitting in Bloch's town hall office, a small but plush space with wood-panelled walls, a dark green carpet and a large framed photograph of Albert Lebrun, the president, upon the wall. Gaspard Bloch sat behind his desk, drumming his fingers. Upon his desk, a photo of his wife and two daughters, or so Leconte assumed. In the corner of the room was a small table with a typewriter. Perrin was back at the station – phoning Nantes.

'Never even heard of the girl,' said Bloch, looking straight at Leconte's eyes. The man, wearing a dark suit, had neatly combed jet-black hair, a strong jaw and was heavily tanned. Not a man to mess with, thought Leconte.

'Are you sure, sir?'

'I know the family, of course. Knew that there was a girl but didn't know her name and never met her – as far as I know. Look, will this take long? I've got a party meeting in a minute. I've got an election to win.'

'Of course. I appreciate your time, sir. It's just that…'

'Yes? What is it?'

'We found this on her bedside table.' Leconte passed him the letter.

The councillor scanned his eyes over it, his face reddening. 'Why, it's got my…'

'Exactly. *I hate you, Gaspara Bloch.* That's quite something to write.'

'I don't understand,' he spluttered. 'Why would she…'

'Did you write the letter, sir?'

Bloch stared at him with a look bordering on hate. 'Don't be bloody ridiculous.'

'Was Nathalie de Chardin your… how should I put this—'

'How dare you! I'm a family man—'

'Exactly as it says in the letter. *I'm a family man. I'm too old for you.*'

Bloch glanced back at the letter. 'Anyone could have written this,' he said, pushing the sheet of paper back across the desk.

'Yes, of course, but not many people have a typewriter,' he said looking over at the small table against the wall.

Unable to stop himself, Bloch also glanced over his shoulder. His face reddened further. 'This is preposterous,' he yelled, rising to his feet. Only then did Leconte realise how tall Bloch was. Trying to contain himself, Bloch leant across the table, snarling at the inspector, his eyes watering with anger. 'I don't think you know who I am. I consider the chief inspector a good friend of mine. If one word of this baseless accusation gets out, one word, mind you, I'll have your guts for garters.'

'I'm only doing my job, sir.'

'You won't have a job by the end of the day.' He sat back down heavily. 'Now get out.'

Leconte stood up. 'Can I ask, sir, where were you yesterday morning?'

Bloch glared at him as if wondering whether to grace the inspector's impertinence with an answer. Eventually, putting his hands on the table, he said, 'I was here until half-ten.' Leconte couldn't help but notice a band of pale skin on his left index finger.

'After that?'

He sighed. 'After that I had a meeting in Sainte-Foy with a business associate, Georges Lescot. No need to take my word for it – ask my secretary.'

He did. On his way out, Leconte asked the secretary and indeed, according to the diary, Councillor Bloch was where he said he was.

*

'So, what have you got?' asked Leconte.

Leconte and Perrin had met in their usual place near the station – a small, deserted café - wanting to avoid Villiers and his growing impatience. Sitting outside beneath a green and white striped parasol, with a coffee and a cake each, Leconte leant down to stroke a large black and white cat, a regular visitor to the café.

'Well, Albert Kahn has got previous all right.'

Leconte choked on his *pain au chocolat* – he hadn't expected that. 'In what way?'

'He got called in about a couple years ago for hitting his girlfriend, this Mirabelle,' said Perrin, stuffing a slice of cake into his mouth.

Leconte waited until his assistant swallowed. 'Was it

serious?'

'No, and no charges,' said Perrin, wiping his mouth with a napkin. 'The neighbours were the ones to call the police. Sounds of it, he got his knuckles rapped and told to go away and not do it again. He never had the chance. She upped and left him soon after, as he told us.'

'And so he came here. I wonder how he found a job with a respectable family like the Chardins.'

'Ah, that I also found out. The chap in Nantes was very helpful. After his job at the factory, he worked as a gardener on an estate and got himself a good reference.'

'So, his woman left him and he came here.'

'Aha. No, not quite. Listen to this… two years ago, some stable hand complained to the police about Kahn, claiming he'd tried to force himself on his daughter.'

'Now you're talking. How old was she?'

'Nineteen.'

'What happened?'

A young couple sat down at the table near theirs. Both men raised their hats at them. They mouthed hello in return.

'Nothing,' said Perrin, lowering his voice. 'The girl refused to talk. I guess that's why he came here – to escape an angry father.'

Leconte was slightly disappointed to see that the cat had slinked away. Finishing his coffee, he said, 'I think we should go talk to our Jewish friend again. Come, let's go.'

*

First, they called in at the house. Madame de Chardin was in bed with a migraine, Monsieur had gone to the funeral parlour in town but Maurice, their son, met them at the front door and said they'd find Kahn in his cottage. 'Oh, before you go, Inspector,' said Maurice. 'Can you wait a minute? Just a minute,' he shouted, running back in doors.

Leconte and Perrin waited, rocking on their feet. One of the tabby cats rushed out of the house. Leconte wondered whether they should attempt to stop it but it was already too late to do so without appearing undignified. Moments later, they heard Maurice's footsteps returning from inside. 'Listen, Inspector, I found this in barn this morning.' He dropped something in Leconte's palm.

It was a ring, a gold band with Saint Francis etched on it. 'Patron saint of animals,' said Leconte.

'Let's see,' said Perrin. 'You don't know who it belongs to?' he asked Maurice.

'Never seen it before.'

'Not your father's?'

'No. But there were a lot of men about yesterday, police, doctors and all that.'

'Or it could have been there for years.'

Maurice de Chardin shrugged. 'Perhaps.'

Bloch came to Leconte's mind – the image of the band of pale skin on his finger.

'Well, if you excuse us,' said Leconte, taking the ring from his colleague.

*

Leconte rapped hard on the door. Still wearing his dungarees, Kahn nervously stood aside to allow them in, the two men ducking beneath the low beam. 'Coffee?' asked Kahn, a tremor in his voice. 'There's some in the pot, if – if you like.'

'So, you make a habit of assaulting women, do you?' asked Leconte.

'What? No. Well, maybe I got carried away once.'

'Twice,' interrupted Perrin.

'To our knowledge,' added Leconte, taking a seat at Kahn's table.

'OK, I admit it. I get jealous. That's why I don't have anything to do with women any more. More trouble than it's worth. What – what are you d-doing?' he asked Perrin on seeing the policeman opening drawers and cupboards, pushing things aside, rummaging.

'Looking for evidence, what d'you think?'

'S-shouldn't you have a warrant or something?'

'Sue me.'

'So what exactly was your relationship with your employer's daughter, eh?' asked Leconte.

'Nothing. Nothing, I swear it.' Kahn kept glancing at Perrin at work.

'Look at me,' shouted Leconte. 'I reckon you made a pass at her. Pretty girl, after all. Way beyond your league, but still, you gave it a shot, didn't you, Kahn?'

'No.'

'And of course, she turned you down. But she was horrible to you in the process.'

'No, really, I never did.'

'You said yourself she was a "stuck-up little madam, spoilt rotten". Those were your words, weren't they? So, your pride's been hurt. How dare she, the bitch? Is that what you thought, eh? Is that what you thought?' The sound of Perrin upturning a box of tools and items onto the wooden floor made Kahn jump. 'You thought, that little miss needs teaching a lesson, didn't you?'

'No!' cried Kahn. 'No, please; you've got it all wrong.'

'But you got carried away, as you just said; you lost control, and before you knew it, your hands are round her throat. You didn't mean to, didn't mean to squeeze the life out of her; it was an accident.'

The man suddenly burst into tears, taking Leconte by surprise. 'I loved her; I admit that, she was beautiful. But I loved her as a man might his daughter. I've never been able to have kids, me. That's why my woman left me.'

'You said it was she who couldn't have children.'

'No, it were me. No lead in my pencil. Listen, Inspector, hear me out.'

'Go on, I'm all ears.' Behind them Perrin was still busy rooting about, searching.

'I had a kid sister. Much younger than me. She was killed. Run over. Just ten years old, she was. I was already twenty-one. Since that day, I've wanted to be a father, to have a daughter. Mademoiselle Nathalie, yes, she could be sharp, but most of the time she was civil to me. Always stopped to say hello. I would never have harmed a hair on that girl's head, I swear it, Inspector. Anyway, she had a boyfriend. Well, a man friend. He was much older than her. I saw them once. House was empty. I reckon they must have thought I'd gone out. I had, but I'd come back.'

'What did he look like, this man?' asked Leconte.

'I don't know. Tall, older, dark hair, suntanned. Had a nice car – a Peugeot. Red.'

'Well, well, well; look what I've found!' cried Perrin, emerging from the shadows of the cottage, his hand behind his back.

'What? What is it, man?'

As Perrin held them up, Kahn gripped the table, the

colour draining from his face.

'Jesus, Perrin, what have you got there?'

Perrin threw the item on the table.

Leconte's eyes widened. There, on the table in front of him, was a red pair of girl's knickers.

*

The following day, Leconte had his usual morning meeting with Chief Inspector Villiers. His boss was in an exultant mood, gulping back his wine and wolfing down his croissant. 'Good work, Nicholas,' he said, leaving Leconte slightly taken aback by the sudden use of his first name. 'Open-and-shut case. He had the motive, the opportunity and the means. The public are off our back and the Chardin family can start to grieve. It's the funeral tomorrow. Thought I'd better go, you know.'

'Sir, I've been giving it a lot of thought. I'm not convinced we've got the right man.'

Villiers coughed. 'You what?' he yelled.

'It's all circumstantial. Nothing concrete. I phoned the offices of Georges Lescot just now.'

'Who?' he asked, sucking his fingers clean of crumbs.

'The man Gaspard Bloch was meant to be meeting at the time of the murder.'

'You said Bloch's secretary confirmed it.'

'I spoke to Lescot himself. He said Bloch cancelled the meeting at the last minute, feigning sickness. Lescot was furious, said he didn't believe him.'

'Careful what you're saying, Leconte.'

'Boss, Nathalie was Bloch's mistress. He also happens to own a red Peugeot. We should get that typewriter tested. I noticed a tiny splodge on the letter 'c', which we need to checkout. And we should check the bank accounts of both Bloch and the girl; see if any money has been transferred.'

'Listen, Leconte…'

'And Nathalie's brother found a ring in their barn, and I've got a feeling it–'

'Stop!' Villiers slammed his fist against the table, causing his plate and glass to jump. 'Are you mad? We've got our man – your little Jew, Alfred Kahn–'

'Albert, sir.'

'Yes, whatever. He has a history of assaulting women, confessed feelings for the girl, and those knickers belonging to the girl, as confirmed by that cleaner woman.'

'But, sir–'

Quickly, Villiers rose from the table, reaching across, pulling Leconte up by his tie. 'Now listen, Leconte. Gaspard Bloch is an important man. A very important man. He is likely to be our next mayor, that is if he can keep out of the sun long enough. And he likes us, champions our cause, if you like. Unlike the toad we've got now who thinks we're all corrupt. If your insinuations ever become public knowledge, his career is dead, and yours, my little Hercule Poirot, will be as well. And that wouldn't be your first misfortune.'

Trying not to show his level of discomfort, Leconte managed to splutter an 'OK'.

Villiers threw him back. Landing in his seat, Leconte turned his head left and right, adjusting his collar and tie.

'You will be called up at the trial. I'll be there. You know what to do. Now get out of my sight.'

*

Nicholas Leconte knew what to do all right.

Eight months later, March 1938, Albert Kahn was tried, pleading his innocence. Leconte gave his evidence, as did Perrin and Florès, the police doctor, and Halimi, the forensics man. It came as no surprise when the eight-man jury, urged by the judge, returned a guilty verdict. Donning his black cap, the judge sentenced Kahn to death. The man was led away, still screaming his innocence.

Another eight months later, during which time Kahn's appeal had failed and a week before the execution was due to take place, Nicholas Leconte was having a coffee in the café near the police station. Sitting inside to warm himself up after a day out in the cold, he read the local newspaper, shaking his head at the folly of a world on the verge, it seemed, of war. Locally, there'd had been a demonstration outside the town hall – farmers objecting to the cost of rising rents. The new mayor, the dashing and popular Gaspard Bloch, justified it on the rising cost of living.

A shadow fell across him. Looking up, Leconte saw the figure of Florès, the police doctor.

'Do you mind if I take a seat?'

Leconte minded very much but nodded a yes. The doctor had changed, thought Leconte. No longer portly, he looked terribly thin and ragged.

'Foul day, isn't it? So cold. They reckon it could snow,' said the doctor, placing his cup and saucer on the table, removing his hat. 'You often come in here, don't you?' His voice, once booming, now sounded reedy.

'Yes.'

Retrieving a flask from his inside coat pocket, Florès unscrewed the cap and added a lug of alcohol to his coffee. On seeing Leconte watching him, he said, 'Makes it go down easier. Cheers.'

Florès told him about his day, about driving to a farm some twelve kilometres away; something to do with a ten-year-old boy, a tractor and an accident. 'You know, I haven't spoken to you since the Chardin murder. Terrible affair. Not one we're ever likely to forget. In fact, not a day goes by when...' He shook his head, stirring his coffee. 'That poor girl, so pretty, so much to live for. I go see the mother fairly regular. Not that there's much I can prescribe for migraines. That boy, Maurice, he's gone off the rails lately. Crashed his father's car the other day. It's hard seeing Monsieur and Madame de Chardin knowing what I know and knowing they don't.'

'What do you mean?'

'You know, about their daughter.'

'What about their daughter?'

'You know.' He paused, looking hard at Leconte. 'Oh, maybe you don't.'

'Spit it out, man.'

'Heck, I thought *you* knew. Well, if I tell you, you'd better keep it under your hat otherwise you'll have Villiers after you. Nathalie de Chardin, at the time of her death, was three months' pregnant.'

*

A week later, a grisly wet November day at the crack of dawn, Leconte attended the execution. It'd been the first in the town since the war, twenty years before. Standing in the prison courtyard, he turned his collar up against the drizzle. The guillotine was ready, a number of prison guards hovering nearby.

Won't you reconsider our situation? The words in Bloch's

letter had haunted him since bumping into the police doctor. Kahn was infertile, no lead in his pencil. Nathalie was pregnant. Bloch was already a father to two girls – Leconte remembered the photograph on his desk. Bloch would have wanted her to have an abortion. She must have refused. He went to see her. A pregnant mistress, half his age, would have left his career in tatters; it would've destroyed his business interests. He probably didn't mean to kill her, as he'd said to Kahn, but he had.

He'd hoped to avoid the Chardins but, returning to the reception area, they were there, drinking coffee. Both had dressed up for the occasion, Madame de Chardin wearing a dark purple skirt and jacket, as if going to a tea party, her face made-up.

On seeing him, Monsieur de Chardin rushed over, waving at him incongruously. 'How I've waited for this day, Inspector,' he said, shaking Leconte's hand rigorously. 'I want to thank you. Justice is about to be done.'

'To think we gave that vile little man a job,' said his wife, joining them. 'A job, a cottage, everything.'

Monsieur de Chardin checked his watch. 'Come, my dear, we must take our place in the gallery. Excuse us, Inspector.' Taking her hand, he led his wife away.

Leconte knew, even now, he could say something; that he could save Kahn's life. Instead, he watched them leave as the bile caught in his throat.

After a few minutes, bracing himself, he made his way outside and took his place on the perimeter of the execution yard. Turning his collar back up, he waited, aware that, above him, the Chardins would be in the viewing gallery looking down on the abysmal proceedings. So what if it was the wrong man? Ultimately, it didn't matter – as long as someone, anyone, paid. He would never have been able to bring Gaspard Bloch to justice. The man had power, he had influence and he had money. Leconte knew the system too well. One way or another, Bloch would have got away with it. And where would that leave the Chardins? They'd be forever scarred by their daughter's death, but now, at least, they could carry on with their lives; they could go to their graves satisfied that, as de Chardin had said, justice had been done.

Dressed in prison garb, Albert Kahn was led out, handcuffed, flanked by two prison officers, a priest three paces behind. This time there were no histrionics. Kahn seemed resigned. He sidestepped a puddle. Even on the point of death, mused Leconte, we don't want to get our shoes wet.

On meeting his executioner, Kahn lifted his handcuffed hands and the two men shook hands. Kahn kneeled in front of the wooden block, his head bowed. Asked if he had any final words, he jerked his head up and looked straight at Leconte. The inspector felt a shot of pain stab him in the heart. 'Yes,' said Kahn, his eyes locked onto Leconte's. 'Tell Mirabelle I always loved her.' He lowered his head as the priest said a final prayer.

Gently pushing him down, the executioner placed Kahn's head against the wooden block. The untying of the rope, the whoosh of the blade. It was over so quickly. Albert Kahn, found guilty of strangling Nathalie de Chardin to death, had been executed by guillotine. He was forty-five years old.

Glancing up, Leconte caught sight of the Chardins, standing up, embracing.

* * *

'You let an innocent man go to his death,' said the doctor. 'I was friends with Doctor Florès. He's dead now. The drink got to him, poor old chap. I bumped into him in a bar once. Drunk as a lord he was, and miserable with it. He told me he'd seen you a few days before the execution. Nathalie had gone to see him. He offered her an abortion. She didn't want one; she wanted to keep it. If the jury had known, I reckon Albert Kahn would still be alive today. When, before the trial, Florès tried to raise it, he was told to keep his mouth shut.'

'It would have left Bloch, the future mayor, in a difficult situation,' said the teacher.

'Impossible situation,' said the doctor. 'It would have destroyed him.'

'So instead, he destroyed her,' said the postman.

'And *you* knew, didn't you, Leconte? The pregnancy, the ring, the typewriter, the car, the cancelled meeting.'

'Circumstantial,' said Leconte, his head in his hands.

'And the evidence against Kahn wasn't?'

'I couldn't do anything; believe me. Not with Villiers against me.'

'Every boss has a boss, Leconte,' said the priest. 'Apart from the Lord Himself. You could have gone over his head. You should have insisted on testing that typewriter, pushed Councillor Bloch on why he lied about that meeting.'

'OK, OK, I know. Don't you think… He's dead now, isn't he? Bloch's dead?'

'Yeah,' said the soldier. 'Everyone knows that. Skin cancer.'

'But that doesn't absolve you, Leconte,' said the priest. 'You were too weak to stand up against the system.'

'And an innocent man died as a result,' added the doctor.

Leconte fell onto his mattress, clutching his throat as he coughed more violently than he'd done for years, his body shaking as he again experienced the taste of poisonous gas on his tongue, his mind throwing him back to 1917.

The church clock struck three.

'We're doing well for time,' said Moreau. 'Do you three want to draw s-straws or do we have a volunteer?'

Gustave Garnier, the teacher, Roger Béart, the soldier, and Father Claudel drew straws. The soldier lost.

Chapter 7:
The Soldier's Story

They'd been riding for days. A battalion of French cavalry, traipsing through the Palestinian desert. The officers knew where they were heading, another camp some 80 kilometres away, but hadn't seen fit to tell the men. Not that it'd make much difference anyway – no one knew one destination from another in this godforsaken place. To Private Roger Béart and his khaki-clad comrades it was all the same, just mile upon mile of desert and sun. He was tired, dead tired, as were all the men, as were the horses and the mules. The monotonous landscape did little to raise their spirits – valleys of sand surrounded by mountains of sand. By day, the men rode their horses, sweltering under the scorching heat, only their wide-brimmed straw hats saving them from the worst. The mules brought up the rear laden with the precious water tanks, one of them pulling the wagon containing the Lewis gun. Water rations were strictly controlled – they had plenty of water but it had to last and one always had to have enough for contingencies. And then there was the sand, the bloody sand. It got everywhere – in their food, their water, in their mouths, their eyes, under their clothes. Jesus, thought Béart, even when you went for a piss, you'd find sand on your cock. Their whole world had been reduced to nothing but sand and sun, both unrelenting, both tortuous.

By night they shivered from the cold. Those lucky enough not to be on guard duty lay on their backs under their blankets gazing up at the limitless glittering night sky, the multitude of stars brighter than they'd ever seen, the moon close enough to touch. Many found the sky at night comforting, putting into perspective man's petty squabbles, but Béart hated it – its vastness frightened him, made him conscious of his mortality.

Béart and his horse, Hector, named, he'd been told, after Berlioz, the composer, had been partners for over two years. They'd got to know each other, he knew Hector's moods, his little foibles. And Béart loved him in a way he'd never loved anyone else. Hector was a gelding, fifteen hands tall, dark brown in colour, almost red, like a red setter, a blaze of white on his nose and one white sock. There was no questioning it, he was a handsome devil. But this war and this unending trek had begun to take its toll on Hector. He was nine years old – too old for this sort of thing, thought Béart. He deserved to be retired off; he'd done his bit for France. His coat was not as shiny as before, he hung his head too low. Man and beast – united in their sufferance.

It was the fifth day. Each day Major Brunet sent a couple of men off in advance to scout for enemy movement. Meanwhile, Béart was fuming. He'd lost half a packet of cigarettes. Some bastard had nicked them during the night. Riding alongside Moulin, he asked, 'Who'd do that to his fellow comrade?'

'One mean bugger, that's who.'

'I'd rationed them all out – four in my pocket for the day, the rest of the pack in me haversack. Now, I've got four left to last God knows how long.' He could tell that Moulin wasn't that bothered about his misfortune. He didn't mention it again. Everything about this place was a misfortune, and there was always that fear of an ambush, of being caught unawares. Bloody slippery fellows, those Turks. Béart's missing cigarettes was not likely to feature highly on Moulin's list of concerns. Moulin's face had blackened from the sun and ingrained dirt and was lined with dried streaks of sweat. His eyes looked vacant; he'd aged twenty years in five days. He'd already grown a beard which he scratched and pulled upon constantly; his clothes were wet from sweat, his palms calloused from holding the reins for so many hours a day. But every man was Moulin; every man looked the same. And Moulin, like everyone else, rarely spoke. Talking required too much effort. Instead, each man fell into his own thoughts, the things that gave him comfort, that reminded him of home. Béart daydreamed about rain. Never again would he complain about rain. He dreamt of cold winter nights at home in Normandy, sitting beside the fire, a dog at his feet, while his mother knitted or, occasionally, played a simple tune on the piano. Then to bed with a hot brick warming the icy cold sheets, snuggling down for the night, the clock ticking on the bedside table.

Béart had been brought up with horses. His mother said he knew how to ride before he could walk. They lived on a farm. His father worked hard, up at dawn, working until late in the evening. One night he didn't come home. His mother searched the outbuildings, calling his name, but couldn't find him. A sleepless night ensued. A labourer found him the following morning – lying face down in a field. Dead. A heart attack. Not yet fifty. No age. Béart was still too young to take the farm over, for which he was thankful – there was no way he wanted to be a farmer. So his mother sold the farm and lived in moderate comfort in the town. She never said so but Béart always suspected that she was happier in town, away from the unrelenting harshness of the countryside. Béart didn't miss it either, but he did miss the horses. As soon as he was old enough he got a job as a stablehand and horses were once again at the centre of his life. In the summer of 1915, he was conscripted. The army, seeing his equine affinity, put him in the cavalry. His mother was delighted. Her son looked so handsome in his uniform. Pity he lacked the education to be an officer, but that was hardly his fault. He'd soon prove himself though; he'd soon be promoted.

Two years on, and Béart hadn't been promoted. Still the lowly private, the lowest of the low, still yet to fire his gun in anger, yet to see the whites of their eyes. But better a private in the cavalry, as he always said, than an NCO in the infantry.

Béart stroked Hector's flank – he too was tired, he could see that. The men often walked, leading their horses by the reins, not only to give the horses a bit of a rest but also to allow the men to use a different set of muscles, and to ease the saddle sores.

Further to his right, Béart saw Private Sarde. 'Hey, Sardines,' he called out. 'Give us a tune.' Private Sarde, or

Sardines, the 'toothless wonder', was in the habit of playing his mouth organ – a couple of ditties every hour or so. Never failed to lift a man.

Sarde shook his head. 'Can't,' he said, running his fingers across his lips. His lips were cracked – everyone's lips were cracked. Poor old Sarde, poor old everyone; no more mouth organ.

It was the sixth day, about ten in the morning, the men were on the move, the sun was already high in the sky, sapping the men of their strength. Their breakfast of bully beef, biscuits and black tea already seemed an eternity ago. The two men sent out to reconnoitre came cantering back, only half an hour after leaving. Major Brunet, on seeing them approach, put his hand up, bringing the whole company to a halt.

'Whoa there, Hector,' said Béart.

'Oi, oi,' said Moulin. 'Something's up. An ill-wind brings them back in a hurry.'

The corporal, his face beneath his hat red with exertion and excitement, reported back to the major. Major Brunet, standing in his stirrups, listened, dismissed the corporal, then, dismounting, called in his officers. Maps were produced, compasses consulted, plans scribbled on paper.

'This could be juicy,' said Moulin.

Even Sardines managed a quick burst on his mouth organ until a lieutenant cut him short. The officers needed to concentrate.

Ten minutes later, Major Brunet was ready to issue his orders. Every man had dismounted, holding their horses by the reins. Gathering round, they listened with keen interest. 'OK, men,' said the major, shielding his eyes, 'this is the situation. Three kilometres south of here is a small

Turk outpost, about a hundred men. Because of the lay of the land, we can't avoid them. The hillocks either side of the valley there are too difficult for the horses, let alone the mules. We have no choice but to face them head-on. "A" Platoon will split into two and on foot detour round the dunes, both east and west. From there, they will lead the attack. The rest of us will follow through. The gradient favours us. A three-pronged attack should do it quite easily. Any questions?'

There were no questions.

It didn't take long for "A" Platoon to get ready. Led by a lieutenant with long whiskers, off they went on foot, bayonets fixed, leaving puffs of sandy dust in their wake.

Galvanised, Béart and his colleagues got ready – a quick clean of their rifles, hats off, helmets on, a check on ammo, the tightening of their belts, a gulp of water, an extra biscuit. 'This is more like it,' said Moulin, grinning, easing his sabre in and out of its holster. 'They won't know what's hit 'em. Got a spare fag?'

'No,' snapped Béart.

Tightening Hector's girth, Béart remounted. Hector seemed to know. He was immediately alert, his ears pricked forward, stamping his hooves. 'Good boy,' said Béart, slapping his neck. Despite the intensity of heat, Béart shivered. Putting his hand on his chest, he realised how fast his heart was beating. He knew what lay ahead would be a mere skirmish, but going into battle upon his horse was what he'd trained for, and he felt both excited and frightened.

The men were ready, the horses geared up. A mule had been packed with the Lewis gun. The major, mounted on his bay stallion, trotted up and down issuing his orders.

'On receiving "A" Platoon's signal, we shall move into place – the furthest we can go without being spotted. We'll move up the Lewis and let them have it. Then, on my signal, we'll charge. Main thing, men, is to fan out, don't group together. Rein your charges in until I give the command. Got it?'

Ten minutes later, the signal, via a mirror reflected in the sun, came flashing from the horizon. 'Right, let's go,' cried the major. 'March at ease, steady as she goes. No talking, no smoking.'

And so, one hundred cavalrymen set off. No sound except the clumping of the horses' hooves on the dry sand, the creaking of saddles and the champing of bits. Béart tried to muffle a cough as more sand lodged in the back of his throat.

The men followed the major two kilometres down the valley, the sun at its worst, boring into them. Behind them, the medical lads, their Red Cross brassards round their arms, their medical kits at the ready, banging against their saddles. Approaching a bend, the major put his hand in the air. The men pulled their horses to a stop. Major Brunet, having given the Lewis gunners the order to prepare, considered the situation through his field glasses, his lieutenants either side of him. Peering through the heat rays, the outpost looked pathetically vulnerable, thought Béart – a few straw huts, sturdy-looking tents, strong enough to resist the desert sand, a Turkish flag limp without a breeze. Men in khaki, some in red fezzes and red sashes across their tunics, pottered about, and, rather incongruously, thought Béart, a couple sat in deck chairs as if at the seaside. A number of men with toasting forks congregated around a camp fire, their rifles slung round their shoulders, the fire emitting wafts of black smoke. Others kept guard over a cannon. Béart almost pitied them – they had no idea.

And then it started – the two portions of "A" Platoon charged down the valley from opposite directions, their guns blazing. Hector snorted, pulling on his bit. Both man and horse were itching to charge, but the major held them back. The Lewis gunners did their work, the guns spewing 500 rounds a minute. The Turks roused themselves immediately, manning their guns, firing back at "A" Platoon.

'Hold it, hold it,' shrieked the major. 'Sabres at the ready.'

The "A" Platoon men had breached the camp; hand-to-hand fighting ensued.

Major Brunet, with his sword poised in the air, keeps his nerve. 'Steady, steady…'

Hector prances on his feet.

With a whoosh, the major brings down his sword, its silver blade catching the sun. 'Chaaaarge!' he yells.

Reins are dropped, spurs dig into horses' flanks. The noise is intense. Leaning forward in his saddle, Béart swings his sword. He screams, his heart pumps with adrenalin and elation. A memory flashes through his mind – galloping through the field at the back of the farm, a blustery autumn day, the wind in his hair, taking a gate at full speed, the joy of flying through the air. Hector, bless him, surviving these last few days on minimal rations, has lost none of his speed. The hooves of so many horses produce clouds of sand. The Turks fire on them, the whistling of bullets, the men meet a hail of lead head on. Someone falls. A horse is hit, falling to the ground with a terrible yelp, his legs caught beneath him. Moulin, riding alongside, his helmet lopsided, is grinning, laughing. A shell whizzes overhead.

Approaching the camp, the men fan out, as the major had ordered. Béart sees a Turk, his rifle aimed right at him. The man fires. Instinctively, Béart ducks. Within a second, he's upon him, cutting him through with his sword. A spurt of blood, a scream, the deed is done in an instant. Béart pulls Hector up, swings him around, looking for someone else to kill. Men shout and curse; rifle fire pierces the air. Hector rears. Bringing him down, Béart catches the sight of Moulin falling from his horse. He sees a comrade bludgeon a Turk on the ground with his rifle butt. More gun fire. There are no Turks left standing.

The guns stop. The silence descends suddenly.

It's over too soon.

Béart, his every sense on full alert, brings Hector down to a trot. Men on prancing, snorting horses search for survivors, their swords at the ready. There's one there! He's injured, his shoulder a bloody mess but he cocks his revolver. Major Brunet leaps from his horse and finishes him off with his sword, the blade slicing through the man's chest. The man arches up as the revolver slips from his hand, then slumps. Using a rag, Brunet wipes the blood from his sword. Dismounting, the men look around for the rest of the wounded, following the sound of groaning and sobbing, and run each of them through with their swords. Screams come from every corner of the camp. Béart, having tied Hector's rein against a tent pole, is desperate to kill one more and is disappointed not to find one.

'I think that's it,' declares Major Brunet after a few

minutes.

Surveying the scene, Béart views all the dead, so many of them, mostly Turkish. But there, amongst them, behind a ragged tent, is Moulin, a crimson hole in his forehead. Béart shakes his head. He wishes he'd given him that cigarette now. Going through his pockets, looking for something he might send home to his family, Béart finds his packet of cigarettes. 'You bastard,' he says, kicking the corpse in the ribs.

The air hangs heavy with smoke and dust and the smell of cordite. Horses snort. The tents, without exception, are torn to shreds, the straw huts burn, the black smoke drifting over the camp. Equipment and weapons lie scattered, a boot here, a fez there, a broken bayonet, pots and pans amongst the debris. Wounded French lie here and there, groaning. One of them screams, holding the bloody, congealed mess that is his thigh, his lower leg shot clean away. Another, his eyes dull, seems on the point of death. The first aid boys are already attending them.

It was then that Béart saw him. A Turk lying facedown on the ground stirring into life. Rubbing the back of his head, he struggled up onto one knee, then the other. Béart, creeping up behind him, drew his sword. Ready to swing, the major shouted at him. 'Stop right there, Private.'

Béart lowered his sword.

Major Brunet approached the Turk, his revolver drawn. Béart held his breath, convinced the man was about to be shot. 'Get up,' said the major, gesturing with his revolver.

The Turk rose slowly to his feet, raising his hands. A tall man with jet black hair, black, piercing eyes and a long, thin moustache, a scar on his cheek, he towered over the major. His tunic was badly torn, his face filthy, but beneath the dirt, Béart could see a young face, his eyes full of pride and hatred. The Turk said something, his voice assertive.

'Private, go call the lieutenants.'

Béart did as told. Stepping over a number of dead Turks, he found one of the lieutenants with his revolver pressed against the temple of a stricken horse. Tears coursed down his cheeks as the man pulled the trigger. A couple of soldiers came running on hearing the sound of the shot. One of them, a sergeant, patted the lieutenant on the back. Béart allowed him a few seconds before approaching him. He found the second lieutenant with a number of men lifting buckets of water from a well. The whole camp, he realized, had been built around this well. The men were happy – the water was clean and fresh, and they could drink their fill and scrub their faces clean. Béart heard the familiar sound of the mouth organ – sitting on an upturned crate, Sardines winked at him.

Béart returned with the two lieutenants to find Major Brunet still with his revolver trained on his prisoner who stood upright, his back straight, his eyes cast far away. A few other soldiers stood nearby, rifles drawn. 'So, how many casualties did we sustain, Lieutenant?'

They both answered at once – 'Three dead, sir.' The taller one continued, 'Plus about a dozen wounded but only one seriously.'

'Does the wog speak French, sir?' asked the shorter lieutenant.

'No, he doesn't. Where's Ozen? He speaks Turkish.'

'Ah. He was one of the three.'

'Dead?'

'Sir.'

'Bloody nuisance.'

'Do you want us to kill him, sir?'

'What? This chap? Certainly not, Lieutenant. He's a captain. We've frisked him. Nothing on him apart from a photo and his ID papers. Captain Hakan Kazaz. We need to get him to intelligence.'

Béart noticed the man's photo lying face-up on the ground at his feet. The major had tossed it away. It was a shot of the man standing behind his seated wife. The woman's beauty caught him by surprise, the hint of Eastern promise, her exotic face, astonishing vibrant eyes – such beauty in this ugly, forgotten outpost.

'What about Dubas?' said the major. 'He speaks Turkish, doesn't he?'

'He only speaks Greek, sir.'

'Oi, Captain,' said the major to the Turk. 'Speak Greek? Or French?'

For a moment, Béart thought he saw the Turk shake his head but then realized he was just glancing between the three French officers in front of him.

'Damn it. I suppose we could just shoot him. We're certainly not taking him with us, far too much of a burden.' The major paced away, stopping in front of a Turkish corpse. Kicking the corpse, he returned. Lifting his revolver, he pointed it at the Turk. The man cowered, knowing his end had come. But then, dropping his arm, the major said to his lieutenants, 'The man's a captain; he'll know stuff, potentially good stuff. We need a caged bird. And he'll talk. Look at him, he's a streak of piss.' Major Brunet spun round to face Béart. Béart stood tall. 'You, Private. What's your name?'

'Béart, sir. Private Roger Béart, number one, six–'

'Shut up.'

'Sir.'

Looking round at the other soldiers, he saw Sardines ambling by. 'Halt, you there, Private.'

'Who? Me, sir?' said Sardines in an exaggerated fashion, pointing at himself.

'Yes, you, sir. What's your name?'

'Jacques Sarde, sir.'

'What's happened to your teeth? Second thoughts, I don't want to know. Stand next to Péart there.'

'It's Béart, sir.'

'Right, you two – take this man back to base.'

Béart's face screwed up in confusion. 'Base, sir?' Did he mean the last place they'd stopped or did he really mean… base?

'Yes, base. Just the two of you. Head due north; it shouldn't take you long. Take a horse each and put Captain Turk here on a mule. That should do it.'

'But… but, sir.'

The major approached him, his moustache twitching slightly under his nostrils. 'Yes?'

'It's… it's five days away.'

'So what? Once back in base, have a day off, then report for further duties. Understood?'

Shooting a glance at Sarde, Béart tried to compute what the major had told him.

'I said understood, Private?'

'Y-yes, sir. Understood.'

'Get Sergeant Berri to kit you up with enough to keep both of you going for the duration. And him. Now listen, Private Péart…'

'It's Béart, sir.'

'Make sure Captain Turk arrives in one piece. It could

be vital. Report to Brigadier Hallier, Intelligence Corps. Tell him I sent you. They'll know what to do with him. Right, off you go, Private, report to Sergeant Berri. You too,' he added, turning to Sarde. As they left, Béart noticed Sarde step on the Turk's photo, whether by accident or design, he didn't know.

Half an hour later, Béart and Sarde and their respective horses were ready. They'd been given enough rations for man and horse for seven days, medical supplies, a couple of flares and spare ammunition. The mule was laden with water tanks, fresh from the well. They each had a map and a compass. All they had to do, they were told, was to retrace their steps and they'd soon find themselves back at base. Simple really.

Béart stroked Hector's muzzle and tickled him round the ears – something which always made Hector grin, exposing his teeth. Béart had always loved the smell of horse, that dry, earthy smell. It made him think of home, of his childhood; like a comfort blanket, it calmed him. The horse looked tired; he too had been through an ordeal. He'd loved a lot of horses over the years but perhaps none as much as Hector with his deep black eyes and his beautiful eyelashes. He loved his colouring, the white blaze and the one odd sock, as if he'd forgotten to put the other ones on.

With Captain Kazaz mounted on a mule, the three men headed off. It was mid-day. Béart half expected a farewell party, a shake of the hand from the major, a 'good luck and thank you'. There was nothing. They left as the medics saw to the wounded, as horses were patched up, and the men made use of the well.

'You got your mouth organ?' asked Béart.

'Course,' said Sarde, grinning, exposing his gums. 'Never go nowhere without it.'

'It's a long way to go.'

'So what? Everywhere's a long way.'

Fair point, thought Béart.

The men rode in silence. It was just too hot to talk. Captain Kazaz kept his place in the middle while Béart brought up the rear. They walked for hour upon hour. The desert, Béart concluded, was a beautiful thing. Beautiful but threatening. A world without end, nature at its rawest, merciless.

Béart felt different somehow and it took him a while to work out why. He'd killed a man; driven his sword through his chest. Like losing one's virginity, it was something one could never undo. He was lucky, he supposed, that it had happened so quickly. He had no recollection of what the man looked like, only that he'd fired his rifle at Béart and so Béart felt no regret. What shocked him though was the degree of his bloodlust that followed, his desire to plunge his sword into another of them, to see Turkish blood upon its blade. He shivered at the thought of his depravity.

Several hours after setting off, as the sun settled, they decided to camp down for the night. They managed to find a boulder on a patch of barren grass. Not much but it'd do. Having fed, watered and rubbed down the horses and mule, they shared out their bully beef and biscuits, and ate and drank in silence. By the time they'd finished, it was already pitch dark, night-time descending quickly. Béart lit the lanterns.

'It's not really fair, is it?' said Sarde, arranging the blankets.

'What's that?'

'Well, Captain Turk here gets a full night's sleep while us two have to make do with half each. Can't we just shoot him? Tell them he tried to run away and we shot him. He probably knows sod all anyway.'

'Orders is orders, Sardine.'

'S'pose.'

Removing his helmet, Sardine stretched his legs, staring up at the night sky. After a while, despite his cracked lips, he began playing a tune on his mouth organ. With his rifle resting on his lap, Béart lit a cigarette and kept his eye on the Turk, the two men sitting cross-legged, face to face, staring at each other. 'Don't look so miserable, you bastard, you was lucky you weren't killed today,' he said to the Turk. 'Just think – you was the only one left alive. You're very young to be a captain.' The man had dark, piercing eyes that seem to bore into him. He was, thought Béart, a good-looking bloke with his black hair and his pencil moustache, his pure, olive skin and his stubble. He wondered how he'd earned the scar. He thought about the woman in the photo, that dark beauty, her eyes, those eyes… 'Here,' he said, 'have a cigarette.'

The Turk looked at him as if suspecting a trick. Carefully, he reached out and took the cigarette and Béart's box of matches. Lighting the cigarette, he exhaled.

'No need to thank me,' said Béart, vaguely offended by the lack of acknowledgement. He realised he felt a little intimidated by this dark-skinned man with his black eyes and steely stare.

'Who are you talking to, Béart?' asked Sarde.

'Him, of course.'

'Captain Turk? You stupid bugger, you might as well talk to your horse.'

The following morning, the three men were up before dawn, breakfasted and ready. Time lost its meaning as the second and third days passed in a haze, merging into one.

On the fourth morning, having harnessed the horses and the mule, they set off just as the hazy sun began to show over the horizon, their shadows stretching before them. 'Still a long way to go,' muttered Béart.

'Bit windy today, ain't it?' said Sarde.

'It'll settle.'

But it didn't. At first, the sand blew round the horses' feet, steadily growing stronger. It was as if the desert was warning them, a warning unheeded by the two Frenchmen. On and on they trudged, hour after hour, the wind swirling around them, the horses having to pick up their feet. Béart pulled down his helmet and pulled his scarf up to cover his mouth but thought nothing of it. Captain Kazaz turned and said something to him, pointing to the horizon. Standing up in his stirrups, Béart couldn't work out what he was talking about. 'Hey, Sardine, Captain Turk's worried about something,' Béart shouted over.

'I'll give him something to worry about if he don't shut up,' came Sarde's response.

'Is it me or has it gone cold all of a sudden?'

'Bloody hell, you're right. Why's it gone so dark? Where's the bloody sun?'

Captain Kazaz shouted something at them, gesticulating.

'Christ, Sarde, he knows something.'

And then it hit them.

In an instant, their world turned yellow.

Seized by terror, Béart grappled with the reins, desperately trying not to fall off. The sand descended as if

God Himself had thrown it in their faces. Screaming, the sand filled his mouth, despite the scarf, the sand blinding him. He had goggles in his pack but where was his pack? The world began spinning, faster and faster, all borders of normality erased, tossed as if he weighed nothing. The noise of the howling wind pummelled his ears; his every sense came under assault. Hector beneath him writhed and screamed. The intensity of it was unremitting. 'I can't breathe,' his mind screamed; 'I can't breathe.' The wind and sand flicked him off Hector like a bowling pin. He felt as if he was falling through space, unending and everlasting, no sense of direction. Utterly disorientated, he couldn't see, hear or feel anything, was only aware of the complete fear and his hopeless vulnerability. The sand whipped his face, as if a million needles were pricking him all at once. 'It's going to bury me', he thought, his every fibre in panic; 'it's going to bury me.' Unable to tell whether he was upright or upside down, the wind blew him down, whipped him, pounded him. He wanted to lie in a foetal position, to close his eyes and make it go away but the fear of being buried alive stopped him.

How long it lasted, he had no idea – it could have been a minute, it could have been six hours. But then, suddenly, it stopped. Breathing manically, Béart tried to open his eyes, crying in pain as the minute granules of sand scrapped his eyeballs. On all fours, he coughed and spat and vomited out the sand, fearing lest he'd never be able to purge his insides of the stuff. Still dark, he looked around him, squinting, and realised with utter dread that nothing was the same. It looked like the surface of a faraway planet. Everything grey. He called out Sarde's name, Hector's, even Captain Kazaz's. His voice echoed back to him, suspended on the calmer but still menacing wind. He put his hand on his head and realised that, despite the strap, his helmet had been whipped off. He reached for his pack but realised that that too had gone, as was his rifle. All that was left was his belt with its holster, his revolver inside. But nothing else. Then the fear seized him round the throat – he was as good as dead. No food, no water, no horse, no compass, nothing. Nothing in a world of nothing.

Standing up, his legs gave way. Grappling round on hands and knees, he cried out for help. It was then he heard it. With renewed strength, he got to his feet. 'Hector,' he yelled, his throat like sandpaper. 'Hector!' He could see the horse's silhouette. Lifting his feet through the sand, he stumbled towards his horse. Hector lifted his head as Béart fell against him, sobbing. And still attached to his quarters was Béart's pack containing his compass, food and a canister of water. The horse looked awful, his hair heavily matted, his eyes coated in sand. Pouring small amounts in his cupped hand, he offered the water to Hector who lapped it up, his tongue and the bristles on his muzzle rubbing against Béart's palm. He tried to remove the worst of the gunk out of his eyes. 'Good boy, good boy.' Hector's forage had gone with the mule. Scanning the horizon, he patted the horse. 'We're going to get out of this, Hector. God knows how but we will.'

The wind had finally died down, but the sky remained dark and a sand-filled mist settled over the dunes. He felt like the last man on earth. Consulting the compass, he started walking, leading Hector by the reins. 'This way's north,' he said, picking his way through the sand. 'Oh, shit, you're limping.' Patting the horse's flank, he said, 'Come on, boy, let's see what's wrong with you.' The white sock was bloodied; he'd cut himself, the gash was deep and ingrained with sand. He had no way of cleaning it — the medicine kit lost to the storm.

He heard a voice, a cry from somewhere. 'Who's that?' he cried. 'Sardine?' The figure came towards him, like a corpse rising from the earth, shrouded in mist. 'Is that you? Sardine?'

'*Merhaba*, hello.'

'Captain Turk, it's you.' Instinctively, he reached for his revolver, unclipping it from its holster.

'Where's your mule? Where's Private Sarde?'

The Turk spoke quickly, pointing vaguely in the distance.

'Where's your pack?'

The Turk mimicked drinking. Reluctantly, Béart allowed him a sip, no more. A rush of anger surged through him, taking him unawares; he hated the man with an intensity he'd never felt before. He realised he was going to have to share what little water he and Hector had with the bloody Turk; and in return the Turk was able to offer nothing. All take, no give. He'd shoot the man; what did he care for saving him, for delivering him for the sake of information which would probably be out of date by the time they got it.

With his revolver he gestured the way forward. 'Walk,' he said. 'Go on, walk.'

The Turk shot him a hateful look.

They walked and walked, how long, Béart didn't know, having no sense of time. Walking, walking, Kazaz in front, the sand sucking their feet, sapping their strength, only the sound of Hector chumping on his bit. They soon felt dead beat. The Turk gestured, asking if he could ride the horse. 'No, you bastard, he's hurt his leg; he's in pain.'

Finally, Kazaz sunk to his knees. Hector snorted, lifting his stockinged leg. 'I know, I know,' said Béart, stroking him. Captain Turk mimed eating and drinking. 'OK, we might as well have a stop.'

Sitting cross-legged, Béart passed the Turk a tin of bully beef from the pack, instructing him to open it. Little insects darted across the sand.

'Enough,' said Béart after the Turk had taken only a couple of mouthfuls. 'Come, pass it back.' Kazaz didn't look keen, tightening his grip round the tin. Béart cocked his revolver. Grudgingly, the Turk passed it back. Scooping out a handful, Béart got to his feet to feed Hector. The Turk screeched in protest.

Béart leapt on him, pushing him back. 'Back off, you bastard. I could quite happily kill you, so if you know what's good for you, butt out. You can starve to death for all I care but that horse – no, he ain't dying for you. Got it?'

Kazaz, his eyes infused with loathing, nodded.

Returning to Hector with the bully beef, he fed the horse. Hector looked exhausted, his eyes had lost their shine, his mouth full of saliva. 'I know it's meat, old boy, but you've got to eat something. Got to keep your strength up, eh? Yeah? Good boy. I'll fetch you some water. I'll get you back, if it's the last thing I do. Just imagine, Hector, you're in a big field back at home. Green, lush grass, and trees round the sides, the sun shining, not like this, just a gentle sun and a few fluffy clouds. Just you and a couple of ladies. Imagine, Hector, imagine that.'

Hector shook his head from left to right; he seemed to

be imagining it.

Sitting back down, Kazaz and Béart eyed each other. He could see his hatred for the man reflected back in the Turk's eyes.

Night fell. Lighting a lantern, Béart sat back down opposite Kazaz, leaning on his pack, his revolver clamped in his hand. Eventually, the man fell asleep. Sarde's words came back to him, but now it was worse. The Turk could sleep but he, Béart, could not, knowing he couldn't afford to take his eyes off him for a second; convinced the man was capable of killing him with his bare hands.

How small he felt under the night sky looming above him in its infinity; how insignificant he felt surrounded by these mountains of sand, everywhere sand, sand, sand. Oh, to be home on the farm, playing in the fields, a hot, cooked meal waiting for him back in the warm kitchen, his mother in that rose-patterned apron, wooden spoon in her hand, greeting him with a kiss on his head. Oh, to be home… so far away, such a long time ago, home…

*

It was a chorus of little sounds that woke him up – the creak of Hector's saddle, a snort, the click of hoof against a stone, the jangle of a water can. Béart opened his eyes with a start – the sun was hovering just over the horizon. He was on his feet in an instant, his revolver still in his hand. 'Oi, stop, stop!'

Kazaz, digging his feet into Hector's sides, pushed the horse on.

'Stop! Stop or I'll fire.'

But he wasn't going to stop, Béart knew that. Lifting his arm, he aimed, squinting against the reddish sun.

Trying to steady his shaking arm, he fired. And missed. He fired again, flustering, once, twice, thrice. Wild shots. The Turk whipped the horse with the reins, urging him on but Hector, who momentarily buckled, was in no hurry. Béart knew he had but one more chance. If he missed again, the Turk would be too far away. His life depended on this. Left eye closed, left hand steadying his right arm, he took aim. The shot rang out. Kazaz slumped. 'Yes!' He watched with thumping heart as the Turk slid from the saddle, landing on the sand in a heap.

Leaving behind his pack, running over as best as he could, Béart found Kazaz breathing, still alive. Hector had come to a halt a few feet away, panting, struggling.

Kazaz, on his back, looked up at Béart's revolver pointing at him, a thin line of blood seeping from his mouth. The image of the man's exotic wife swept through Béart's mind. Too young to be a widow.

'Please… shoot me,' said the Turk between breaths.

'You… you speak French?'

'Yes, I speak French.'

'You speak French.' Of course, he remembered the Turk's reaction when surrounded by the major and the lieutenants. 'You mean, we didn't have to do this. If the major had known… We wouldn't be here. You… you bastard, you bloody bastard.'

'Fuck you, Frenchman.' He snorted, a sort of laugh. His eyes glazed over.

Stiffening his arm, Béart pressed his finger against the trigger. Holding his breath, he urged himself to do it, to kill him, to kill the bastard… But he couldn't. Instead, summoning every ounce of his strength, he swung his boot in, catching the Turk in the ribs.

But the man was already dead.

'Hector? Hector.' The horse had slumped to the ground, lying on his side in the sand. Clambering over, losing his footing in the sand, Béart reached the horse, brushing his forelock from his eyes. 'Hector, what's the matter? What's the matter?'

Hector was panting heavily, occasionally emitting a strange gurgling noise; his eyes awash with fright. Béart ran his hands down his flanks. 'Don't do this to me, Hector; we've come too far for it to end like this. Please, Hector, get up, eh? Stop this, will you? I'll get you some water. That'd be nice, hey?' He slipped the bit from the horse's mouth, loosened his girth and tried to brush off the worse of the sand. It was then he noticed it. 'Oh, shit. Oh, shit, no...' A circle of blood on his hindquarters attracting vile little flies. 'Please, God, no...' The enormity of what'd he done hit him like a kick in the stomach – one of his stray bullets had caught him. 'Oh, God, I'm sorry,' he sobbed, burying his face into Hector's neck. 'I'm sorry, Hector, I'm sorry...'

And there he remained, for how long he didn't know, but the sun had fully risen, burning into the back of his neck. Hector was dying, but he was dying slowly. His whole body quivered continuously, his mouth frothed-up with discharge and bile. He was in agony. Béart wanted to cry but no, he had to remain strong, even if just for another few moments.

He checked the revolver barrel – two bullets left. One each, he thought. He swallowed. This time, he knew, he only had the one chance – if he lost his nerve, he'd never get it back again. He kissed the horse over the eye, tasting the sand and dirt. He tickled the horse's ears. This time there was no grin. He clicked the revolver.

'Just think, eh, Hector. Soon you'll be in that field. The one with all the girly horses to keep you company in your old age. Think of all that moist grass, as much as you can eat, and there'd be a river; yes, a river with cold, fresh water. That'd be nice, wouldn't it? The sun will shine, a nice sun, not like this one, and you can shade under the trees.' He pressed his finger against the trigger. 'And after the war, after all this is over, I'll come and visit you. Yeah? I promise, I'll visit you every day. It'd be perfect, eh? Everything will be just perfect, my friend.' The horse looked up at him, his huge black eyes reflecting the sun. He seemed to know. 'My dear friend…'

And then he squeezed.

✱ ✱ ✱

'Thank you, Roger,' said the priest. 'You've been very honest.'

'Oh, come on, Father,' said Leconte, the policeman. 'That's because he doesn't appreciate the severity of what he did.' Turning to look at Béart, he narrowed his eyes. 'You shot an unarmed man in the back.'

'It wasn't like that.'

'Sounds like it.'

'So what? I shot him. I had to; I had no choice.'

'Someone who could have provided useful intelligence to your commanders? Whatever the circumstance, doesn't sound right to me.'

'And what would you have done, eh, Inspector?'

'Shot the horse down, and kept the Turk alive.'

'I did shoot the horse; I just didn't mean to. I loved

that horse, I really did, you know…'

'And then a patrol found you?' asked the priest.

'Yeah.' Béart sighed. 'I was ready to put a bullet through my head but, yeah, they found me – and they found the Turk too.'

The church clock struck four. 'We've got two hours left,' said the doctor. 'It's just you two,' he said, pointing at Garnier and Father Claudel.

'OK, no need to draw straws again,' said Garnier. 'I'll go next; get it over and done with. Is that OK with you, Father?'

'By all means, Gustave; by all means.'

Chapter 8:
The Teacher's Story

Gustave Garnier told the gathering of his career as a teacher, of the children he'd taught over the years, many of whom went on to achieve great things in life. He confessed, hand on heart, of the impure thoughts he had for one of the mothers. Three minutes later, he was ready to sit down again.

'Wait a moment, Professor,' said the priest. 'Tell me, did your school have a secretary by the name of Mademoiselle Artaud?'

'Why, yes, we did. Why do you ask?'

'Ah,' said the priest, stroking his chin. 'It's just that I had an interesting chat with her once. She was of my Sunday regulars. She mentioned your name. Something about a school play and the art teacher; now what was it she said…?'

* * *

Gustave Garnier arrived at school early, as was his habit, to grab a cup of coffee before the kids arrived. The secondary school was quite the largest in the town; modern, recently built, with some 300 pupils, it was the envy of educational establishments across the region. The reason for Garnier's early starts was that Mademoiselle Bouchez, the maths teacher, was another early bird. Garnier found Mademoiselle Bouchez terribly attractive in her pencil skirts, high-heeled shoes and her black-rimmed spectacles. Far too glamorous for a teacher. Each morning, they ran through the same routine – both making their coffees, his with milk and sugar, hers without, then he would sit and read the paper in the staffroom while she took hers to her classroom. So their only time together, much to Garnier's disappointment, lasted a matter of a couple of minutes. Garnier always hoped that she'd stay and talk. But she never did.

He knew the reason – six months before, long before the Germans had arrived (a lifetime ago), Garnier had asked her out. He'd planned it for weeks, waiting for a sign that his advances may be accepted. No sign came and, frustrated with waiting, he'd decided to force the issue and ask her right out. It'd been quite the hardest thing he'd ever done. This was when she still took her early morning coffee in the staffroom. They were quite alone. Only the headmaster was around and he was, as usual, ensconced in his office. It was a Wednesday. He had planned to ask her Monday but lost his nerve; ditto Tuesday. In the end, he went for it with a 'what's the worst that can happen' attitude.

'Mademoiselle Bouchez, have you seen that new film by Jean Renoir – what's it called? *Rules of the Game*, that's it.

Rules of the Game. It's meant to be very good, so I'm told. I wondered if…, I mean, if–'

She looked at him through her spectacles as if he'd just run over her cat. 'Yes?' she asked nervously.

'Well, whether you'd… we could go together; to the cinema, I mean.'

'Oh, erm. It's kind of you, Monsieur Garnier, but I'd…'

'No, of course. I understand. Oh, look, here's Paul.' Never had he'd been so pleased to see Paul Dauphin, the art teacher, with his multi-coloured cardigan and arty, unkempt hair. 'Hello, Dauphin,' he said gushingly, causing Dauphin to raise his eyebrows in surprise. 'Have you seen *Rules of the Game*?'

'Yes, it's meant to be shit.'

Despite herself, Bouchez laughed.

'What's so funny?'

'It's nothing,' she said, shooting Garnier a furtive look.

*

A week later, Dauphin buttonholed Garnier in the gents' toilet. 'Hey, Garnier, you were right about that film,' he said, standing at the urinal.

'Film?' asked Garnier, washing his hands.

'*The Rules of the Game*, it's very good.'

'You saw it?' He looked at his reflection in the mirror.

'I was told it was rubbish, but it's excellent. Nora Gregor is great in it.'

'That's good.'

'Yeah, and guess what? Mademoiselle Bouchez enjoyed it too.'

*

That was all of six months ago. It was now July 1940. The Battle of France was over – the nation had fallen and surrendered to the triumphant, swaggering Germans. The future had never seemed so uncertain.

The end of the school term was fast approaching – only a couple of weeks to go. Half past eight – the schoolkids piled into their classrooms, the German occupation had done nothing to dampen their boisterousness.

Garnier, literature teacher, waited for his charges to settle down. Garnier knew he was a popular teacher but could never work out whether it was because the children actually liked him or simply because they found him a bit of a pushover. The classroom was large, overlooking the school entrance. The morning sun shone through the window catching dust motes thrown up by the movement of pupils and chairs. Along the side wall was a map of the world plus several portraits of famous writers from down the ages – Victor Hugo, Voltaire, Jules Verne and others. In the corner, near the door, a display of poems his pupils had written under the theme, 'Reflections'. The poems were, almost without exception, fairly atrocious. But for this, he couldn't blame them. The kids may still have been boisterous but the war and the arrival of the enemy had unnerved them, and himself, to varying degrees. A couple of them had lost family members – fathers, brothers or cousins, killed or taken prisoner. These were not the easiest of times. The illustrations many had added were, by and large, of much better quality. Paul Dauphin, the art teacher, damn him, was bloody good at his job. He could make an artist out of a blind man.

'So, I trust you all managed to memorise a sonnet.

Michel, remind the class, if you'd be so kind, what constitutes a sonnet?'

Michel, one of Garnier's keenest students, did as told with, thought Garnier, perhaps a little too much elaboration.

Mid-morning, the children had their break. Monsieur Pérec, the head, called a meeting, allowing his staff three minutes to get their coffees. The staffroom, akin to a waiting room filled with armchairs, was full. Its walls were decorated with a number of Monsieur Pérec's notices that no one ever read. The aroma of sweat and fresh coffee wafted across the room. The shops were fast running out of real coffee so people savoured every sip, thinking it might be the last. Every teacher crammed in. Given the lack of chairs, most had to stand and Garnier had arrived early in order to claim one. Like an actor making his entrance, Monsieur Pérec made his appearance. Clearing his throat, he glanced round his audience. 'I've had a visit,' he announced without preamble. A bald-headed man with looming eyes behind large round spectacles, Pérec had been the school head since its opening a few years back. He wore his usual light brown suit, with the corner of a white handkerchief poking out of his breast pocket. Folding his arms, he continued, 'A small delegation of Germans came to see me this morning.'

A wave of titters and murmurs arose. 'Did you not show them the door?' asked Paul Dauphin, putting his hand up.

'No, Dauphin, I did not. The fact is… It's very warm in here,' he said, wiping his shiny head with his handkerchief. 'Mademoiselle Bouchez, would you mind opening the window?'

Removing her glasses, Bouchez said, 'Are you asking me because I'm a woman?'

'No, Mademoiselle Bouchez, I'm asking you because you're closest to the window.'

With a sigh, Bouchez opened the window, teetering in her high-heels, while Pérec tried to rearrange his handkerchief neatly into his breast pocket. Garnier tried to distract himself from staring at Bouchez's arse. Dauphin, sitting next to him, nudged him in the ribs, wagging his finger at him.

'Thank you,' said Pérec, stuffing the handkerchief into his trouser pocket. 'Where was I?'

'Our German friends,' said Monsieur Jobert, the chemistry teacher, fanning himself with a leaflet, a young man with a large moustache who lived life with a perpetual sweat.

'Ah, yes. They were in fact rather pleasant.' More murmuring. 'All right, calm down, calm down, everyone.'

'Absolutely,' said Jobert. 'Best thing that's happened to our nation. We need a bit of discipline.'

Dauphin, shaking his head, muttered, 'He's made a pact with Satan.'

'What was that, Monsieur Dauphin?' asked Pérec.

'I was just saying, Headmaster, that you can't always hate 'em.'

Bouchez giggled.

'Yes, well.' Adjusting his glasses, Pérec continued. 'The fact is that there are certain school texts that our new masters disprove of.' Reaching for a pile of papers on the table behind him, he said, 'They seem most particular about this, and it affects most of you.'

'Even chemistry?' asked Jobert.

'And maths?' added Bouchez.

'Well, maybe not the sciences or maths. You are to take these lists for your subject, and ensure your classrooms are free of these texts.'

'You're joking, right?' said Dauphin.

'Do I look like a comedian?' said Pérec.

'Makes sense to me,' said Jobert, looking hotter by the minute.

'You would say that,' said Dauphin. 'You're half German, aren't you?'

'That I am and proud of it.'

'Which half? The German half or the idiot half?'

'What about the compilations and anthologies, Headmaster?' asked Garnier.

'Use your common sense, Garnier. Rip out the offending pages but leave the rest intact. Right, that is all. Get your pupils to do the work but make sure it's done by the end of the day.'

Garnier returned to his classroom in time for the next class, scanning the list of authors who, for one reason or another, had to be removed from his bookshelves. On Pérec's suggestion, he got his pupils to find the books and pile them up on his desk at the front of the class. Garnier marked them off – 'Hemingway, Karl Marx, André Gide, Victor Hugo.'

'What's wrong with Hugo?' asked Michel.

'I don't know, Michel.'

'The bells, the bells,' said another, adopting a stoop in an attempt to impersonate Quasimodo.

'Yes, thank you, Jean. Now, let's get to the anthologies.'

'So, you really want us to rip out the pages, sir?'

'That's right, Yvonne. As simple as that.'

'Doesn't seem right to me.'

'Ours is not to reason.'

And so the class set to. Half an hour later, the waste paper bin was full with discarded books and pages. Yvonne shook her head. 'How dare they?' she said.

'Ours is not to reason, Yvonne.'

'You said that already, sir.'

At the end of the school day, Garnier bumped into Dauphin and Bouchez in the staffroom. 'Well, did you do it?' asked Bouchez, gathering her things.

'No, I bloody didn't,' said Dauphin, buttoning up his cardigan.

'Oh, Paul,' said Bouchez, pulling on a strand of hair. 'I'm impressed.'

Pursing his lips, Dauphin smiled. 'One does what one can, Claire. We must show these people we're not going to roll over every time they click their fingers.'

'Indeed. I never realised you were so…'

'Yes?'

'Oh, I don't know, so… so strong, I guess.'

'My name, Mademoiselle B, is Spartacus.'

She laughed.

They seemed to have forgotten his presence, thought Garnier, hoping to slip away unnoticed. But, just as he'd reached the door, he heard Bouchez ask, 'What about you, Monsieur Garnier?'

'Me? What?'

'Did you refuse?'

'Refuse what?'

'Refuse to defile our culture, that's what,' said Dauphin, slinging his haversack over his shoulder.

'Well, no, I mean, it was an order, wasn't it? I mean…

the headmaster said.'

Garnier found himself holding the door open as Dauphin and Bouchez sidled passed him. Shaking his head, Dauphin tutted at him, while Bouchez, looking at him over her spectacles, mouthed the words 'Shame on you.'

Feeling thoroughly disgruntled, his briefcase in hand, Garnier was pleased to be heading home, but before he could make good his escape, halfway down the corridor, he was called back by Pérec. Lurking behind him was Monsieur Jobert, the corridor too narrow to accommodate both of them side by side.

'He hasn't done it, you know,' said the head, waving a sheet of paper in the air.

'I'm sorry?'

'That fool Dauphin. He hasn't gone through his books and now he's buggered off home.'

'I'd have him shot,' said the chemistry teacher, the sweat shining on his forehead.

'Yes, thank you, Jobert. You'll have to do it,' said Pérec, slamming Dauphin's sheet against Garnier's chest.

'Hey, what? That's not fair.'

Jobert laughed.

'You may spend all day with your students, Garnier,' said the head, 'but you don't have to talk like one of them. If the colonel comes back tomorrow morning and finds all these books by degenerate artists, as he called them, we're in trouble. Now if you'd be so kind…'

'He sure would appreciate it,' added Jobert, standing on his tiptoes behind the headmaster.

'Jobert,' said Pérec, spinning round, 'have you not got anything better to do than follow me around all day?'

'But I wanted to get home,' said Garnier.

'Your home will still be there when you return, Monsieur Garnier. We don't work to a timesheet when it comes to the Germans, so get to it, if you please.'

Monsieur Dauphin's classroom was as chaotic as any art teacher's, examples of his pupil's work on every available inch of wall. Glancing at them, Garnier had to twist his head this way and that just to try and understand half of them. Some of it, most of it, was eye-poppingly explicit – flesh, so much flesh – writhing, pulsating, naked flesh; phalluses, flowers all open, red and inviting like… like… If this wasn't degenerate art, he didn't know what was. What was Dauphin trying to teach these kids? He felt embarrassed even to stand within this small temple of teenage artistic wantonness. In a cupboard behind the desk, he found the books – dozens and dozens of them. This, he thought, could take a while. There goes his evening of doing nothing. George Grosz, Wassily Kandinsky, Paul Klee, Marc Chagall, Max Ernst. God, he hadn't heard of any of these artists but, flipping through the pages, he could see why the Germans wanted them banned. You can't show impressionable youth stuff like this. Show them stuff like this and they end up… oh, they already had, thought Garnier, looking back at the artwork adorning the classroom walls. Dauphin was singlehandedly attempting to corrupt France's youth. It takes bloody foreigners to mend our ways.

Galvanised by irritation, Garnier took a pair of scissors and a utility knife from Dauphin's pot of materials and set to work – cutting here, slashing there, hacking at degeneracy, pornography, all this filth dressed up as art.

'You can't fool me, Dauphin, nor the Germans. "Oh,

Monsieur Dauphin, I'm so impressed,"' he sung, pretending to suck on his hair, coiling invisible strands of it around his finger. "'You're so strong." "My name, Mademoiselle B, is Spartacus,"' he said, adopting a deep voice. "'I am Spartacus. I am Spartacus,"' he said, thumping his chest. 'Ha, I'll stuff a crown of thorns up your arse, then we'll see if you're Spartacus, you prick.'

'Is everything OK in here, Garnier?'

'Oh, good God, I'm sorry? Yes, thank you, Headmaster, everything's fine,' he said, slipping on a discarded book open on the floor. 'Whoa, I almost fell. Sorry, Headmaster. Just finishing.'

'I didn't mean you to make such a mess. Looks like you've had a bunch of kindergarten kids in here.'

'Haha, yes.'

'It wasn't meant to be funny, Garnier.'

'No, sir, you're not a comedian.'

'Don't play the smart alec with me. Now, get on with it and clear all this up, would you?'

'Yes, of course, Headmaster.'

In clearing up, he threw all the discarded pages in the bin. Then, about to leave, he retrieved all the pages from the bin and surreptitiously put them in his briefcase.

*

'Was it you?' bellowed Dauphin, charging into the staffroom the following morning.

'What's that?' asked Garnier, his face redder than the sky at night.

'It bloody was. You pig, you traitor, you... you...'

Garnier had expected nothing less – Dauphin was beside himself with rage. He'd been to his classroom a few minutes before school was due to start while Garnier waited in the staffroom, sipping his coffee, pretending to read the newspaper, waiting with increasing nervousness for the explosion of anger once the art teacher realised. It didn't take long. He heard Dauphin's footsteps pounding up the corridor. Unfortunately, Bouchez chose that moment to return to the staffroom, tottering in on her high-heeled shoes, and so saw Garnier's moment of humiliation.

'What on earth's wrong, Paul, love?' she asked.

Love? thought Garnier, she calls him 'love'?

'This... this...' he stuttered, pointing at Garnier hunched up in the armchair in the corner, trying to hide behind the newspaper. 'He's cut out pages from my textbooks.'

'Oh no,' said Bouchez, casting Garnier a withering look of contempt and disappointment. 'How could you, Monsieur Garnier?'

'I... I had no choice; Headmaster made me do it.'

'Headmaster made me do it,' said Dauphin, mimicking Garnier's weedy voice. 'You'd jump in a fire if he asked you to.'

Dauphin came over to Garnier. Garnier shrunk back, fearing he was about to be hit. Leaning over him, his hands on the chair's armrests, Dauphin whispered into his face, 'One day, once we've got rid of the Krauts and the day of reckoning comes, you, you turncoat, you quisling, you'll be the first against the wall. At least Jobert is open about his love for the Boche, but you're like a little slithering snake in the grass.'

*

A few months later, on the morning of 22 October 1940, the kids came to school in a state of high excitement. The evening before, many of them had listened to the radio as Winston Churchill relayed a speech in French to France from London. 'What did he say? What did he say?' asked the ones who'd missed it.

'He was funny,' said Michel. 'He said the Brits were waiting for the Boche invasion, and he said, "So are the fishes" in a funny accent.'

'He sounded like my granddad,' said Yvonne.

The staffroom during morning break also talked about it.

'Me and Perrier have got an idea,' said Dauphin, pouring his ersatz coffee. Real coffee was now but a luxury available only to those who could afford it. 'We're going to join forces and do an exhibition and a play, a short one, mind you, and we're going to call it *So are the fishes.*'

'What a good idea,' said Bouchez, polishing her spectacles. Garnier had noticed – whenever she spoke to Dauphin, she wore the same silly, soppy expression. Nauseating. He knew they were dating but were trying to keep it a secret. Monsieur Pérec wouldn't approve.

'Sure is, Mademoiselle B,' he said with a wink.

'You are clever.'

'I think you should be careful,' said Jobert. 'Whatever that drunkard Churchill says, it'll soon be the Brits' turn. The Germans will ring their necks like so many chickens, you mark my words.'

'You would say that, you half Kraut,' said Dauphin, settling in his chair. 'I can never get used to this coffee, it's disgusting. What do you think, eh, Garnier?'

'Me? I don't drink the stuff.'

'No, I mean will the Germans invade Britain?'

'I don't know,' he said, quietly.

'No, you wouldn't.'

'Does the head know about your *little* project?' asked Jobert.

'I haven't told him yet.'

'He won't like it.'

'He will when I tell him.'

But Dauphin never did tell the headmaster. Instead, he launched straight into the project. It certainly galvanized the kids but it took up all his time – Monsieur Perrier, the drama teacher, had taken ill, so the whole endeavour fell on his shoulders. He got his class to write up a ten-minute play while others began work on producing paintings around the theme of Churchill's speech.

One Friday morning, on his way to class, Garnier popped into the school office to collect his post from his pigeon hole. He found the school secretary at her desk, typing, laughing to herself. 'Morning, Mademoiselle Artaud,' he said cheerfully. 'Something's amusing you.'

'Oh, Monsieur Garnier, good morning to you. It's this play Monsieur Dauphin's class have written. I'm just typing it up. It's so funny.'

'Is it?' said Garnier, grumpily.

That same morning, Monsieur Pérec finally caught wind of Dauphin's project and immediately brought it all to an end. In a typed memo circulated to all staff, he said it wasn't for teachers to exploit the children into provoking the German authorities.

Dauphin took it quite well, thought Garnier. He drank his usual ersatz coffee in silence, reading a newspaper. He didn't speak and no one, not even Bouchez, spoke to him.

That afternoon, about to go home, Garnier returned to the office. The place was deserted; he could hear Mademoiselle Artaud's voice coming from the headmaster's office. Finding nothing new in his pigeon hole, Garnier noticed the typewritten play on her desk. Picking it up, he saw two carbon copies. Before he had time to think about it, he swiped the bottom copy and, folding it into two, quickly stuffed it into his jacket pocket.

That evening, back at home with his cat lying on his lap, he read the play. 'So Are the Fishes, a play in one act,' he read aloud. Consisting just one side of foolscap, he read it quickly. 'It's not funny at all,' he said on finishing it. 'You could do better, Mimi,' he added, stroking his cat. 'You are clever, Paul,' he said, mimicking Mademoiselle Bouchez's voice. 'So bloody clever.'

It was only as he was going to bed that the idea came to him. Grinning at himself in the bathroom mirror, he said, 'Yes, that's it. That's it! I'll show you, you clever, smug bastard.'

For once, he went to bed happy.

*

A week later, a delegation of Germans arrived at the school in a convoy of three cars.

'The Boche are here,' said Yvonne in a high-pitched voice, halfway through Garnier's effort to instil in his pupils an appreciation of French nineteenth century poetry.

Immediately, the whole class rose as one from their seats and rushed over to the windows. 'Sit down,' shouted Garnier in a futile attempt at maintaining order.

'Look at that car,' said a bespectacled boy called Henri.

'Citroën 11 CV. Beautiful.' 'Why are they here?' asked Michel. 'Perhaps they've come to arrest Headmaster.' 'There're enough of them.' 'That one's got an eye patch.' 'Yeah, he looks like a pirate.'

Unable to resist it, Garnier joined them at the window. A few soldiers hung around the vehicles, one of them pulling the creases out of a pennant, while a colonel wearing a greatcoat, accompanied by a couple of privates, approached the main school entrance.

The bell signalling the end of class rang. 'OK, you may gather your things and leave in an orderly fashion. I said an orderly fashion. Tomorrow we will be continuing…' By the time he'd come to the end of the sentence, every child had gone, a loud, chaotic exodus of overexcited schoolkids. The classroom door swung shut, a piece of paper floated to the ground, the air settled. '… by looking at the poetry of Paul Verlaine,' said Garnier quietly.

Garnier quickly made his way to the staffroom. The school was abuzz with news of the Germans' arrival.

'The colonel's talking to Headmaster,' said Jobert, the sweat pouring off him. 'In his office – with the door closed,' he emphasised.

'What do you think they want?' asked Bouchez, brushing her hair, her head tilted to one side.

'How should I know?'

Various teachers came and went. Dauphin came in, almost staggering, as if he'd just survived a stampede. 'Bloody kids have gone feral,' he said, catching his breath.

Bouchez went up to him. Laying her hand on his chest, she said, 'You all right, Paul?'

'Yeah, sure I am.'

More teachers came in, all as excitable as the children,

speculating on the German presence within the school, laughing nervously. The place soon filled up. Jobert looked down the corridor. Barely able to contain himself, he announced, 'They're coming. The headmaster and the colonel.'

Conversations stopped short mid-sentence, a sudden silence descended; everyone stood still as the door swung open. 'This way, Colonel,' said Monsieur Pérec.

The colonel stepped into the room, a fair-haired man with a bright red face as if his collar was too tight and a stomach overhanging his belt. Jobert, Garnier noticed, stood straight, his chin up, looking as if he might salute any moment.

Pérec hopped around behind the colonel, his usual confidence absent. 'This is our staffroom,' he said, quietly, aware of all eyes upon him. 'It's a bit small for all the staff we have.'

The colonel, not responding, said, 'Well?'

'Yes, of course, erm…' Scanning everyone, he caught Dauphin's eye. 'Paul, erm…'

'Are you Paul Dauphin?' asked the colonel.

'What of it?'

'I have to ask you to come with me.'

It was only then that Garnier noticed the presence of the German privates outside the staffroom door and, behind them, a number of schoolchildren trying to see round them.

'Why?'

'It is best you come with me.'

Bouchez sidled up to him, looping her arm through Dauphin's. Pérec raised his eyebrows. Her presence emboldened the art teacher. 'Not until you tell me why.'

The colonel considered him for a moment, as if weighing up his opponent. 'Have it your way.' Retrieving a sheet of paper from his inside pocket, he said, 'This has come to my attention.'

Even from afar, Garnier recognised the sheet of paper straightaway. 'This is what I wanted,' he thought to himself. So why, he wondered, did he feel so sick?

'What children wrote this? One child or more?'

Dauphin didn't hesitate. 'None of them,' he said firmly. 'I wrote it all myself. Good, isn't it?' More schoolchildren had converged outside the staffroom, the ones behind standing on tiptoe.

'None of the children had any part in writing this silly play?'

'If it's so silly, why are you so worried about it?'

The colonel clicked his fingers. Immediately, the two soldiers appeared, the kids directly behind them almost falling through the door. 'Take him,' said the colonel.

'No,' screeched Bouchez.

One of the soldiers pushed her aside. Dauphin put up no resistance as the two men grabbed an arm each. 'Hey, hey, steady; mind the cardigan.'

'Leave him be,' said Bouchez.

'It's OK, Mademoiselle B. I'll be back soon; you'll see. Spartacus, remember?' he said with a wink. Shaking his arms free of the soldiers, he told them he'd go willingly. The colonel nodded his consent.

Garnier didn't know who'd started it but suddenly everyone was clapping. He joined in, had to, he thought. Only Pérec and Jobert refrained, their faces reddening. And the applause got louder as the two soldiers escorted Dauphin out of the staffroom. The children at the door stood aside. They had also began applauding. Starting with Mademoiselle Bouchez, the teachers, including Garnier, followed them out, still clapping while, in turn, the kids followed them. Dauphin's ovation got louder as more and more children joined the procession, following the teacher and his escorts down the corridor, past the offices and outside onto the school drive.

Outside, the clouds hung heavy, the atmosphere dank, the branches of distant trees swayed in the wind. On seeing the mass of staff and students coming towards them, the soldiers leaning on the cars stood. One ground a cigarette into the gravel. At their prompting, Dauphin headed for the second car. On reaching it, he turned to face his audience. Smiling he bowed and waved. Bouchez with tears in her eyes clapped even louder. Garnier felt dizzy, the ground in front of him going in and out of focus. I'm Spartacus, he thought; I'm Spartacus. Last out of the school came the colonel and the headmaster, followed by Jobert. The colonel and the headmaster shook hands. Garnier noticed the headmaster surreptitiously wipe his hand on the back of his trousers. Jobert pulled a face. Approaching the car in front, the colonel nodded at his men. The back door of the second car opened and Dauphin, with a final wave, was bundled in.

And still, the clapping continued. Bouchez, with tears streaming down her face, began singing: 'Arise, children of the Fatherland, The day of glory has arrived.' On hearing the familiar tune, the children nearest her joined in. 'Against us tyranny raises its bloody banner. Do you hear, in the countryside?' One by one, they all joined in. Soon, the whole drive reverberated to the sound of singing, the voices becoming bolder with each line. 'To arms, citizens,

Form your battalions, Let's march, let's march!' The colonel gazed at them all, shaking his head as if in disbelief. With his adjutant holding open the car door, the colonel climbed in. Still singing, the children and teachers watched as the three cars started up and leisurely drove down the drive, through the gate with its granite gateposts, and out and away. 'Let the impure blood water our furrows.' And then came the silence. Monsieur Pérec didn't need to say it, the children turned and slowly traipsed back indoors, back to class. Rooted to the spot and with the tune of *La Marseillaise* still ringing in his ears, Garnier watched them all leave, one by one, followed by the teachers. No one spoke. But everyone could feel it – the solidarity, the strength in the silence, the determination in their hearts. Garnier knew then, at that moment, that one day, maybe many years in the future, but one day, the French would prevail and France would be France once again. History would prove the Dauphins of this world right. And with it came the realisation that he'd never be able to look at himself in the mirror again. His Pyrrhic victory brought no pleasure. His own sense of shame made him wince. Turning round, he realised that Bouchez had been standing right behind him. 'Oh, Mademoiselle Bouchez, I'm…' He didn't know what to say. Her eyes bored into his, penetrating his very being. He wanted to lie, to say it was Jobert's fault, that Jobert had sent them the transcript of the play, Jobert the collaborator. But there was no point; she knew. He could see it in her eyes – she knew. Suddenly, she threw her head back and spat at him. He stood stock-still, feeling her spittle dribble down his cheek. Pushing past him, she walked back into the school, her high heels crunching in the gravel. It was only as he heard the door slam shut he realised he was crying.

* * *

'Phew, so you let a man get arrested out of nothing more than petty jealousy,' said Roger Béart, the former soldier. 'What happened to him?'

'They let him out of course,' said Garnier, trying to sound upbeat about it. 'So it was no big deal, you see?'

'And then he married your Mademoiselle Bouchez, didn't he?' said the priest. 'I know… a friend of mine married them.'

'Yes, so you see… all's well that ends well.'

'Well, not quite, Professor,' said the priest.

'W-what do you mean?' said Garnier.

'Your school secretary told me, Mademoiselle Artaud. One day a few weeks later, a German soldier was shot and killed in the street. You may not have heard about it. They hushed it up. Anyway, according to Mademoiselle Artaud, your Monsieur Dauphin was one of those they shot in reprisal.'

'But that was nothing to do with me; you can't–'

'Perhaps not, Professor, but once he'd been arrested, the Germans had his card marked. So when they came looking for people to execute, they came knocking at his door. I think it's fair to say that if it hadn't been for your treachery, Monsieur Dauphin would still be with us.'

'No, I couldn't have –'

'Actions have consequences, Professor,' said the doctor, repeating the teacher's earlier words back to him.

Roger Béart shook his head. 'Oh dear, Garnier. It

doesn't look good.'

'Look at the time; it's five o'clock already,' said Le Vau, the doctor, on hearing the church clock strike the hour. On looking up at the barred window, they could see the first hints of misty light, could hear the first birds singing their tunes. They listened, as if each aware that they might never hear the birdsong again, knowing that the following morning, the birds would be here again, singing, but they would not.

'Gentlemen,' said Father Claudel, 'I believe it is my turn.'

Standing up, taking his place centre stage, he looked suddenly bashful, as if caught in the act of doing something shameful. 'I won't mess around. I did lots of good things. I'm a priest; it's my job. Instead, I'll tell you the one story that makes a mockery of my position. May God forgive me,' he added quietly, crossing himself. 'It took place during the summer of 1935…'

Chapter 9:
The Priest's Story

'Take, eat. This is my body. Do this in remembrance of me.' From the corner of his eye, Father Claudel saw the distinctive figure of Maria Pigalle at the church entrance. With her bright red headscarf and her voluminous dress, you couldn't miss her. The woman never stepped into the church unless she wanted something. She was a self-confessed hater of God because, before Jesus had entered his heart and taken him, Claudel and Madame Pigalle had been lovers. But that was some thirty years ago, when they were still kids, when she still called him Ju-ju. She hadn't called him that since. Her presence at the far end of the church, caught in the sun, was distracting. He needed to ignore her and finish his work. He'd done the Eucharist a thousand times; he could do it standing on his head with his eyes closed, but still, he needed to concentrate. 'This cup is the new covenant in my blood. Do this, as often as you drink it, in remembrance of me.'

Finally, on finishing, the old ladies, for they were all

female and elderly at this time of the morning, came up to him to shake his hand, to grumble and pass comment, usually a disparaging one, on their husbands or their kids or grandchildren. Daughters-in-law were usually favourite targets. These girls were never good enough for the old women: they were lazy, they were lower class, they were terrible cooks, didn't know how to keep home, they wore their skirts too short, their blouses unbuttoned. Father Claudel listened and smiled and sympathised while all the time aware that Madame Pigalle was waiting for him. 'Well, ladies, if you'll excuse me…' he said, trying to escape their clutches.

Walking swiftly down the aisle, his bible still in his hand, he caught Madame Pigalle's eye. She smiled that smile of hers, the one where she narrowed her eyes, and he knew she had something to import. 'Jean, have I got some news for you.'

'Please, Maria, I'm Father Claudel to you. You know that.'

'For goodness sake, listen to you. The priesthood's made an old man of you.'

'So you frequently tell me.'

'Come, walk with me.'

It was a glorious June day in 1935, the sky blue, the shadows long. A couple of young mothers passed, pushing their prams; in the middle of the square, shaded by the trees, a group of older men egged each other on in a game of bowls amidst laughter and shouts of encouragement. Maria hadn't lost her looks over the years; she still had that spark in her eyes, those luscious lips. Strands of her hair, once black, now streaked with grey, peeked out from beneath her headscarf.

'Well, what is it?' he asked, perhaps more brusquely than intended.

She stopped. 'Aren't you going to ask me how I am, Father?' She rooted round in her handbag, retrieving a packet of cigarettes. 'Want one?'

'Don't be silly.'

'I'm very well, thank you, Father. My new boyfriend doesn't beat me quite as often as he used to, my son refuses to talk to him, which is great, 'cos it means fewer arguments, and I've managed to stop drinking on Sunday mornings. Thank you for asking.' She put her cigarettes away without taking one.

'Maria, please…'

A cheer erupted from the bowls game.

'It's your job, isn't it? Listening to people's woes all day, giving them the answers to life when you've never lived in the real world. Anyway, talking about jobs – I know something you don't, and I've come all the way over here to tell you about it.'

'Maria, you only live over there,' he said, pointing over her shoulder.

'Bishop Bossuet is dead.'

It took a second before he took in what she'd said. 'What did you say?'

'Bishop Bossuet. Dropped dead halfway through mass. Can you imagine?'

She was enjoying this, he thought, revelling in her knowledge. 'But… how? He was no age.'

'Sixty, I heard. Dodgy heart, they say.'

'This is awful news.'

'For him, yes, but for you, Jean-Paul, your time has come.'

'I don't know what you mean,' he said, knowing exactly what she meant.

'Here's René,' she said, waving to her approaching son. 'Bishop Claudel. Hmm, has a certain ring to it, don't you think?'

'Hello, Father,' said René Pigalle, a heavily-tanned, good-looking young man with a hint of a beard and a sweep of black hair.

'René. How's work?'

He glanced at his mother. 'Got the sack, didn't I?' he said, kicking a stone.

'Oh, I'm sorry to hear that.'

'But it wasn't you, was it, darling?' said his mother. Turning to Father Claudel, she explained that her son had been falsely accused of stealing eggs from the farm he worked on. 'René wouldn't do that sort of thing.'

Yes he would, thought the priest. If René Pigalle should ever step foot in the church, not that he had since the day Father Claudel had baptized him eighteen years before, he'd be keeping an eye on the silver.

'So now he's got plenty of time to help his old ma with the shopping.'

'Yeah, alright,' said René.

Father Claudel watched them saunter off.

Rushing back into the cool interior of the church, Father Claudel slipped down the side aisle, hoping to escape the attention of the old ladies now ambling out, chattering loudly to each other.

'Bishop Bossuet is dead,' he said to himself, closing the door to the vestry behind him. 'He's dead.' He paced to the window, glancing out at the familiar view, the churchyard encircled within the stone wall, a clutch of small, whitewashed houses beyond. Maria, damn her, was right; he'd been waiting for an opportunity like this. There were six churches within the diocese, six priests. Surely, one of them would be appointed bishop, surely they wouldn't look beyond. He considered the others, his rivals. They were all good men, outwardly more pious, more dedicated than he. But he was the oldest, the most experienced. That had to count for something. The diocese committee would meet several times and discuss in detail the potential candidates. One didn't lodge one's candidacy; one didn't apply in the normal sense of the word, one waited for an invitation to help 'review future developments'. It was all very polite – but ruthless. The name that came to him was Charles Jacquot – his benefactor. Jacquot, a generous donator to the church's coffers, had huge influence throughout the diocese.

*

Monsieur Jacquot certainly lived in the grandest house around, a decent-sized nineteenth century chateau at the heart of the village consisting of several bedrooms, a grandfather clock in the hallway and ground floor rooms with high ceilings and ornate fireplaces. Father Claudel had a pleasant enough if rather false rapport with Monsieur Jacquot. He'd been to his house for dinner several times over the years and had got to know the man and his family. Anyone looking at their relationship from the outside would have thought of them as friends, but Father Claudel knew that, as priest and landowner, theirs was very much a business relationship. He knew that if he was to be replaced for whatever reason, not that it would ever happen, but if it did, then he'd never step foot inside

Chateau Luff again. He never felt truly at ease in the Jacquot's company, there was always a hint of malevolence about the man, a malice hidden behind a veneer of cordiality. Seventeen years ago, the priest had baptized the Jacquot girl, Beatrice. He'd watched her grow into a perfectly normal, polite, God-fearing young girl, now maturing into a confident, vivacious and frankly voluptuous young beauty, capable of turning heads both young and old. She'd reached an age where she'd become aware of her sexuality and its power but not old enough to know how to use that power responsibly, or indeed to appreciate just how powerful it was. In fact, the priest's most recent visit to the Jacquot household, about six weeks previously, was to discuss Beatrice's impending nuptials. 'I can tell you, Father,' Monsieur Jacquot had said, pouring himself a large whisky, 'it's a huge relief. My daughter attracts boys like bees to honey. Now at least she's accounted for.' They sat in the Jacquot drawing room with its baby grand piano in the corner, its lid open, and a huge portrait of Monsieur Jacquot's great-grandfather in a gold frame staring down at them from above an elaborate mantelpiece.

'And to such a nice, young man,' added Madame Jacquot, moving round the drawing room in squeaky shoes, lighting candles. Father Claudel could see where Beatrice had got her looks from – the same curly, black hair, the same upturned nose, the same dimpled smile. 'He's a lawyer already. Only twenty-two. A lovely boy. Have you got any more matches, Charles?'

'We know his family,' said Monsieur Jacquot. Luckily for her, Beatrice didn't take after her father with his pug nose and his eyes slightly too close. 'Good, upright people.

Hardworking. Educated.'

'Like your good self, Monsieur.'

'Ha, save your breath, Father. You don't win me over that easily.'

'So, when were you thinking – the marriage, I mean?'

The drawing room door opened and in came Beatrice, breezing in as if floating on air.

'Ah, speak of the devil.'

'What's that, Papa? Good evening, Father,' she said with a little bow.

She looked quite divine, thought the priest, with her dark, deep eyes, and her blue blouse. She reminded him of Maria as a young girl. This lawyer boy was one lucky chap.

'Father Claudel was just asking when the big day will be.'

'Not for another year, not until she turns eighteen,' said Madame Jacquot. The candles lit, apart from one, she sat down with a satisfied sigh in a squashy armchair. 'And we've got so much to organise, haven't we, Bee?'

Turning to the priest, Beatrice said, 'I was rather hoping for a small, intimate wedding, Father. But I can see there's little chance of that.'

Charles Jacquot laughed. 'We want the best for our little angel.'

'Yes, well, your little angel has to go out for now.' She leant down to kiss her father. 'I'm meeting Robert for dinner.'

That was six weeks ago. Meanwhile, the date had been set and the church booked.

With the news of Bishop Bossuet's death, Father Claudel rushed back to Chateau Luff, hoping to catch Jacquot at home. The maid showed the priest through to the study where he found Jacquot replacing the telephone receiver in its cradle. 'Ah, Father Claudel, I've just come off the phone – have you heard?'

'If you mean, Monsieur, the terrible news about Bishop Bossuet, then yes.'

'Yes, shocking news. I'm saddened, I really am, even if Bossuet and I didn't always meet eye to eye.'

Father Claudel knew exactly what Jacquot was referring to. Three or four years back, Jacquot had tried to buy some church land that was lying neglected. Bossuet showed him the door. Jacquot was furious – he'd donated a lot of money to the church over the years, money that had helped, in no small part, to build a church school. Rumour had it that although grateful, Bishop Bossuet had wanted it built in one village but, through Jacquot's insistence and influence, they built it in another.

'What you need, Monsieur, is someone more accommodating to your needs.'

Jacquot looked at him. Yes, thought the priest, the two of them understood each other.

That night at the rectory, having eaten and thanked his housekeeper, Madame Dumont, for her cooking, Father Claudel sat down to read. The death of Bishop Bossuet had brought it home to Claudel just how much he was bored by life. The work of a provincial priest brought few rewards; enough, perhaps, for a man of limited ambition, but after almost thirty years, he was desperate to move on, to experience of bit of real life, as Maria Pigalle would call it. The pay here was also abysmal. He had to think of his retirement. A priest's pension wasn't enough to keep a dormouse warm. But a bishop's pension, that would do nicely. The diocese committee would listen to Charles

Jacquot; they always did but would Jacquot forgive him over that misunderstanding a couple of years back?

Father Claudel had set up a fund to repair the church roof. Jacquot had offered a sizeable donation on the condition that Claudel used a certain contractor. Claudel met the man, a shifty individual who called him 'chum' and who wanted too much money for the job, more than Jacquot's donation. So, acting on his own initiative, Claudel had got someone else to do the work at 75 per cent the contractor's quote. Jacquot was not happy. And Jacquot was not a man who forgot – or forgave – easily.

Beatrice's forthcoming wedding had helped restore their relationship but Claudel was still worried – what if it wasn't enough? Their conversation that morning had helped but he needed something more; something that would earn Jacquot's undying gratitude; something to ensure Jacquot would back his nomination as Bishop Bossuet's replacement.

*

Bishop Bossuet's funeral took place at his church in the neighbouring town some four kilometres away on a beautiful July morning. Every seat was taken; the archbishop had come a long way from his parish to lead the service and deliver a eulogy full of poetry and pathos. Afterwards, at the wake, the six diocese priests found themselves gravitating towards each other. Trying not to spill their glasses of sherry and plates of sandwiches and sausage rolls, they shook hands, expressed their sadness at Bishop Bossuet's sudden death and praised the archbishop's eulogy. Claudel was particularly pleased to see Father Dion, a jolly man who liked to shock people with his use of the vernacular. He and Dion had known each other at school and although their paths crossed rarely now, he still considered the man someone he could talk to, although you had to be a little careful – Dion liked to talk and would think nothing of telephoning for a gossip. One by one they began recounting anecdotes about the bishop, tales about the times he'd been supportive, wise or even just funny, each one subtly trying to outdo the others in claiming the deceased bishop's affections. And here, Father Claudel knew he'd failed; he had no stories with which to impress his rivals. The question that hung in Father Claudel's mind was did they want the bishopric for themselves? One couldn't ask – it'd be too unseemly to expose one's ambition. 'Ambition' was a dirty word, and to be seen harbouring any ambition would be frowned upon. It was obvious to Father Claudel that three of them, including Father Dion, were happy where they were. The other two… well, he wasn't so sure. One of them in particular worried him – Father Castellio, dashing and ruthless, loved by his congregation, loathed by his fellow priests, especially Dion, as an upstart who thought himself superior to everyone else. The committee would see him as young and thrusting, someone with charisma who would appeal to the youth. But surely, thought Father Claudel, surely age and experience counted for more. But no, looking at Father Castellio over his glass of sherry, he wasn't so sure.

*

Three, four, then five weeks passed and Father Claudel was no nearer to securing Charles Jacquot's support. He'd been to his house one more time, invited by Madame

Jacquot to discuss wedding hymns, but the man of the house was out on business, as indeed was Beatrice. Together, they sat in the drawing room, sipping tea. Beatrice, Madame Jacquot told Father Claudel, was more than happy to leave the choice of hymns to her. As he was about to leave, shaking Madame Jacquot's hand at the front door of Chateau Luff, Beatrice returned. They both saw her walking quickly up the drive and round the fountain, her heeled shoes crunching in the gravel.

'Your daughter looks keen to be home,' said Father Claudel.

'Beatrice, are you OK, dear?'

The girl looked upset, her hair dishevelled. The priest noticed a faint smudging of her lipstick. He stepped back, allowing her room to pass, as she bounced up the stone steps leading up to the front door.

'Bee?' Madame Jacquot's expression creased with concern.

The girl didn't respond, didn't look at her, or at him. Like a tornado, blowing them to one side, she barged into the house.

'Beatrice!' her mother called after her. 'Beatrice, where are your manners?'

They watched as she ran nimbly up the stairs and out of view.

'Father, I don't know what's got into her; I do apologise…'

He put his hand up. 'Madame Jacquot, please, there's no need. She's obviously upset about something. She's young, the young get upset easily. I shall leave you to it. Good day, Madame, and let me know when you've made your final choice for the hymns. But no hurry.'

He'd got to the end of the drive when he remembered he'd left his pen in the chateau's drawing room. He wondered whether to go back for it, it was after all only a pen. But it was his gold pen, a gift bequeathed by a grateful parishioner. Yes, he thought, he'd go back. The maid let him in. 'No need to disturb Madame,' he said in a whisper, a finger at his lips. 'I'll be quick as a flash.'

Finding his pen in the drawing room, exactly where he remembered leaving it, he made his way out, taking note of the piece of Chopin sheet music opened on the piano and winking at Monsieur Jacquot's great-grandfather's portrait as he closed the double doors behind him. He heard her voice from the landing upstairs. She was sobbing. 'He'll tell everyone, won't he?' she gasped between sobs. Father Claudel slowed down; he couldn't stop, the maid was watching him from the door. He pretended to check his watch against the grandfather clock. 'Then everyone will know, and Robert will know, and I'll never be able to get married.' He heard a door slam, Madame Jacquot's squeaky shoes, a plaintive cry, 'No, Beatrice, wait, my love…'

'I found it,' said Father Claudel in a whisper as he approached the maid, holding up his pen. She nodded. No smile though. 'Sorry to have disturbed you.'

For the rest of the day, Father Claudel tried to work out what exactly Beatrice had meant. As so often these days, he found his lack of experience of 'real life' a definite handicap. He wanted to ask Maria for help – what had Beatrice meant. But he couldn't; he didn't want to give her the satisfaction.

But, as it was, he didn't have to wait too long before he found out.

Ten o'clock the following morning, the church was empty. Father Claudel had finished morning matins, had seen off a sales rep trying to sell him a new set of prayer books and was thinking of popping to the bakery to buy a sweet pastry. As he left the church, stepping into the heat of the day, checking his cassock pocket for change, he bumped into René Pigalle.

'Oh, hello, René, I didn't see you there.'

The boy looked worried, his brow wrinkled, although his eyes were hidden behind a pair of sunglasses. 'Father, can I have a word with you?'

'Yes, er, of course. I was only… it doesn't matter.' The pastry would have to wait. 'So, how can I help you?'

'I mean in private.'

'Right, yes. You'd better come in then.' He led René into the church, René's feet shuffling on the flagstones behind him. 'However hot it is outside, it always stays cool in here. It's those thick sandstone walls, you know.'

'Father, can I do a…'

Father Claudel stopped to look at him 'Yes, René, what is it?'

He looked down. 'I need to confess.'

Trying to disguise his surprise, the priest said, 'Yes, naturally, if that's what you want.'

René removed his sunglasses. Looking round, he said, 'What I tell you, you don't, I mean…'

'What you say is between you, me and God; that is all. You understand?'

He nodded.

'Come then…'

René paused outside the confessional box, as if unsure whether to commit himself to it, as if frightened of entering its dark interior.

'If you don't want to…'

René glanced at him. 'I have to.'

'Good.' Pushing aside the purple curtain, Father Claudel entered the confessional box, sat down and waited. He could hear the sound of René's breathing from outside the box. Eventually, he entered, his darkened outline visible through the latticed grille separating the two compartments.

'In the name of the Father, and of the Son, and of the Holy Spirit. Bless me, Father, for I have sinned,' René muttered *sotto voce*.

'And how long has it been since your last confession, René?'

'What?'

'You're meant to tell me that.'

'I can't remember.' He said it loudly then, remembering where he was, repeated it in a whisper.

Father Claudel suppressed a smile. 'It doesn't matter.'

'Father, I…'

He paused. Prompting him, Father Claudel said, 'Yes, René? What is it? You can tell me and God will listen.'

'But will He forgive me, Father? I mean properly?'

'If you are serious about repenting, then yes, God always forgives.'

'OK. Well…' He coughed. 'It's like this, Father. I didn't mean to, really, but I got carried away. There's this girl – she comes round to my house to teach me how to read, you know. Every now and then. She doesn't want paying or anything, so I used to get her eggs, nice fresh ones, you know. Can't now though. Lost me job, didn't I? Anyway, she still comes round. And she's so pretty, she's like a vase, you see? A delicate vase. I can read a bit now, thanks to her. Nothing difficult, mind you. So… I thought she liked me. The way she speaks to me, and she has this smile. I thought… Yesterday, Ma was out. And I tried to… you know, I kissed her. We were in the kitchen. I pushed her down on the table. She tried to stop me but I thought she was just playing. So I kissed her some more. She was wearing this skirt. Oh God, I shouldn't have, I know that now. I can't… I can't tell you no more.'

Father Claudel heard him sniff. Through the grille, he could see his head was bowed. 'Are you all right, René?'

'Yeah. No, not really. I don't know.'

'René, did you… did you do more than just kiss her?'

After a while, came an answer.

'I didn't hear you, René.'

'I said yes, Father, I… I did. The Devil took hold of me; I didn't mean to hurt her like that, but something inside me, it… it seized me. God, forgive me.'

'It was Beatrice, wasn't it? Beatrice Jacquot.'

'Yes.'

'Oh, René, René. You know she's engaged to be married?'

'Yes.'

'What you have committed, René, is a mortal sin. It is good you have confessed otherwise you would have gone straight to Hell. You must tell me that you feel contrite for having committed this act?'

'Contrite?'

'That you feel sorry.'

'Yes, Father, I do. I feel sorry, believe me, Father.'

'OK, good. Go home now, and contemplate your sin, say three Hail Marys. I forgive you and through your confession, God will absolve you of your sin. Go now, in the name of the Lord.'

'Thank you, Father. Thank you.'

René Pigalle's confession troubled Father Claudel. He liked the boy; he was, after all, the son of the only woman he'd ever shared a bed with, back in his darker days. He was a simple lad, a bit of a tearaway, had always been a worry to his mother, but his remorse had been genuine. And he'd grown fond of Beatrice Jacquot, such a pretty girl, soon to be married. He hoped Beatrice would find it in her heart to forgive René. If she went to the police, it'd break Maria's heart. He had to go see how Beatrice was, to try and get an idea of how she might react.

Madame Jacquot answered the door. She looked tired, he thought. He was just passing, he said, and wondered whether he'd left his pen behind yesterday. It's only a pen, but a gold one, a gift he rather treasured.

'By all means, Father,' she said tonelessly. 'Come in.'

'I haven't disturbed you?'

'I was just... no, not at all.'

'How's the family?' he asked as he stepped into the hallway. 'How's Beatrice?'

'Beatrice?' The question seemed to take her by surprise. 'She's fine.'

'She's not bloody fine,' said Charles Jacquot appearing behind his wife. He also looked ragged, thought the priest, unshaven, his top button undone. 'A word with you, if you please, Father.'

Jacquot led him through to his study, a large, book-filled room that had the air of being perpetually dusty despite it being spotlessly clean. Closing the door behind them, Jacquot said, 'Something's come up, Father. Take a seat.'

'Thank you.'

'What I have to tell you is in the strictest confidence.'

'Of course, Monsieur.'

'It's to do with Beatrice. My honour has been besmirched. She's been… been…. God damn it. She's an attractive girl as you know and popular with the boys. Problem is she encourages them; far too friendly. And now she's been… what's the word? Seduced. No, not seduced, violated. Yes – violated,' he said, thumping his desk. 'Less than a year to her wedding, and she lets herself get violated by some ruffian from the village.'

'I'm sorry to hear this, Monsieur.'

'It's her own stupid fault. I've warned her in the past, many times, but she doesn't listen and now it's happened.'

His telephone rang. Ignoring it, he continued, 'By God, if she's pregnant…' He put his head in his hands. 'It doesn't bear thinking about. I've told her, she's not to go to the police. We'll sort this out ourselves.'

Father Claudel tried to disguise his relief, fanning himself as if he was suddenly too hot.

'Problem is,' continued Jacquot, 'she won't tell me the name of the bastard who did this to her. I'm telling you, Father, if I ever get my hands on him…'

The image of René's bowed features came to the priest's mind.

'But she refuses to tell us. So, you speak to her, Father. She might listen to you.'

'Oh dear me. I doubt–'

'I'd be most grateful, Father. I've got a diocese meeting next week.' Cocking his head to one side, he added, 'Need I say more?'

'Will I find her in her bedroom?'

'Yes. Third on the right. Pink door.'

✳

'Go away,' came Beatrice's response on hearing a knock on her door.

'It's me, Beatrice, Father Claudel.'

He waited. After a while, the door opened a fraction. She peered at him through the gap and after a moment's hesitation, let him in. Wrapped in a pink dressing gown, she'd been crying, her eyes puffed up and red, a handkerchief in her hand.

The room certainly had the stamp of a young girl – a four-poster bed plumped up with numerous red and purple pillows and teddy bears, a bookshelf with a decorative surround, and the walls plastered with photographs of Hollywood stars. The priest sat on the chair in front of her dressing table, a table laden with bottles of perfumes and lotions. He was unused to so much femininity. Catching his reflection in the mirror, he saw how incongruous he looked in his black robes in this pink haven.

Sitting on her bed, she said, 'Maman's choosing all the hymns.'

'Yes, I know but that's not the reason I've come to see you. You see, Beatrice, I understand you've been, how should I put this… upset. I saw you when you came home yesterday, and your father tells me–'

'Well, he shouldn't have.'

'Perhaps, but he's concerned for you, my dear.'

'Concerned about the family name more like.'

'Again – perhaps, but he's also concerned for you.

Your father's worried, and your mother, that you might be…' He couldn't do it; he couldn't say the word.

'Well, I'm not,' she said impatiently.

'No, good. Right then. Yes. Are you sure? So soon?'

'If I'm wrong I'll let you know. I'll put an advert in the local paper.'

Clark Gable stared down at him with his seductive smile, flanked either side by Joan Crawford and Carole Lombard.

'Who did it, Beatrice? You can tell me.'

She blew her nose and let herself be distracted by the view from her window.

'Beatrice?'

'Yeah, I can tell you, and then you'll go straight downstairs and tell my father.'

'Well…' He shifted on the chair.

'I'm not telling you,' she said, pulling on a loose thread from her dressing gown.

Again, Father Claudel felt a surge of relief. Nonetheless, he had to maintain the charade. 'But, Beatrice, this boy, whoever he is, needs to be punished for what he's done to you. You must understand that.'

'Yeah, and then everyone will know, the whole village, and Robert will know. And his parents. I'll be tainted, won't I? Robert won't marry me, no one will, and that'll be it. I'll die an old maid.'

'I see,' he said, trying to disguise his exasperation. 'So, you won't tell me.'

'No.'

He made to leave. Stopping at the door, he turned and said, 'If you ever change your mind, Beatrice, you know where to find me.'

She didn't answer.

Father Claudel found Monsieur and Madame Jacquot waiting for him at the bottom of the stairs. 'Well?' asked Jacquot.

'She won't say.'

'Damn it.' He spun round in annoyance. 'Stubborn girl; I'll wring it out of her myself.'

'Charles, no.' Madame Jacquot gripped his wrist. 'You will do no such thing.' Turning to Father Claudel, she said, 'Bee's been terribly upset. She refuses to eat or to come out of her room. We don't know what to do.'

'She'll come round in the end,' said the priest, adopting a sympathetic smile.

'She'd better,' said Charles Jacquot. 'Keep your ear to the ground, Claudel, and let me know if you hear anything. Remember, this is to do with my honour.' Catching his wife's eye, he added, 'our honour.'

He almost told him there and then, almost told him that it was René Pigalle who had defiled his daughter, that had 'besmirched' his family's honour. Instead, looking away, he said, 'I'll let you know.'

'Good, and who knows, I'll put in a good word for you next week. I assume you're interested in becoming our next bishop?'

'Oh. Monsieur,' he said, shrugging his shoulders. 'What an idea! I've not given it much thought if I'm honest with you. But now you mention it, it would be an...' He didn't want to use the word 'honour'; that was Jacquot's word. '...privilege. Yes, a great privilege.'

'A privilege. Yes, I thought as much.'

*

Days passed. If there was one thing Father Claudel was sure of, he was not going to tell Jacquot René's name. Sure, what he had done was despicable but René was aware of this; he knew he'd sinned and he'd learnt his lesson. Bishopric or no bishopric, it wasn't worth breaking the confessional vow for the sake of career advancement. No one would know if he broke the vow, but *he* would know and, what's more, God would know. God knew everything.

One evening, having dismissed his housekeeper, Madame Dumont, for the night, the telephone rang. It was Father Dion, his old school friend, whom he hadn't seen since Bishop Bossuet's funeral.

'Greetings, Jean-Paul,' said Dion. 'You want the bishop's job, right?'

'Well, I don't—'

'Don't give me that, Jean, we've known each other too long; I know what you're like. So, listen, a nod to the wise. I was speaking to a friend of mine, well, not really a friend, but he told me in confidence that the diocese committee have already been talking about the bishop's replacement although they haven't officially met yet.' He emphasised the word 'officially'.

'What friend?'

'Never you mind. Anyway, the word is Father Castellio is virtually a shoo-in.'

Father Claudel couldn't help but groan loudly.

'Exactly. That's my response. Castellio's got the police chief as his sponsor. Now, I don't know about you but I can't abide the thought of that man being my boss. At least Bossuet gave us a free rein but that's not Castellio's way. If you as much as fart in church, he'll know about it.'

'What can–'

'Get yourself a better sponsor, that's what you have to do. Police are all very well but there's no money there. Now, you're friends with that landowner bloke, aren't you?'

'I'm marrying his daughter.'

'Are you, be Gods? You're a dark horse.'

'Don't be silly, Georges, you know what I mean.'

'Ha! That's good though. Do whatever you have to do, Jean, just make sure you get your landowner friend to speak up for you. Last thing we want is for Castellio to be bishop.'

'I'm not sure…'

But Dion had hung up.

'It doesn't make any difference,' he said aloud. 'I can't break my vow; a confession is a confession.' But Dion was right – the thought of Castellio stealing what Claudel had come to see as his right was too much to bear. Castellio was almost half his age; his time would come. But this was Father Claudel's last chance. He had to be bishop.

He tried not to think of Maria but invariably did. He was only nineteen when he broke her heart. They'd been a couple for a few years, they were engaged, they had the rings on their fingers. She called him Ju-ju, a nickname intolerable from anyone else, but adorable coming from the lips of Maria. Life was panning out until the day it happened. He'd gone away for the weekend with his parents to a family friend's house on the coast. It was late spring; they'd got the boats out and were out on the water every day. After a few days, Claudel, with the arrogance of youth, felt himself confident in his handling of these little yachts. It was one late afternoon when, against everyone's advice, he went out on his own. A sudden wind whipped up, he got caught in a current and before he knew it, he was in trouble. To this day, thirty years on, he could still remember the panic seizing his heart, the terror clouding his mind, the bile in the back of his throat. With the rain lashing his face, the sky darkening, he truly thought he was living his last few moments. And so he prayed, as his mother had taught him, he prayed. 'O, Lord, help me now,' he remembered bellowing into the wind. 'O, Lord, can you hear me? Spare me my life. Let me live and I vow to thee that I shall devote the rest of my life to thee.' He remembered repeating it again and again, screaming into the elements, his face wet with rain and tears, his heart wrenched with fear. 'O, Lord, I beseech thee; spare me my life.'

And the good Lord did spare him his life; Claudel was rescued by a homebound fishing trawler.

He woke up the following day and he knew that from that moment on, he belonged to God… and only God.

Maria, understandably, took it badly. She moved away and rebounded into the arms of another, a man totally unsuitable, then to another and another, finally, after ten years, returning home and marrying an equally unsuitable man and bearing him a son whom he had no interest in. The man was now gone but Maria remained, as did the son, taking the virginity of a young girl that, by right, should have been her future husband's to take.

Very occasionally, over the years, he regretted his haste in striking such a deal with God. But then, he'd look around at his peers and see the path that their marriages had taken, and realised that almost without exception it was the same path – a path blighted with vague disappointments and seething resentments. And he knew that however much, thirty years ago, they'd loved each other, a marriage with Maria would have inevitably traversed that very same path as everyone else's. God, on the other hand, never lets you down. Day after day, He was always there. If anything, He never ceased to surprise Claudel with the extent of His munificence.

The whole business with René, Jacquot's bribery, and now Father Dion's phone call had put Claudel at a crossroads in his life. Confessional vow or no vow, it was René's future or his. One of them had shamed himself and had shamed his mother and the whole community; the other had done nothing but serve God these last thirty years. And all he wanted to do now was serve God in a more meaningful way. It seemed so unjust that his noble ambitions should be ruined by a lustful, egg-thieving reprobate.

Before going to bed, Father Claudel settled at his desk in his study, turned on the desk lamp, and wrote a short anonymous letter to Monsieur Jacquot telling him the truth about his daughter's violation:

Dear Monsieur Jacquot,

Sometimes life necessitates that we tell the truth as we know it, whatever the consequences. Truth must always win out. Justice must be done. I know, monsieur, who defiled your daughter.

His name is René Pigalle.

Yours sincerely,

A friend.

Then, realising anonymity would serve him no purpose, he crossed out the words 'a friend', and added his signature. He re-read the letter several times and each time recoiled at seeing his name at the bottom. It was as if the Devil himself had signed it. 'No,' he said aloud. 'I can't do this.'

He screwed the letter up and threw it into the waste paper bin.

*

The following day, the heavens opened. Sheltering under his umbrella, trying to keep it from blowing inside out, Father Claudel made his way to church, breezily wishing passers-by good morning. He hadn't broken his vow and he felt jubilant. He'd done the right thing; this he knew from the depths of his soul. God had been his guide, and God had guided him down the rightful path. He marched into the church, shaking the excess rainwater from his umbrella, determined more than ever to spread God's work. Even if it meant staying put in this backwater of a French village for the rest of his days. He didn't care any more. For once, for the first time in years, he felt good about life. And for that he had God to thank. As always.

*

Two days later, a Monday, Father Claudel had just returned to the rectory after morning matins. Madame Dumont wasn't due for half an hour by which time he would be heading back to church. Sitting at his desk in the study, opening his morning post, he gazed out over the garden, the shadows of the trees encroaching on the lawn, the sun filtering through the branches. He watched as a robin bathed itself in his birdbath. He breathed easily, knowing he'd done the right thing. A bishopric would serve him well in this life but breaking the confessional vow, whatever the justification, would damn him for evermore. A rabbit came into view, sniffing round, its big black eyes blinking. The priest smiled. Yes, he'd done the right thing. A knock on the door brought him back to the present.

He stuttered on finding Charles Jacquot on his doorstep. 'D-do come in, Monsieur.'

'Are you alone?' asked Jacquot brusquely.

'Yes, Madame Du–'

'Good,' said Jacquot, striding past Father Claudel and into the house.

The priest showed Jacquot through to his drawing room, realising that the man had never stepped foot in the rectory before.

'Do… do take a seat.' Being at the back of the house, the sun had yet to permeate the drawing room, and the priest felt conscious of the smallness of the room, of its drab colours and cluttered appearance, its musty smell. 'Can I get you something, Monsieur? A cup of coffee, perhaps?'

'I won't be staying for long.' Father Claudel took the armchair opposite Jacquot. Jacquot continued, 'I just wanted to thank you, Father. I won't forget this.'

'I beg your pardon, Monsieur?'

'No one will ever know. I promise you that.'

The priest's eyes narrowed. 'I'm not sure I follow.'

'I'm attending a diocese meeting later this week. They will know that you have my full support.'

Claudel couldn't help but smile. 'Well, thank you, Monsieur. That's wonderful. But I don't understand…'

Abruptly, Jacquot rose to his feet. 'And that is all I

wanted to say. To say thank you. I will never forget. Now, I mustn't detain you any longer.'

'But I–' Father Claudel also rose to his feet.

'No, don't worry, Father, I'll see myself out.' He shook the priest's hand. 'Good day,' he said.

Claudel watched him leave but as he reached the drawing room door, Jacquot stopped. 'Here, you better have it back.'

'I'm sorry?'

Jacquot handed him a piece of folder paper. 'Burn it.'

And with that he was gone.

His hands shaking, Father Claudel unfolded the slightly crumpled sheet of paper. His vision blurring, the words jumped out at him… *Sometimes life necessitates that we tell the truth as we know it, whatever the consequences … His name is René Pigalle. Yours sincerely, ~~A friend~~. Fr. Claudel.*

The priest fell to his knees. 'No, no, no. My God, no.'

A shadow fell on him. 'Father, what on earth's wrong?'

'What?'

It was Madame Dumont. 'What are you doing on the floor, Father?'

'I… I don't know.' And then he knew – the piece of paper, only slightly crumpled, in his waste paper bin… Madame Dumont… she would have… She must've fished it out; she must've have…

*

Two months later, September 1935.

The postman gave Father Claudel his morning post. 'Lovely day,' said the postman.

'Indeed it is,' he replied. But he wasn't sure; his heart was thumping, his palms wet with sweat, for today was the day he was fully expecting the diocese letter formally informing him of their decision regarding Bishop Bossuet's replacement. Over the preceding weeks, he'd been invited to two diocesan meetings; the committee had been to his church and sat through two services, taking notes. 'Oh, God,' he said aloud on seeing the official diocesan stamp on the back of a brown envelope. 'Oh, God, oh God.' Using his letter opener, he sliced open the envelope and with trembling fingers pulled out the letter…

*

That evening Father Claudel was halfway through evensong, the slanting sun shining through the stained-glass windows leaving colourful patterns on the flagstones. Hands together, he led the congregation in prayer, dimly aware of a commotion outside, of police cars speeding by, their bells ringing manically. 'Our Father, who art in Heaven; Hallowed be thy name…' By the time he'd come to the end of the Lord's Prayer, he'd already forgotten about the commotion outside. Nothing mattered any more. In one month's time he was due to start his new position as bishop. He'd floated through the whole day, unable to believe his good fortune, pinching himself. Frustratingly, the appointment was subject to utmost secrecy until the committee had received his written acceptance. He couldn't wait until, in a few day's time, he could tell everyone, the whole world. He especially couldn't wait to tell and thank Jacquot – thank God he never acted on that information carelessly handed to him by Madame Dumont. He'd have a party, one great big ecclesiastical knees-up!

It was only as Father Claudel was preparing to go home

after a long but memorable day that the church doors opened. He sighed; if he was a shopkeeper, he could tell them he was closing up for the night. But as a priest, he couldn't – the church was always open.

It was Maria – that was good, he thought, he could tell her his good news, as long as she kept it to herself. But no, something was wrong, she was crying, her eye make-up had run, she looked hysterical. 'Jean, Jean…'

'Maria, what on earth–'

'Jean, it's… it's…' She could hardly get the words out. 'It's René; he's dead.'

The world stopped for a moment. 'Dead?' he gasped.

She fell into his arms, sobbing into his chest. Between muffled sobs, she blurted the details, 'Dead, Jean. Murdered.'

His knees gave way. Freeing himself, he staggered to a pew, propping himself up.

'No. No, this can't be.'

'They slit his throat, Jean.'

'Slit his… Please, no,' he said, crossing himself. The words came back to him… 'O, Lord, I beseech thee; spare me my life.'

'My boy, my baby boy. Who'd do this to him, Jean-Paul? Tell me, what sort of person would do this?'

* * *

'I remember that boy's murder,' said Leconte, the policeman, accompanied now by the full dawn chorus of birdsong. 'Not that I was assigned to it. They never did find the murderer. So, after all these years, Father, you're saying it was Charles Jacquot? Or at least it was done under his orders?'

'I don't know. I couldn't tell the police because I couldn't be sure.'

'You didn't have to be sure,' yelled Leconte. 'It was for you to report your suspicions.'

'Yeah, but how could he?' asked Moreau, the postman. 'Without admitting he'd broken his vow.'

'My God, I thought we were bad,' said Garnier, 'but this, this is worse.'

'So why aren't you a bishop then, Father?' asked Doctor Le Vau.

Gazing at the floor, the priest said, 'How could I? I was not worthy of carrying out God's work to such a high degree. I wrote to the diocese thanking them but declining their invitation. It broke my heart.'

'My heart bleeds,' said Béart.

'You all judge me harshly, as indeed you should. But believe me, no one hates me as much as myself for what I did back then.'

Wearily, the priest returned to his mattress.

Chapter 10

The early morning sun streamed through the barred window, leaving its imprint on the stone floor, the strands of straw, caught within its glare, rendered gold. Outside, the birds had finished their singing and instead the faint din of traffic had started up. The six men sat in silence, each lost in his own thoughts. None had meant to voice the thing that had damned them the most, having hoped to pass off lighter sins. But they had. And now they each sat in their own halo of shame. Yes, they had each thought about it before, many times over, tried to come to terms with their guilt. But before, when the shame bit too deeply, they could always shake it off. A telephone call, something to eat, a knock on the door – something always saved them. Not any more. Here they were, just six, forgotten men, all but one of them just an hour or so from death. Their darkest hour had come back to haunt them at the very last. They'd each done one thousand or more good things during their lives; but now, at the end, they counted for nothing; it is the one terrible thing that men do that dominate their minds when time is at an end. No one could save them from the things that pained them the most, the things they carried through their lives, always there, as intrinsic to their being as their flesh and blood. The six Frenchmen weren't born as the doers of bad things. But they happened; they'd made their choice, whether out of malice, selfishness, greed or simply carelessness, they acted as they did, and things, consequences, foreseen or unforeseen, happened as a result.

They each, in their own way, asked for forgiveness. But there was no one there to forgive, and so they asked God. Whether God listened, they didn't know, but it helped. And after a while, they began to feel different. Slowly. So slowly they didn't realise it at first. But then, as if the body had been rid of its cancer, their minds felt a little freer, their souls purged of the one thing that had for so long tormented them.

It was Doctor Le Vau who first rose unsteadily, like a new-born calf, to his feet, feeling quite peculiar. It felt as if, either side of him, Madame and Claudia Aubert's arms were linked into his as together they strolled through the winter streets of the town decked-up with Christmas decorations, their faces buffeted by snow. They were laughing, the three of them, wishing passers-by a merry Christmas. Then Henri Moreau, the postman, followed suit, tears of happiness coursing down his cheeks, hearing in his mind the happy voices of Lilly and Marguerite. He was on a train station platform, holding a suitcase. They were there on the opposite side, holding hands, chortling, calling his name. Dropping his suitcase, he rushed up the stairs of the bridge linking the two platforms, joy filling his heart. Nicholas Leconte, the policeman, also felt different but didn't know why. It felt, strangely, as if Albert Kahn had forgiven him and, standing at the door of his little workman's cottage, was inviting him in, a smile on his face. Leconte entered the cottage, ducking below the low beam, smelling the heavenly aroma of fresh real coffee. Roger Béart rubbed his eyes, convinced he'd just seen Captain Kazaz walking beside his exotic wife leading Hector, the horse's white blaze cleaner and fresher than snow; the Turk reuniting Béart with his faithful old horse, shaking his hand as he handed over the reins. Gustave Garnier kicked away the cramp in his left foot, convinced the Paul Dauphin had taken the torn pictures from Garnier's briefcase and had stuck them all back into their books and, having done so, hugged Garnier in a manly embrace, while Mademoiselle Bouchez watched on with a kindly smile. And last of all, rising to his feet feeling dizzy, Father Claudel knew his piety was nothing to that of René Pigalle who, standing above him on a small boat tossed on the raging seas beneath a storm of biblical tempestuousness, offered him the body and blood of Jesus Christ, our Lord.

The six men looked at one another. Silently and with their eyes clouded by tears and their hearts bursting with love, they hugged each other, each man hugging the other five as if his life depended on it.

Then, almost with a jolt, their minds snapped back to the present.

*

'Whoa. I feel odd,' said Dr Le Vau.

Moreau muttered the words, 'Six sizzling sausages,' and realised he'd lost his stutter.

'Yeah, I feel better somehow,' said Leconte. He put his hand to his chest, expecting to cough. But there was no cough.

'So, what do we do now?' asked Béart. 'Do we vote?'

'Seems a bit churlish now,' said Garnier.

One by one they agreed.

'What time is it?' asked Béart.

'It must be almost time,' said Leconte. 'I heard the clock strike half past about twenty minutes ago.'

'I thought it was about five minutes ago,' said Moreau, the postman.

'In that case, it's almost six,' said Le Vau, fiddling with his finger that once sported one of his rings. 'Colonel Geist could be back any moment.'

It was, for all of them, a horrible thought.

'It's strange,' said Le Vau, 'but the idea of death doesn't seem as frightening as it did six hours ago.'

'Yes, I feel the same,' said Moreau, the postman.

'But one of us can still live,' said Garnier. 'It doesn't matter who, but we can't let the swine murder all of us if we can help it.'

'If we can't decide over six hours, how can we decide in five minutes?' asked Le Vau.

'We'll draw straws,' said Leconte.

'That means we've come in a full circle,' said Moreau. 'Six hours and we're back exactly where we started.'

The men fell silent.

'I can't bloody do it,' said Béart. 'I can't take a straw that will decide whether I should live or not.'

'In that case we all die,' said Garnier. 'You're very quiet, Father; what do you say?'

Father Claudel looked at all of them in turn. 'Yes, the

time has come to decide. I feel that if we don't, we will be breaking some unseen force. We will have disobeyed the colonel's orders. Yes, if we had to choose just the one man to die, then I'd be happy for it to be me, but since five of us must be killed, then I suggest we stand together as brothers... and die together. After all, what would life be like for the sixth man? It wouldn't be a life worth living.'

No one spoke but they all knew the priest was right. Why should they have to decide? Silently, they all agreed. Together, they would go to their execution, side by side, united, as we all are in the end, by death.

*

The church clock struck six. Standing in a semi-circle, the square of sunlight in front of them, the six men held their breaths on hearing the three pairs of boots on the stone-floored corridor outside. Involuntarily, they each took half a step back on hearing the turning of the key in the heavy wooden door. The door pushed open. A bolt of fear pierced each of them as they braced themselves for the appearance of Colonel Geist. But it was not Colonel Geist now standing before them – it was Lieutenant Lowitz, and behind him his faithful corporal, Schmidt, with his rifle slung, as usual, over his shoulder, and a private who made his presence felt by sneezing. The latter two brought the prisoners their breakfasts – the usual fare of bread spread with a hint of margarine and a cup of water. Although they knew it made no difference, they were all rather relieved that it was the lieutenant and not Colonel Geist who had come to see them.

'Good morning, gentlemen,' said the lieutenant, looking fresh after a good night's sleep. 'I trust you all slept well.'

The six men glanced at each other, thinking, 'Is he being serious?'

The lieutenant, momentarily put out by the lack of any response, continued, 'Eat, drink and I'll be back in five minutes.'

The six men sat on their straw mattresses, balancing their trays on their laps.

The priest began with a prayer. In forty years he had never failed to thank the Lord for the meal in front of him – not since the day he was rescued from that storm.

'Why are you bothering?' asked Béart.

The priest didn't answer.

'Not much of a last supper, is it?' said Le Vau.

'What day is it?' asked Moreau.

'Tuesday, you idiot,' said Garnier.

'Don't know why they're feeding us when we'll be dead within the hour,' said Leconte.

Following their meagre breakfasts, the men took turns at the piss bucket.

'I feel oddly calm,' said the doctor.

Wiping his hands on the back of his trousers, Garnier nodded. 'I know what you mean. I knew a chef once...'

Again, they could hear the tread of boots approaching. 'This is it,' whispered Béart.

With Corporal Schmidt behind him, Lieutenant Lowitz addressed them. 'Right, gentlemen, I hope over the last six months you have had time to reflect on your situation. The German authorities will tolerate no sedition or attempts at undermining its war effort. Let this be a lesson to you.'

No one spoke; the air hung heavy with their silence. Garnier shook his head. Leconte kicked a stone.

'The time has come. You will follow me, please.'

One by one, the men followed, each one glancing behind one last time at the room that had been their shelter for their last night on earth. Corporal Schmidt brought up the rear, the clink of his rifle against his belt.

Down dark and dank corridors they followed the lieutenant, past cell doors, and up a spiral stone staircase, where the air felt progressively lighter. The lieutenant delivered them to a reception area with its checked floor tiles and the sun streaming through the open door, and disappeared. The men stood in a corner, Corporal Schmidt nearby, and waited silently, their spirits quashed by fearful anticipation, their hearts dulled by resigned acceptance. Looking round, they felt momentarily disorientated by the normality of it all – the receptionist with her painted nails and her hair in a bun, a German captain leaning on the counter flirting with her, a delivery man with a pencil behind his ear popping in with a parcel needing the receptionist's signature, an elderly French couple asking about visiting times. A poster on the wall featuring a Wehrmacht soldier with a baby in his arms proclaimed France was safer with the Germans in control. Outside, under the early morning sun, people went about their business, going to work, coming back from night shifts, the hustle and bustle of a normal working day. How the six men envied them.

Lieutenant Lowitz soon returned and handed each man a slip of folded paper.

'What's this?' asked Le Vau.

'Your train passes.'

Train passes? Did they hear him right?

'Our what?' asked Leconte.

'Six of them?' asked Moreau.

'You won't be able to get on the train without them.'

'The train?' 'But...' 'Are you...' They looked at their passes, and yes, today's date, the seven o'clock train to Saint-Romain.

The lieutenant screwed his eyes. 'Anyone would think you weren't keen on leaving. What's the matter with you all?'

Father Claudel spoke for all of them. 'We... we don't understand, Lieutenant Lowitz. Are we all catching the train – *now*?'

The lieutenant looked puzzled. 'Why, yes, of course. I told you last night. Why... why are you looking at me like that?'

'But we thought...'

'You thought what?'

The priest shook his head. 'No, nothing. Nothing at all.'

Their hearts beat like a thousand drums. Béart's mouth gaped open like that of a fish; Garnier was trying not to cry; and Moreau had to grip Leconte's arm for support.

'You're a strange bunch, you really are,' said the lieutenant. 'Anyone would think you were sorry to leave here.' Puffing his cheeks, he continued, 'Right, when you're quite ready, see the receptionist and she'll get your belongings for you.'

The men did so in the highest of spirits, hugging each other, kissing each other on the foreheads, patting each other on the back, while the receptionist, infected by their happiness, chortled and fetched them their things wrapped up in envelopes.

'I can't believe this is happening,' said Leconte.

'I can't wait to have that drink,' said Garnier, the teacher, rubbing his hands with glee.

'And I can't wait to see my missus,' said Béart, the soldier, an erection stirring in his pants.

'And I'm reserving the best table in town for tonight,' said Le Vau, slipping his rings back on his fingers, his mouth salivating at the thought of eating.

'Yeah, and me, I'm going to have the longest bath known to mankind,' said Moreau, the postman.

'I've never seen so many happy men,' said the receptionist.

Father Claudel, checking his envelope for the chain and crucifix they had confiscated on his arrival, replied, 'There is no greater gift than the gift of life, my dear. We all know that, but we don't always appreciate it. Today we do.'

'I s'pose. Sign the paper, please,' she said, pointing to the dotted line with a long, painted fingernail.

Even Lieutenant Lowitz and Corporal Schmidt, watching this circus from the side, tittered and shook their heads at the absurd happiness of the six mad but rather likeable Frenchmen.

'What idiots,' he said. 'Let's go. We've got a train to catch.'

'We're happy to follow, Lieutenant,' said Leconte.

'Before we go,' said the lieutenant. 'You are still technically prisoners until we reach Saint-Romain, which is why you'll still be under guard until you pass the ticket barriers there. I know you won't try anything silly now, but that is why you'll still be under escort. I do apologise.'

'Why, thank you, Lieutenant,' said the priest.

One by one, the six men shook the lieutenant's hand.

*

Twenty minutes later, having walked through the town, breathing in the fresh air and having every passer-by stare at this haggardly and foul-smelling but cheerful group of men, they arrived at the station. How joyful it was to see the sun, to feel the breeze on their faces, to breathe in the smells of the town, of ordinary life. Once at the train station, they got their passes stamped and, with the lieutenant and the corporal, waited on platform three while the cleaners finished their task on the stationary train.

Commuters off to work waited nearby, men puffing on pipes, others reading a newspaper, women filing their nails, a small group of young German soldiers laughing. The men watched as a train eased into the station on the opposite platform, emitting large puffs of black smoke, its brakes screeching. Doors swung open, people jumped off, many in a hurry to get to work.

Eventually, the men boarded the front carriage of their train, a first class carriage usually reserved for soldiers of the Wehrmacht. Lieutenant Lowitz showed them to their compartment. Settling down, the men took their places on the purple padded seats and stretched their legs. A sign on the door said 'No Smoking' in both French and German.

'Right then,' said the lieutenant, standing at the door and checking his watch. 'Try not to get the seats dirty. The train leaves in about ten minutes. We should get to Saint-Romain at eight o'clock. Corporal Schmidt will remain outside your door. Two years in this country and the good corporal still can't speak a word of French. Still, he will find someone to escort you should you need the toilet. I'll be in the compartment just up the corridor. I've got paperwork to read through. Any questions?'

Clearing his throat, Nicholas Leconte asked what was on all their minds. 'You managed to fix the line quickly.'

'What line?'

'The railway line – you've got it fixed already. I mean, the trains seem to be running on time. We were told it was buckled beyond use.'

'Buckled? I wasn't aware of it being broken.'

'The bombing yesterday morning,' said Moreau.

'What bombing?'

Béart, sitting forward, said quickly, 'The train blown up on the Saint-Romain line at seven twenty-two yesterday.'

'Seven twenty-two?' The lieutenant laughed. 'No, I'm sorry, you must be mistaken. I would know about it – obviously. There were no acts of sabotage last night, nor for many weeks, believe me.'

'But…'

The men glanced at each other.

'Are you sure?' said Leconte. 'The colonel said.'

The lieutenant looked puzzled. 'Colonel? What colonel?'

'Colonel Geist,' said Béart and Le Vau in unison.

'Colonel Geist?' The lieutenant laughed again.

'Yes, Lieutenant,' said Father Claudel. 'Colonel Geist came to see us last night, just before midnight, to tell us about a train being blown up.'

'You're mad.'

'Yeah,' said Moreau excitedly. 'Five Boche, sorry, I mean Germans, were killed and five French.'

The others nodded their agreement.

'Enough of this,' said the lieutenant, slicing the air with his hand. 'What do you think you take me for? Colonel Geist is no longer with us. He left over a year ago, transferred east.'

'No, that can't be,' said Garnier, his eyes popping in confusion. 'He said that…'

'Shut up. What's more, Colonel Geist was killed six months ago, stepped on a landmine in Stalingrad.'

'That can't be,' muttered Béart.

'And from what I heard, there wasn't enough bits of him left to bury. So, enough of this stupid talk.'

Father Claudel, rising to his feet, spoke. 'Lieutenant Lowitz, let me assure you that we saw your Colonel Geist last night as real as you are now. He told us a train had been–'

'Stop. Just stop. Sit down. You're mad, all of you. Prison's made you go potty. One more word about this and I'll have you back in your cells quicker than your feet can carry you. Do you understand?'

They didn't understand, none of them did, but they knew not to pursue it. Satisfied but still clearly annoyed, the lieutenant turned on his heel and, muttering something to the corporal, left.

Outside on the platform, amidst shouting and the blowing of the station guard's whistle, the last passengers jumped onto the train, slamming the doors behind them. With a lurch and a puff of smoke, the train began to move. It was exactly seven o'clock.

The six Frenchmen in their compartment with purple seats looked at each other with confusion writ large on their faces. 'But we saw him…'

'Yes, as clear as day.'

'Of course, he spoke to us.'

'But the lieutenant said he's dead. Blown to bits.'

'Maybe there're two Colonel Geists?'

'That's ridiculous.'

'We must've imagined it. I mean, we're still here, aren't we? We're still alive.'

'It must be six months in prison – you start imagining things.'

'But if we imagined it, how did we know his name? Did any of us ever meet him before?'

'No. So if we imagined it how come we invented the name of a man who actually existed?'

'Yes, and who worked in that same place.'

'We can't have all imagined the same thing; that's just plain idiotic.'

Jumping out of his seat, Béart said, 'I'm going to ask the corporal.' Sliding open the door, the corporal swiftly reached for his rifle. Béart, putting his hands up, said, 'Eh, Corporal, where's Colonel Geist?'

Corporal Schmidt grimaced as if he didn't comprehend the question. Then, mimicking the cutting of the throat, he grunted, 'Colonel Geist – kaput.'

Béart returned to his seat.

'He didn't have an escort, did he?' said Leconte.

'What do you mean?'

'The Boche never go anywhere unescorted, understandably. They always have an ape with a rifle behind them. But he didn't, not the colonel.'

'Good lord, you're right,' said Garnier. 'He was alone.'

'Yeah, and he had no gun on him,' said Moreau. 'The officers, they always have a revolver in a holster, don't they? He didn't.'

'Shit, I just thought of something else strange,' said Béart. 'He knew all our names.'

'Oh yes, old chap, you're right, he did,' said Doctor Le

Vau.

'We didn't tell him,' said Béart. 'And he'd never seen us before. So even if Lieutenant Lowitz had told him, he wouldn't have known one of us from the other.'

'Apart from Father Claudel here in his cassock,' said Garnier.

'So, how did he know?' asked Leconte.

'I remember his eyes,' said Father Claudel, staring out of the window at the passing town. 'They made me shudder. I've never seen eyes like his, it was almost as if he was…'

'Yes?'

'Well, it sounds silly, but as if he was possessed in some way.'

'Perhaps he was a ghost,' said Leconte jovially, forcing a smile.

'Oh my God,' said Doctor Le Vau.

'What's the matter, André, you've gone all pale,' said Garnier.

'Oh my. I've just remembered my schoolboy German. Colonel Geist…'

'Yes, go on, André,' said the priest. 'Say it.'

The doctor swallowed. 'Geist – that's the German word for ghost.'

*

All alone, Lieutenant Hans Lowitz sat back in his first class train compartment at the front of the train, his officer's hat on the seat next to him. If he shifted forward a bit, he could just about put his feet on the chair opposite. Despite the sign, he lit a cigarette. He enjoyed his work in France – long may it continue, he thought. He'd been here right from the start, back in the summer of 1940. He took part in the invasion. He'd been wounded – nothing serious, just a bullet through the thigh, but enough to keep him in France. He was still single but had had a few French girls along the way. He abhorred them – the thought of a good German girl throwing herself into the arms of the enemy… well, it wouldn't happen, they had too much pride. Not these French floozies, with their lipstick and garters. Perfectly happy to sidle up to any German they thought might help them out in some way – extra bread, half a chicken to put in the pot, a packet of cigarettes. The mothers were the worst; perhaps they were doing it for the children. Still, while he despised them, he was happy to accommodate them. Life in France was sweet. What he dreaded, what they all dreaded, was a transfer to the Eastern Front. Going east was as good as a death sentence. As indeed had happened to Colonel Geist, his old commanding officer. He liked Geist, a decent man, a bit of a father figure. A little too puritanical at times, liked people to know their rights from wrongs. And a bit too moralistic, thought Lowitz, but a decent man nonetheless. When the call came through that he was to be transferred east, he took it well. Calmer than any other man he'd seen. His last words to Lowitz as he left were, 'What will be will be, Lieutenant. Death holds no fear for me.' And then he was gone. Lowitz never saw him again. Six months later, Geist was dead.

Strange, thought Lowitz, why those French blokes thought they'd seen Geist; really rather bizarre. They were quite the oddest group of prisoners he'd come across. Considering they were about to be released, he'd seen men about to be shot display greater happiness than those six.

And then, later, in the reception area, they were so happy Lowitz truly thought they'd gone mad. And then, just now, this weird obsession that they'd seen Colonel Geist and a train being blown up. After three years in France, he thought he'd worked out how the French mind worked. But not this lot, as unpredictable as a sack of cats.

He remembered their arrest – catching them in the church's vestry in the middle of their first meeting. They didn't exactly resemble a threat to the German order. Six inadequates, barely able to pose order on their own miserable lives, let alone anyone else's. It was Madame Dauphin, once Mademoiselle Bouchez, who had given them away. Gustave Garnier, the teacher, had let it slip, probably showing off, trying to make out he was going to be a grand hero of the resistance. Garnier's faith in Dauphin had been a miscalculation; she was more than happy to denounce him and his friends.

He drew on his cigarette. He was supposed to be reading up on some paperwork. Damn it, he thought, he worked hard enough. He looked at his watch, a twenty-first birthday present from his parents back home in Dortmund. It was seven twenty-two; another forty minutes or so to Saint-Romain. He was just happy to put his feet up, smoke his cigarette and admire the passing view.

This is the life, he thought, this is the life.

*

Such was the intensity of the blast, Lieutenant Lowitz never knew. Catching the full impact of the bomb, the lieutenant was killed instantly, blown to smithereens.

He never felt a thing.

Chapter 11

He opened his eyes. Gradually, the white ceiling came into focus, an electric bulb hanging down, its flex covered in cobwebs. With his eyes, he followed the line of a crack zigzagging across the ceiling like a dried river bed in a desert. He could hear voices, German and French, groans, men complaining. The smell of disinfectant wafted in the air. Turning his head left and right, he realised he was in a hospital. A row of beds either side and opposite, each filled with bandaged-up, frail and battered-looking men. Outside, it was dark. His legs throbbed with pain, his head pounding. He lifted his right arm, how heavy it felt, and rubbed his eyes. A couple of tubes had been attached to his left arm. He sighed and tried to remember but could recall nothing – just a blinding white light and the feeling he was flying, no, floating through the air. Why did his legs hurt so? His knees felt as if they were on fire. He tried to sit up, but a shot of pain pinned him to the bed. Pulling up the sleeves of his pyjamas, he realised his skin was covered with a patchwork of scorch marks. His hair felt dry and matted.

Turning to his right, he saw the swing doors at the end of the ward fling open and a familiar figure emerge, walking towards him. Was that…? Yes, my word, it was.

'Hello,' she said softly. 'You're awake. Welcome back to the world of the living.' She sat on a little wooden chair next to his bed. Taking his hand, she asked, 'How are you feeling?'

Finding his voice, he croaked, 'Terrible.'

'You lost a lot of blood.'

God, his head hurt. 'What day is it?'

'Tuesday.' She looked at her watch. 'Coming up to ten. You must be thirsty. Here, take this…'

'Ten in the morning?'

'No, it's night.'

He drank the water, much of it dribbling down his pyjama top, soaking his chest hair.

Things started to come back to him… the train, the others, Corporal Schmidt, the blinding light, the ear-shattering explosion. 'What happened?'

Placing her hand over his again, she said quietly, 'There was a bomb. They blew up the train. It was terrible, there was so much damage.'

'Seven twenty-two. That was the time it went off, wasn't it?'

'Yes, seven twenty-two this morning, that's right.'

'I know, the colonel said.'

She cocked her head. 'The colonel?'

'Colonel Geist.' He paused, closing his eyes. He could see him clearly as if he was in front of him at that moment with his deep, measured accent, and his piercing blue eyes that made him shudder, the jawline scar shaped like a bolt of lightning. 'Colonel Ghost.'

'Are you OK, Ju-ju?'

Ju-ju. She called him Ju-ju. It'd been forty years since she'd called him that. He took another sip of water. 'Five Germans were killed, yes?'

'Yes, including the two men escorting you. How did you know that?'

'Corporal Schmidt and Lieutenant Lowitz?' He shook his head. 'And… and five Frenchmen were killed?'

She tried to speak. Unable to, she nodded.

'André Le Vau, the doctor; Henri Moreau, the postman; Nicholas Leconte, the policeman; Roger Béart, the soldier; and Gustave Garnier, the teacher. What a shame, terrible shame.'

'Yes.'

'That leaves just me, the sixth man. But it wasn't meant to happen this way; we should have done as the colonel ordered.'

'Darling, what on earth are you talking about?'

'We should have drawn straws after all, anything, but we should have chosen.'

A man opposite laughed as a nurse tried to give him a bed bath. An orderly passed through the ward pushing a trolley of medicines.

He sighed. He may have just woken up but he felt so very tired. 'Tell me, Maria, I've lost both my legs, haven't I?'

Again she nodded. 'I'm sorry.'

He remembered his words to the colonel, *Oh my, poor fellow, both his legs.* 'He did say.'

'Who said?'

'Colonel Geist. It's all exactly as he said. We were dead

men from the start but we were due to go to our deaths with clean consciences, unburdened by the things we had done. Sure, we were aware of them, felt bad, et cetera, but only superficially. He made sure we confronted our sinful deeds full on; he made sure we went to our deaths aware of their consequences.'

'Deaths? But you're not dead, Jean-Paul.'

'I know.' Turning to her, he reached over and gripped her hands. 'I'm sorry, Maria, I'm truly sorry for everything. I should never have turned my back on you.'

'Oh, Jean, that was forty years ago now. I think I've just about recovered. Thank you all the same.'

And yet, thought Father Claudel, you're crying. 'And René?'

'Now, that is something I will never recover from. It's been ten years but the pain never goes, not for one second.'

'I know. I'm sorry; truly I am.'

'I will never rest until his murderer is brought to justice. Every day, I hope, I pray, that the police will come to my door and tell me they've caught the devil who slit my son's throat. Every single day, Jean. My only wish in this life is that I can go to my grave knowing justice has been done.'

'Maria…' He tightened his grip on her hands. 'Oh, Maria, my only love, there's something… something I need to tell you…' A shot of pain kicked him in the knees. It took his breath away; it traversed up and through him, pain like a bolt of lightning.

'Jean? What's the matter, darling?'

Arching his back, he screwed up his face, his breath coming in short, panicked bursts. His furious heartbeat pounded in his head. The pain, such pain… Then, gradually, very gradually, it receded, slowly fading away. Catching his breath, he relaxed his back and felt himself sink into the mattress.

'Jean, are you OK?'

How tired he felt; so, so tired…

'Jean? Jean, speak to me. Jean…' He could hear her voice drifting away, further and further away, drifting ever so distant, drifting like a leaf in the wind… 'Nurse, nurse! Nurse, please, quickly, something's wrong here… Ju-ju, darling, wake up. Please, what's the matter? Wake up, Ju-ju, wake up…'

*

Father Claudel opened his eyes, feeling quite peculiar. The pain, at least, had gone. He was still in the hospital ward but everything had gone – Maria was gone, so the nurses, all the other beds and their occupants. And everything seemed bathed in white, a white hazy mist. A figure emerged from the mist, a man with a military cap. The man stopped in front of him, removing his cap, exposing a full head of neatly-combed strawberry-blond hair. 'Oh, Father Claudel,' said Colonel Geist in his deep, carefully articulated French. His scar had disappeared. The German fixed his gaze on the priest with his piercing blue eyes, causing the priest to shudder. 'You failed me. You would have lived; it would've been you, Father. The five Frenchmen killed in the explosion, yes, they all died instantly, like I said. But the sixth one, the sixth man, the one who lost both his legs; yes, him. He would have lived, Father, contrite perhaps, crippled for sure, but a *better* man, a better servant to God, more aware of man's failings, the failings inherent in all of us. Despite your sin perhaps being the gravest, they would have voted for you, the man of God. You would have lived and you would have lived for God in a more sincere way. Did I not say if you couldn't decide, you'd all die? You never decided. And so the sixth man had to die. Yes, Father, you died later that same day.'

THE END

Note from the author

At the end of the classic 1955 French film, *Les Diaboliques*, the director, Henri-Georges Clouzot, pleaded with his viewer: "Don't be devils! Don't ruin this film for your friends. Don't tell them what you've seen. On behalf of your friends, thank you."

I hope you enjoyed this short novel. Do leave a review on your preferred online store. But if you do, in the spirit of *Les Diaboliques*, **don't tell your friends what you've read!**

Thank you,

Rupert Colley,
April 2017.

The Woman
on the Train

Rupert Colley

Part One

The Woman on the Train

Chapter 1
Annecy, September 1982

I was expecting a visitor. The first, perhaps, in years. I can't remember. I had a tidy up in recognition of this momentous occasion – threw away newspapers that should have been thrown away weeks, if not months, ago, cleaned the toilet, pushed the vacuum cleaner around. At five minutes past one, the doorbell rang. He was five minutes late. Not that I blamed him – trying to find this address in this backwater French provincial town near the Swiss border is no mean feat. And he'd come some distance – over 500 kilometres, all the way from Paris.

He'd phoned me a few days earlier. His name was Henri Bowen, a Frenchman with an English name, a journalist from one of the nationals, I forget which now. He'd said he was writing an article about people who'd made a name for themselves during the sixties but had since faded from public view. A sort of 'where are they now?'-type piece. I had hesitated and told him I would consider it and ring him back. And I did think about it – in fact, I thought of nothing else all day. I was tempted, of course; it appealed to my vanity, a trait I thought I'd repressed years ago. Obviously not. For I was once a very vain man. But I was comfortable with that – to be a leading light in one's chosen profession, a degree of vanity is a necessity. But since my downfall, no, let's call it retirement, many years ago, I'd been content to fade into obscurity. Did I want to be remembered? Of course I did. The chance may never present itself again. The following day, I phoned up this Monsieur Bowen and, as I knew I would, told him yes, I'd be happy to be interviewed. He seemed delighted.

And here he is, sitting in my living room, the place smelling of air freshener. Good-looking fellow, slicked-back hair, positively shiny, tall, very pale, wearing a dapper cream-coloured suit, firm handgrip. 'It's lovely to meet you, Maestro.'

'Oh please, Monsieur Bowen, less of the maestro. I'm a plain old Monsieur now, and happy to be so.'

He refused my offer of tea and biscuits, and, at my invitation, sat down on my settee which sucked him in, leaving him looking slightly awkward. He took in his surroundings and, I have to confess, despite my efforts at cleaning up, I felt a prick of shame. There was no denying it – I lived in such a mundane place. The chintzy carpets, the turquoise curtains, the squashy settee, the old-fashioned radio – nothing wrong with any of it but it must have seemed very ordinary to a thrusting young man like

Henri Bowen. Given my former fame, given the respect I used to command, he must have expected a lot more. I could see the words written all over his face – 'how the mighty have fallen'. He tried his best to cover up his embarrassment. 'My parents had all your records,' he said, almost falling over his words. 'They loved everything you did. I think the Richard Strauss was their favourite.'

I sat down opposite him, crossing my legs. 'Your parents had fine tastes, Monsieur Bowen.'

He laughed politely. 'As far as they were concerned, if it had your name on it then it had to be good.' So, what happened? He didn't say it – but from the expression on his face, he might as well have done. 'Do you have any of your own records?'

'No.' His reaction obliged me to explain. 'One's musical direction changes all the time. What I felt was right twenty years ago, now makes me cringe. With age, I look back at my cavalier approach, and at the liberties I took, and I feel, well, if not embarrassed, then certainly a little bashful. I fear my younger self had a rather inflated opinion of himself, thinking he knew better than the composers he was trying to interpret.'

'Do you listen to much music now?'

'No, not often. I prefer Moroccan music nowadays.'

'That surprises me. Do you mind if I take notes?'

'Be my guest. Tell me, Monsieur Bowen, I don't mind, but how long do you think this'll take? It's just that everyday at three, I like to pop over and visit an elderly neighbour. I like to make sure they're OK.'

'Plenty of time.'

As he organised himself with pad and pen, rummaging in his briefcase, he mentioned a photographer. 'It'd only take a few minutes,' he said. 'She's very good. Based locally. I'll get her to give you a call.'

'I used to have my photo taken every few minutes. This will be the first for many a year.' I wasn't sure how I felt about it. Part of me was, for sure, thrilled, but the idea of the whole country seeing me, as I am now, a shadow of my former self, perturbed me.

'You look different from the photos.'

'We all get older, Monsieur Bowen.'

'No, it's not that – it's something about your nose, I think. Sorry, that sounds rude.'

'It's a long story.'

'Would you mind if I smoked?'

'I would.'

He took this little setback in his stride. 'I read about you in the papers. I know, before your success as a conductor, you were a hero of the resistance.'

'A hero? I may have exaggerated a little.' Drumming my fingers on my knee, I tried to explain. 'The words resistance and hero are too often merged together, as if by merely being in the resistance automatically made you a hero. Yes, I was in the resistance, as you know, but I never did anything remotely heroic.' Bowen tried to speak. I cut him short with my hand in the air. 'Yes, if I had been caught it would have been unpleasant but I was, how do you say these days, small fry. I was not on any list; I knew nothing. Occasionally, I'd be given an errand which might have carried an element of risk but that was about it. I would do my task, without fuss, and go home again.'

'Yes, I read about what you said. Nonetheless, they must have been difficult times.'

'Oh yes. One had no control over one's life. I'd always

wanted to conduct. Before the war, I had secured myself a place at a music college but the Germans invaded before I had chance to take up my place. After that… well.' I waved my hands in the air. He understood. 'Instead I was forced into conducting invisible orchestras while I played Vivaldi or Elgar, or whatever was that week's favourite, on my father's gramophone player. Before the war, we listened, as a family, to concerts on the radio but once the Germans took over, radios were banned.'

'In case you listened to the BBC, or something like that.'

'Precisely that. We had to hand our radios in. That was a sad day for me. But, really, Monsieur Bowen, about my war years, I have nothing to say that could be of interest to you. Except perhaps…'

He sat forward, his pen poised over his pad. 'Go on.'

'I met a woman once.' He raised an eyebrow, a sort of man-to-man acknowledgement. 'No, no, nothing like that.' I laughed inwardly. If only it had been that simple, I thought. But no, this woman was to have a far greater impact on my life than any wife or mistress could ever have had.

'Ah yes, the woman on the train. Of course, this is what our readers want to know – how you feel about it now, all these years later.'

'It's strange, isn't it, how an innocuous meeting can have such repercussions, in this instance, many, many years down the line. She was much older than me for one thing. It was the summer of forty-two. I was just twenty years old. Still a boy really, although at the time I thought of myself as a man.' I paused.

'Are you OK, Monsieur?'

'Yes. Just give me a moment.'

He leant back in the settee and gazed round the room, pretending to show an interest in the landscape paintings I have framed on the walls. Obscure paintings of no value by forgotten artists. Placing my fingertips against my temples, I tried to think. Did I really want to share this story with, in effect, the huge readership of a national newspaper? I had lost everything, pride was all that remained, and now I seemed on the verge of losing that too. I knew that for many people of my generation I was one of those 'Whatever happened to…' personalities. Was it not better for it to remain that way; to allow my former achievements to speak for themselves? I would regret it, I knew I would, but that vain streak was too strong to resist. I had had my years in the limelight followed by many more in obscurity. I thought I was old enough, mature enough, not to be tempted by the lure of fame any more. Could I resist one last passing shot at being at the centre of attention, at being the name on people's lips? No, sadly I couldn't; this was my one last grab at the chalice of infamy.

'Monsieur Bowen?'

'Maestro?' He sat up, trying unsuccessfully to hide his enthusiasm.

'You're right, somehow my whole life has been influenced by, as you call her, the woman on the train...'

Part Two

The Woman on the Train

Chapter 2
Saint-Romain, August 1942

I'd bought my train ticket and waited at the far end of the platform, pacing up and down. It was almost midday on a warm but dull summer's day, heavy clouds dominating the sky. Above me, a large hanging sign with the word *Sortie*, 'Exit'. The train was due any moment. Patting my pockets, I checked for my identity card and the paper permitting my travel – I was visiting my old piano teacher, and that was the story I had to keep to. I was indeed visiting a former piano teacher in Saint-Romain, so if checked, my story would hold. Nonetheless, my stomach flittered with butterflies. Nearby, a couple of mothers with pushchairs shared a cigarette, passing it from one to the other, while talking animatedly. Further along, also waiting, was a group of German soldiers. The sight of their uniforms always made me shudder, today especially so. But they seemed in a jovial mood, as if they were a group of sightseers out on a day trip. Perhaps they were. They seemed so young, no older than me. I knew if my nation hadn't been defeated

11

so quickly I would have been forced to join up by now. Craning my neck, I spied a couple of older ones, further along, who seemed to view their younger colleagues with a degree of exasperation. It seemed strange to think that, unbeknownst to them, I was working with the local resistance, doing tasks, albeit minor ones, that would help undermine their authority. I hated it, having too nervous a disposition for such gallant deeds, but when I was asked, what could I do? This was the second time I'd been sent on such a mission – to take information written on a sheet of paper and deliver it to fellow resisters in the town of Saint-Romain, a train ride of less than half an hour. I needed to think of an excuse to avoid any further missions. The man I'd replaced, a twenty-year-old, like me, had been caught, supposedly tortured, and sent to Germany to work in a labour camp. A death sentence in all but name.

I could see the train approaching, a huge, ugly thing with its fender protruding from the front. I didn't have to worry about having to share a carriage with the Boche – they always had their own carriages, the first class ones, reserved for their exclusive use. The station guard appeared, a busy-looking fellow with his green flag tucked under his arm. The train puffed large clouds of black smoke into the high rafters. A couple of men jumped off before the train had fully come to a stop and embraced the two young mothers. I boarded the last carriage as, further up, the soldiers pushed and jostled each other like a bunch of overexcited kids. I found a near-empty compartment. Sliding the door open, I asked its sole occupant, an older woman sitting by the window, if I could join her. She waved her hand by means of saying yes, fine. I sat in the middle of the row of seats, not wanting to sit directly opposite her. No one joined us and after a few minutes, the train pulled out of the station.

Soon, we were out in the open countryside. I twirled my thumbs, crossed and uncrossed my legs, feeling sick to the core, knowing I was carrying information that could land me in front of the Gestapo. The compartment smelt slightly of the woman's perfume. After a few minutes, I opened my satchel and retrieved my reading material – the sheet music to Wagner's opera, *Tristan and Isolde*. I didn't feel like reading but I was told to – it'd make me look more *normal*. So, I thought, if I had to read, it might as well be music. I wasn't a big fan of Wagner, far too Teutonic and self-important for my liking, but my man in the village had persuaded me that, if questioned, it'd look better to be reading something German than French. I was tempted to sneak a look at the contents of the illicit envelope handed to me, the one causing me such anxiety, now nestled in my satchel. I had no idea of its contents. All I knew was that I had to deliver it to a woman who worked at the station at Saint-Romain. I wouldn't miss her, I was told – she was African. I puffed my cheeks – this was awful; this was not my calling. I'd been placed here on this earth to conduct music. My time, I knew, would come. The war had hindered my grand plans, but it couldn't last forever, and when, finally, men braver than me had driven the Germans off our land and defeated them, then I'd be ready.

I'd not gotten far in the score, no more than the end of the opening scene, when I considered the woman opposite. She had her eyes closed, her hands on her lap, a large handbag, more like a briefcase, at her feet. She wasn't as old as I had originally thought – middle aged, in her fifties, perhaps, nicely dressed with a burgundy-coloured jacket with heavy black stitching and a large-collared white blouse. Her skin looked tough, as if many layers deep, yet surprisingly smooth. She had jet-black hair swept up in a bun, with matching, prominent eyebrows. She had a solid-looking nose, deep-set eyes and a prominent forehead, and downturned lips. She reminded me of a bad-tempered schoolmistress. She opened her eyes, taking me by surprise, and looked straight at me – as if aware I'd been scrutinising her. I tried to turn away but too late. I felt her eyes bore into me; this time it was her turn to consider me. When I stole a glance at her, she was still staring straight at me, unblinking, with a distinct look of disapproval. Unnerved, I returned my attention to the Wagner and pretended to read.

'What is that you're studying?' Her voice confirmed the image of the old schoolmistress – loud, sharp and well-articulated, like someone in a hurry.

'I, er, it's Wagner,' I stuttered, unable to meet her eyes.

She didn't answer for a few moments, as if considering this morsel of information. Eventually, she asked. 'Why not a French composer?'

Oh, the irony, I thought. 'I study them as well. Debussy, Ravel, Bizet–'

'You don't have to list them, I am perfectly aware of who they are.'

'Yes. Sorry.'

'There's no need to apologise,' she said. 'You study music?'

'Not at the moment but one day I will be a conductor.'

'Oh, you will, will you? You sound very sure of yourself.'

This time, I looked at her directly as I said firmly, 'Yes.

A conductor.'

Finally, she took her eyes off me. 'I wish you the very best of luck,' she said, looking outside the window at a passing woodland.

I returned my attention to the score but although she seemed, thankfully, to have lost interest in me, I could no longer concentrate. For some reason, our short conversation had unsettled me.

I looked at my watch – we'd be there in less than quarter of an hour.

A few minutes later, the compartment door was slid violently open. I jumped. Standing at the doorway, deeply intimidating, were two German soldiers. 'Papers,' barked the first one, a tall man with small, steely-blue eyes, wearing a peaked cap, and a swastika on an armband. I'd been in this situation before and got away with it. This was worse – my exchange with the woman had made me nervous. I knew it was obvious but I lacked the strength to control my trembling hands. While I fumbled in my pockets for my card and papers, the woman passed her documents to the German. He glanced at them and with a nod of the head returned them to her. '*Dankeschön*,' she said, putting them back in her inside pocket.

'And you,' he said to me, while his squared-headed colleague hovered behind. I passed them to him, knowing that I had guilt written all over my face. He considered my card carefully, glancing from the photograph to me and back again, his eyes narrowing. I tried to calm my nerves conscious of the sweat forming on my brow. 'Why are you going to Saint-Romain?'

'To visit–'

'The real reason.'

My stomach caved in. I didn't know what to say.

'Well?'

It was the woman who spoke next – in German, talking quickly.

He considered her words for a few moments, bowed in a slightly exaggerated fashion, and exited, pushing away his colleague, who slid the door firmly shut behind him.

The woman looked at me again, without expression. I wasn't sure what to say. If I thanked her it would only confirm my guilt. What had she said to them, I wondered.

We sat in silence as before – me pretending to read the score, she gazing out of the window. I knew I was far from safe – I still had to run the gauntlet of getting past the guards at the station.

Finally, the train began slowing down – we were approaching Saint-Romain. She stretched her arms and took a deep breath. I realised then that she too was getting off here. I returned the music to my satchel.

The station came into view, a much larger place than our local one, boasting several platforms with trains coming and going. We both stood. While checking the contents of her briefcase, she spoke: 'As we pass the guards on the platform, you'll have to walk beside me. Have your documents ready. Say nothing.'

I nodded. Clicking shut her briefcase, she waited for me to open the door.

The platform here was far busier – lots of people, both French and German, some with heavy baggage, boarding, a few alighting. A porter rushed passed us, pushing a trolley laden with suitcases, a newspaper vendor enjoyed a brisk trade, as did a kiosk selling tobacco and sweets. The woman strode briskly, sidestepping others, while I tried to keep up. At the far end of the platform, I could see the barrier decked with swastika flags and manned by numerous Nazis in their ugly uniforms, with Alsatian dogs straining on their leashes. It was a foreboding sight. They had stepped up their presence since the last time I'd been here. I knew I could never have done this alone, and I was relieved to have my newfound companion at my side. We had to queue for some time as the guards ahead of us were stopping everyone and frisking them and searching their bags. I looked round for a bin in which I could ditch my incriminating envelope. The woman, sensing my concern, looked at me and mouthed, 'Don't worry,' before staring straight ahead again.

Slowly, we reached the head of the queue. My companion passed over her documents and signalled me to do the same. Again, she spoke to them in that same authoritative voice in German, and again it did the trick. The guard bowed, returned her papers and indicated to his colleagues to let us through. No one, apart from one of the dogs, even bothered to look at me. We were through to the main part of the station with its high, curved roof and the hustle and bustle of so many people. I felt a surge of relief, almost of adrenalin. This time, in my enthusiasm, I did thank her.

'Please, do not say another word.'

'I'm sorry.'

I think she may have smiled a moment. 'This is where we part.'

'Yes.' I offered my hand. She didn't take it.

'Can I ask your name?' I asked, lowering my arm.

'No.' She turned to leave. Before she left me, she stopped and, turning, said, 'I look forward to watching you conduct one day.'

'Yes, I'll…' But she'd gone, disappearing into the crowd.

*

So, now I had to find the African woman and deliver my message. It wasn't difficult, she knew someone would be looking for her, and I saw her, a large, short black woman in her railway uniform with its peaked cap, carrying a pile of envelopes. She watched me as I approached her.

'Can you tell me the time of the next train to Rennes, please?' These were the words I was told to say.

'Not for at least another two hours, Monsieur.' And those were the words I was told would be said back to me. 'Follow me,' she said, in her thick African accent. She led me to the back end of a newspaper kiosk, checking round her in, what I thought, a rather obvious fashion. 'Have you got something for me?' I think she said.

'I'm sorry?'

She rolled her eyes. 'Are you not listening? I said–'

'Oh, yes.' I fished the envelope from my bag and passed it her.

'Good,' she said, inserting my envelope into the middle of her pile. Without another word, she spun on her shoes and walked briskly away.

'Thank you very much,' I muttered under my breath. Nonetheless, I was hugely relieved to be shot of the offending document. Now, at last, I could breathe easy. I saw her enter an office with the words *Personnel Seulement* written on the door.

I sauntered towards the station exit. Two French policemen stood either side, eyeing the crowds. Above the

18

large doors was a framed portrait of Marshal Pétain, the head of our collaborationist government, bordered by a couple of French flags. I stopped to check the address of my piano teacher on a slip of paper, while people rushed past me. A mother, carrying a small but bulging suitcase, yelled at her child to hurry up; two men bumped into each other, and had started arguing. 'Why don't you look where you're going,' said the taller one, scooping up his hat off the ground. A station announcement broadcast the time of the next train on platform two; two men on ladders were affixing a new poster on the station wall.

I was about to leave, when I heard another commotion behind me. The door to the station office was opened. I saw the back of a German uniform; I heard shouts in German-accented French, competing with the argument between the two Frenchmen who had clashed into each other. Had something happened to my African woman? I had to see if anything was wrong. Approaching, I heard a German say, 'We can do this here or you come with us to HQ – it's up to you.' Others, like me, had come to see what was happening. We could see inside, the African women, dwarfed by two German officers, unable to escape their clutches. She caught my eye, her expression one of confusion and fear. One of the Germans followed her gaze. He saw me and the two of us remained frozen for a second, staring at each other. Then, instinctively, I ran. I heard the German yell, 'Hey, you, stop.'

The two French policemen had heard it too but they had moved away from the exit, having become embroiled with the two men arguing. I sprinted out of the station, zigzagging past people, porters and pigeons, and ran down the street, pursued by a number of men in uniforms. 'Out of the way, out of the way,' I heard one shout. 'Stop right now,' screamed another. I turned up a street on my right, running across the road. A car screeched to a halt, the driver sounding his horn. I had no idea where I was; I only knew I had to keep going. 'Stop or we'll fire!' A warning shot rang out. People in the street screamed. A mother pulled her child in as she pinned herself against a wall. I knew the second shot would be aimed at me. I had no choice and came to a halt, putting my hands in the air, my chest heaving as I tried to catch my breath. I refused to turn around but I heard their heavy boots on the tarmac rapidly approaching me. One of them pushed me against the wall next to a baker's. 'You're fast,' he said, breathlessly as his colleagues caught up, 'but not fast enough.' He thrust his revolver into my back. 'Up against the wall. Legs apart.'

The baker waved at me from within the shop while a second German began frisking me, his fat hands inside my jacket, against my shirt, checking every pocket. Grabbing me by the shoulder, he turned me around. 'Open your bag.' There were three of them, their revolvers drawn.

'Is this code?' he asked, holding up the score.

'No, it's sheet music – Wagner. He's German.'

'Mm. You've got nothing on you,' said the second once he'd turned my bag inside out. 'So why are you running away, eh? What are you hiding?'

'Nothing.'

'Nothing? You run away for nothing?'

'I'm in a hurry.'

'Don't try to be funny. Right, you're coming with us.'

'But I haven't done anything wrong.'

'We'll soon see about that.'

Passers-by stopped to stare as I was marched back to the station, my hands still above my head, my three Germans behind me. Those coming towards me stepped off the pavement to let me pass, concerned looks upon their faces. An older woman in black winked. Perhaps she thought I was some sort of a hero.

We were almost back at the station when I heard what was now a familiar voice shouting in German. 'Halt,' said one of the soldiers.

And there she was – the woman from the train, berating the Germans while showing them her ID. They passed it from one to the other as she launched into a long tale, speaking quickly in that authoritative tone.

One responded in a quiet voice. The exchange continued in German while I watched them daring to hope that I'd get away from this.

The Germans answered as one, sounding apologetic. Turning to me, the woman said, 'I've explained to the gentlemen and they realise they've made a mistake. You're free to go.'

I opened my mouth not sure what to say or how to thank her.

'Accept our apologies, Monsieur,' said one of the soldiers.

'Oh, yes. Easy mistake to make,' I said with a confidence I didn't feel.

I bowed to the woman and even clicked my heels. 'Thank you, Madame.'

I quickly returned back to the station. Stuff my piano teacher, I thought; I was heading back home.

Chapter 3
Paris, November 1966

A conductor bears a huge weight of responsibility – a poor conductor can render a magnificent work mediocre, reduce an esteemed orchestra to that of a confused rabble, and can flaw even the greatest of singers. The composer, who has spent possibly years writing and perfecting his work is then entirely in the hands of the conductor who brings it to life. They say that even Beethoven, blighted by his deafness, ruined his own work as a conductor. The orchestra is as dependent upon their conductor as a newly-born child is dependent upon its mother.

Conducting an eighty-piece orchestra in the confines of a recording studio is a very different prospect to a live venue. One feels restrained; it is not a natural setting. In a live situation, the conductor and musicians feed off the audience and the environment; there is a natural energy that spurs us on to higher deeds, to a greater performance. Not so in a studio, with its muted, artificial air. All spontaneity is destroyed. As a conductor one must spur one's charges to produce a music that is beyond mere workmanship. Theoretically, a studio recording allows one to stop and re-record as much or as little as necessary; it provides one with the opportunity to attain perfection. Yet, in reality, it does exactly the opposite – it acts as a stop on creativity, it renders both the musicians and the conductor too self-conscious. We follow the music, not our hearts. Therefore, one has to work ten times harder to try to produce a work that is worthy of one's name and the composer's expectations.

Then, from the recording studio to the editing suite, where technology plays its part, where one can lift a performance to something near what one hears in the head. At the end of the process, one is left with a perfect rendition, perfect but soulless. My first studio recording, with my new Parisian orchestra, was Brahms's First Symphony. It almost caused to me to suffer a breakdown, not least because I carried the burden of expectation. The orchestra and I had been signed up by a big American record label. They expected great things from us, and from me in particular; they expected a return on their investment. I had a recording budget which, although on paper might have seemed generous, was never going to be enough. In the end, it was money, not time, that forced me to declare the work finished. The label executives were delighted, congratulating me on such a fine piece of work. I accepted their thanks with dignity while I suffered sleepless nights knowing full well that I had not even begun to capture the work as I had intended.

I spent a day being photographed for the record sleeve. My good looks, they said, would help shift sales. Shift? Words failed me. Was I selling a cereal, I asked them. They insisted and I had no choice. But, I'll admit, the final result was impressive – me with my hands in the air, gripping my baton, the glow of artistic perspiration on my brow.

Then came the day of release – I expected the worst, and wished I had been selling cereals after all. I need not have worried – it sold beyond expectations. I finished with the year's bestselling classical release in all France. My name was known the country over. My American bosses were delighted; my bank manager and my wife even more so. French record companies, who had failed to secure me, outbid by their American competitors, hinted at my lack of patriotism.

The following year, I was back in the studio – several times. The Americans had their golden goose and they were going to make damned sure they made the most of it. I never did learn to enjoy working in a studio, but I quickly learnt to enjoy the fruits of my labour. Michèle and I bought a grand new home in an affluent southern suburb of Paris, far bigger than we needed. I bought two fine cars, new clothes, the latest gadgets and innovations. My recordings won prizes, I was interviewed, my face appeared on the front of magazines; I was asked to endorse various products, enhancing my income even further.

Michèle and I had married in 1956. A subdued affair; I was still the conductor of a small, provincial orchestra, and my pay was meagre. Michèle was its violist. But, unlike me, music was not her obsession; it never permeated to her marrow. She played moderately well and music was a means by which to earn an income. The viola was, to her, merely the tool of her trade. She was petite with heavy eyelids, a sharp nose, dimpled cheeks and a most pleasant smile. I'd met her a decade after the war. She too had been in the resistance but a much more active member than I. She'd been arrested and brutally tortured by the Gestapo. She never told me the details suffice to say that, as a result, she'll never have children. Such was my love for her, I didn't mind. Alas, I always felt that our love was rather one-sided, that the Gestapo, as well as leaving the scars, had also stripped her of her ability to love.

Ten years on and I was at the top of my career. Things could not have gone better. It never occurred to me, not even for a moment, that it might all, one day, pop like a balloon. It was in Paris, November sixty-six. I'd just conducted Mahler's Fifth, always an exhausting affair, when I received a visitor. I was in my dressing room, backstage at the *Salle Pleyel*, still wearing my tuxedo, my bowtie undone. It was one of those traditional dressing rooms with light bulbs around the mirror. On the dresser in front of me, a bottle of champagne in a bucket of ice, half empty, having already consumed three glasses in quick succession. I was sprawled back in my chair, still catching my breath, replaying the music in my head, smiling inanely at my reflection and congratulating myself on another success when there was a knock on the door. 'Would Maestro be prepared to accept a visitor?' asked a pale member of the theatre staff. 'Would it be convenient?'

'Yes, yes, show them in,' I said, half expecting a reporter or a music reviewer.

'Good evening, Maestro,' said the stranger.

I spun round in my chair. I opened my mouth to say something but the words wouldn't come. Standing in front of me was not a reporter, not a reviewer, but the woman from the train all those years ago. She looked smart in a tailored mackintosh and a silk scarf. She'd aged a little, after all it'd been twenty years, a few lines on her face, her black hair, now much longer, was streaked with grey, but otherwise she looked much the same.

'Have you got time?'

'Yes, of course,' I said, almost falling out of my chair to invite her in. She offered her hand. I took it. 'What a surprise. How… how did you find me?'

She laughed. 'It wasn't difficult – your face is everywhere.'

'I suppose.'

She looked me up and down, seeing what time had done to me in the intervening years. 'You look well. You're doing well.'

'Yes, perhaps. I'm sorry – do take a seat.' I offered her my chair in front of the mirror but instead she sat in the little chair in the corner of the room.

'This will do fine,' she said, looking slightly absurd as she nestled her bottom on the tiny seat.

'Can I get you a drink? Champagne perhaps?'

'No, no, I don't want to take up your time.'

'Did you… I mean, were you here for the concert?'

'Oh yes. In fact, I've been to several. I've been following your career with interest. I always remember our conversation on the train. You said that one day you'd be a conductor. I may have doubted you. For that, I apologise, for here you are. Not only a conductor but the most famous one in France. I congratulate you.'

Usually, I can take compliments in my stride, I was well practised by now, but this time I felt genuinely bashful. 'Thank you. And you, Madam, you look well.'

'I am, thank you. I never did tell you my name. Let me

introduce myself – *Mademoiselle* Lapointe. You must call me Hilda.'

'And my name is–'

'Oh, I know your name. The whole country knows your name by now.'

'Ha, you make me sound like one of The Beatles.'

'Oh, please, Maestro, there's no need to compare yourself to those delinquents and their Negro music.'

I didn't like to say I rather admired the four boys from across The Channel. 'Mademoiselle Lapointe–'

'Hilda, please.'

'Hilda – I still, after all these years, appreciate how you helped me that day. I've never forgotten it. I admit, I was carrying some papers that… well, if they'd been discovered…'

'Would have been compromising?'

I smiled. 'Yes, exactly.'

'It's all water under the bridge now.'

'Yes. Yes, it is.'

We sat in silence for a while, remembering a time that seemed so distant and so alien to seem unreal now.

I cleared my throat. 'Would you care, Mademoiselle, Hilda, for a spot to eat? There are so many–'

She held up her hand. 'No, no. It's very kind of you, Maestro, but no. I just wanted to…' She rose to her feet. Rearranging her scarf, she said, 'I don't know – to say hello, I suppose, and to say how pleased I am that things have turned out so well for you.'

'Well, thank you. If it hadn't been for you, it could have turned out very differently.' She seemed pleased with that; pleased with the acknowledgement. 'But what I've always wanted to know, is what exactly did you say to them?'

'Let's just say I used my powers of persuasion.'

'Yes, but what—'

'I must go. It's been lovely seeing you again.' We shook hands again, and I showed her out of the door and passed her to the theatre boy to escort her back outside.

Closing the door, I slunk in my chair and smiled at my reflection. Yes, I thought, perhaps if she hadn't intervened all those years ago, if she hadn't offered her protection, things might well have turned out very differently.

I poured myself another glass of champagne and toasted myself and my continued success. It was late. Time, I decided, to order a car to take me home.

Chapter 4
Paris, August 1944

My activities in the resistance fairly well came to an end that day in August 1942. The whole episode confirmed for me that I lacked the necessary qualities for such work; it was far too risky for the likes of me. About a week after my last assignment, my man in the village asked me to deliver another missive to his colleagues in Saint-Romain. I made excuses – told him my mother was ill. A month later, following another request, I told him I had a piano exam. He criticised my 'lack of commitment' and never asked me again. My lack of commitment may have been cowardly but, as it proved, sensible – about six months later, the Gestapo swept through the village arresting a number of men and women, my man included. Most returned after a few months, looking a lot worse for the experience, but my man, as the ringleader, had been executed.

The occupation carried on around me but never impinged on my life. I was frequently stopped as I went about my business and asked for my identity card, but apart from that I was free to pursue my interest in music. I was desperate to leave my sleepy village. My mother irritated me, and my father had died when I was young. I felt no ties to the place and wanted so much to go out and explore the world. But I learnt to be patient – I knew my time would come. I may have lost my place at music college, but I went to see my piano teacher in Saint-Romain. Occasionally, I played a recital at the local church. Starved of entertainment, it always attracted a good turnout, including a number of appreciative Germans.

Paris was liberated in August 1944, the Nazis finally driven out. Immediately, I bade my mother farewell and headed for the capital. I drank in the celebratory atmosphere. I watched the American tanks on the streets and, along with hoards of others, cheered the soldiers. The atmosphere was contagious; never had I seen people so happy. I fell in with a group of students, made friends, drank, went to parties and waved the flag. I shared my story of resistance, inventing a whole new persona for myself. No one doubted me for a moment. I watched as women accused of having slept with Germans, 'horizontal collaborators', as they were known, were hunted down by angry mobs, stripped and had their hair hacked off. People laughed and called it the new hairstyle of '44. Many were branded with a swastika on their bare heads or their breasts. I watched as male collaborators were marched down the streets with signs hung round their necks, signs that attested to their guilt. I joined my new-found friends to jostle, shout abuse and spit at them. They were giddy times. After four years of occupation, the future seemed unending with possibility and awash with opportunity.

My musical career beckoned.

Chapter 5
Paris, May 1968

After years of recording and performing, of going on concert and promotional tours, I needed a break. The novelty of fame and the strain of being in constant demand had begun to take its toll. I was due to start work soon on a live performance and a new recording of Berlioz's Second Symphony, along with some supplementary pieces. But first, Michèle and I went on holiday to Morocco. I fell in love with Moroccan music with its erratic rhythms and earthy roots. We spent hours browsing round the souks of Marrakech, buying knick-knacks, drinking strong coffee, eating tagines, indulging the street children and their nuisance. After a week, we relaxed on the coast, going on camel rides, boat trips, reading and idling the hours away in the local cafés. I thought that perhaps, just perhaps, my wife had begun to learn how to love.

We returned to find Paris in a state of turmoil. People had taken to the streets, fighting the police, overturning cars, building barricades. Revolution was in the air as demonstrators preached liberty and socialism. Students occupied their universities, workers downed tools. President de Gaulle teetered. The country was in a state of anarchy. Public transport, postal services, the whole infrastructure crumbled.

I was at work, having begun rehearsals on the Berlioz, when, one morning in early May, a small delegation of students came to see me – earnest, young men and women, with long hair and high ideals. They wanted me to speak on their behalf, my fame would give the movement credibility, they said. I wasn't sure – I was an establishment figure and rocking the boat had never been my thing. But they were so persuasive and motivated – how could I turn them down? I admired the strength of their convictions and their belief in the justice of their cause. I realised how blinkered I'd been all my life. Michèle was dead set against it. I'd be risking my career, she said, I'd be setting my stall against the very people, the conservatives and the elite, who saw me as one of their own. And what, she asked, would the record label make of it? They paid me to make music, not bring down governments. I told her not to be so dramatic; the students had legitimate concerns, they had principles; who was I to turn my back on them? I knew the real reason – I'd been given the chance to atone for the guilt I felt at my lack of gumption during the war.

I did wonder why they had approached me. There were many far more suitable men in the public eye who would have made a better spokesman for their cause than me. It didn't take long to find out. The orchestra had recently recruited a new cellist, a talented young woman named Isabelle. She had long, dark hair, often decorated with a little bow, wide puppy-dog eyes, thin, painfully so, and fine cheekbones. She was also earnest, impressionistic and idealistic – she was one of them. She'd approached me one day, holding hands as she spoke to me with a sandal-wearing, long-haired, bearded youth I presumed to be her boyfriend. She introduced him as Jacques. I said I'd already been asked and was considering it.

The following day, after rehearsals, I called her over and told her yes, I would do it.

'Thank you,' she said, almost skipping with enthusiasm. For a moment I thought she was about to hug me. 'I hope you're not cross with me for asking.'

'No, no, not at all.'

'We all thought you'd be such a good choice. People will listen to you.'

'Am I not too conservative for you?'

'No, you're old enough to remember the war and to have witnessed its injustices but you're young enough, just about, to still be relevant.'

I thanked her for this backhanded compliment.

'So, how are you enjoying your work?' I asked.

'I love it. I've always wanted to work for you, Maestro. It's a dream come true for me,' she said, grinning.

'Good. You play well. More importantly, you know how to listen. I've noticed this.' I asked how old she was, where she'd come from, where she'd studied. Questions I'd asked when I interviewed her, but this time I listened. She reminded me of myself as a 22-year-old – confident, aware of her own abilities, and what she wanted from life. She was certainly attractive, if rather thin for my liking, but I had no intention of being unfaithful to my wife just as things were changing for the better. Anyway, she had a boyfriend, the bearded, Jesus-like chap I'd met the day before – a student, she told me, at the Sorbonne.

It was a fine spring day, when, surrounded by thousands of students and workers, I stood on a platform to the side of a park and was handed a loudhailer. Nearby, two upturned cars lay smouldering, thin veils of smoke adding to the surreal atmosphere of a city under siege. I was nervous – this was to be the most frightening performance of my life so far. In front of me, a sea of expectant faces, banners held aloft plastered with revolutionary slogans. I spotted Isabelle, her arms linked with her student boyfriend. She gave me a little wave. I tried to smile. Policemen with riot gear kept a careful eye on us. I mumbled through my speech, written for me by one of the student leaders, criticising the state for treating its citizens like children, demanding greater social justice, a greater share of the prosperity produced by the masses but enjoyed by the few. I understood little of what I read; I knew nothing about these things. Reporters took notes; photographers did their work. I realised that I may have been a great conductor but I was no talker. Yet, my speech was greatly applauded and cheered, and as I descended the platform, I was greeted with appreciative slaps on the back, and hearty thanks from those who had organised the demonstration.

'Well done, Maestro, that was great.' It was Isabelle. I wondered whether she was being entirely honest. Her boyfriend, Jacques, invited me to a meeting. I thanked him but said no – I had done enough revolutionising for one day. I knew my performance had been below par but, nonetheless, relieved it was over, I returned home in a state of high excitement. Even Michèle's rebukes didn't blunt my enthusiasm. The deeper understanding we'd gained of one another, forged in Morocco, had already evaporated, and we'd quickly returned to our normal selves – acknowledging each other's presence but maintaining a perpetual distance. I only realised, many years later, that my insistence on helping the demonstrators had so annoyed my wife that it had destroyed whatever small stirrings of affection we'd found in Marrakech.

The following day, unusually for me, I bought a newspaper and was surprised to see a picture of myself at the bottom of the front page. *Has the Maestro lost his marbles?* screamed the headline. The article made for grim reading: *He may be able to lift a baton and lead an orchestra of talented musicians, but the Maestro's attempts to lead the masses on a merry dance of revolution fell on deaf ears yesterday. He mumbled through a speech ridden with clichés and empty rhetoric that would have embarrassed a ten-year-old. The Maestro may be a demon on the rostrum but as a rebel he is as effective as a decrepit church mouse. Stick to what you know, Maestro. The students can mess it up just as easily without you!* I just hoped the article didn't echo Isabelle's opinion.

I threw the paper away; I had no wish for Michèle to find it. Nevertheless, I followed the progress of the demonstrations with a keen interest, buying various newspapers everyday and exclaiming at the papers' pro-establishment stance and the scorn they heaped upon the demonstrators. Despite the drubbing I received, I felt the urge to join them at the barricades. But I resisted it. I didn't want to push my luck too far with my American bosses. A pity, for I felt that for the first time in my life, I had found a purpose that wasn't solely based around me. It was during this euphoric time, however, that I received the letter.

I had a secretary that dealt with my post, and my travel arrangements and appointments. She had a stack of postcards featuring a sombre black-and-white photograph of me, an official shot taken in a studio, and signed by her with my name. She answered my fan mail and batted off all but the most important correspondence. This letter she deemed worthy enough of my personal attention. Postmarked locally, it read:

My dear Maestro,

A huge misfortune has fallen on me. I know you are terribly busy and I wouldn't normally bother you unless it was extremely important. I have been arrested and accused of all sorts of fanciful things.

I desperately need your help.

I ask you to remember our short journey together on the train to Saint-Romain all those years ago. Please, Maestro, if you could contact my lawyer, M. d'Espérey, on the telephone number above, he's expecting to hear from you.

I beseech you to help me in my hour of need.

Yours sincerely,

Hilda Lapointe (Mademoiselle).

I re-read it several times. I knew I had no choice – I had to respond. If nothing else, I was intrigued; I had to know. '*Accused of all sorts of fanciful things.*' I rang Monsieur d'Espérey, her lawyer, but he told me little except that his client had been arrested and was due to stand trial. He asked me to come see him at his offices in the sixteenth *arrondissement* but to keep it to myself and not to tell anyone. No fear of that, I thought; I certainly had no intention of telling Michèle.

At eleven o'clock the following day, I found myself in the offices of *Messieurs d'Espérey et Cotillard*, a plush office on the fourth floor of an ornate nineteenth century block, with red leather armchairs and a mahogany desk and a brass lamp. Sitting behind the desk in a pinstriped suit was Monsieur d'Espérey, a man in his sixties with a thin, grey moustache and rimless glasses sliding off the end of his nose.

'I believe you know my client, Mademoiselle Lapointe?' he said, in a baritone voice.

'I wouldn't say I *know* her – I've only met her twice. And that was over a course of twenty years or so.'

He considered this for a few moments. 'Nonetheless, I understand she, how shall we say, she helped you out once. During the war. Got you out of an awkward situation,' he said with upturned palms.

'Well, yes.'

'Can you describe this occasion?'

I did, relating briefly our encounter on the train during the years of occupation. He listened intently, his head tilted to the side.

After I'd finished, he scribbled a few words on a notepad on his desk. 'Good.'

'Is it?'

He looked up at me. 'Oh yes, it'll help. My client is due to appear in court on the second of June. We will enter a not guilty plea, after which we will be assigned a date for trial. Probably sometime in September. My client and I have no illusions, she is likely to be found guilty but it is the sentence that concerns us. I would like you, if you would agree, to stand as a character witness. If she is sentenced, your testimony could help lessen the severity of the punishment.'

'I – I don't understand. I don't know what Mademoiselle Lapointe has been arrested for.'

He threw his hands in the air. 'I apologise. I assumed… no matter. Mademoiselle Lapointe, my client, is standing trial for war crimes…'

I swallowed. 'War crimes?'

'Yes, during her time at the Drancy camp, particularly in her treatment of its Jewish inmates.'

I stared at him, goggled-eyed. 'Drancy? Wasn't that…?'

'A concentration camp right here in our city – yes. You had no idea she was a camp guard?'

I shook my head, speechless.

'OK, let me brief you. You understand this is all highly confidential. If you were to–'

'I understand.'

'Very well then.' He sighed before launching into the tale. 'Mademoiselle Lapointe worked as a guard at the Drancy internment camp from June 1942 until its liberation in August 1944. I don't know how much you know, but the Vichy wartime government carted off Jews, both foreign born and French, to Drancy where they were interned in appalling conditions before being deported to the death camps in the east, mainly Auschwitz. Some seventy thousand were sent. Very few returned.'

'I remember now,' I said quietly.

'I think we are all aware of it; it's just that not many of us want to think about it. We deliberately want to forget; it is too much of a stain on our memory. Like any job, Mademoiselle Lapointe, or Irène d'Urville as she was then, started at a lowly position at the camp but with time, she was promoted. However, after the war, she managed to disappear. She changed her name, lived in the south for a while. She was small fry – it wasn't difficult. However, she was discovered, just recently, quite by chance.'

'But… I thought you said she was not guilty.'

'She's not denying that she worked there but she denies the charges levelled against her – that she meted out unfair and brutal punishment on inmates.'

'I see. Monsieur d'Espérey, I won't be able to attend on June second; I have–'

'That doesn't matter. As long as you are available to give your testimony. That's when it matters.'

'OK, I'll be there. Can I visit Hilda?'

'Of course. She's been remanded on bail. I don't want to give out her home address, so leave it with me. I'll arrange something.'

*

Monsieur d'Espérey was a man true to his word. A week later I found myself sitting opposite Hilda in a small, rundown café within sight of the Sacré-Cœur. Despite its advantageous location, the place was nearly deserted as we sipped our coffees. With untreated brick walls, uncomfortable chairs, wilting plants and sullen staff, the lawyer couldn't have found us a more dingy place had he tried. 'Come here often?' I joked.

Hilda didn't laugh. She looked like a woman under strain. Gone was the blustery woman who had come to my dressing room two years before; here was a thinner, older-looking woman in a drab, blue-grey cardigan, her hair scraped back, her eyes dulled.

'I went to see your lawyer. He told me the story, well,

the outline of it. What happened, Mademoiselle?'

She gazed beyond me to the world outside.

'So, that's how you got me through that day – you were one of them.'

She nodded, still unable to look at me.

'You were one of them,' I repeated for effect.

This time, she reacted, looking straight at me. 'Yes, I was one of them, as you say,' she snapped, leaning forward. 'But I saved you, didn't I? That's the point. I'm painted as this terrible person, as evil personified. And yes, I did some things I'm not proud of. But life isn't always black and white, is it? This is why you must help me now, Maestro. You have to help me.'

'I don't know if it'll make any difference but yes, I told your lawyer, I will speak on your behalf. But you must tell me… something that has puzzled me these last 26 years – why did you help me? I was nothing to you, so why?'

The owner of the café appeared before us, asking whether we wanted a refill of coffee. We both gladly accepted. We waited while he poured fresh, steaming coffee into our mugs and brought us a little jug of hot milk. We thanked him and as he returned to his counter, the café door opened and a young couple holding hands came in, hovered at the door, and backed out. I saw the searing look of disappointment on the owner's face.

'Very well then,' she said eventually. 'I will tell you, then you can judge whether I am as bad as they make out. That day I met you on the train, I was on leave. About the only leave I got while I worked at that place.'

'Drancy?'

She nodded. With her eyes still focused elsewhere, she told me her story. 'I was on my way to visit an old friend of mine in Saint-Romain. You came into that carriage and started reading that sheet music of yours. You were humming the tune aloud – I don't even think you were aware of it. I was impressed. I thought it's so rare to see a youngster practicing such noble pursuits. I thought how proud your parents must be of you. And then, of course, the Germans came in wanting to see our papers. I saw straightaway that you had something to hide – it was written all over your face. Normally, I wouldn't have intervened. I was a collaborator; I freely admit that. It was wrong of me, I know, but at the time I felt I was doing the right thing. You, on the other hand, were clearly working for the resistance.'

'I was only delivering a message.'

'Nonetheless. You were still very young – you hadn't learnt the art of disguising your body language. I felt sorry for you. Perhaps, deep down, I knew that if they searched you and then arrested you, we would have risked losing one of our finest musicians. I knew, instinctively somehow, that you deserved a second chance. So, it was simple, I showed the guards my Drancy card that stated my job and told them you were with me.'

'As simple as that?'

Now, finally, she looked at me. 'As simple as that. I told them you were a trainee, and again, when they caught you in the street.'

'A *trainee*? In that place?'

'It saved you.'

'I was only a messenger.'

'Maybe, but I wasn't to know that. Still, they would have asked you for names, and I'm sure you know what that would have meant.'

'Yes.' I thought of the boy who did my job before me. Deported to a work camp somewhere in Germany. He never came back. Worked to death at the age of twenty-one.

'Remembering how you were, I don't think you would have withstood it very well.'

'You're right. I doubt I would today.'

'Exactly.'

'What happened after the war? What did you do?'

'It wasn't difficult.' She drummed her fingers on the tabletop. 'There was so much confusion. Accusations and claims and counter-claims, collaborators who pretended to have been in the resistance. I put on some old clothes, made myself look like a peasant woman, and made my way to Saint-Romain, and stayed with my friend there. We became close. She vouched for me and together we invented a new history for myself.'

'And your papers?'

'I told them they'd all been destroyed in the war.'

'Perfectly feasible, I suppose.'

'Oh yes. Lots of people did it.'

'So how were you found out?'

She sighed at the regrettable memory. 'I was recognised. I've been living in Paris a number of years now. I knew there was always the risk and sure enough, one day, I was shopping in a big department store in the centre of town when someone, a horrible little man, a Jew, of course, came up to me and said "Hello, Madame d'Urville", that was my name then, not that I was married. Never have been. Like you on the train, I was unable to hide my reaction. I should have been on my guard. I tried to back away but I knew there was no escape. He yelled

42

the place down. The store manager came down and forcibly took me to his office and from there he called the police. The silly thing is, had I'd been arrested at the time, after the war, I would have been one of many. But now, by myself, I'm exposed. But you know, I am no more than a scapegoat for a country still too ashamed of its wartime guilt to look at itself in the mirror.'

'Is that how you see it?'

'Of course. Yes, we are now a country full of resisters but we all know it's not true. Especially at the beginning – had it been put to the vote, ninety per cent of us would have voted for the collaborationist government. At least I'm being honest. I worked for them; I regret it, of course, but I don't see why I should play the part of the sacrificial lamb.' I tried not to laugh – a scapegoat and a sacrificial lamb. I wondered how many other farmyard animals she could conjure up.

'And I saved you. Can I be that bad?'

'I don't know, Hilda, you tell me. What happened in that place?'

'In Drancy?' She looked away, scanning the café with its empty chairs and unoccupied tables. Behind the counter, the owner polished a glass, a cigarette stuck to his lip. 'We had to maintain discipline. It was war.'

'Discipline?'

'It was not a holiday camp.'

'But what do you mean – discipline?'

'So many questions. Am I on trial already?'

'No, Hilda, but you soon will be.'

43

Chapter 6
Paris, September 1968

It'd been a difficult summer. Rehearsals for the Berlioz symphony were arduous and took every ounce of my energy. I would return home at night exhausted and bad-tempered, hoping for some sympathy from my wife, but finding none. At her insistence, Michèle and I had begun sleeping in separate beds proving, for once and for all, that our holiday in Morocco had been a false dawn. One evening, she told me to my face – she was fond of me, she said, but she didn't love me, she never had, she never would. She apologised. I politely accepted her apology. It was, under the circumstances, the most cordial of exchanges, as if we'd agreed to disagree on what film to go see. It felt so final. I had failed her; failed to make her love me. I bowed, left the room, retired to bed and sobbed.

The riots had finished – the workers returned to work and the students went back to college. President de Gaulle won convincingly at the June elections but, in light of the May riots, promised reform. A letter from Monsieur d'Espérey confirmed that Hilda had indeed pleaded not guilty to the charges against her. A second letter, the following month, asked me to appear in court on the twenty-first of October.

One Friday evening, we finished early. Rehearsals had gone well and I was pleased with how hard everyone had worked and allowed them home early to start the weekend. For me, however, work was never finished. I wrapped up some business and grabbed a bite to eat from the theatre restaurant.

An hour or so later, I decided to disappear to a local bar; less chance, I thought, of being disturbed. Although it was still only four o'clock, *Le Bar Rocco*, as it was called, was already quite busy, small groups of people chatting, elsewhere a couple held hands over the table top. The place was big with a large central area encircled by a number of booths. Gentle jazz and soft amber lighting added to the relaxed atmosphere. The staff were all young and good looking. I wondered how many of them had taken to the streets four months earlier. I sat down in a booth tucked away in a quieter corner and, having spread out my papers, ordered a beer. The issue that was taxing me at this point was the availability of a studio engineer I particularly valued. He was much in demand and my American bosses had seen fit to assign him to work on another, to my mind, minor project. I composed a letter, decided it wasn't persuasive enough, screwed it up and started again. I was nearing the end of my third attempt when a familiar voice said hello to me. Looking up, I was surprised to see Isabelle standing at the end of my table. I was taken aback by how delighted I was to see her. 'I won't disturb you,' she said. 'I can see you're busy. I just thought I'd say hello.'

'It's very nice of you. Are you here with… I'm sorry, I forget your boyfriend's name.' The image of Jesus flashed across my mind.

'Jacques. No, he's at college revising. He's got a big exam coming up. I'm here with my girlfriends,' she said, motioning behind with her head. Near the bar was a group of four fashionably-dressed girls of Isabelle's age, leaning in towards each other, all talking at the same time in high-pitched voices.

'So I see.'

'They're a bit loud, aren't they? I'll ask them to keep it down a bit.'

'No, don't do that. They're perfectly entitled to be as loud as they want. If I wanted peace and quiet, I would have gone to a library.'

She laughed. 'I'd better get back.'

'Yes, of course. Have a lovely evening.'

I ordered a second beer and tried to focus on my letter but instead I kept glancing up at the girls. How I envied them – to be young, in the capital and living in such prosperous times. When I was their age, we were still an occupied country, our lives restricted by the lack of opportunity and blighted by boredom. They were all attractive in their own way, attractive by the mere dint of being young. I eyed Isabelle, seeing her outside the orchestral environment for the first time, being herself. She was a person who spoke with her hands, gesticulating wildly, emphasising her point. I knew then how attracted I was to her. I had been from the moment I first saw her at the interview but then I was still a man who yearned for the love of his wife. I realised then, in that bar, with

Isabelle and her friends nearby, that I felt lonely. I had a wife, so many friends, and was adored by the multitudes, and yet… I had no one. Being a conductor is, ultimately, a lonely job – you are the boss and the musicians treat you as such; polite, respectful but always at a distance. I knew too that I had somehow been weakened, unwittingly, by Hilda. She existed in my mind as two people – the woman I'd met twenty years ago and the person I knew today. I felt, somehow, sullied by my association with her younger self while, at the same time, deeply sorry for the woman she was now. Her downfall had left me feeling vulnerable. For the first time in my life, I felt sorry for myself.

An hour passed.

'Maestro, you look like you have the world on your shoulders.'

'My word.'

'I'm sorry, I didn't mean to make you jump.'

'It's fine. What happened to your friends?'

'They had to go. I was about to leave but I thought…'

'Well, join me.'

'I wouldn't want–'

'No, do. I'm bored of being on my own.'

She glanced behind her, as if ensuring her friends had left, then, with a little shrug of the shoulders, slid onto the bench beside me.

'I'll get you a glass of wine.'

'I shouldn't; I've had too many already.'

'Come now, one more won't hurt.'

And so we talked for two, maybe three hours. The bar became steadily busier and louder, and after a while we had to raise our voices to hear each other. A group of drinkers asked if they could share our table which, for me, seemed like a good time to call it a day. Isabelle escorted me as I returned to my office in the theatre from where I phoned through for a car.

Sliding open the glass partition, I ordered the driver to take me home via Isabelle's. We sat in the back, Isabelle grinning and stroking the leather seats. 'I'm not used to such luxury,' she purred.

'Let's call it a perk of the job.'

We talked some more as the car meandered its way through the streets of Paris and out into the suburbs. The car smelt of leather and Isabelle's perfume. I enjoyed her company and, for the first time in an age, found myself laughing.

'We're here already,' said Isabelle as the car slowed down. 'That was quick. It's just at the end of this road.'

I told the driver where to stop.

'Well, thank you, Maestro,' she said, buttoning up her coat. 'It's been a lovely evening.' I couldn't see her expression in the dark but her tone sounded sincere.

'Yes,' I said, 'we must do it again some time.'

'Maestro, would you like, I mean, if you have time; what I want to say is…'

'Are you inviting me in for a cup of coffee?'

'I wouldn't want to speak out of turn.'

I leant over and kissed her hard, taking her, and myself, by surprise.

'Oh,' she breathed. 'I'll take that as a yes.'

'I'm sorry,' I said, biting my fist. 'I don't know what… I'm really sorry–'

She took my hand from my mouth, stroking it. 'Shush now, it's fine, it's OK. Come and have a coffee.'

'Won't your boyfriend be in?'

'We don't live together.'

'I'll tell the driver to wait.'

A street lamp illuminated her eyes. Hesitantly, she said, 'Send him home.' She smiled.

The car came to a halt. I saw the driver's eyes in the rear view mirror. Leaving the engine on, he darted out and opened the door for her. I followed her out, telling myself that I mustn't give in, that I had to resist. But she doesn't love you, I told myself, never had, never will. I felt the anger rise within me, a tightening in my chest. So why the hell did she marry me, then? Why the pretence all these years? I gave the driver a few francs as a tip. 'Thank you,' I said. 'You can call it a day now.'

Involuntarily, he shot a look at Isabelle who had wandered off to wait from a discreet distance. He nodded. 'Thank you, Monsieur.'

'Come,' she said, as the car drove off, an intense look in her eyes. 'Let's go up.' She took my hand. After just a few steps, I stopped and glanced back to see the tail lights of the car recede into the distance. 'Are you OK?'

'Yes,' I said. 'I'm fine.'

She lived in a small apartment on the fourth floor of a fine Art Nouveau block with ironwork balconies. She unlocked the door and pulled me in. Slamming the door shut behind me, she pushed me against it and kissed me with an urgency I'd never experienced before, her cold hands pulling my shirt free of my trousers. Ripping off our coats, she led me to her bedroom, her lips never leaving mine. By the time we got to her bed we were already half undressed, a trail of discarded clothes and shoes, hers and mine, littering the floor. She threw me onto her bed and reached over and switched on her bedside lamp. Straddling me, grinning in anticipation, she removed her bra.

*

Afterwards, I lay on my back, catching my breath, and felt a deep sense of contentment. She lay on her front, nestling into my neck; her arm drooped across my chest. 'Well, Maestro, that was quite something.' I felt the warmth of her breath against my skin. 'I bet you sleep with all your female musicians.'

'No, not at all!'

'Ha! I don't believe you.'

'No, really. You're the first.'

'Anyway, I don't mind. You're very good for an older man.'

I laughed at another backhanded compliment. 'If you could just pass me my walking stick?'

She thumped me playfully on my chest. 'What about your wife? Won't she be missing you?'

'You know I'm married?'

'Of course. You wear a ring.'

I held up my hand, inspecting my wedding ring and sighed. 'No, she won't miss me at all.' If she did, I thought, I wouldn't now be in this situation.

She fell asleep lying next to me while I took in my surroundings – its high ceiling, stripped blue wallpaper, a large dresser adorned with make-up and jewellery boxes, a framed Picasso print and, in the corner, a cello case. It was, I felt, a room full of love and warmth, perfectly reflecting my pretty young cellist. Resting my hand on her back, feeling the defined outline of her ribcage, I looked down at her, this delicate little thing, the wisps of hair covering her face, her arched, finely-plucked eyebrows, her flawless skin, this vulnerable, beautiful girl, and felt quite overcome with emotion.

*

We awoke the following morning, a Saturday, and made love again with the autumnal sunshine streaming through her curtains, the constant hum of city traffic from below.

'What are your plans today?' I asked, as finally, having showered and dressed, we ate a breakfast of boiled eggs and toast and strong coffee in her living room. The radio played English pop music in the background.

'Jacques and I are going to the new Kandinsky exhibition at the Louvre.' I tried not to wince on hearing the name of her boyfriend.

'Is he one of those painters that produces mishmashes of shapes and colour?'

'It's lovely, so vibrant.'

'Yes.' I thought it best, at this point, not to reveal what I thought of this type of art, that is, if one can call it art.

'And you, Maestro; what are your plans?'

'Huh, I'll do what I do every Saturday – I shall lock myself away in my study and work.'

'All you do is work,' she said, dipping a piece of toast into her egg. 'You must give yourself a day off sometime.'

'I know, you're right.' Yet, I thought, working was the only way to keep out of Michèle's way.

A large fireplace dominated the room, candleholders on the mantelpiece, a gold-framed octagonal mirror above it; in the centre of the room a low oval table piled high with fashion magazines and, to the side, a copy of *Le Monde*.

'What's this song?' I asked on hearing something on the radio I hadn't heard before.

'Oh, it's good this, isn't it? It's *All or Nothing* by a band called The Small Faces,' she said, pronouncing the names in an exaggerated English accent.

'Very good, Isabelle, you'd make a good English disc jockey.'

She laughed. 'Thank you kindly, Monsieur Conductor.' A sudden movement of her hands knocked over the saltcellar. 'Silly me,' she said.

'I didn't know there was a new Kandinsky exhibition.'

'Yes, it's got of a good review in *Le Monde*,' she said, pointing to the newspaper. 'Did you read the paper yesterday?'

'No, I never get the time,' I said, scraping out the last of the egg.

'So you wouldn't have read about this case coming up with that woman from the war?' she asked, wiping crumbs from her fingers.

I stirred in an extra spoonful of sugar into my coffee. 'What woman?'

'She's only just been found. She was a guard at Drancy, you know?'

I spluttered on my coffee.

'Are you alright?'

'Yes, yes,' I said, thumping my chest. 'Drancy, the concentration camp?'

'Yeah. A right bitch, by the sounds of it, working for the Nazis – doing their dirty work.' She picked up her coffee bowl. 'I hope she pays for it.'

'Careful, Isabelle, we have no right to pre-judge.'

Slowly, she placed the bowl on the table. 'I can,' she said in a flat voice. Her eyes changed, their brightness dissolving into something altogether darker.

'What do you mean?'

She held her breath and cast her eyes down at the tablecloth. 'My father was sent to Drancy. He was on one of the last transports out of there to Auschwitz.'

'Oh.' I wasn't sure how to proceed.

'I'm Jewish.'

'I see. I didn't know.'

She pulled a face. 'So what? Does it change anything?'

'No, of course not.'

We sat in silence for a while. I wanted to ask whether her father had survived. Instead, I watched her as she made a circle of salt with her fingertip. 'I'm twenty-three; born at the end of 1944. I never met my father.'

'I'm–'

'My parents were hiding out in a village up in the hills above Lyon. They were staying with good people, a whole community of farmers who wanted to protect the Jews. But it was getting more difficult. Twice, the Germans had come on searches, offering rewards to those prepared to denounce the Jews. My parents got away with it but they knew it'd be only a matter of time. And then Maman fell pregnant with me. This would have been in the last few months of the occupation, spring forty-four. They decided they had to do something before she became too, I don't know, incapacitated. They tried to get over the border into Switzerland. Lots of people had already gone that way. But someone denounced them, and they were arrested and sent to Drancy, where they were separated. They were kept in inhumane conditions, and beaten for no reason. The article says the camp was run by the Nazis. The French ran it at first until the Germans took over but they don't mention that. Too ashamed, I suppose. Maman never saw

Papa again. He was put on a train to Auschwitz, that much she knew. She was kept in Drancy. She always thought she'd lose me, they were all so undernourished. But she survived, and I too, as you can see, survived. I was born terribly premature. Explains, I guess, why I've always been so skinny.'

'You're perfect, Isabelle.'

She smiled and reached for my hand across the table.

'You're too kind, Maestro. So you see, no one who worked at Drancy can be innocent.' She rose from the table and fetched the newspaper. Flicking through the pages, she found the article. 'Here it is. Her name's Hilda Lapointe. Look at her, she looks like a right monster, don't you think?'

She passed the paper over the table. My mouth went dry on seeing her police mug shot. I was shocked by the intense coldness of her eyes, her thin lips, the solid outline of her jaw. Isabelle was right – she did look like a monster.

I read the opening paragraph:

She has escaped justice for over two decades, but next month, at Le Palais de Justice, *68-year-old Hilda Lapointe, a former guard at the wartime internment camp in the Parisian suburb of Drancy, will finally come face-to-face with her accusers. Nicknamed 'The Lady with the Truncheon' by her victims, she was infamous for wielding her club against the Jewish inmates at this Nazi-run camp.*

Unable to read any more, I folded the paper and placed it neatly on the table.

'Are you OK, Maestro? You look worried about something.'

'No, I'm fine. Just fine,' I said quietly.

*

I spent the afternoon locked in my study, brooding. The article in Le Monde had deeply shocked me. I had no idea Hilda's case would attract any attention at all, let alone the attention of a national newspaper. When Monsieur d'Espérey had asked me to speak on Hilda's behalf, I had no perception whatsoever that people and the media might be interested. I rang the lawyer straightaway.

'What did you expect, Maestro? Of course something like this would cause interest.'

'But it was the war, for God's sake, twenty-three years ago. Haven't people moved on?'

He laughed but not in a way that implied he'd found anything funny. 'Twenty-three years is not so very long, Maestro. You, Monsieur, conduct music hundreds of years old so surely you must appreciate that.'

'I just didn't think... I didn't realise... Oh, it doesn't matter. Anyway, my point is, I don't think I can help you any more.'

'Meaning...?'

'I mean...' He knew damn well what I meant – he merely wanted to make it difficult for me. 'Mademoiselle Lapointe, I can't.... Damn it, man, I've got my reputation to think of.'

Immediately, I regretted using the phrase and he picked up on it. 'Your reputation, Maestro?'

'The woman worked in France's most notorious concentration camp, you said yourself that she was guilty of... war crimes, didn't you say? I'm well known, you know that, I can't be seen condoning the actions of some sadistic camp guard.'

'Our case lies on the fact she was coerced to act the way she did, both by her masters and the environment, that she was an unwilling accomplice. Look, she is a woman who's always kept herself to herself. She has no friends, no family. She is alone in the world, alone and very much afraid. If you can stand up for her and say, look, she may have been bad but she wasn't all bad, it will help us prove that, at core, she was a good woman led astray by circumstances. We can't do it without you, Maestro.'

'What about her friend, the one she lived with in Saint-Romain after the war.'

'Yes, I know. Alas, she died.'

'Oh.'

'Yes, exactly. She has you and no one else. You know, she's hinted at… at doing away with herself. Those were her words.'

'Really?' Well, I thought, that would solve everything. 'Do you think she would?'

'No. She was a bully, and we all know bullies are, essentially, cowards.'

I didn't know what to say. Picking up on my silence, the lawyer continued. 'Naturally, it's your choice but this reputation you mention, and I do understand, was built on the fact you survived the war. And I'm sure you'd agree with me that your survival was in no small part secured by the woman who now depends on you. But, as I say, it's all your own choice, Maestro.'

*

My conversation with Hilda's lawyer had left me in a constant state of anxiety. People had been sent to their deaths from Drancy; people had died there. I thought of Isabelle's parents. Who knows, perhaps the paths of Hilda and Isabelle's parents had crossed. What was Hilda's role at Drancy; to what extent was she guilty of terrible things? Perhaps she was no more than a scapegoat, like she'd said.

We worked hard on rehearsing the Berlioz and a couple of supplementary pieces but, for the first time in my life, I had difficulty applying myself. I even had difficulty getting up in the morning. I missed my wife. We had always led separate lives but now, after her announcement, I felt as if I was sharing a house with a stranger. Morocco seemed like a long time ago. Meanwhile, every day at work, I had to see Isabelle, a member of my team, awaiting my instruction. I felt self-conscious in front of her – and went out of my way to not over praise or criticise her, convinced that others would see through our body language. Yet, I certainly did not regret having her as my mistress – not now. After that first day, I returned and slept the night a second time soon afterwards. I found Isabelle a delight to be with; I loved her company. She was witty and intelligent, and could hold her own in any discussion. And she was still a valued member of my orchestra.

The fact that we were both being unfaithful caused her, I think, no concern – until one Sunday afternoon. We were lounging on her settee, warm with the afterglow of sex, reading the papers, listening to the radio, the sort of things I had always envisioned doing with Michèle – just *being* together, silently enjoying each other's company, when her doorbell rang. She sprang up from the settee, swearing. 'It's Jacques,' she shrieked.

'How do you know?'

'He has a special ring. Christ, put your shoes on. Shit, what do we do?'

'You're not going to make me stand on the balcony, are you?'

'You've come over because of work,' she said, knowing I never went anywhere without a work file in my briefcase. 'Turn the radio off,' she said as, quickly, she tidied up the magazines and newspapers. She leapt over to the intercom, still buttoning up her blouse and straightening her hair, and pressed the button to allow her boyfriend up.

By the time he caught the lift up to the fourth floor, Isabelle and I were sitting at the table, with paper and sheet music scattered round, looking the part. She welcomed him in with a lingering hug and a sloppy kiss while I averted my eyes and tried to sit on my jealousy. We shook hands as she re-introduced us. He grimaced in an attempt at a smile and I knew he suspected that something was amiss. I had to make my excuses and leave as soon as I could.

It was only as I was putting on my coat I realised I'd left my tie in Isabelle's bedroom. I could not think of a single plausible reason why I should need to go into there, and unless Jacques went to use Isabelle's toilet, I wouldn't be able to speak to her alone. I had no choice – I would simply have to leave and hope to God that if they did decide to go to bed, that it would be Isabelle and not Jacques who found my tie of many colours. The thought of Isabelle taking Jacques to her still-warm bed left me feeling quite nauseous.

I caught the Métro home. Catching the Métro had become part of my daily routine now, allowing me to connect to real people. I had come to realise that I was too closeted from the world – from home to the theatre, and from the theatre back to home, in a luxury car with its own driver. The journey allowed me too much time to think, to dwell on problems that offered nothing by the way of solution. In the confines of the car, I felt suffocated by thoughts of Hilda, of knowing what had happened to Isabelle's parents. The Métro with its anonymity and all its passengers allowed me an escape which even music could no longer provide.

*

Seeing Isabelle at rehearsals was wonderfully tortuous – my heart would surge upon seeing her and as much as I wanted to sneakily take her to one side and kiss her, I knew I couldn't. I could tell the other men in the orchestra found her attractive as well but, I thought gleefully to myself, she's mine!

We were having a break, and I stepped out onto the patio for some fresh air. Autumn was well on its way, one could feel it in the air. Groups of my musicians congregated. It's always amused me how musicians stick to their own – the woodwind players in this corner, the percussion in that. Isabelle was out there with some of her string players, laughing, twiddling with a bow in her hair. She looked beautiful in a knee-length dress with a lace hem, her thin legs and her freckled arms dangling with bracelets. I was desperate for her to come talk to me. Instead, I watched her with her colleagues, laughing, young, so full of life. I ached with desire yet, at that moment, observing her, I knew it would never last.

People nodded at me but I remained, as always, alone. No one, unless they want something, wants to speak to the boss. Power places one on a lonely pedestal.

I turned my back to view the city below, gripping the balcony, and realised how much I missed my wife. Isabelle was beautiful but I knew, given the choice, I wanted

Michèle back. Looking up at the clouds, I realised I had tears rolling down my cheeks.

*

Hilda's trial was due to start on the Monday and was expected to last most of the week. I had been scheduled to appear on the Wednesday. The recorded concert was due to take place the following Saturday. I asked Michèle whether she'd like to attend the concert. No, she said, she had other plans. I tried not to show my disappointment – it'd been years since she'd come watch me perform. Her lack of interest had always hurt, but never as much as now. But, oddly enough, she suggested I go see a dentist ahead of the performance, saying that my teeth needed a professional clean. But I'll have my back to the audience, I said. No one will see my teeth, apart from the orchestra, and they've seen them many times before. She insisted; she knew of a dentist who could whiten them up for me.

We should have been rehearsing every day in the lead up to such a momentous performance but, in order to attend court, I had given the orchestra the whole of Wednesday off. I didn't tell them why, and I certainly didn't tell Isabelle. It felt like a dirty secret. I knew I had to tell her at some point – after all, she'd find out soon enough, what with the media waiting on the sidelines, sharpening their knives.

Monday came and went. I knew Tuesday's papers would carry a report from the first day of the case but I chose not to buy a copy. I felt worried enough as it was without having my confidence, or lack of it, undermined any further. The rehearsals were a painful affair, my concentration now shot at, not by Isabelle's presence, but by this black cloud that followed my every step.

On Tuesday evening, after work, Isabelle and I retired to *Le Bar Rocco*. It was still early, the music quiet and the place largely deserted. We sat in the same booth as before and ate a mediocre meal and drank passable wine. She seemed subdued, as subdued as I felt. We barely talked, although I did ask her whether she thought my teeth needed whitening. Eventually, as we were finishing our desserts, she said quietly, 'He found your tie, you know.'

My spoonful of crème caramel stopped half way to my mouth. 'Oh.'

'Yes.'

'What did you say?'

She almost laughed as she told me. 'I came up with the most ridiculous of excuses. I said you'd spilt coffee down it earlier in the day and I said I'd wash it for you, and just threw it in the bedroom until later.'

'That's terrible.'

'And what would you have said off the cuff that would have been any better?' She wasn't laughing now.

'You're right. I'm sorry.' After a long pause, during which I contemplated my dessert, I asked, 'Did he believe you?'

'He pretended to.'

We didn't speak for a few minutes as we struggled through the rest of our desserts. I asked whether I should call for the bill.

She didn't answer. Instead, she said, 'I'm going to court tomorrow, for that case we read about in the papers. The guard at Drancy.'

I felt my face redden. I had to dissuade her. 'But why, Isabelle?' I reached for her hand. 'It'll make it worse for you.'

'I have to know. I need to know what went on there. If I had time, I'd go every day.'

'Would your mother thank you for it?'

'She won't know.'

'It's not for me to say, Isabelle, but… I don't think it's a good idea.'

'You're right.' I enjoyed a moment of optimism until she looked straight at me. 'It's not for you to say.'

I got the bill.

*

I returned home. If I was worried about appearing in court before, now I was panicked. I found Michèle watching TV. I poured myself a beer and slumped on the settee next to her and pretended to take an interest in a documentary about President Kennedy. I wanted to tell her everything, she was still my wife after all, but the words wouldn't come. I wondered how we'd become so estranged. Hadn't I given her everything? I looked round our living room in all its glory – the leather three-piece suite, the Turkish rugs, the chandelier, our own cocktail cabinet, despite my preference for beer, the gold-framed mirror, the yucca plant. Upon the mantelpiece, various souvenirs from Morocco, including a decorative tagine and a brightly-coloured teapot with a long, curved spout. God, how ostentatious it looked, and how, all of a sudden, I hated it. I wondered whether she too had seen Hilda's story in the papers. After all, she had also suffered at the hands of the Nazis. Our lack of children was the result, her inability to love me another. The documentary came to an end. She shuffled to the kitchen to make her cocoa and fill a hot water bottle, despite it still being warm, and we retired to our separate bedrooms.

Lying in bed, I picked up the telephone. I had to tell Isabelle the truth. Better now, I thought, than she found me in court, standing up for the woman who represented those responsible for her parent's maltreatment and her father's death. She answered on the second ring. 'Jacques?' she said.

Swallowing my disappointment, I said hello. 'I... I wanted to make sure you were OK.'

'Of course.' She yawned and I couldn't help but wonder whether she would have done so had it been Jacques at the end of the line. 'Why wouldn't I be?'

'It's just... well, you seemed a bit quiet tonight, a bit pensive.'

'I'm worried, that's all, about tomorrow. It's a big thing for me, this court case. I'm nervous about how it might affect me, you know?'

'Yes.' It had to be now. 'Listen, Isabelle, about tomorrow–'

'I know, I'm just being silly. Ignore me; it'll be fine. Look, it's good of you to call, but I'm really tired. I have to go now. I'll see you on Thursday, Maestro.'

'But, Isabelle, wait...'

She'd hung up. I held the receiver for a while, its buzzing noise permeating my brain until, in a fit of frustration, I slammed it back into its cradle.

Chapter 7
Paris, October 1968

Monsieur d'Espérey wasn't expecting me until the afternoon session. I got myself ready and, in my haste, cut myself shaving. Never had I felt in such a state of anxiety. Even the biggest and grandest of concerts hadn't reduced me to such a wreck. I deliberated over what to wear and finally opted for all black – as if going to a funeral. For a dash of colour, I added a fake carnation to my lapel then, deciding it inappropriate, removed it. Even Michèle, who never took an interest in my comings and goings, commented on my suit. A meeting with the record label bosses, I told her. She too was off out for the day and we made an elaborate dance of ensuring we didn't leave together.

Le Palais de Justice, a grand grey-stoned building in central Paris, is a spectacular if intimidating place. I'd heard that Marie Antoinette had been imprisoned here before being executed. I made my way to the chambers, as instructed, and there, sitting on a bench in the corridor, waited for Monsieur d'Espérey and Hilda. Finally, they appeared, following a break, and, for only the fourth time in my life, I met Hilda. She looked drawn and pale, her lips the same colour as her skin, but determined, having the air of someone ready to do battle. I spoke to them politely but couldn't bring myself to act friendly. I wanted them to know I was doing this under sufferance. She looked smart for the occasion – a matching deep-brown jacket and skirt, a collared shirt with a black necktie. She shook my hand firmly. 'I can't thank you enough,' she said.

'What's the matter with your face,' asked Monsieur d'Espérey.

'What? Oh, I cut myself shaving. So, how's it been going?'

He glanced at Hilda. 'Not too well, if I'm honest.' He removed his wig and, inspecting the inside, said, 'The prosecution have chosen their witnesses well – they're all articulate, have good memories, and they each hold a deep-rooted hatred for Hilda here.'

I had to stop myself from saying, "what did you expect?" Instead, I asked, 'Am I next then?'

'No, they're running behind time. They have one more to go. I fear they've saved their best for last.' Giving his wig a shake, he continued, 'All the more reason why you must play your part, Maestro. You and the others.'

'Others? I thought–'

'We managed to dredge up a couple of Hilda's former pupils.'

'Pupils?'

'I used to be a teacher,' said Hilda, with a wry smile. 'Music.'

'You were a music teacher?'

She pulled a face. 'Before the war. At a Catholic girls' school. Did I not mention it?'

'No. No, you never mentioned it. I think I would've remembered.'

'Well, we all have a few surprises, don't we?'

*

'Madame Kahn, how old were you at the time of your arrest?'

'I was fifteen.'

'Why were you arrested?'

She shrugged as if it was a silly question. 'Because I'm Jewish.'

'And when was this?'

'Fourth December 1943.' A thin woman with sunken cheeks, Madame Kahn pulled on the beads around her neck.

'Were any other members of your family arrested at the same time?'

'Yes, my parents, my grandmother and my younger sister.'

'What happened to them?'

'Suzanne, my sister, and I were separated from our parents and–'

'Forcibly?'

'Yes. It was… horrible. We tried to cling onto them. Suzanne became hysterical, well, we all did. There were hundreds of families like us, all being pulled apart. They kicked us and beat us with their sticks, and used water hoses against us. The noise, the screaming, will live with me forever. That's when I first remember seeing her.'

'Her? The accused?'

She pointed at Hilda, who sat impassively, without expression. 'Yes, her.'

'Irène d'Urville or, as she is known today, Hilda Lapointe.'

I glanced around at my surroundings. The courtroom lacked the style of its exterior. A plain wall-to-wall brown carpet and wood-panelled walls made it all seem rather bleak. The public sat either on a raised platform behind or in a gallery above. Every space was taken. Without wanting to make it too obvious, I searched for Isabelle but couldn't see her. Perhaps she hadn't come after all. On the walls, various framed portraits of serious-looking men in wigs, while behind the judge, a larger portrait of President de Gaulle with his long nose, his knowing eyes and slightly-contemptuous stare. To one side sat the twelve men and women of the jury. The judge, a gaunt man with thick glasses on the end of a thin nose, listened intently as the prosecutor asked Madame Kahn his next question.

'Now, could you tell the court what Madame d'Urville was doing at the point you first arrived at Drancy?'

'Shouting and ordering her staff around.'

'Did you see her use force?'

'No, but others were on her orders.'

He paused a moment to look at his notes. 'Did you see your family again?'

'Suzanne and I were kept together. I never saw my mother or father again, or grandma.'

'What happened to them?'

'At the time I didn't know but after the war I learnt they'd been deported to Auschwitz.'

'And…?'

She bowed her head and muttered, 'They were gassed.'

'All three of them?'

'Yes.'

'Did your sister survive?'

'Yes but she…'

He lowered his eyes at her. 'Go on.'

'She took her own life – five years ago.'

'I see.'

She looked to the floor and quietly produced a handkerchief which she held tightly in her hand. He allowed her a few moments to compose herself. 'Madame Kahn, how long were you incarcerated at Drancy?'

'Eight months.'

'Could you please describe for the court the conditions there?'

'Yes. It was terribly overcrowded. I found out after the war that the place was designed for 700 people yet there were 7,000 of us crammed into there at any one time. We slept fifty to a dorm. The lucky ones had bunk beds or even just planks to sleep on. Others slept on straw on the floor. We were fed abysmally – watery soup that tasted like soap, no protein. People died of malnourishment. There was hardly any fresh water and only two toilets.'

'Two toilets for 7,000 inmates?'

'Yes, you can imagine what it was like. People fell ill all the time and many of them died. There was little electricity so during winter we were always very cold, shivering constantly.'

'Was the security tight?'

'Of course. There was barbed wire everywhere, searchlights, watchtowers, and men with machine guns. As Jews, we weren't allowed to look at any German or French guard in the eye. If we met a guard, say, on the staircase, we had to stop and push ourselves flat against the wall.'

'And during these eight months, did you have much contact with the accused?'

'We saw her almost everyday. Some of the guards were OK, some were nasty only occasionally, as if it was expected of them, but she was the worst. We were all very frightened of her.'

'In what way exactly?'

'Well, if… I mean, whenever you saw her, you were on tenterhooks in case she lashed out at you.'

'Perhaps you gave her reason to?'

'No, not at all. She…' The woman turned to face Hilda. 'She didn't need a reason.'

'Could you tell the court the reasons for your fear?'

'She carried a truncheon and she used it all the time, whether you deserved it or not. Everyone called her "the lady with the truncheon".'

The judge spoke, 'Did you say a truncheon?'

'Yes, it was a wooden one with a leather strap.'

'I see. Carry on.'

The prosecutor cleared his throat. 'Madame Kahn, could you describe what happened one morning in early February of 1944?'

'Yes. Every morning we had to line up for roll call. We had to stand there, in lines of five, absolutely still, usually for about two hours, whatever the weather. It might not sound much but when you're starving hungry and weak, possibly ill, and cold and frightened, then I can't describe how difficult it is.'

'Do continue.'

'On this particular morning in February, Madame d'Urville said that someone had stolen food from the kitchens. No one admitted to it. Probably because it didn't happen–'

'But you can't be sure of this fact?'

'No. We were starving, like I said, so it could've happened.'

'What did she do?'

'She… she made us undress. All of us.'

'Down to your underwear?'

'No.' She cast her eyes downwards. 'Naked.'

'It was cold?'

'Yes, it was snowing and there was ice on the ground. It was February after all. We had to remain totally still. If anyone moved, Madame d'Urville would hit us with her truncheon.'

'On what part of the body did she hit you?'

'Usually, across the breasts.'

He raised his eyebrows. 'Carry on.'

'She would walk up and down in her thick coat and boots, watching us like a wolf, while we stood there humiliated in our nakedness. Every half an hour or so, she would return to the staff quarters to warm up for a few minutes and some other woman would come to take her place.'

'Do you remember this other woman's name?'

'No.'

'Did this other woman hit you?'

'No, in fact she even allowed us to wrap our arms round ourselves. We were all shivering like crazy. But with Madame d'Urville we had to stand with our arms at our sides. Many of the girls started crying. The girl next to me lost control of her bladder. I remember trying to step in her urine just to warm up the soles of my feet. Another one became hysterical.'

'What happened to this woman?'

Madame Kahn glanced from the lawyer to Hilda and back again. 'She slapped her across the face then hit her several times until she fell. I mean, she hit her really hard with her club. Then she carried on hitting her across the… the backside and over her head, everywhere, and kicking her. The woman curled up in a ball on the ice, all naked. I remember the sound of her boots cracking her ribcage. She, Madame d'Urville, lost control; she looked like something possessed. She hit that poor woman until blood poured from her mouth and ears. Then, suddenly, it stopped, and Madame d'Urville looked, I don't know, exhilarated.' She closed her eyes. 'Madame d'Urville ordered two of us to take her to the infirmary.'

'You were one of them.'

'Yes, me and the girl who had peed herself, about my age. I took the woman by the legs and the other girl by the arms. She was covered in blood and some of her bones…'

'Yes?'

'Some of her bones were sticking out at odd angles.'

'I see.'

'Although she was rake thin, so were we, and we hardly had the strength to lift her and we were blue with cold. I remember…'

'Yes?'

She sighed. 'Once we were out of Madame d'Urville's vision, we put her on the ground so we could catch our breaths. We felt awful, just leaving her heaped on the ground like that, like a sack of potatoes, naked and all bloodied. We embraced each other, really tightly, to try and warm up a bit. We were both crying and our teeth were chattering. We took her to the infirmary and even they felt sorry for us, and gave us a blanket each.'

Speaking slowly, the lawyer asked, 'Did you know the woman you carried?'

'I had spoken to her but I didn't know her name. She wasn't young; perhaps about forty. But it's difficult to tell a person's age when they're almost dead from starvation.'

'Do you know what happened to this woman?'

'I heard she died a few days later.'

'As a result of the beating?'

She cast her eyes at the judge. 'I wouldn't know that for sure, but it couldn't have helped.'

The lawyer nodded knowingly. 'Thank you, Madame Kahn. No more questions.'

The judge looked at Monsieur d'Espérey who shook his head. He had nothing to ask.

The judge called for a brief adjournment.

*

I spent a few minutes in the lavatory, staring at myself in the mirror. Madame Kahn's story was upsetting, naturally, and now I was expected to stand in front of a packed courtroom, full of reporters, and tell the world that Irène d'Urville wasn't such a bad sort. I had a headache, I felt nauseous, my mouth felt dry. What had brought me to this place? If I'd known, all those years ago, that I'd now be in this situation, I think I would have taken my chances with the Gestapo. I combed my hair and took a gulp of water. But still, I felt sick.

Leaving the lavatory, I bumped straight into Isabelle. We stood in the corridor, simply staring at each other. She too had dressed up for the occasion, wearing a slim-lined grey skirt and a matching jacket, her hair pulled back. Eventually, she asked what was I doing there. 'Just been to the toilet,' I said, hoping to inject a lighter note.

'You've come to support me,' she said, with the faintest of smiles. 'Jacques is here though. You look very smart for the occasion.'

'I'm a character witness for the accused.' There, at last, I'd said it.

She tilted her head, as if better to understand. 'What did you say?'

'It's a long story but–'

'You're a character witness? For *her* – that bitch in there?'

A couple of court clerks passed by, laughing. I watched them as they made their way down the corridor. 'I'm sorry.'

'I… I don't understand. Do you *actually* know her?'

'Well, not really. It was during the war. I, erm…'

'No, wait; let me get this straight. You are about to go in there and say something nice about the woman who worked for the regime that killed my father? Is that right? Because if it is…'

'Isabelle.' I reached out for her but she stepped back.

'So it's true – that's what you're doing here.' She looked at me with utter contempt and I felt myself diminish under her hateful gaze.

I was almost tearful as I croaked, 'I have no choice–'

'No choice?' She spat out the words. 'My parents had no choice; Madame Kahn in there had no choice, but you do. You have a choice.'

D'Espérey appeared. With a quick nod, he said a curt hello to Isabelle. 'Maestro, we've been called back in.'

'I'm sorry, Isabelle.' I followed the lawyer back into the courtroom.

*

'You are well known, Monsieur; a conductor of some repute,' said d'Espérey, his thumbs hooked into his waistcoat.

'I like to think so.'

'Could you speak up?' said the judge.

'I'm sorry, Your Honour. I said I'd like to think so.'

He asked me to relate my background story – my age, where I was brought up, my interest in music, my training. I spoke at length, hoping to come across as a decent human being, hoping to delay the inevitable. Then it came to my activities during the war, I confessed I was little more than a messenger but I embellished the importance of what was within those missives, how the information I delivered on a 'regular basis' had provided the necessary means of communication in order to launch attacks against the German occupiers. Lucky, I thought, that my man in the village had been executed. I wondered what had happened to the train guard from Africa. I emphasised how I had to use my cunning to pass by the Germans without ever rousing their suspicion. 'On one occasion,' I told them, 'I had to rush to the train toilet in order to escape them. When they knocked on the door, I had no option but to rip up the paper and throw it out of the window. They searched me and found nothing.' It was a complete lie. Looking up, I saw Isabelle, sitting towards the back of the courtroom, Jacques next to her.

'Quite the resistance hero then?'

'Well, I wouldn't go quite that far.' I hoped Isabelle was

paying attention at this point.

'And it was in this capacity as a messenger for the resistance that you met the accused, Hilda Lapointe?'

'Yes, but only the once, and I didn't know her name.'

'Did you know where she worked?'

'No, not at all.' I glanced over at Hilda, who sat there, her eyes fixed on me.

'Could you tell the court about the occasion your paths crossed?'

And so I told the court the story of that day in August 1942, 26 years previously. I started with a preamble about how a messenger, like me, had been arrested and tortured – I needed to emphasise the risk I was running. It felt strange – I was used to telling stories with music but here, for the first time, I was using words and I felt as if I had no control.

'She could quite easily have turned you in. From what you say, she suspected you, but she said nothing to the German guards.'

'Yes, I've thought about it many times since.'

'But she didn't,' he said loudly, turning to the jurors. 'She did not hand him over to the Germans.' Stroking his chin, Monsieur d'Espérey considered his next question. 'Did she gain anything from intervening on your behalf?'

'Not that I know of.'

'Do you think it fair to say that without the accused's intervention that day, your life might have turned out very differently?'

'Objection!' shouted the prosecutor. 'The question is pure speculation.'

'Quite,' said the judge. 'Objection upheld. Monsieur d'Espérey, may I remind you that a court of law deals in facts, not "what-ifs".'

'Of course, Your Honour. I do apologise. Speculation it may be, but we know of many, many cases when young men, sometimes boys, were cruelly tortured by the Nazi occupiers and frequently executed, whether they provided information or not. We also know that earlier in the war, those arrested were usually imprisoned for a while and, except for the ringleaders, released. But by the summer of 1942, many more were being executed, often for the slightest transgressions. It is speculation, but my point is that my client knew that without her intervention, this young man, as he was then, would have been under very great danger of torture and possibly execution.'

When asked, I told the court how, after the war, Hilda had come to see me just the once, in 1966, and that was it. In other words, we were not acquaintances in any sense of the word. 'Yet, in that conversation, I am right in thinking that you acknowledged your debt to the accused?'

'Yes.'

'Thank you. No more questions.'

*

Next came the prosecutor. He paced up and down in front of me, hands behind his back, as if collecting his thoughts. 'You were here this morning, were you not, so you would have heard the testimony of Madame Kahn. All week, we've been hearing similar stories – of habitual beatings, cruelty and maltreatment at the hands of Hilda Lapointe. What did you make of it?'

'I thought… I thought it was appalling.'

'Hmm, interesting. Yet, you are still prepared to stand in a court of law to act as a character witness for the woman who is accused of such barbaric acts?'

A titter of voices rose from the public galleries. 'Only because she may have saved my life. I wasn't to know–'

'But you do now! You've known for months, unless you live a life of a hermit, which we all know you do not. Yet, despite this knowledge, you still agreed. You could have said no at any point. You can still say no right this instance!'

'They were only accusations.' Someone booed.

'Silence!' said the judge.

'Only accusations? No, not accusations – facts. Her defence here is not that she didn't commit these crimes, but that she was under orders. So, leaving aside the second point for a moment, these acts are things that actually happened.'

'I… I suppose because I felt I owed her.' People hissed at me. I felt their loathing for me.

'You *owed* her? So because you were the beneficiary of this one single act of kindness, you feel you have the right to dismiss all these scores of victims.' Turning to the jury, he said, 'I repeat what I said at the beginning of this trial – the number of victims and witnesses number over eighty. Under court instruction, we have asked only a sample to come here this week to give evidence.' He returned his attention to me. 'So, despite what we all know to be fact, do you still feel that you *owe* the accused?'

I stood there, opened mouthed, shaking. I could feel Isabelle's eyes bearing down on me; I thought of her parents, of her murdered father. I saw Madame Kahn, gently shaking her head, living every day of her life with the memory that her family had been gassed, of picking that poor woman up from the icy ground. I felt the whole world looking at me, despising me for what I'd become.

'Well, Monsieur, we await your answer.'

I looked at Hilda and I hated her. Why had she done it, why had she intervened? I remembered our conversation: *One day I will be a conductor / Oh, you will, will you? You sound very sure of yourself. I wish you the very best of luck.* My life had come full circle, yet here I was consumed with a visceral hatred I'd never experienced before. How could she have done those things? To those poor, abused people.

'A simple yes or no – do you still feel that you owe the accused?'

I felt myself tremble as quietly, so quietly, I answered, 'Yes.'

*

I don't remember leaving the witness stand or how people looked at me. But often, since, I've had dreams in which a thousand angry faces leer at me, pointing, hissing, frothing at the mouth, blood seeping from their ears. I see scratch marks against the brown wooden panels of the courtroom. I see the judge donning a black wig. I see Isabelle's father leading me away to somewhere unknown and dark. I see Monsieur d'Espérey writing the word 'reputation' with a quill pen. I see Jesus Christ and I call for him and I reach out for him. He sees me and he turns his back on me.

It took me years to work out the meaning of those scratch marks until, one day, I came across a photograph of the inside of a gas chamber – its walls were covered in those very same scratch marks.

I know I rushed out of the courtroom and staggered down the deserted corridor, lurching from one side to the other, falling against the walls. I went to the lavatory and, locking the cubicle door, lent over the toilet and was sick. What had I done, I asked myself again and again, what had I done?

I didn't stay to hear Monsieur d'Espérey call in Hilda's former pupils from her girls' school, and I certainly didn't hang around to watch Hilda's turn in the witness box. I had seen enough; I'd repaid my debt and now I wanted nothing else to do with it. The woman could go to Hell and rot, for all I cared.

I returned home, got drunk, and went to bed.

*

The following day I felt a little better, despite the hangover. But I was dreading having to face Isabelle. Surely, she would see that I had been put into an impossible situation; that, despite what the prosecutor had said, I had had no choice. I was last to arrive, and the whole orchestra were already at their places, tuning their instruments. The combined effect of eighty musical instruments being tuned at the same time made my head throb. Clasping my temples, I yelled at them to stop. A sea of bewildered eyes turned to face me. I searched for Isabelle and couldn't see her. I went to get myself a cup of tea, and the cacophony started afresh. I made sure I was away long enough to ensure that by the time I returned, they had finished.

'I can't see Isabelle,' I said to no one in particular.

A fellow cellist stood, a middle-aged woman whose work I always valued. 'Maestro, I'm afraid to say Isabelle's phoned in to say she's resigned from the orchestra.'

'What?' I yelled. 'But surely, she'll do the concert.'

The woman shook her head. 'With immediate effect,'

she said.

'She can't do that – her contract… Did you speak to her?'

'No, it was the office. Someone just came in to pass the message on.'

I almost pulled a fistful of hair from my scalp. We were two days from the concert and she was leaving me in the lurch? And what about us, me and her? Did this mean we were finished? God, I hoped not; I liked her too much to lose her.

I turned to my first violinist and asked her to take over from me while I went off to make some phone calls.

Settling myself in my office, I tried ringing her. She didn't answer; I hadn't expected her to. I rang the record company and, being put through to my agent, told him what had happened. His reaction was much the same as mine. 'Her contract explicitly states that she can't do this. We could take her to court over this.'

'Maybe, but the question is who can we bring in at this stage?' I said frantically. I suggested the name of France's leading cellist.

'Him? You're mad – he'll cost a fortune, more than all the others put together.'

'He's the only reliable alternative we have at this stage. I've worked with him before; he's the only cellist I can think of who could pull it off. What choice do we have?'

I heard him sigh. 'You're right; we have no bloody choice. OK, I'll get on it.'

'Thank you.'

'Listen, Maestro, before you go, have you seen today's papers?'

My heart sank; I knew what was coming next. I heard

him rustle the newspaper. 'The headline reads, "Conductor Condones the Collaborator".' He laughed. 'I love the alliteration. I congratulate you, Maestro.'

'You do?'

'If you weren't famous enough already, then this ensures there won't be a Frenchman anywhere who doesn't know your name. This'll make marvellous publicity.'

I returned to the orchestra, and for the rest of the day, we struggled on – hardly the ideal preparation for such a big occasion.

On the way home, I couldn't help myself and bought a copy of *Le Figaro*. My agent was right – the report on Hilda's third day in court was damning of both her and myself. Her former pupils were not even mentioned. I may have helped the resistance out, the article said, but in sticking up for the guard, I was no better than a collaborator. Hilda Lapointe will be damned for all eternity, it said, and I will be condemned alongside her.

I found the house empty; Michèle still being out. I tried phoning Isabelle again but still no answer. I made myself a basic meal and settled down for an evening of pointless television. Surely, I thought, Isabelle would come round at some point; she couldn't remain angry with me forever. I liked her so much; I couldn't bear the thought of not seeing her and taking her into my arms. Isabelle was everything I wanted in a woman – beautiful, funny, intelligent, and a talented musician. God, I missed her.

I went to bed and dreamt of making love to Isabelle.

*

It's one of the great joys in a conductor's life – the start of the concert. The orchestra is ready; the audience is seated and awaiting your appearance; silence descends, edged with anticipation; the lights are dimmed. It is now, as a conductor, one makes one's appearance beneath the spotlight. It's Saturday night and everything is ready. Our replacement cellist, costing a small fortune, has stepped into Isabelle's shoes, all the top brass from my American record label are present, together with an assortment of music reviewers and even a couple of politicians. Every ticket has sold out; I heard rumours of tickets being sold on the black market for four or five times their face value. It is the biggest musical occasion of the year. I am a professional and all thoughts of Hilda, Drancy, and Isabelle have been banished from my mind. I confess, I have butterflies but I know that on picking up the baton that I shall live for the music and the music alone. I hover in the stage wings. The stage manager uses a walkie-talkie to communicate with the lighting guy. All is set. He gives me the thumbs up. It is time.

I step out onto the stage and wait for the applause to hit me. There is an inexplicable delay. Then, instead of applause, I'm greeted with a slow handclap. I feel the panic rising within me. I can't tell what's happening out there – the glare of the spotlight blinds me. Someone even has the audacity to boo me. How dare they? Don't they know who I am? I pick up the baton from the music stand and I realise I am shaking. I try to breathe away my nerves, to call on my inner resources. But I am stumbling; I feel my confidence seep away like water down a drain. I face my orchestra; I can see their concerned faces. I daren't turn around. I just need to start and allow the music to do the talking for me.

Two gruelling hours later, and we finish. I am sweating from every pore; I have never put so much effort into conducting and I am trembling with exhaustion. The audience doesn't clap. Finally, I turn around, panting heavily with the exertion, and peer out into the auditorium. It takes a few moments for it to sink in but, like a punch into my stomach, I see half the seats are empty. I don't understand. A rage descends over me. Throwing my baton down, I storm off the stage and into the side wings where I see the stage manager and my agent. 'What was that about?' I yell at them. 'I thought we'd sold out.'

'We didn't want to tell you, but the box office told us they'd been inundated with people demanding their money back.'

'What on earth for? Why?'

'We don't know exactly... some sort of boycott, we think.'

'A what?' I know I am screaming but I can't help it.

'We think it's to do with your appearance in court.'

I put my face in my hands and scream. I storm to my dressing room and, slamming the door shut behind me, pace up and down unable to believe that it had come to this. I pour myself a whisky and gulp it down in one. I stand there with the empty glass in my hand, shaking from head to foot while my throat burns. I catch my reflection in the mirror – a man in a tuxedo, bow tie undone, his face red with anger and sweat, a man contaminated, and for the first time in my life I hate what I see. I fling the glass at the mirror, shattering it.

Half an hour later, having ordered another glass and drunk too much whisky, there was a knock on the door. 'Leave me alone,' I shouted.

'Maestro, sir,' came the nervous voice from the other side. 'There's someone to see you.'

'Tell them to—'

'They say they've got something of yours and that it is important.'

I hesitated but of course who can resist something like that. I staggered to my feet, feeling distinctly woozy, and opened the door.

'Good evening, Maestro,' he said, walking straight past me to stand in the middle of my dressing room. He took in the mirror but said nothing.

'Jesus, what are you doing here?'

'I've come to give you this back,' he said, holding something curled up in his hand.

'What is it?'

He opened his palm and let something unfurl from his fingers. 'It's your tie.'

'Yes,' I said, transfixed by its many colours.

'Isabelle wanted you to have it back. She said you weren't to try and contact her again. Also, she asked me to give you another message.'

I looked at him expectantly. 'Yes? What is it?'

'It's this.'

Hell, the pain. It felt like a sledgehammer had slammed into my face. I fell back, falling against my chair and landing awkwardly amidst the shards of broken glass. My whole face felt as if it had ballooned, pulsating with pain. My vision blurred, blood poured from my nose and from a cut in my hand where I'd landed on the broken glass. Jacques transformed himself into two before throwing the tie at me, spinning on his heels, and leaving.

Chapter 8
Annecy, March 1969

I knew my career would be in tatters but I hadn't expected it to be torn apart quite so spectacularly. On the Monday morning following the disastrous Saturday concert, my record bosses telephoned me to tell me they were due to have discussions about my future. I could expect to hear from them the following week. That same day I went to see my doctor about my broken nose. Meanwhile, on Wednesday, after two days of deliberations, the jury returned their verdict on Hilda Lapointe. Unsurprisingly, they found her guilty of war crimes. The next week, my record label called me in for a meeting. Having asked what had happened to my nose, they told me that through my association with a war criminal, I had become a liability both to myself and, more importantly, to the label. They had no option but to release me. When I hinted at compensation, they told me I was lucky they had decided against suing me. Apparently, there was a standard clause in my contract about not bringing the label into ill-repute.

Two days later, Hilda was back in court to hear the sentence – she got five years. The papers led the public outcry, saying it was far too lenient. They reckoned she'd be out within three years. It was a national disgrace, they said, a slap in the face for those who had suffered during the war.

I received no word from Isabelle. Not that I had expected to. I missed her terribly and spent weeks pining for her.

Things got worse. If I thought my royalties would keep me afloat, again I was to be disappointed. My record sales dried up entirely. I had no work and no income.

The case, and the sentence, also upset Michèle, bringing back too many painful memories of the war. Her indifference towards me deepened, first to resentment then anger. How could I have spoken up for her, she kept asking, how could I have done it. I had no answer; I didn't truly know myself. I wanted to use words like 'honour' and 'debt', but they sounded too hollow, too inadequate.

Come Christmas 1968, Michèle announced she was leaving me. I'd been half expecting it. I thought I'd be devastated but, in the end, it came almost as a relief. She'd been seeing someone else, she said, a dentist, someone she was very much in love with and someone she wanted to marry. Of course, I thought, the wonderful dentist. I wondered how he'd managed to bring out her love when I, after so many years, had failed.

Oddly enough, we got on better in those last few weeks than we had for years, with the exception of our holiday in Morocco. It was probably the relief. We reached an amicable settlement, sold the house and split the proceeds. With my share, I bought a modest little house with a small garden in a tiny village outside the town of Annecy, near the Swiss border, about 40 kilometres south of Geneva. With its low ceilings and stone floors and old-fashioned wooden furniture, the house is what one might describe as rustic; a far cry from Paris. Here, in this village, stuck sometime in the previous century, no one recognised me. I was yesterday's news and already forgotten. Also, my longer hair and newly-shaped nose acted as a disguise. I bought a puppy, a short-legged Jack Russell, and called him Claude – after Claude Debussy. In March, I found a job in a warehouse in town, and tried my best to adapt to my new circumstances.

The town of Annecy lies on a lake and on Sundays, Claude and I would walk round its perimeter, admiring the views, soothed by its calm waters. In the evenings, with Claude nestled on my lap, I'd watch television, read the papers or the monthly classical music magazine, *Diapason*, and go to bed to dream of Isabelle.

But it was Hilda that occupied my thoughts.

Chapter 9
Rennes, October 1969

In April 1969, Charles de Gaulle resigned as president. Elections for his successor took place in June. I went to the polling station in Annecy to cast my vote. I handed over my identification to the old woman working there. Having found my name on her list, she looked up quizzically at me and asked, 'Aren't you–'

'No,' I snapped. 'We just share the same name.'

'You look like him.'

'No, I'm far more handsome.'

I voted for Georges Pompidou for no other reason than I liked his name. He duly won and became our new president.

Every day I thought less of Isabelle and more of Hilda. I constantly wondered how she was getting on. She'd been incarcerated at the *Centre Pénitentiaire de Rennes*, a women's prison in Brittany. I hoped she was suffering. I hated her for what she'd done to me, and resented the idea that she'd taken the credit for supposedly having saved me but none of the flak for having, in effect, destroyed me. I was determined she should know, that she should apologise for having caused all my misfortune. Some nights, unable to sleep, I relived Madame Kahn's testimony, visualising those poor women naked on the ice while she whipped them across the breasts. Sometimes, I fantasised about killing her. I would buy poison, I decided, strychnine perhaps, and administer it to her via a homemade cake. After all, they say Alexander the Great was killed by the stuff. But I am no murderer. Yet, the thought of seeing her began to obsess me. I wanted to see her in prison, miserable, repentant for all the things she had done.

Unable to bear it any more, I wrote a letter to the prison authorities in Rennes, expressing the desire to visit my "old friend", and, having posted it off, waited for the reply. It came two weeks later. Yes, it said, Hilda Lapointe would see me. I was given a specific date and time.

And so, at the crack of dawn on a bright but chilly autumn day in October 1969, I embarked on the seven-hour train journey to Rennes, changing at Montparnasse in Paris. It was the first time I'd been in the capital since my departure a few months before but I had no desire to see it, and remained in the station platform's waiting room until I was able to board the train to Rennes. The return train fare was not cheap. This, in itself, was a new sensation – I'd never had to worry about money before, I just had it. Now, things were different – I was having to budget and mind the centimes.

I settled down on the train, and, eating my cheese baguette, began to read the latest edition of *Diapason*. I may have been shunned but I was still interested in reading about the world of classical music. I knew, from the previous edition, that the Americans had found a replacement for me in whom they had high hopes. On the day of his first performance, I even sent him a telegram wishing him luck. I tried to mean it but, in truth, I rather hoped to see him fail. The magazine helped pass time on the train. But then, having reached page thirteen, my mouth hung open, my mind whirling – there, looking stunning, was a photograph of Isabelle. My heart thumped as I read the accompanying interview, barely able to take in the words. I'd absorbed enough to see that she been taken on by my old label as a soloist and was due to record her first record soon. *Gifted with a natural talent,* concluded the article, *Isabelle has a bright future in front of her. And she'll enjoy the support of her new husband and manager, Jacques. We wish them both well.* I threw the magazine to one side and felt myself overwhelmed with a sense of longing and regret.

Rennes, at a cursory glance, seemed an attractive town. But ignoring it, and with no time or desire to explore, I caught a taxi straight to the prison. There, I had my bag searched, my magazine flipped through, and went through all the other security checks. Satisfied, the guard then took me to a bare, grey-bricked, airless room and told me to wait. I took a plastic seat and sat with my hands on my lap, watching as various people and prison staff came and went. Only now did I begin to regret my haste. Yet, I knew, having come this far, I had to go through with it. I felt as if I couldn't get on with my new life until I had confronted her and finally put the whole sorry episode behind me. I had wanted an apology but I knew that was expecting too much. I wanted something from her, I just couldn't work out what it was. Perhaps if I had stayed in court that day, I would have heard what I needed to hear.

Half an hour later, I was called through. My heart skipped a beat on hearing my name. I followed the female guard across a courtyard, up a flight of steps, and through a maze of corridors, stopping behind her as she unlocked and relocked numerous doors and gates. The guard escorted me into a large room full of tables and chairs, some already occupied by fellow visitors, and told me to take a seat. Was this it? I wondered. I rather expected a partition between us and them, but no, we were to share a table as if enjoying a coffee in a café, albeit a bleak one.

A door opened at the far end of the hall, and in came two guards followed by a number of prisoners, each wearing handcuffs, and all dressed identically in grey prison overalls. There were waves and embraces. I searched for Hilda and found her, last in the queue. On seeing me, she nodded and strode towards me. She sat on the opposite side of the table from me, leaning back on the chair, fixing me with a steely stare.

'Hello, Hilda. How are you?' Stupid question, I thought.

'I'm fine, as you can see.' She had managed, somehow, to have gained weight, although it might have been illusion in the shapeless overalls. But her shoulders looked square, her jaw likewise. She had the pallor of someone lacking sunlight on her skin, her face was almost grey, her eyes deep-set.

'Why do you want to see me?' she asked, bypassing all small talk.

'I don't know,' I stuttered. 'I suppose I wanted to see how you were.'

'I'm fine – I told you and, as you can see, I am here, and I am well, all things considered.'

'Are you... are you treated well?'

She pulled a face which I interpreted as a reluctant yes. 'What happened to your nose?' she asked.

'I walked into a wall.'

I felt unnerved by her attitude, the unsmiling way she was looking at me, sitting there with the handcuffs round her wrists. 'Do you get any other visitors?'

'No, you're the first.' After a pause, she added, 'And no doubt you'll be the last.'

I'd come all this way for this?

'What you really want to know is have I repented for my sins?'

I laughed nervously. 'You make me sound like a priest.'

'They sent a priest to see me – I sent him away. What use have I for a priest? OK, as you're here, I'll tell you. I shall never say it again. Had you stayed in court and listened, you would know.' Exactly what I'd thought. 'What I said, and still say, is that I had no choice. I had to be severe, it was expected of me, and of course, I feel sorry for the women I hurt as individuals but we mustn't forget, Maestro, that they were Jews. Don't you remember what it was like before the war? Perhaps you were too young. We had that Jewish prime minister and the country was going to the dogs. Decadence, lack of morals, debauchery, corruption – that's what we had. Leftism, too much leftism. It took the Germans to bring us back into line. Of course, it's highly unfashionable to say that now, especially now that we know what we know.'

'The death camps?'

She nodded.

'But–'

'No, I may have helped the Jews onto the train but I

swore in court that I didn't know what was going to happen to them. "Re-settlement" – that's all I knew. I knew not to question orders.'

'Do you regret–?'

'It's not for you to ask me that.'

We glared at each other. Eventually, I said, 'You told me once that when you saw me on that train, you thought it rare to see a youngster pursuing such noble pursuits.'

'Yes, I saw that you weren't one of *them*, a leftist, that you had a cause, a decent one. You were reading your music and I saw in you the future of France.'

'Me? Decent?' I shouted. 'Huh, I'm sorry, but you got that wrong.'

'No, I did not. You conducted beautiful music, you helped introduce the masses to what's good in life – culture, appreciation, refinement.'

'Do you really think that? You talk about the lack of morals and debauchery – that was me,' I yelled, jabbing myself in the chest. 'I may have conducted some of the finest French composers but my God, I lived a life of indulgence.'

One of the guards came over. 'Is everything OK here?' she asked.

'Yes, thank you, we're fine.' I realised that others were looking our way. 'I'm sorry.'

She walked away slowly, keeping her eyes on us.

'You can't mean that,' whispered Hilda.

I leant towards her. 'You have no idea the amount of money I earned. Obscene amounts. And did I use my wealth to help others? Did I donate to charity; did I become a benefactor of people less fortunate than me? No, I never gave it a thought. I paid my taxes, and that was all, and even that reluctantly. I had no interest in anyone, no concern for the masses, as you call them. As long as I had my wealth, and constant admiration and gratitude, I was happy. I was unfaithful to my wife and went to bed with a beautiful younger woman. So you see, you were wrong. The young man you saved that day proved to be the very definition of what you hated. Those women you so cruelly beat had a greater sense of morality in their little fingers than I have in my whole being. You took it out on the wrong people, Hilda. It was all for nothing, everything you ever did was all for nothing.'

'No, I cannot believe this.'

'And now I've fallen from grace, cast aside, and I have nothing.'

'Oh please, now you're going to tell me that with nothing, you're happier than ever; that you lead a more fulfilling existence.' She laughed.

'No, I'm not – I'd have it back in an instant. Who wouldn't? But I would want to be younger, and be in a rock band, and take drugs, and go to orgies.'

'Do you really think I believe that? You're pathetic. Your circumstances may change but you can't change who you are.'

'You said it, Hilda, you said it.'

She leant back in her chair. 'Thank you for taking the time to visit me, Maestro.'

'Fine, I'm happy to go.'

'Good.'

I rose from my chair. The guard came over, perhaps to ensure I didn't start shouting again. I turned to leave. 'Oh, I almost forgot. I brought you a cake. Reception said it'd be OK.' I placed the box on the table, removing its lid. 'I hope you like it. It's, erm… homemade.'

*

By the time I'd returned to Annecy, it was dark and raining. From the station, I caught the bus back to my little village. All the way home from Rennes, I asked myself time and again, whether I'd been honest with Hilda – would I want it all again? Perhaps, I thought, perhaps. All I did know was that, having seen her, I would never see her again.

Exhausted after such a long day, I opened the door to my house and was greeted by an over-excited and hungry Claude. I let him out for a pee and then fed him. Having dried him off, I put on some Moroccan music and settled down for the evening with Claude on his back on my lap, and felt a surge of affection for my little home. As I tapped my foot and tickled Claude's stomach, I realised it had taken the whole day but Hilda had given me the answer I was looking for after all – I had no desire to go back to my old life.

The Woman on the Train

Part Three

The Woman on the Train

Chapter 10
Annecy, September 1982

'I think perhaps, after all, I will have that cup of tea.'

'And why not, Monsieur Bowen, why not.'

I left him sitting in my squashy settee, reading his notes. 'So, you weren't tempted to get another dog?'

'Yes,' I shouted from the kitchen as I poured water into the kettle. 'But it's too soon. Claude only died earlier this year. He was fourteen, poor old thing.'

I made the tea and found a packet of biscuits and arranged a few on a plate.

'Sugar?'

'No thanks.' I handed him his tea and the plate. 'Thank you. You never re-married then, Maestro?'

'No. I'm still waiting for Isabelle.'

'Are you?'

I laughed. 'No, sadly not. I never heard from her again but I know she's still doing well.'

'Still married to that Jesus fellow?'

'Jacques. No. I heard they'd divorced. Recently. That

came as a surprise.'

'You seem to know a lot about her,' he said, tackling a biscuit.

'I look out for her, and she's often mentioned in that music magazine.'

'Yes, she's considered the country's top cellist.'

'Indeed. Here's to Isabelle and her continued success,' I said, raising my cup of tea.

'And you, Maestro – you've never been tempted to return to music?'

'No, not now. I'm too old now anyway.'

'Nonsense, you're only what – sixty?'

'Sixty, going on eighty.'

'But, of course, what I really want to know, is what happened to Hilda Lapointe. We know you didn't actually poison her!'

'No! Tempting as it was.'

'And that she was released in 1971–'

'Yes, she'd served three years.'

'But after that, whoosh – she just vanished.' He took a sip of his tea. 'I asked the prison whether they knew where she was but they didn't know, or, more likely, they didn't want to tell me. Do you know, Maestro?'

'Me? No. I never did go see her again. She probably changed her name again. She'd be 82 now.'

'If she's still alive.'

'Exactly.'

He glanced at his watch. 'Well, Maestro, I've taken enough of your time and I've got a long way to go.' He slipped his pen into his inside pocket and put his notepad into his briefcase. 'I know you have to pop out soon.'

'What?'

'You said you have to go and see a neighbour, or something.'

'Oh, yes, of course. I ought to go and do my duty.'

'Very good of you.' He struggled out of the settee. Pulling the creases out of his jacket, he offered me his hand. 'It's been a real pleasure.'

'The pleasure's all mine, Monsieur Bowen. Now, have you got everything? Good. I'll see you out.'

'Thank you.'

'I think it might rain soon,' I said, stepping outside with him. 'When do you think the article will appear?'

'After the photographer's been over. I'll get her to give you a ring. Then probably a week or so after that.'

'That's fine. I look forward to reading about myself,' I said, aware that I'd let slip a hint of my old vanity.

'Yes, well. Thank you for the tea.'

'Have a good trip back.'

'I will. Thank you. Goodbye, Maestro.'

'Goodbye, Monsieur Bowen. Goodbye.' I watched him leave, in his dapper cream-coloured suit, and thought, what a charming fellow.

*

Returning indoors, I ate another biscuit and finished my tea. Yes, I thought, I'd better go – it was almost three. She doesn't like it if I'm late. Not that she ever goes anywhere, but she likes the routine.

I felt strangely content – as if I'd just purged myself of something unpleasant. I felt lighter somehow. Is this how Catholics feel after confession, I wondered. Donning my overcoat and taking my umbrella, I closed my front door behind me, and made my way down the road. I told

Monsieur Bowen I was visiting a neighbour but in fact, they lived right at the far end of the village. I strode across the village square and past the church, and along another street lined with picturesque cottages and well-tended gardens, a spring in my step, waving to various people whom I knew by sight. I was wrong about the rain – indeed, the sun was appearing from the clouds. I stopped by at the village shop and brought a newspaper, a dozen eggs, powdered milk and a small assortment of vegetables. What a fine day it'd been. I thoroughly enjoyed unburdening myself. And what a pleasant young man was Monsieur Bowen, Henri. I was sure he would do the article justice. And here it is, the house. I pushed open the gate and admired the front garden which I had, just a few days previously, spent some time clearing and weeding, dead-heading the plants and flowers. Having my own key, I let myself in.

'Only me,' I shouted as I closed the door behind me.

'I'm in here,' she shouted back from the living room. Not that she'd be anywhere else.

'I got you your paper and the groceries you asked for.' I said, handing her the newspaper. She spent the whole day in her living room, sitting in an old armchair with a blanket over her knees, a small space cluttered with too much furniture and too many paintings on the wall, and a mantelpiece adorned with cheap horse figurines. In the corner, opposite her, the television was on, the volume turned down. Next to her, on a high, small table, a blue-coloured budgerigar in its cage. 'How's Pompidou?' I asked.

'A bit quiet today, aren't you, Pompy? Next time you pass the shop, can you get me some more birdseed?'

'Sure.'

'And some more headache pills.'

'Again?'

She glanced at the paper's headlines. 'I don't know why I read the paper,' she said. 'It's nothing but bad news.'

Stepping into her tiny kitchen, I packed away the groceries. Returning, I asked her how she was.

'I feel very stiff today.'

'Well, I keep telling you, Hilda, you ought to get up and about. Walk up to the square and back. It'd do you the world of good.'

'I know, I know,' she said, readjusting her blanket.

'Are you warm enough? Can I make you a cup of tea?'

'Maestro, I'm fine. Will you stop fussing?'

'Well, you know, I like to make sure you're OK. None of us are getting any younger.'

She attempted a smile. 'You're so kind. I don't know how I would cope without you.' The words were appreciative, and she said them occasionally, but I always felt as if she was saying them for the sake of it; because she felt she had to; it never felt as if it came from the heart.

'Ah, it's nothing,' I said, playing my part.

'It's been many years now, hasn't it?'

'Yes, I suppose it has. But someone had to look after you, eh?'

'Did you say something about a cup of tea?'

I laughed. 'Coming right up, Hilda, coming right up.'

.

Chapter 11
Annecy, October 1982

A couple days after Monsieur Bowen's visit, came the photographer. A young woman in a hurry. She declined my offer of a drink and kept her mackintosh on, its belt flapping behind her. She did her business quickly and efficiently, thanked me and left. I was rather disappointed how little time it took.

Each day, I bought Hilda her paper and quickly flicked through its pages to see whether my interview had appeared yet. I did wonder what she'd make of it. I feared she'd be cross but she knew what I was like, and, heck, I thought, the world had given her up for dead; it had no interest in her any more.

I hadn't been quite honest with Monsieur Bowen. I did visit Hilda in prison again. A week or so after my first visit, I received a short letter from her. It merely thanked me for the cake, saying how delicious it was. I was so pleasantly surprised that, a few weeks later, I made another and set off all the way to Rennes to deliver it to her. And that's how it started. Despite the distance and the effort, not to mention the cost, I went once a month for the rest of her sentence. I didn't like leaving Claude by himself for so long a day, but, as I told him, it wasn't often.

Once there, we talked about the news, the gossip and even, to my surprise, sport. She read the papers everyday, devouring what was going on in France and around the world. She was fascinated by the on-going war in Vietnam; she adored the cyclist, Eddie Merckx, who had won the Tour de France that year, and liked to pour scorn on Georges Pompidou and the work of his government.

Towards the end of her sentence, I brought up the subject of where she was going to live following her release. Although she still had her apartment in Paris, she was determined never to return to the capital. I knew the feeling. I helped her sell the flat and, with the proceeds, bought a little cottage in the same village as mine near Annecy. In October 1971, after exactly three years in prison, Hilda was released. I met her at the prison gates, and took her to Annecy and her new home, fearful of what she'd think of it. She liked it. Almost immediately, however, she became a recluse, rarely venturing out, content to sit at home all day, or sitting out in the small garden at the back, reading the papers. I suggested she buy a pet and took Claude round to visit. She wasn't the slightest bit interested in the dog and asked me never to bring 'that mongrel' round again. But she did buy a budgerigar – the first of many.

Eleven years later, little had changed but now, aged 82, she suffers from her age.

*

Ten days after the photographer's visit, it was there! My interview. I was already half way from the shop to Hilda's cottage, when I saw it. *Whatever happened to the Maestro?* said the headline. *Once, he was renowned and feted throughout France as the future of classical music. Yet, just when his star was at its zenith, just when it seemed he could do no wrong, the Maestro, as he was commonly known, stood by a former guard from the wartime concentration camp at Drancy. It proved a fateful mistake and left him with his career in tatters, forcing him to disappear. Now, 14 years on, we've tracked him down and sent our top music reporter, Henri Bowen, to see him. After so many years of silence, the Maestro finally has his say…*

I didn't like the photo, though. I hadn't realised how old I looked. But here, in this black and white photo, I looked thin and drawn and grey. Nonetheless, excited, I rushed over to Hilda's, deciding to buy myself a copy on the way back.

I didn't stay too long at Hilda's, just long enough to give her the paper and make sure she was all right. I didn't mention the interview – she'd find it soon enough.

I returned to the shop and to my utter disappointment, found they'd sold out of the newspaper. Not to worry, I thought, I'd read Hilda's copy the following day.

*

First thing the following morning, I rang her to ask if I could come and visit her straightaway. Having delayed it a day, I couldn't wait to read the interview. To my surprise, she didn't answer. Perhaps it's bath day, I thought. I decided not to wait – I'd simply walk over now.

I let myself in. 'Only me,' I shouted. 'Hope you don't mind, but I've come early. I have to pop out later, so I thought I'd come see you now instead.' No answer. 'Hello? Hilda?'

It was past nine o'clock – she wouldn't still be in bed. No, she'd been up – I noticed her post propped up on the mantelpiece. Surely, she hadn't gone out. Hilda never went out unless necessity forced her into it. It was now that I felt the first real pangs of concern. 'Hilda?' I shouted again.

She was nowhere downstairs, nor in the garden. Coming back indoors, I ran up the stairs, knocked on her bedroom door, and, having received no reply, opened it. She wasn't there. Her bed was made, everything was as it was supposed to be.

From there, I tried the bathroom door. It was locked. I tapped gently on the door and again called out her name. Still no response. I knocked harder, then harder still, shouting her name, to the point I was thumping on the door, rattling the doorknob. I'd become frantic. I had no choice – I had to break down the door. Bracing myself, I barged against the door with my shoulder. It didn't budge. There was no way I was going to force it open by jumping against it. Having an idea, I ran downstairs and back into her garden and to her shed, where I knew I'd find an axe.

I suffered a moment's hesitation at the thought of ruining a perfectly good bathroom door. 'Hilda, are you there? Are you OK?' Silence. 'For heaven's sake, answer me.' I swung the axe, splintering the wood. Again and again, I hacked at it, getting faster all the time, my breaths coming in panicked bursts. Eventually I'd made enough of a split to be able to see. Peering through the gap, I could see her – in her bath, the head thrown back, an arm dangling over the side. She was wearing her clothes. 'Hilda, what have you done?' I slashed further at the door until, finally, I was able to squeeze my arm through and, after a bit of fumbling, managed to unlock the bolt. I almost fell in, slipping on the fragments of wood on the bathroom tiles.

'Hilda?' I held my breath. She had had a bath fully dressed. The water, up to her neck, was coloured red.

Chapter 12
Annecy, November 1982

Aged 82, Hilda Lapointe, *née* Irène d'Urville, had committed suicide. Somehow, the papers had picked up on it and published the story. They reckoned that, finally, after almost forty years, her guilt had caught up with her. They were utterly wrong. She'd never felt guilt.

The post I thought I saw that morning, propped up on her mantelpiece, was in fact one single envelope – addressed to me. A policewoman brought it round to mine later that day. Using a letter opener, I sliced it open and, in front of the policewoman, nervously unfolded the single sheet of paper. The note contained just five words. It read: *Don't forget to feed Pompidou.* 'You bitch,' I screamed.

Shocked, the policewoman asked if I was OK.

I apologised and groaned – for I knew she'd tell her colleagues that I'd sworn and what an unfeeling, nasty man I was.

Over the days that followed, I arranged a funeral for her. She had enough money in her account to cover it all.

There was to be a delay, however. The local coroner had ordered an autopsy. I think they wanted to ensure that she had really taken her own life and that I hadn't killed her off. I remembered her lawyer all those years ago telling me she once talked of suicide.

What little money was left over, including the house and its contents, was, according to her will, to be passed to a nephew of the woman she used to know in Saint-Romain after the war. Someone who, as far as I knew, had never visited her, never wrote, not even a Christmas card. I was disappointed but not surprised; I hadn't expected it to come my way. There wasn't much of it anyway. I knew full well that she'd been using me these last eleven years. I'd become her cleaner, her shopper, her cook, her gardener, her unpaid skivvy. She'd never once, in all that time, thanked me. The occasional, insincere word of appreciation, perhaps, but never a 'thank you'.

The autopsy returned a verdict of suicide by the cutting of the wrists and an overdose of headache tablets. So, that was why she kept making me buy them. She'd planned it, slowly hoarding the pills. Why had she done it? I wasn't sure but it wasn't guilt. But I do know that my interview in the newspaper had tipped her over the edge. That was my intention, perhaps not to kill herself, but to hurt her, to make her see that still after all these years, people would remember her for what she was – a cruel, sadistic woman who never expressed any remorse for the dreadful things she did. And through the interview, I'd ensured that people would *remember*.

I felt no pity yet, in a strange way, I rather missed her. I missed the routine of going round to see her day after day.

*

Hilda's funeral took place on a cold and breezy but sunny November morning, the clouds moving briskly across the sky, the late autumnal colours a joy to behold, the graveyard awash with a carpet of orange-brown leaves. Hilda had never shown the slightest interest in the church. Still, we have to do these things. There were just the three of us – me, the priest and, to my surprise, the nephew, Gérard, a tall, slim man in his fifties with a pointed chin, sporting a watch chain across his waistcoat. I think he, at least, had been driven by guilt. Before the service began, he apologised for never having visited. I gave him Hilda's keys and told him to deal with the house as he saw fit. We shook hands and stood next to each other as the priest did his bit.

We therefore commit Hilda's body to the ground; earth to earth, ashes to ashes, dust to dust…

Afterwards, the three of us stood with our hands clasped in front of us, and looked down at Hilda's coffin inside its grave. I thought of Madame Kahn, and the poor woman Hilda had beaten to death on the ice; I thought of her sitting impassively in court, her eyes cold while those around her wept; I thought of me as a young man on that train.

The church clock struck twelve. As the last peal faded away, the priest asked to be excused, and Gérard and I watched as he scuttled off, his cassock caught by the breeze, exposing a pair of trainers.

'Well, that's it,' said Gérard.

'Yes.' I sighed. 'That's truly it.'

'Have you noticed something?' he said, his eyes still fixed on the coffin.

I shook my head.

'Don't make it obvious, but the whole time we've been here, there's been someone watching us, standing next to the elm tree behind us.'

I hadn't noticed. Slowly, the two of us turned round. Gérard was right – there was someone, a woman dressed in funereal black, right down to a veil over her face.

'Is it someone you know?' he asked.

'Yes,' I said, squinting my eyes against the autumn sun. 'I think it is. You'll have to excuse me.'

Slowly, I walked towards her, my hands behind my back, my shoes crunching the dried leaves underfoot. I watched her as she stepped away from the long shadow of the tree. Lifting her veil, she said quietly, 'Hello, Maestro.'

I smiled. 'Isabelle. I'd hoped you'd come. How lovely to see you again.'

THE END

The White Venus

Rupert Colley

Chapter 1

Xavier passed him the chicken. 'Go on then, you do it. Like you say, it can't be that difficult.'

Pierre gathered the hen in his arms and stroked its head, trying to keep it calm. Her sister hens and cousins ambled around the yard, pecking, their shadows long in the late afternoon sun, circling the various monuments dotted around – statues and memorials half completed. It was here, at the back of the house, that Pierre's father did his work.

'It's all right for you,' said Pierre, 'she's not part of your family.'

Xavier, sitting in an old rocking chair Pierre's mother no longer wanted in the house, guffawed. 'It's a chicken, Pierre, not your grandmother. Go on, two seconds and it'll be done with.'

'Yeah.' The chicken jerked its head. 'Right then, Madeleine.'

'Madeleine? You call it Madeleine?'

'Yeah. So what? All the chickens have names.'

'How quaint,' said Xavier, shielding his eyes from the sun. 'You give it a name, it's part of your family, as you say, like a family pet, then your dad tells you to kill it.'

'She's old. She's not laying any more. And Papa, well, he thinks I'm *of an age now*,' he said, adopting a pompous tone. 'This one's called Marion,' he said, pointing to another hen. 'That one Marlene, Monique...'

'Wait, do they all start with M?'

'Mmm. Maman's idea.'

'Your parents are strange.'

'Papa wanted to name them each after top Nazis – Goebbels, Goring, Rosenberg, but Maman wouldn't let him. Said it'd be bad taste, especially if he was heard calling out the names.'

'She has a point. So, which one's Hitler?'

'He's the cock behind you – on the fence. But he's called Maurice.'

Xavier turned round to view the cockerel. 'So what would Madeleine have been?'

'I don't know. Perhaps Bormann.'

'Well, hurry up then, kill Martin Bormann, even though she's a girl. They could be here any minute.'

'And we can't be late for our special guests.'

'Exactly. The swine. They couldn't have chosen a hotter day for it. All this white stone – it hurts your eyes. How do you see to work?'

'Sunglasses, Xavier. Sunglasses. What d'you think?'

'What's this block of stone going to be?'

'It's sandstone. It's mine to practice on. Papa said I could have it.'

Xavier ran his hand down the stone. 'What's it going to be?'

'A chicken.'

Xavier laughed. 'Oh, really? A fucking chicken? A metre-high chicken? I'd like to see that when it's done.'

'Yeah, a chicken with a Hitler moustache pecking your eyes out.'

'Very funny. Well, look, your Madeleine's going to die of old age before you get to wring her neck.'

'OK. It can't be that difficult.' Pierre placed two fingers beneath the bird's head. Securing its body under his armpit and clamping it against his chest, he tightened his fingers. All he had to do was pull. Pull hard. He'd seen his father do it several times. It took but a second. One solid pull; that's all it took. The bird squawked. He had to do this. It was part of growing up. He had to have it done before his father came out. He regretted now having invited Xavier over to witness the occasion. He thought it would give him courage but instead it only made things worse. It was like inviting someone over to watch you lose your virginity. He felt self-conscious, pressurised by his friend's presence. Some things should be done in private. Bracing himself, he started to count down in his head. Five, four, three…

The door to the kitchen flung open. It was his father. Pierre's fingers slackened, his body slumped. 'They're here,' said Georges.

'What, already?'

'Come on, we ought to go.' Uncharacteristically, Pierre's father was wearing a collar and tie and his best beret, his shoes polished, his moustache waxed. 'Hello, Xavier. You can come with us if you like, or are you going with your parents?'

'I said I'd meet them there.'

'Let's go then. After all, we don't want to keep them

waiting.'

Pierre wondered what to do about the chicken. His father spotted his hesitation. 'What are you doing with Mirabelle?'

'Mirabelle?'

'I said wring Madeleine, not Mirabelle.'

Pierre dropped the chicken as if he'd burnt himself. The bird flapped its wings as it landed, causing billows of dust, and ran off, squawking.

His father sighed. 'Please don't tell me you were about to do away with one of our best layers?'

Xavier stepped forward. 'No, Pierre wanted to show me Mirabelle, that's all.'

'Thank the Lord for that.' He straightened his tie. 'Well, let's go. Let's see what the future of France looks like. You ready then, boys?'

*

It was like a carnival. The whole population seemed to have converged on the town square. The clock on the town hall showed five. The sun beat down on the assembled crowd. Whole families had turned out together. Children ran around the square, their shadows chasing after them. The cafés, although still open for business, were empty; their staff in their black and white uniforms waiting outside, craning their necks like so many penguins. There was laughter but also a deep sense of apprehension. No one wanted to admit it but Pierre could feel it; could see it behind everyone's outward smiles. Ahead of them, in front of the town hall and the war memorial, they had erected a stage, a wooden platform, with large speakers to the side. Centre stage, a microphone in its stand. The war memorial, dating from the Franco-Prussian War of 1870-71, featured a bronze statue of a French soldier high on a plinth, one hand holding a rifle, the other shielding his eyes as he gazed into the distance. The locals affectionately called him 'Soldier Mike'. The French tricolour hung limp on its flagpole above the town hall; there was no wind to stir it.

People stood on the benches. Pierre's mother stood on tiptoe, the better to see. She too had dressed up for the occasion, wearing a bright blue dress that came with a belt and a simple straw hat. It was her 'going out' dress, her only one. She wore it rarely. A kingfisher brooch acted as a button. Pierre noticed her take her husband's hand. His father wouldn't like that. Sure enough, after a few seconds, he leant over to talk to his friend, thereby having the excuse of letting go. Kafka, his father's friend, chewed on his pipe, scowling as Georges whispered in his ear. Pierre heard Kafka utter the word 'bastards'. Georges rolled his eyes and nodded knowingly. 'Georges…' said Pierre's mother, remonstrating that her husband should allow his friend to swear in public.

Xavier nudged Pierre in the ribs. 'Well, this is better than murdering innocent chickens.'

'I wish they'd hurry up; it's getting hot.'

'Look who I see. Our lovely librarian.'

Pierre followed his friend's gaze. Involuntarily, he let slip the word 'fuck'. His mother, thank God, didn't hear. Claire looked gorgeous. She was wearing a white blouse, its buttons like daisies, her breasts clearly defined, and a swirling yellow skirt. Her auburn hair, held with a band, reflected the sun. As if aware of Pierre looking at her, she turned and caught his eye. A flicker of a smile.

5

'Here he comes,' said Georges, breaking the moment. Pierre saw the mayor climbing the steps onto the platform. He looked back towards Claire, but she had gone.

The mayor, wearing his red robes, tapped the microphone. Clutching a sheet of paper, he waited as mothers called their children back. A wave of silence descended across the town square as the hum of conversation died away, broken only by the cawing of a pair of crows perched high on top of Soldier Mike.

'*Bonjour, messieurs, mesdames.*' The microphone squealed. The mayor stepped back, a clear look of annoyance on his face. Someone to the side of the platform offered advice. Adjusting his spectacles, the mayor, now standing a little further back, continued. 'My friends, citizens of this glorious town; we live in momentous times. France may have been defeated but she is still France and we are still her children. Yes, we have fallen at the feet of the enemy and yes, Marshal Pétain has asked the Germans for an armistice. The Battle of France is over. You may ask is it unpatriotic to accept so meekly the German in our midst, to bow down before him? I tell you instead to ask is it patriotic to want to throw thousands, hundreds of thousands, of young men to be slaughtered like lambs? Is it not patriotic to want to save our future generation from futile resistance? Most of us remember too well the horrors of the last war. A war we won, but at what price?' He shook his fist, causing his chin to wobble. 'So many men and boys killed; leaving behind a generation of young widows; children growing up without ever having known their fathers. Those of you who remember, look now at the children, the young men amongst us. Would you want them to suffer as we suffered twenty years ago in the name of victory?' Pierre and Georges exchanged glances. His father, Pierre knew, had been in the war. His father had never mentioned it to him – not once. And Pierre had never, until this moment, thought to ask him. 'No,' continued the mayor, the sun reflecting off his glasses, 'this is no shameful defeat; this is peace. Compromised maybe, but better a compromised peace than a victory awash with so much blood.'

'Bollocks,' someone muttered. People nearest turned around. That someone, Pierre knew, was Kafka. Pierre's mother pursed her lips, tutted, noticeably affronted by Kafka's language. Georges grimaced, as if responsible for his friend's outburst.

'I, Claude Marchel, will remain your mayor. You elected me to serve four years. And four years I will serve. With your blessing, perhaps more. But now, as from today, I will have at my side, the *Ortskommandantur* at Saint-Romain. Together, Colonel Eisler and I will ensure the smooth running of this town and its surrounding area. We shall work together to maintain peace so that we, the good people of this proud town, can coexist in tranquillity with our guests.'

Pierre feared another outburst from Kafka. Thankfully, the man held his tongue. Pierre could see this Colonel Eisler hovering at the side of the stage, waiting for his cue.

'I have asked the colonel to deliver a few words.' Removing his spectacles, the mayor motioned the German to take his turn. Pierre noticed that the crows had gone but, with a start, he saw a line of German soldiers at the edges of the crowd. Left and right, they were there, stock still in their grey-green uniforms and steel helmets, their rifles at their sides. Georges had noticed too and visibly stiffened.

The mayor stepped back to allow the colonel centre stage. A tall man, in his fifties, thought Pierre, but still lean. Even from a distance, the man had a presence; his immaculate uniform a stark contrast to the mayor's ceremonial garb. 'Thank you, Monsieur le Maire.' Pierre had half expected a deep authoritative voice, and, although heavily accented, was surprised by its normality. 'This town and its surrounding area are now under the jurisdiction of the German High Command,' said the colonel without an introduction. He paused as if allowing his audience to absorb the import of what he had said. 'While we have nothing but scorn for your government and its feeble-minded politicians, we have nothing but respect for the French people.'

'So why in the hell did you invade us, then?' came a loud voice to the side. It was not Kafka, but the man was nodding his agreement. The colonel ignored the taunt and continued his speech, extolling the need for Franco-German cordiality. Pierre noticed the German soldiers nearest the dissenter shuffle forward, squeezing in the crowd. They had seen the man, Monsieur Touvier, the town's blacksmith, and they were watching him.

Pierre saw his mother take his father's hand again. 'All guns, in whatever form, are to be handed in to the town hall by noon tomorrow. There are to be no exceptions. Likewise, all radios are to be handed in by the same time. From today, we will be observing German time, so you will need to adjust your clocks and watches by one hour in advance.' Pierre felt rather than heard the collective groan. 'From today also, you will have to abide by a curfew. This curfew will change with the time of year but for now, with

8

the days at their longest, it will be nine o'clock – German time. Anyone found outside their homes from nine to five the following morning will face consequences.' The colonel scanned the audience in front of him, looking at people, one to another, as if daring anyone else to make a comment. No one did. The soldiers nearby, Pierre noticed, were still watching the blacksmith.

'The day-to-day running of this town will remain with Monsieur le Maire. My staff and I will be based in Saint-Romain. Most of my men will be based there but a few will remain here. Some of those remaining will be billeted in your homes. It will not be for long – perhaps a month at the most. The noticeboard behind me has a list of residents who can await a lodger. I expect those listed to make my men feel welcome; and I fully expect my men to treat you with the utmost courtesy. I bid you all good day.'

The rumble of voices began immediately, rising to a crescendo of speculation. The mayor returned to the microphone but his attempts to call for attention were ignored as his face reddened to the same colour as his robes.

'I hope we don't get someone staying with us,' said Pierre's mother.

'I'll bloody show him the door if we do,' said Georges, pulling on his moustache.

'Don't swear, Georges.'

'He's right, though,' said Kafka. 'Any German staying in my house will sleep in the outside toilet.'

'Kafka, you live alone – they won't send anyone to you.'

Pierre noticed two soldiers squeezing into the dissenter. Holding his arms down, they took Monsieur Touvier to one side, trying their best not to cause a commotion.

'What are they going to do him?' asked Xavier.

'They're going to make him pluck chickens as a punishment.'

Pierre's mother called out to them. 'Boys, why don't you go check the noticeboard? Let us know the worst.'

*

Xavier had got there before Pierre, pushing his way through the throng of people crowding round the noticeboard. Pierre watched as people came away, either with a look of relief or dread emblazoned on their faces. Someone, he noticed, had wrapped a French flag round Soldier Mike's ankle. He caught sight of Claire again. He waved and although she was looking in his direction, did not see him, leaving him feeling rather foolish with his hand mid-air.

Xavier re-appeared from the scrum of people, looking slightly dishevelled but grinning.

'Well?'

'Don't worry, my parents are in the clear.'

'Well, that's nice. I'm so pleased for you. And, erm…'

'Oh, sorry, Pierre, I forgot to look for your name.'

'You're an idiot.'

His friend laughed. 'I'm only joking. I did look.'

'Oh, the suspense. Well, go on then, tell me.'

Xavier could not contain his glee as he imparted the news. 'Yep, my dear friend. You are to expect a Major something-or-other at some point in the next couple of days.'

'Oh great. Sod it. A major?'

'Yeah. What rank was your father?'

'No idea. So what's his name?'

'I've forgotten. Something beginning with an H.'

'Major H, welcome to our humble home. I'd better tell my parents.'

'Ah, don't worry. I'm sure he'll be a very nice Kraut, and I'm sure you'll all live happily ever after together.'

'Yeah, thanks, Xavier. You're still an idiot.'

*

Xavier had, at last, found his parents and disappeared with them into the throng of people now meandering back to their homes. Heading home down a side street, Pierre walked alongside his mother while his father walked behind, talking to Kafka. Pierre had told them the news – they were to expect a lodger. They took it rather well, he thought. 'What does it all mean, Maman?'

'The Germans? I don't know. Maybe the mayor was right; maybe it is for the best.'

'What? To have a bunch of Germans telling us what to do?' Further ahead, they saw two German soldiers peering through the window at the baker's.

'I remember the last war, Pierre,' said his mother quietly, as if the soldiers might hear her from twenty metres away. 'They were terrible, terrible years. The Marshal knows what he's doing; he'll find a way.'

'What, Pétain? That old goat?'

'Pierre, please. Keep your voice down. You don't know what you're saying. He saved us once; he'll save us again.' The soldiers, sharing a joke, were now heading towards them, ambling leisurely, looking around them as if sightseeing in the sunshine.

'But the lad is right,' bellowed Kafka from behind.

'Pétain *is* an old goat; he's sold us down the river.' The soldiers were getting closer but Pierre feared that Kafka was far from finished. 'In sucking up to the Krauts, he's signed a pact with the Devil.'

The soldiers had heard Kafka's shouting. They were watching him as they strolled past them in the lane. Pierre's mother turned to Kafka, 'Keep your voice down.'

'No, sorry, Lucienne; I cannot hold my tongue. Pétain has betrayed us and betrayed his country.' This time the Germans had clearly heard him. Pierre saw their faces harden. 'And so now we have to tolerate having these Krauts telling us what to do.'

'Hey, you; watch your tongue,' said one of the soldiers in German, a man with a boxer's nose, gripping his rifle in front of him.

'Fuck off back to Germany.'

It took but a second – Kafka was on his knees on the tarmac, clutching his stomach. The soldier had hit him with his rifle butt. Lucienne screamed; Georges's face turned white; Pierre had taken his mother's hand. The soldier was leaning over Kafka, screaming at him: 'You filth! You talk like that again you're dead; you got it?' The second soldier kicked Kafka, catching him in the arm. People stopped, shocked, open-mouthed.

'Please don't say anything else,' Pierre whispered to himself.

The first soldier had his rifle poised, ready to butt Kafka a second time. Pierre held his breath, gripped his fingers over his mother's, but a voice rang out in German: 'Hey, stop right this instant.'

Kafka spat as a German officer ran onto the scene. 'Stop right now, Private. What's going on?'

The second private spoke. 'This piece of shit was insulting us, sir.'

'What was he saying?'

'I don't know, I don't know that much French.'

'He's got a bad attitude, sir,' said the other, lowering his rifle.

Kafka rose unsteadily to his feet, still holding his stomach.

'That's enough now,' said the major. Pierre released his mother's hand.

Georges helped his friend up. 'You're OK, Kafka?'

'I can manage,' he said, shrugging Georges off.

'Kafka? What sort of name is that? Are you a writer?' asked the major in perfect French. Turning to his soldiers, he said in German, 'OK, men, you can go now.' The two soldiers looked at each other. One shrugged and with a half-hearted Hitler salute headed off, the other following in his wake. 'I apologise for the men,' he said to Kafka. 'After a month of fighting, they're a little twitchy. Are you OK?'

Kafka puffed out his cheeks. 'A month of killing Frenchmen, eh? My heart bleeds for them.'

Pierre could see the major's goodwill rapidly draining away. 'What is your name?'

'Kafka; I told you.'

'Your real name?'

Kafka stretched, as if trying to rid his stomach of the pain.

'I asked you what is your name?'

'Foucault, Albert Foucault.'

'But they call you Kafka?'

'Looks like it. Can we go now?'

The major stared at him for a few moments. Then with a quick bow to Pierre's mother, turned to leave. They watched him head briskly back towards the town square.

'Oh, Kafka,' said Lucienne. 'When will you learn?'

'Thanks for all your help, Georges.'

'I – I wanted to but…'

'But what?'

Lucienne, still agitated, fanned herself with her hat. 'I think we should go now. Come, Pierre.'

But Kafka, rubbing his stomach, wasn't finished. 'Still a little smitten with the German race, eh, Georges? Still in awe of their biological superiority after all these years?'

Lucienne took Georges's hand. 'Let's get you home, dear,' she said, dragging him away, trying to save her husband from further embarrassment. 'And you, Kafka. Go home and have a bath, even in this heat. Hot water will do your stomach some good. Help ease the pain.'

Georges huffed. 'Take a few days off, Kafka. Go to your island on the lake, have a rest.'

'I might well do that. And thank you for your concern, Lucienne; I'll do exactly as you say, a hot bath, even in this weather.' He was smiling now, a smile without affection. 'I'll see you soon, Georges; and Pierre…'

'Yes?' said Pierre nervously.

'You know, you don't always have to grab your mother's hand at the first sign of trouble.'

Chapter 2

While Lucienne waited for the kettle to boil on their large, black stove, she washed her hands thoroughly, still determined, she'd said, to wash away the dirt of the previous day. Pierre was familiar with this habit of hers – this obsessive washing of hands whenever she felt under a strain. He remembered exactly when it had started.

Eventually, with the tea made, they sat and sipped in silence, Lucienne smelling of carbolic soap. His parents sat on the bench at the kitchen table, the table with its rose-patterned oilcloth, while Pierre sat back in the kitchen armchair. His eyelids felt heavy. His eyes scanned the familiar items on the chest – the crucifix at its top, the china cups hanging on hooks, the ones rarely used; the saucers on display with a picture of the Eiffel Tower on a white background, the Tower, adorned with a smiling face, leaning to one side as if exercising. There was one missing – Pierre had broken it years back; he must've been about eight or nine. It was the only time he ever recalled his mother spanking him. He cried, naturally, but not from the pain – there wasn't any, but from the fact he'd so upset his mother. On the wall opposite the chest, two framed photographs – one of a man on a tightrope and the other of a young boy aged about five wearing a flat cap too big for him and baggy trousers, the definition of a cheeky but sweet boy.

While his mother had made tea, he had sat there with his father. Neither spoke a word yet he'd wanted so much to ask. But his father seemed so diminished it didn't seem right to bring it out in the open. Kafka knew something that Georges would rather forget. Perhaps, at some point, thought Pierre, he would broach the subject with his mother. And then of course there was the little matter of his own abject humiliation. He tried to persuade himself that he had taken his mother's hand to protect her. But Kafka knew the truth. And so did he.

Finally, Pierre's mother broke the silence. 'What about your gun, Georges?'

'What about it?'

'You have to hand it in.'

'Why? Because they said so?' asked Georges, stirring his tea although he had almost finished it.

'Of course. We can't keep it, especially with a German staying in the house. If they find it…'

'There'd be serious consequences,' finished Pierre.

'Yes, thank you, Pierre,' said his father. 'For God's sake, it's only an old shotgun. I use it for the rabbits and crows. That's it.' Pierre didn't like to say that, despite numerous attempts, he'd never seen his father kill anything. 'And I've had it for years. It's virtually an antique.'

'Yes but they don't know that, Georges. You have to

hand it in. Think of us, all of us.'

Georges finished his tea. 'I'm not handing it in,' he said, placing his mug on the table.

Lucienne rose from her seat and went outside. 'She's gone to get it,' said Georges to Pierre. 'You wait.'

Sure enough, moments later, Lucienne returned carrying the shotgun at arm's length as if it was emitting a terrible smell. 'It is safe, isn't it, Georges? You haven't left it loaded or anything?'

'No, of course not. Bloody hell.'

She looked up worriedly at the crucifix. 'Please, Georges, don't use profanities.'

Gingerly, she placed the gun on the table. They looked at it. Pierre had never really considered it before. It was a fine piece of craftsmanship, he decided. Elegant, sleek yet solid. He knew nothing about guns but could see that this thing could cause some damage. He realised that his father knew he had to hand it in but couldn't face another indignity. 'I'll take it if you want.' The idea of walking through the town with this in his hand was thrilling.

His parents looked at each other and silently reached the same conclusion. 'Good idea,' said Lucienne. 'Yes, you take it. But do it now – in case this Major H turns up early.'

Pierre picked it up. He weighed it up and down. It was heavier than he expected. 'It's lovely.'

'Just take it, Pierre,' said Lucienne.

Pierre pointed to his father's wartime helmet that hung from the back of the kitchen door. It'd been there for as long as he could remember. 'Can I wear your helmet, Papa?'

'No, you cannot. Is there not a bag of some sort he

could put it in?' asked Georges.

But Pierre was already out of the door. As he closed it behind him he heard his father shout, 'Get a receipt for it.'

*

Pierre couldn't resist it. He called in on Xavier to show him the shotgun. His friend was suitably impressed. 'So what are you doing with it?'

'I'm off to shoot a few Germans. Do you want to come?'

'Right we are.'

'For every German we take out, there's one less to worry about.'

'Yep – simple. Let's go.'

It was strange walking down the street with a huge gun. People couldn't help but notice and many backed away. Monsieur Tautou, the carpenter, saw them. 'That's the spirit, boys.'

They took turns with the gun, carrying it as a soldier would on parade. The walk from Xavier's house to the town hall was but a few minutes but the boys took several detours so that soon hardly a street in the whole town had not been visited by the two boys and their heavy shotgun. 'Hey, Pierre, let's take it into the woods and see if we can kill something. Or we can sneak into the back of the mayor's house and kill his rabbits.'

'Xavier – it's not loaded.'

'Oh.'

'You think my dad would let me walk down the street with a loaded gun? Anyway, imagine firing this thing; it'd dislocate your shoulder.'

'Let's go to the library – go see the lovely Claire,' he

said in a sing-song voice. 'I'm sure she'd be impressed with something that size.'

'It's closed now.'

'Barriers, barriers. That's all you do; create barriers to everything I say.'

Pierre laughed. 'It's not my bloody fault that the gun's not loaded and the library is closed.'

Wrapped up in their banter, they hadn't noticed the pair of German soldiers approach them. 'What are you doing with that gun?' said one in German, his rifle trained on them.

The boys looked up. 'Oh, shit,' uttered Pierre, recognising the soldier with the flattened nose. 'What did he say?'

'I don't know.'

'Put that gun down,' said the first German.

'Don't you understand German?' shouted the second.

'I think he wants you to put the gun down, Xavier.'

'Yeah, you're probably right.' Carefully, he placed it on the road.

Pierre pointed in the direction of the town hall. 'We hand it in to the mayor.'

'What did he say?' asked the first German to his comrade.

'I think he says they're going to shoot the mayor.'

On hearing this, the first one leapt into action, lifting his rifle to eye-level and, advancing, aiming it straight at Pierre's head. 'Get down, you frog, on your knees now.'

'Whoa,' cried Pierre putting his hands up.

'Get down.'

The boys understood and went down on their knees, then, after furthering gesturing, lay on the road on their fronts.

'I think they're going to kill us,' said Pierre.

'But I haven't had my dinner yet.'

'You could ask him to come back later.'

'Stop talking,' yelled the first as the second German began frisking Xavier.

'We've got an audience,' whispered Pierre. Sure enough, a small gathering of people had emerged, forming a circle around the spectacle. Someone shouted, 'Leave them alone.' Someone else added, 'They're only kids.'

'No, we're not,' said Pierre.

The second soldier had begun frisking Pierre, kicking his legs apart, and running his hands down his trousers, into his pockets, and down his socks. Craning his neck, Pierre saw a light green skirt. Fantastic, he thought; Claire couldn't help but be impressed. Here he was, only two days in, and he was already a resistance fighter. If only she'd step a little closer with that swirling skirt.

'What are you doing?' she asked the soldiers in German.

'Are they friends of yours?'

'I know them.'

'We caught them on their way to kill your mayor. They confessed.'

'Really?' She laughed. 'Hello, Pierre, Xavier. So, you were off to assassinate the mayor, were you?'

'Erm, yes,' said Pierre.

'Don't listen to him,' said Xavier. 'Of course we weren't. Tell her, you idiot.'

Pierre told her the truth as the soldier frisked his shirt. People in the crowd sniggered as they turned to leave. Claire, in turn, told the soldiers.

'I'm not so sure,' said the first. 'They look suspicious to me.'

'Do you really think–'

'Nonetheless, we'd better escort them,' said the second. 'Just to make sure. Get up!' he yelled at the boys.

'What did he say?' asked Pierre.

'He said, "prepare to die, you filthy sons of dogs",' returned Xavier.

'He said all that in just two syllables?'

'Boys, you can get up now,' said Claire. 'These kind soldiers are going to escort you to the mayor's office.'

'What – Fritz One and Fritz Two? That's awfully decent of them,' said Xavier, brushing away fragments of tarmac.

'They don't have to; we know the way.'

Claire shook her head and smiled.

*

Pierre felt rather excited, walking to the town hall with two German soldiers behind them, pointing their rifles. One carried his father's shotgun. He hoped everyone in the town would get to see them. Indeed, they received many admiring glances and shocked ones too. It was turning out not to be such a bad day after all. Outside the town hall, the Germans had already erected a notice: *Whoever commits acts of sabotage against members or property of the German armed forces, or found to be in possession of arms of any type, will be shot.* Xavier caught Pierre's eye, raising his eyebrows.

Inside the town hall, the reception area was brimming. With its high ceiling and marbled floor, voices echoed. Men in German uniforms marched in and out; well-dressed women carrying envelopes or pads of paper busied themselves; telephones rang; a deliveryman appeared pushing a large cardboard box on a trolley.

The two German soldiers deposited the boys at the main desk, handing the shotgun over to the receptionist. She took it, leaning it against the desk beside her as they briefed her. On the wall behind the desk, a large portrait of Marshal Pétain wearing his peaked hat decorated with gold braids, his grey moustache almost white, his eyes fixed resolutely on the viewer, his chin defiantly prominent. The boys looked at each other. Subtly, Pierre shook his head, warning Xavier not to say anything. As the soldiers left, the first one slapped Xavier on the back and said, 'There we are; wasn't too bad, after all.'

'What did he say?' asked Xavier.

'He said next time you're dead.'

'Severe.'

It took Pierre a whole five minutes to fill out the necessary paperwork and receive, in return, a receipt. As they turned to leave, his mother suddenly appeared, throwing open the double doors of the town hall and standing there, catching her breath while trying to find her son. 'Pierre, thank God,' she said upon seeing him. 'I heard you'd been arrested.' She threw her arms round him.

'Maman, please.'

'Were you arrested? I heard all sorts of tales of you being led away at gunpoint. What happened?'

As they left and Pierre began recounting the tale, Xavier told them to look behind. They stood and looked up at the flagpole above the town hall. The French flag that had been there as long as anyone could remember had gone. In its place, flapping gently in the breeze, was the swastika.

'It's no joke, is it?' said Xavier.

'No,' said Pierre.

*

Having said their goodbyes to Xavier, Pierre and his mother slowly walked the rest of the way home.

'Maman, what did Kafka mean by saying Papa was still in awe of the Germans?'

Lucienne stopped. She sighed. 'I don't know. Your father fought in the war. You know that, he's got the medals. And that helmet on the back of the door. They were in the same unit. But, like a lot of men, your father never talks about the war. I only met him in 1920. We married a year later, so I didn't know him as a soldier. But something happened; I don't know what but something between Kafka and your father. Whatever it was, your father has always seemed as if he is still in debt to Kafka. He says Kafka is his friend – but friends don't blackmail each other.'

'Blackmail?'

'I don't mean with money. Just – emotionally, somehow. I remember, about ten years ago, Kafka moved away for a while. I think he moved to the city to be with his father who was dying. He was gone for about six months. I'd never seen your father so happy. He was like a different man. Then, Kafka came back and it was as if a big shadow had fallen over him again. I tell Georges just ignore him but, of course, in a town of this size, it's almost impossible.'

They had come to the house now. They lived in a bricked bungalow painted green, with large windows and a wooden porch that had three steps leading up to the front door. Either side, on each step, a blue enamel pot of flowers, which Lucienne watered every day. More pots hung from the porch. At this time of year, especially, their porch was ablaze with colour.

'Before we go in, let me say – don't mention any of this to your father. And be careful of Kafka. You know what he's like; we saw it yesterday. He's unpredictable. Stay away from him. For whatever reason, your father can't – but you, Pierre, you can.'

Chapter 3

The following morning, Georges was in the yard, working on another memorial engraving, while Lucienne had just returned from her daily visit to the churchyard and a shopping spree, complaining about prices already going up. Pierre was sitting on the bench at the kitchen table drawing – sketching out his ideas for a grand statue. He'd just had his daily dose of cod liver oil and the foul taste still lingered in his mouth. He decided then and there he would never take the stuff again. He was too old for it now. A tray with three Eiffel Tower china cups and saucers lay at the end of the table.

It was exactly ten o'clock when the knock on the door came. They had been expecting it but had not mentioned it. Lucienne, carrying a pallet of mushrooms, ran a hand through her hair. Quickly, she removed her apron, and smoothed out her blue dress. Pierre wondered why his mother had worn her best outfit again, right down to the kingfisher brooch. Again, she smelt strongly of carbolic soap. She opened the door. Immediately, Pierre recognized the German's voice speaking immaculate French.

'It's no inconvenience; do come in,' he heard his mother say. 'Mind your head.'

And then, there he was – this tall German officer standing in the middle of the kitchen, his big, shiny boots on the red tiled floor, his cap in hand, carrying a small suitcase. It was the major from the gathering; the one who had intervened in Kafka's argument.

'Such a lovely house… oh, hello there.' The man offered Pierre his hand. 'My name is Major Hurtzberger, Thomas.'

'Major H.'

'Yes; if you like. And your name is?'

'Pierre. I'll get my father.' He heard his mother offer the German a cup of coffee as Pierre stepped outside. It was another hot day. He found Georges with his goggles on, chisel and mallet in hand.

On seeing his son, Georges took off his goggles. 'He's here?'

Back inside, Pierre found the German looking at the ornaments and the pictures, paying particular attention to the photographs of the tightrope walker and the young boy in the flat cap. Sitting back at the table, Pierre watched as the three of them, his parents and the German, danced through a series of apologies and polite platitudes. 'It should only be for a month or so; I do apologize for the inconvenience.' He was over six foot, dark-haired, thin nose, pronounced cheekbones, and here he was, with his Nazi uniform with its German eagle, epaulettes, and medal ribbons, sitting at the kitchen table. The polite occupier; the enemy within their midst, being offered coffee.

Pierre twirled his pencil around his fingers. He noticed

that the German wore a gold signet ring on his left hand.

'What amusing cups,' said the major.

Lucienne laughed. 'Yes, it's the Eiffel Tower.'

'Yes, I can see.'

Georges shook his head.

Lucienne complimented the German on his French; mentioned that Pierre had done well in his English lessons at school.

'You speak English?' asked the German in English.

'No,' replied Pierre in French; annoyed to have been brought into the conversation.

'Don't be silly, Pierre. Go on, say something in English,' said his mother.

'Leave the boy alone,' said Georges.

'What is it you're drawing?' asked the major.

'Nothing really.' Subconsciously, he scribbled over his drawing, leaving an impression on the oilcloth beneath.

The kettle steamed on the stove while Lucienne prepared the coffee.

'Almost ready, Major.'

'Please, Madame Durand, you must call me Thomas.'

'No,' interrupted Georges. 'I think for the sake of propriety, we should stick to more formal use. I hope you understand, Major?'

'Y-yes. Yes, if you like.'

Changing the subject, Georges asked the German whether he had been to France before. He had once, as a child, with his parents, in about 1922, he said. Loire Valley – all those lovely chateaus. Had Georges been to Germany? 'No.' came the quick reply; too quick, causing a moment of awkwardness.

'You'll be pleased to know, you won't see too much of

me. I'll be working most of the day – every day.'

'No peace for the wicked?' asked Lucienne. She flushed red and subconsciously glanced up at the crucifix. Georges groaned.

'Well, yes. Erm. We're not all so wicked. And don't worry about food – I'll be eating all my meals at the canteen. I will endeavour to restrict my intrusion into your home to a minimum.'

'That's perfectly OK,' said Lucienne. 'You'll be sleeping in our third bedroom. You'll just have to ignore all the toys in there.'

'Toys? Oh, I'm sorry, I wouldn't want to take Pierre's room–'

'No, it's not Pierre's room. He's too old for toys now.' She poured him his coffee. 'Sugar, Major?'

'No, thank you.'

Oh, please, mother, don't say it. 'Sweet enough already, Major?' She'd said it.

He looked suitably embarrassed; as did she for saying it. Nerves. Pierre ground his pencil onto the oilcloth, breaking its nib. 'Are you all right, Pierre?' asked his mother.

'I need to go out. I said I'd go see Xavier.'

'Well…'

'You go, if you want,' said Georges.

'Yes, please, don't stay on my account,' said the major. 'You must all try to act as if I wasn't here.'

'Right,' said Pierre. A stern look from his mother stopped him from saying anything else.

*

'Well?' asked Xavier. 'Has he moved in?'

They were heading towards the town square. 'He's moved in all right. My mother couldn't be more creepy than if the Queen of Sheba had arrived. *It's no inconvenience, Major. Can I get you a coffee, Major? Sugar, Major? Sweet enough, Major? Can I stroke your hair, Major?* It's sickening.'

'You ought to send Kafka over. He'll sort it out. What about your dad?'

'He doesn't say much – as usual.'

'No guns today, boys?' asked a passer-by, Tautou, the carpenter.

'Why does everyone find this such a joke?' said Pierre. 'We're swamped by Krauts and we have to pretend nothing's changed.'

'What can we do?'

'You said it just now.'

'What?'

'Kafka. He'll know.'

'He's bad news, that man. My father told me to stay away from him.'

'Funny that, that's exactly what my mother said. Everyone's frightened of him all of a sudden.'

'Good God, look at the cafés; we've been taken over.' They had reached the square and the cafés dotted round the perimeter were all doing a brisk business – but not a Frenchman amongst them; every outside seat seemed to be taken by Germans. The mood was jovial, much laughing as the soldiers relaxed, helmets on the back of their chairs, smoking and drinking their coffees in the sun. With a jolt, Pierre spotted Claire. She was outside Café Bleu standing next to a table full of Germans. She had their undivided attention. With a laugh and a wave, she bid them goodbye and made to cross the square, a smile on her lips, a bounce in her step.

She saw Pierre and his friend. 'Hello, boys.'

'Hello, Claire,' said Pierre. 'What are you doing?'

'Me? Nothing. Oh, that.'

'You were–'

'Keep your voice down. I'm going to the baker's. Come with me.'

The boys accompanied her to the baker's and accepted her offer of a macaroon each. They waited outside while Claire went in. A girl of about eleven passed on a red bicycle. 'I'm surprised the Germans haven't requisitioned that,' said Xavier.

'Ha; don't give them the idea.'

'Here we are,' said Claire, reappearing with a baguette and three macaroons.

'Are you buying our silence?' joked Pierre as they walked on.

Glancing up and down the street, Claire seemed to take the accusation seriously. Speaking quietly, she said, 'It's Kafka's idea. He told me to get friendly with the enemy. He'd said I'd be an asset with my German and… well, whatever. Better to know what they're up to, he said.'

'And what are they up to?' asked Xavier.

She waited for an old woman with a walking stick to pass by. 'That's not for me to indulge.'

'Are you working for Kafka now?'

'No, of course not, I still work at the library. I need to go. I have to open up. What's the time? My watch's wrong.'

Xavier shook his head. 'They've changed the time, haven't they? We're on German time now.'

'I forgot. Oh no, that means I'm an hour late.'

'Don't suppose anyone will notice.'

'Nonetheless, I have to go.'

The boys watched her go towards the library, her hair bouncing, her skirt flowing behind her.

'Wait here,' Pierre told Xavier. Running, he caught up with Claire.

'Did you not enjoy your macaroon?'

'Claire, can I work for Kafka?'

She stopped. She ran a finger softly down his cheek. Her touch, however soft, sent a little surge of electricity through Pierre. 'Don't,' was all she said before walking off again.

Pierre ran up beside her. 'I don't understand. Why on earth not?'

'You're too young, Pierre.'

'I'm almost seventeen.'

'Exactly. Anyway, think of your mother; what would she say?'

'She'd–'

'She'd be horrified.'

Pierre watched her leave, waving to a friend across the street. Claire was new to the village; she'd come from Paris, apparently wanting to escape the capital and its Germans. She'd merely swapped one set of Germans for another. Pierre wondered whether the Germans in Paris were any different to the ones in the town. More pertinently, he wondered how long she'd stay. A couple of soldiers passed by on bicycles, one of them wolf-whistling at her. Xavier appeared at his side. 'What was that about?' he asked. He had speckles of crumbs on his upper lip.

'She reckons I could work for Kafka,' he said.

'What do you mean *work for*?'

'You know.'

He wiped his mouth with the back of his hand. 'No.'

'No, nor do I. But I intend to find out.'

*

Producing a sculpture is, foremost, a matter of patience. Occasionally, the family of the deceased wanted something different from the stocks of memorials Georges had at the ready. They wanted a different kind of angel, or Virgin Mary, or Jesus. And they had the money to pay for it. This, then, meant you had to work to a deadline, for no family wanted their loved ones to be deprived of their headstone for too long. But even with a deadline, one had to have patience. Remember, this was a monument that would remain in place for evermore; long after they themselves were dead and forgotten. This was the message that Pierre's father had instilled in him. The sculptor's art was unique, he said frequently, in that it involved both hard, physical work, yet a finesse of touch. They were labourers and artists; lackeys and craftsmen. Theirs was a job that came with great responsibility. After all, they were putting the full stop at the very end of someone's life. They had been given a solemn obligation by the ones left behind; one that came with an expectation that, with their craft, they honour the memory of a life now gone with a memorial that would last for eternity; a testament to the worthy life once lived. In accepting the obligation, they, as sculptors, had formed a bond with the departed.

He hadn't heard the German open the back door but he knew from the chickens running away that he had company. 'So, is this how you spend the day?' asked the major, holding a cup of coffee.

'Yeah.' He kicked away the tarpaulin lying at his feet.

'It's a beautiful spot.' Shielding his eyes from the sun, the major scanned the view. Pierre noticed the signet ring on his left hand, holding the coffee cup. The design was of a horse with a wild mane. 'How big is that woodland?'

'Fairly big.'

'Hmm. You have two sheds?'

'Yes, that one over there with the bike against it is where we keep the stone, the marble and the granite and stuff. Papa calls it the warehouse.'

'Is that your bike?'

'Yes. And this shed is for tools and things.'

The major opened the door of the nearest shed. 'Oh yes, a workman's paradise in here. What a lot of tools, and so much paint.'

'Papa wants to paint both sheds.'

'What colour?'

'Red.'

'Certainly bright. Do you mind if I sit for a while?' asked the major taking a seat on the rocking chair. Pierre shrugged with what he hoped was marked indifference. He was aware of the major watching him at work, chiselling away at the stone. 'So, is this to be a memorial?' the German asked, removing his cap.

'Yes.'

Why, wondered Pierre, had he not told the German the truth? After all, it was not a big deal. He wasn't doing anything wrong. But the man was a German; he had no right to be in his house, his yard, let alone his country. There again, he was but a man, an annoyingly nice man who washed his cup after he'd finished with it; something neither his father nor he had ever done; a man who rose to his feet whenever his mother walked in the room; why, he even put the toilet seat down and rinsed the sink after he'd had a shave. Pierre had been brought up believing the Germans to be a race of barbarians; brought up on stories of how they'd behaved during the last war; of atrocities committed; of nuns raped and children butchered. The image and reality differed in the extreme.

'It's not a memorial,' he said eventually. 'Papa reckons I'm not ready for a real memorial, although I have helped him lots. This is just for me.'

'Just for you and for your father – to show him you're perfectly capable.'

Pierre looked at the major – what right did he have to read his mind?

'And may I ask what's it going to be, this sculpture? Or is it an artistic secret?'

Indeed, Pierre had intended on keeping it a secret, but as neither his mother nor father had shown any interest it hardly warranted being classed as such. And the German had acknowledged that Pierre was embarking on a work of art.

'You don't have to tell me.'

'Venus.'

'Venus, indeed?'

Pierre got up, went to the tool shed and returned carrying a large book. Opening the pages at a bookmark, he passed it to the major.

'*The Birth of Venus* – Botticelli,' said the German. 'Sandro Botticelli. I have seen it.'

'You've seen it – in the flesh, the real thing?'

'Why yes. In Florence, the Uffizi. It's beautiful, of course. And so big. It's almost three metres long.'

'You've been to Italy?'

'Yes. In my early twenties. The Uffizi is the most wondrous place. One day you must go. It's perhaps even grander than your Louvre. Well, perhaps not so grand. You've been to the Louvre, yes?'

Pierre felt a prick of shame as he had to confess he had not; had not even been to Paris.

'Don't worry; you're still young. One day, when all this… this is over, you'll go – both the Louvre and the Uffizi, and you'll see Venus in the flesh, as you say, the real thing. Meanwhile, what you are doing is a grand endeavour; it's certainly ambitious. I'm impressed, Pierre.'

Pierre shuddered as a feeling of warmth cascaded through him, inducing such an unexpected wave of pleasure it left him momentarily disorientated. It was the way the major had said his name – not as a grown-up would but as an equal, a fellow lover of art.

'I have to go now; work to do.'

Pierre nodded; he wanted to say thank you but found it was simply too difficult.

The major stood and pulled the creases out of his tunic. 'I shall leave the artist to get on with his work.'

Pierre smiled.

Putting his cap back on, the major turned to leave. As he opened the kitchen door, he turned round. 'What do you plan on calling your sculpture?'

Pierre hadn't actually thought about a name. He stroked the dry sandstone and, on eyeing the thin layer of white dust on his palm, the name came to him in an instant. Grinning, he turned to the major and said, '*The White Venus.*'

Chapter 4

It was perhaps a week later. Already the family and their new guest had settled into a routine. True to his word, the major was out all day from eight, sometimes earlier, to about seven at night. He would return tired, having already eaten with his colleagues, sit quietly in the living room, reading a book, and retire early. On the fourth evening, much to everyone's delight, although Georges and Pierre tried not to show it, the major returned with a small joint of pork. The town, as a whole, was slowly becoming accustomed to the sight of the grey-green uniforms, the strangers within their midst. Sometimes people had to remind themselves that they were under occupation. The Germans went out of their way to be polite, speaking to the locals, accepting without complaint that shops charged them twice or thrice the going rate for every item on sale.

Meanwhile, while his father was out, Pierre worked on his sculpture, pulling off the tarpaulin each morning and chipping away at the stone, slowly bringing out a recognisable shape. It was still early days; it was going to be a long, rather daunting job.

One morning, Xavier burst in, barely able to contain himself. 'You have to hurry. They're coming through any minute. The whole town is gathering. Still working on your lump of stone, I see. Come on, hurry.'

Together with Lucienne, the boys joined the procession of people heading to the square. Again, thought Pierre, there was that same sense of carnival as the day the Germans had arrived. Was this the same feeling they had in medieval times when crowds gathered to watch an execution? Again, all the shops had closed down; the town had come to a standstill so they might witness the coming spectacle. It was well past one o'clock; Pierre was hungry. Strange, he thought, how quickly they had grown accustomed to the new time.

'Pierre, could you not have changed?' said Lucienne.

'I hardly think it matters, Maman.'

'Oh, but it does; impressions count on occasions like this – the whole town will be there, the mayor included.'

'And a lot of Germans,' added Xavier.

'Well, yes; best not to think of that.'

'Your Major H might be there.'

'I'm sure he wouldn't be involved in such things.'

Xavier pulled a face.

They joined the crowd of onlookers half way down Rue de Courcelles, one of the main arteries leading off the town square. Every few yards, standing guard, was a German soldier. Pierre recognised the soldier nearest to them, Fritz One. Xavier had seen him too. The man looked painfully hot in his tunic and buttoned shirt, standing to attention under the full glare of the sun. His colleagues opposite, at least, were in the shade.

Lucienne pushed through the crowds, suggesting they cross the road to the other side. The soldier put his hand up, preventing her from moving. The two of them, Lucienne and Fritz One, locked eyes for a moment. Pierre was impressed although he knew there could only be one outcome. Sure enough, she stepped back. Fritz One moved on a few yards. Muttering, Lucienne rummaged in her handbag and produced a fan. And there they stood; ten, fifteen minutes and more. Georges appeared, slipping through to join them. 'You look like you're going to the opera with that fan,' he remarked.

'Shush.'

It was only with his mother's shush, that Pierre realised the whole crowd was deathly silent. He heard the two o'clock chime from the town hall clock. Somewhere a dog barked.

And then they heard. A faint, faraway sound; the rumble of a motorbike and the shuffle of a thousand feet. Slowly, the sound became louder, the shuffle of feet nearer. Occasionally, a shout punctuated the air; occasionally a motorbike revved its engine. They were moving through the square; soon they'd be coming round the bend and down the street. Pierre's heartbeat quickened. But what was that noise; that new sound? With a jolt, he realised women were sobbing. And still the shouting; nasty, barked commands in German. People craned their necks as the first shadows appeared at the bend. A group of four German soldiers emerged, marching slowly, followed by the motorbike, mustard green in colour, with a machine gun mounted in its sidecar, its engine rumbling uncomfortably in first gear. And then came the mass, the pitiful mass of defeat. Lucienne held her hand over her mouth; Georges's eyes seemed to be on stalks; Xavier muttered a *merde*. There were so many of them, marching not as soldiers but as a shamble of ghosts, their khaki uniforms in tatters. Pierre watched, his stomach caving in with emptiness, as the parade of prisoners of war passed. And passed. The minutes ticked by yet still they came, hundreds and hundreds of men, Frenchmen; each and every one of these broken men had fought for France. The wailing of sobs spiralled like a funnel, gathering a momentum of its own. Pierre had never experienced such an outpouring of grief. He turned to see that his mother was openly crying. The Battle of France had waged a mere few weeks yet it had totally passed by their sleepy town. Although never too far off, it seemed to be happening somewhere faraway. Not any more, thought Pierre. He watched, uncomprehending, the dark, dirty faces, the haunted eyes. These men, united in defeat, were his countrymen, his brothers. Yet they did not seek the solace of the onlookers, the citizens. These men seemed unaware of their presence, unaware of anything. The crowd might as well not have been there. Marching alongside them, at regular intervals, were more Germans, their rifles drawn, bayonets glinting in the afternoon sun. But these weren't like the Germans in the town; their uniforms were black, altogether more sinister; somehow more serious. And still they came.

A woman standing next to Lucienne, Madame Philippe, the butcher's wife, slipped through the cordon of soldiers and placed a bucket of water at the side of the column. Her action was met by a murmur of approval. Lucienne fanned herself more vigorously. A PoW, his eyes wide as can be, scooped down with cupped hands. A soldier in a black uniform rushed up, shouting at him, and pushed him away. Despite this, another PoW tried also to snatch a few driblets of water. The German kicked the bucket over; it was too much for the prisoner who, exhausted, sank to his knees, causing the men behind him to crash into one another, to lose their rhythm. 'Get up, get up!' shouted the German. The Frenchman didn't get up. Lucienne took Pierre's hand. Xavier was crying. 'Get up, you bastard; get up.' Pierre knew he had to look away; knew he would forever regret it if he didn't. The German swung his rifle around and hit the prisoner with the butt, smashing it onto his back, followed by a vicious kick into the ribs. The Frenchmen fell onto his front and groaned. Pierre saw how hard the German's boots looked; steel toecaps capable of breaking bones.

The column moved on. No one stopped, sidestepping their fallen comrade. The German swung his rifle round again. A collective grasp echoed round as the German plunged his bayonet into the man's back. A splash of crimson but no sound. Using his foot against the Frenchman for leverage, he pulled the blade out; a streak of blood glistening on the steel. Women screamed. Many started crying. The German in his black uniform marched on, his rifle with its bloodied blade against his shoulder, the other arm swinging. Someone vomited. Men muttered words like animals, beasts, murderers. Madame Philippe tried to reach the stricken prisoner. She escaped the clutches of her husband, who implored her to get back, but failed to get past Fritz One, who pushed her back. 'For the love of Jesus, let me through,' she screamed. She tried again. This time Fritz One slapped her with the back of his hand. Madame Philippe fell, her hand against her cheek.

Lucienne put her arm around her. Madame Philippe's cheek was bleeding; a cut from a ring, thought Pierre. She glared angrily at her husband.

The hopeless column of men continued for another twenty minutes or more. No one took any notice of the dead man lying in a heap, the circle of blood on his back. Finally, the last men staggered by, followed by another motorbike and sidecar. The crowd watched quietly as they advanced down the street, round the bend and out of view. Everyone remained in place, too dazed to move, listening to the fading sounds of shuffling feet, boots and the motorbike. So many people, thought Pierre, but the air hung heavy with silence. The local Germans nodded at each other; their task for the afternoon done. Fritz One prodded Georges with his gun. 'Take him away,' he said in German, pointing to the body. Georges nodded. Monsieur Philippe, the butcher, offered to get an old door he had lying in his shed, pleased perhaps to appear to be doing something after his earlier humiliation. The door, he said, could be used as a stretcher. Georges thanked him; said he would wait. As the soldiers dispersed, Lucienne and Madame Philippe, and others, went to the body. Pierre watched them. They came away, shaking their heads, their eyes filled with tears. He was dead all right.

Kafka appeared and shook hands with Georges. 'Are you OK, boys?' Pierre and Xavier nodded. Turning to Georges, he said quietly, 'Was that convincing enough for you? We need to talk.'

'I need to remove our friend here first.'

'I'll help you.' While they waited, Kafka puffed on his pipe. He offered Pierre and Xavier a drag. They both declined.

Monsieur Philippe reappeared struggling with his door, its green paint peeling off. 'Can you manage?' he asked the men.

'We'll manage.'

'Good. Right oh. Er, I'll be off then.'

The stench filled the nostrils, a mixture of dirt and sweat. Xavier gagged as, taking a leg, he helped lift the body onto the door. 'God, it's heavy,' said Pierre, immediately regretting using the word 'it'. The trouser leg slipped away, leaving Pierre holding onto the man's leg. He recoiled at how dry it felt, how flaky the skin.

A small crowd of spectators had congregated, including Pierre's mother, clasping a handkerchief to her mouth, although he wasn't sure whether it was because of the smell or the emotion. 'Careful,' urged Kafka as they eased the body onto the wood. And there he lay; a nameless soldier heaped face down on an old green door. It didn't seem right.

'Take him to Monsieur Breton,' said Lucienne.

'No, take him straight to the church, hand him over to Father de Beaufort,' said another voice from the crowd.

'What do we do?' asked Kafka. 'The undertaker or the church?'

'Cut out the middleman, take him to the church.'

'The funeral parlour is there for a reason, Georges; to clean him up and all that.'

'The church is nearer.'

'Not sure we should use that as a criterion.'

'Perhaps we should have a vote on it.'

'But people are coming and going all the time.'

'Only men should vote.'

'And those over twenty-one.'

'Oh, for goodness sake,' said Lucienne. 'Georges, you were given the responsibility – you decide.'

Xavier whispered in Pierre's ear, 'Your mother should be the mayor.' Indeed, thought Pierre, feeling a rare surge of pride for his mother.

'The undertaker it is. Should we not turn him around?'

'You might be right,' said Kafka.

'More dignified.'

'OK, boys. We'll twist him clockwise.' The four of them tried to turn the body clockwise which meant Pierre and Xavier, at their end, going the opposite direction of the men. 'No,' said Kafka. 'What I meant…'

For the first time they saw the man's face; his dark but sallow skin, the hollow eyes, still open.

'He's from North Africa,' said Kafka. 'Algerian. Perhaps Moroccan.'

'He might have his papers in a pocket.'

'We'll leave that to Breton.'

'We need to close his eyes.'

But no one did. Instead, they stood and looked down at the man, the man from North Africa who had tried to keep France free. He had failed. They had all failed. Pierre thought of the German who had done this; how he so easily took another man's life; how he kicked away the water, denying the man everything. And then he had walked on; just walked away. Pierre couldn't understand; how could a man do that; how could life be so cheap? How did one become so hard? It was why France had lost. We're too soft. To win meant beating the Nazis at their own game; to toughen up. But how in the hell do you go about achieving that?

And so, it was to Monsieur Breton they went; one man

at each corner, the boys at the back with the feet, the lighter end. As they carried their heavy but precious cargo, people stopped. Men took their hats off; women crossed themselves and shielded the eyes of their children. Pierre felt as if the body, with his eyes still open, was staring at him. He tried not to look back. After five minutes, panting in the heat, they arrived at the funeral parlour but, like every business in the town, it was closed; the shutters pulled across the window. 'We'll have to wait,' said Kafka. And so they did; the body on its door, on the tarmac. Kafka re-lit his pipe. Pierre and Xavier pulled a face at each other; they were both thinking the same: it didn't need all four of them to wait for Monsieur Breton's return. But to say so seemed disrespectful. Neither could bring themselves to say it and so they remained. It was almost thirty minutes before Breton returned.

'My word, sorry to keep you waiting. What does it take to get a drink around here? Were you here long?'

'About–'

'Let's get him in, the poor chap, away from all these people. This way,' he said, unlocking the door. After the brightness of the day, it took a few seconds to adjust to the darkness inside. Monsieur Breton flung open the shutters, and blades of sunlight filled his reception area. 'Just bring him through to the back.'

Having laid out the body on Breton's marble slab, Georges took the door. The four men made to leave. 'Can I ask, gentleman,' said Breton, 'to whom I should present my bill?'

'Your what?' snapped Kafka.

'I don't work for free, you know. Would you? Work for nothing?'

Kafka and Georges exchanged glances. 'He died for you,' bellowed Kafka, 'fighting for your country. Is that not enough?'

'No, frankly, it is not. I work in a relatively small town. Not enough people die; I barely scrape by. You may live off the fat of the land, Monsieur Kafka, but I have a family; I can not.'

'My heart bleeds, but may I suggest, Monsieur Breton, that for a man who fought for your freedom, you waive your fee in this instance?'

'Fought for my freedom? What sentimental nonsense. Did you see that rabble?' said Breton. 'What a sad sight. Made me ashamed to be a Frenchman. No wonder we lost.'

'I suggest you hold your tongue.'

'You suggest a lot, Kafka. But whatever you say, we lost and it's no wonder. Who knows, a bit of German discipline might do us some good. Our children could do with a dose of it. Help toughen up young lads like these two.' Pierre was surprised to find Breton feeling his upper arm. Was he meant to flex his bicep, he wondered?

It happened quickly. Kafka pushed Breton against the wall, grabbing the undertaker by his throat. 'That poor sod died fighting for the likes of you.'

'Fat lot of good it did us, eh, Monsieur Kafka?'

Kafka tightened his grip. Breton spluttered, his face reddening, sweat breaking out on his forehead.

'Papa, stop him,' urged Pierre in a whisper.

Georges grabbed Kafka's wrists and pulled them away. Kafka relented, let go, snorting. Breton coughed and eased the pain from his throat. 'You... you maniac,' he gasped. 'Get out!'

'We're leaving alright. You just make sure you prepare this body properly; no short cuts. Understand?'

Kafka stormed out. 'What fine company you keep, Georges Durand,' said Breton. 'What a fine example to these boys.' Pierre and Xavier glanced at each other.

'He's a patriot, Breton; something you don't appreciate. Come on, boys, let's go.'

Pierre opened the door as his father struggled out with the green door. As he was about to leave, Georges said, 'Monsieur Breton, if I can also suggest something, you could present your bill to the mayor.'

Kafka was waiting further up the road, his back to them, a haze of smoke circling above his head. 'Here, you boys take this,' said Georges leaning the door against a building.

'Where are you going, Papa?'

'Kafka and I have business to discuss.' Pierre watched his father walk up to Kafka. Together the two men headed off.

'Jesus,' said Xavier. 'What a day. Do you want a cigarette?'

'You smoke?'

'I do now. Nicked them from my dad. Here, I have two.'

With cupped hands, Xavier lit both cigarettes, passing one to Pierre. The smoke hit the back of Pierre's throat, taking him by surprise, making his eyes water. He swallowed down a cough. The whole sensation was rather unpleasant. His legs felt woolly; he felt the need to sit down. But no, he wasn't going to give in. It was time to be a man.

They'd almost finished their cigarettes when Xavier

said, 'Watch out, here comes your mother.'

'Shit. Where? Here, take this,' he said, hurriedly passing his cigarette to his friend.

'Pierre. Hello, Xavier, again. Here you are. Did you manage to take the…?'

'Yes.'

'I can't find your father anywhere and I would like to go home now. Would you escort me, please?'

'The house is only over–'

'Pierre.'

'Yes, OK. OK.'

'Pierre, have you been smoking?' she asked, intensifying the use of her fan.

'No,' Pierre said, quickly.

'It's me, Madame Durand,' said Xavier stepping forward. 'I smoke.'

'You must be very addicted, Xavier, to have to smoke two cigarettes at a time.'

'Y-yes. Its… it's been a difficult day, Madame Durand.'

'Yes, it has. Come, Pierre, take me home now.'

'Yes, Maman,' he said, trying to suppress a sigh.

*

That evening, the atmosphere at home was equally subdued. They sat in the kitchen, Pierre and his father reading while Lucienne knitted, the click clack of her knitting needles being the only sound. Georges lit a cigarette; Lucienne pushed an ashtray towards him, a gentle reminder not to drop his ash on the floor. Pierre was flicking through a book on French artists, skim-reading a passage on the life of Auguste Rodin. A shiny plate featuring Rodin's *The Kiss* took up a whole page.

Pierre studied it, turning the book this way and that, admiring such a piece of work that somehow combined the classical and the modern. But the more he studied it, the less he saw and the greater the image of the bayonet, the crumpled figure on the road, the blazing sun, the German killer. Somewhere, faraway in Algeria, a woman, a mother, had no idea that today, in a small town in northern France, her son had been murdered. In cold blood.

They heard footsteps. Georges stubbed out his cigarette. A gentle knock on the door. 'Hello, only me.' The door opened. It was Major Hurtzberger. A round of 'good evenings' ensued, offers of something to eat, a cup of coffee perhaps. A coffee would be very nice, thank you. Do take a seat, Major. 'Pierre, get up, let the major have the armchair.'

'No, Pierre, it's fine, you sit. I'm alright at the table.'

But no, Pierre got up, insisted. He knew what was expected of him. The major sat, a buff-coloured folder on his lap, and let out a sigh of tiredness. He took his coffee. No one was quite sure what to say, so, for a while, they said nothing. Pierre's father picked up his book, and his mother resumed her knitting. The major leant back, cup in hand, his eyes closed.

Eventually, it was Pierre who spoke. 'A difficult day, today,' he said to no one in particular, repeating Xavier's phrase.

'Yes,' said the major. 'Quite a day. These things happen in war. I understand there was an incident. I hope you weren't witness to it.'

'Witness? It happened right there in front of us, Major,' said Georges. 'We had ringside seats.'

'Georges, don't trivialise it.'

'Oh dear,' said the major.

'Oh dear indeed.'

'I'm sorry you had to witness such a thing, Monsieur Durand. It was unfortunate. The men who were escorting the prisoners, the one who killed the man, they weren't Wehrmacht, like I am, like all the garrison here. They are SS.'

'They're still German. They're still one of you.'

'Yes but we have no jurisdiction over them. And they are, how shall I say, very committed to the cause…'

'Committed to the–'

The major put his hand up. 'Please, Monsieur Durand, I beg you to say no more.'

Georges look confused. 'Say no more? In my own home? I'll–'

'Georges, stop,' said Lucienne. 'I think what the major is saying is that however cordial we may act within these four walls, he is German, we are French, and it is best if we remember that.'

'Your wife, Monsieur Durand, is a wise and intelligent woman.'

'She is also,' said Lucienne, 'a very tired woman. I'm off to bed. Georges…'

'What?'

'You must be very tired too. And you, Pierre.'

'You're telling us when to go to bed now?'

'It might not be a bad idea, Papa.'

Chapter 5

The following morning, Georges left early to catch a bus to Saint-Romain and arrange a new delivery of marble; after all, he'd said, they'd have a new addition to the graveyard soon, once Monsieur Breton had done his work, and the poor blighter will need a headstone of his own. Pierre decided to make the most of his absence and work on his sculpture. The yard was mainly in shade. With a slight draft, he felt chilled enough to wear a smock. The chickens pecked around him – Mirabelle, Madeleine, Marion, and the rest. All the M's. He knew at some point he'd be joined by the major. Sure enough, after little more than ten minutes, the back door opened and the major appeared holding a steaming Eiffel Tower cup of coffee. The chickens flapped and fussed. 'Your mother makes a fine coffee,' he said. 'Good morning, Pierre. Should be another fine day. So how's it going with the White Venus? It's beginning to take shape, I see. You work fast.'

Yes, thought Pierre. It was a matter of confidence as his father always told him. The more you chipped away, the less there was of the stone left standing and the more important the work. This is the point where things could go wrong. But too much caution can be counter-productive; can act as a break on creativity. This is where you had to firm up your plan and have the conviction in achieving it. No holding back.

'Listen, Pierre, I was thinking. Once it's done, your work, would you like to see it displayed at the town hall?'

'The town hall?'

'I could have a word with the mayor. I'm sure he would be accommodating.'

'Well, yes, I suppose so. That'd be good.'

'Excellent! Consider it done.'

'But he might say no.'

'I'm sure he won't.'

Pierre might have imagined it but he thought he saw the major wink. He tried not to show it but Pierre was staggered by this. That it could be so simple. He knew full well that if he, or his father, approached the mayor with such a request, they'd be laughed at. But not the major. A click of the fingers and it's done. This, in a small way, was the meaning of power. He tried to resume his work but felt too conscious of the major's presence. At least it meant he didn't have to look at him, so he carried on, making inconsequential chips.

'Thank you,' he said in a whisper.

'That's OK. I have a son like you, Pierre.' He took a large gulp of coffee and stared out over the fields towards the woods. 'He's quite a lot like you, really. Joachim. A bit older though. Just turned nineteen. In two years, for his twenty-first, I'm going to give him this.' He held up his hand, showing Pierre his signet ring.

'A horse?'

'Yes. Generations of my family were cavalrymen. It's a family tradition to be given the ring on one's twenty-first birthday. Well, the boys. Joachim's just joined the army. He had no choice really. Not now. He's already finished his training. When I joined up, we had months of training. Joachim had just a few weeks. Hardly ideal, in my opinion, but these are far from ideal times. The army needs men; the Führer needs men. And Joachim is a man now. He wanted to be a vet. I told him he'll have plenty of time to be a vet when it's all finished. When all this is finished. I'd have preferred it had he joined the Luftwaffe. Now there's a glamorous job. His mother would have preferred it too. But no, he's in the army, infantry, a foot soldier like me. Here, would you like to see a picture of him?'

Frankly Pierre did not but as the photograph was thrust at him, he had little choice but to 'oo and err', as his mother would say. The corner of the photograph was creased, otherwise it was intact. It wasn't just the boy but the whole family – the major and the boy standing behind his wife and a girl, seated. The girl must have been about ten, her hair in plaits, wearing a white, collared shirt with a cravat. For reasons he didn't understand, Pierre found the image revolting even though, as individuals, they each seemed pleasant enough. Father and son were in uniform, everywhere little swastikas, on all four of them – a badge, a brooch, a tie, an armband.

'It was taken about two years ago. Unfortunately, his mother and I are no longer together. Brigitte, my daughter, lives with her mother. Joachim was in the *Hitlerjugend*.'

'The what?'

'Hitler Youth. Brigitte is in the *Jungmädel*; that's for girls ten to fourteen. Or is it fifteen? I can't remember.'

'Yes, very nice.' The boy looked big, as tall as his father, broad in the shoulders, proud to be in his uniform. A fine Nazi family. He handed it back. The major looked at it, the familiar picture, smiled, and returned the photograph to his breast pocket.

'It's nice to carry a reminder.'

'Yes.'

'Yes, anyway, I ought to be going. Work to be done and all that. Do you ever use your bike?'

'Occasionally.'

He finished his coffee. 'Nice to talk to you again, Pierre. You're a fine lad. See you this evening.' He made to leave but then, at the kitchen door, stopped. 'I've been meaning to ask – who's that man on the tightrope in the photograph in your kitchen?'

'That was my Uncle Jacques. He was killed when I was small. Hit by a car.'

'Oh. And the photograph of the boy? The boy with the cap?'

A flash of memory shot through Pierre's mind – a teddy bear with a yellow waistcoat and green trousers. 'No one,' he said firmly.

'And those toys in my room?' he asked hesitantly. 'Do they belong…?'

'No one.'

The major considered his answer for a moment; nodded and left.

More images appeared unwanted – a haversack in the water, bubbles, a bucket of worms. He shook his head, trying to free his mind of the memory.

It was only after the major had left that the thought

occurred to Pierre that they had no need for any more marble. He checked the shed at the far end of the yard, the warehouse, as his father called it. He was right; there were several slabs of it, enough for many new headstones. So where exactly, he wondered, had his father gone?

*

Later, Pierre found the major talking to his parents. His father was still upset over the killing of the Algerian. 'There is such a thing as compassion, you know, Major Hurtzberger,' said Georges. 'Even in war.'

'Of course, I realise that.'

'My husband fought in the last war,' said Lucienne.

'I know – I can see the medals from here. And the helmet.'

Pierre was so used to his father's framed display of medals, he'd quite forgotten they were there.

'Yes, so don't tell me about the necessities of war, Major; I was there. I know what it's like to be expected to kill another man; I know what it's like to expect to be killed. I once tried to show compassion. Did your father fight? Was he there?'

'Yes.'

'Perhaps it was him then. Him or someone very much like him. After all, none of us are that different, are we? Whatever side we fight on; whatever cause. I tried to show a man, a German, compassion. I had a choice. That's what compassion is, isn't it? You have a choice and you make a decision. A moral choice for which you have a second to decide. I decided. I thought I'd done the right thing, taken the right path, as the church tells us. A moment of compassion, Major Hurtzberger. Unfortunately fate intervened...'

'Georges, come, dear, you're being too hard on yourself.'

'What appals me is that your man acted as if he had no choice. He had every choice. The prisoner was unarmed and harmless. A defeated man. Your SS man murdered him. That wasn't the act of a soldier; that was the work of a barbarian.'

'Monsieur Durand, I advise you to be careful. You put too much faith in me. I can appreciate your distaste–'

'Distaste?'

'Let me finish. We have reached an understanding, you and I, your family. I regret we've had to meet under such circumstances. But I will not tolerate such denigration of Germany's forces. I have my superiors to answer to. I'm sure, as a former soldier, you understand that.'

'Yes, I understand, Major Hurtzberger.'

With a bright smile, Lucienne asked, 'Another coffee, Major?'

He laughed. 'Most kind, Madame Durand, but no thank you.'

*

Pierre was queuing in the baker's. After twenty minutes, it was almost his turn. A number of people were behind him. Outside, several children played. Behind the glass-fronted counter were Madame Gide and her ten-year-old daughter, their hair bunched up in hairnets, their aprons dusted in flour, their fingers white with the stuff, looking increasingly flustered with the unending queue of demanding and complaining customers. Until just a few weeks ago, the glass cabinet boasted vast arrays of cakes and cream buns. Not any more. Now it was bread and nothing but bread. And not much of it. Everyone knew that it wasn't Madame Gide's fault but still they took the opportunity to chastise her, as if she, and not the Germans, was responsible. Pierre just hoped there'd be some left by the time he got to the front of the queue. They'd heard that the Germans would soon be issuing coupons so that everyone had a fair share. He just hoped they'd hurry up because Madame Claudel, the locksmith's wife, three in front of him, seemed to be buying up the whole shop. It was stiflingly hot inside, with so many people, and the sun streaming through the large window, exposing myriad streaks of grease on the glass. Behind him stood Madame Clément who kept tutting at the amount of time it was taking and complaining to Madame Picard behind her, while her child had a continual sniff which, after a while, Pierre found mildly irritating. If he'd had a handkerchief, he would have given it to her. Madame Picard pulled away her dog, a white terrier, from Madame Clément's child. But time, at least, now passed quickly as everyone discussed in hushed but animated tones what Monsieur Gide, the baker, had just heard on the BBC in London. While his wife and daughter continued serving their customers, he had been at the back clandestinely listening to the radio. He came out and told everyone, loudly, what he had just heard, and he was not happy about it. 'How dare he?' he said.

'Who?'

'I don't know; some general. Never heard of him. But he was on the radio – just now. Talking nonsense about carrying on the fight.'

'What did he say exactly?'

'I'll tell you, I wrote some of it down. Listen.'

The queue gathered together, becoming not so much a line but a circle of people, all eager to hear what Monsieur Gide had heard.

'Of course, I didn't get all of it but I got the gist.'

'Go on then.'

The baker adjusted his rimless spectacles and cleared his throat. He was enjoying this, thought Pierre; more concerned he should not lose his place in the queue. 'He said, "France is not alone". That with our empire and the British, we can defeat the Germans. He said, "Is defeat final? No." Then later, he said, "The flame of the French resistance must not be extinguished." Or something like that.'

'Was that it?'

'No, of course not, Madame Claudel, there was a lot more, but I'm not a secretary taking a dictation, you know. He spoke quickly.'

Madame Claudel huffed. 'So where he is, this general?'

'In London.'

'London?' came the chorus.

'Shush, keep your voice down.' Emerging from the sudden silence, Madame Clément's child continued sniffing. 'Pierre,' said Monsieur Gide, 'keep an eye out the door, make sure no Boches are passing.'

'What? Me? But I'll lose my '

'Go on, boy,' said Monsieur Gide, waving his arm. 'If anyone comes, shout, *What, no more baguettes today?*'

'You want me to shout that?'

'Do as he says,' said Madame Bonnet, standing next to her husband, the chemist.

'Such insolence,' agreed Madame Clément.

'So what's he's doing in London, this man on the radio?' asked Monsieur Bonnet.

'Telling us to fight.'

'Oh, that's awfully decent of him. Easy for him to say that safely tucked away in England.'

Pierre stood at the door, keeping it ajar, trying to listen while glancing up and down the street. In the distance, he could see Xavier ambling with a hefty book under his arm.

'Gide, you must remember his name.'

'It sounded French.'

'No surprise there, Gide; we're all bloody French.'

'Monsieur Bonnet, please mind your language in front of my lady customers.'

'My apologies, ladies,' said Monsieur Bonnet, removing his beret in a sweeping movement.

'I think his name was Gaulle. Or *de* Gaulle. That was it – General de Gaulle.'

'I see what you mean, that *is* a French-sounding name. So this General de Gaulle in London says we're to rely on the British?' said Bonnet loudly.

'Keep your voice down, man. But yes, in essence.'

'The British?' shrieked Madame Picard. 'Well, we've seen what the British can do.'

'That's right,' said Bonnet. 'First bit of trouble and they're scrambling back home, sobbing all the way from Dunkirk. We lost the war because of them. Traitors.'

'They fought to the last drop of *French* blood before running away.'

'My husband says we lost the war because of the communists,' said Madame Claudel.

'How's that then?'

'And the Jews,' shouted Madame Picard. 'Despicable

lot.'

'Exactly. The Jews stole all the petrol.'

'The Bernheims are Jewish and they're quite nice,' said Madame Bonnet. 'Very nice, in fact.'

'Wolves in sheep's clothing,' muttered her husband behind his hand. 'Don't trust them, my dear.'

Pierre beckoned his friend over. 'Psst, Xavier, come here.'

'What are you doing?'

'Buying bread, you fool. What do you think I'm doing? Listen, I dare you to shout out, *What, no more baguettes today?*'

'Why would I want to do that?'

'Go on. Double dare.'

'What, no more baguettes today?' he said.

'No, that's no good; no one heard. Do it louder.'

Xavier shrugged his shoulders and repeated the phrase with volume.

Inside the shop, customers clashed into each other as a surge of panic took hold. 'Quick, they're coming.'

'Back in line,' urged Monsieur Gide. 'Back in line. Quick, quick.'

'I was before you,' Pierre heard Madame Clément say.

'No, you certainly were not.'

Another woman moaned, 'I wasn't this far back,' as she was pushed past Pierre and out into the street. 'This is outrageous.'

'Have you not bought enough already, Madame Claudel?' said a voice inside. 'There are other people, you know.'

'I have a big family.'

'And whose fault is that?'

'I beg your pardon?'

Still at the door, Pierre and Xavier started laughing. He heard Madame Picard's voice. 'Good God, your child has just wiped his nose on me.'

'It was an accident.'

'Disgusting child. Can't you wipe its nose?'

'But, Gide,' said Monsieur Bonnet, 'you still have loads of baguettes.'

'For goodness sake, did you not hear me say? That was my code for the boy Durand.'

'But he didn't say it, that other boy did.'

Suddenly aware of all the faces turning round, Pierre pulled on Xavier's sleeve. 'I think we should go,' he whispered. 'Quick, run.'

'Oi, you two, come back here, you scamps.'

A minute later, having escaped the bakery, they stopped running. Two German soldiers passed, walking slowly.

'Morning,' said Xavier between breaths.

No response. Pierre whispered, 'Tell them to check out the bakery.'

'You are a sod.' He waited until the soldiers were out of earshot, then asked, 'So, what was all that about?'

Pierre laughed. 'I'll tell you later. It's strange, though, everyone seems to have changed in the last few days.'

'The whole world's changing; hadn't you noticed? Soon there won't be a Europe; we'll just be one vast German Empire, the swine.'

'Yeah, you're right. So, what do we do about it?'

'Go to the library. My mum told me to hand this book back in.'

'It's big.'

'Marcel Proust.'

'That's big.'

'It's called *Remembrance of Things Past*. Looks dead boring to me.'

'It's big.'

'Stop saying that. Anyway, why were you at the baker's?'

'Buying a skirt.'

'You are an idiot as well as a sod. Come on, you can come with me. You'll get to see Claire stamping books.'

'Do you think she'll say *shush* for me?'

'Tickle her feet, she might.'

The library stood alone – a small, solitary building beneath a looming oak tree at the end of a quiet street. It was known less for its books than for the surrounding garden that the previous librarian had tended with much care. The path leading up to the library entrance cut through an abundance of summer flowers, the names of which Pierre didn't know. But what made him stop in his tracks was the sight of his father walking briskly in front of him. He was about to call out but thought better of it.

'What's he doing here?' asked Xavier.

'No idea.'

'Maybe he fancies Claire.'

'Piss off; she's mine.'

'Yes, right.'

'She just doesn't know it yet.'

'Well, let's find out what your dad's doing there.'

*

After the heat of the morning, the library felt deliciously cool. Pierre and Xavier found Claire, wearing, thought Pierre, a fetching blue frock, behind the counter, running her finger down the spines of a pile of books. 'What brings you two here?' she asked. A skylight in the roof allowed in a slither of light, illuminating tangles of cobwebs, behind Claire's counter, mounted on the wall, another portrait of Marshal Pétain.

Xavier handed over the Proust while Pierre strolled round the library looking for his father. The shelves backed high against the wall, beneath the small square-shaped windows. A couple of stacks jutted out, books either side. It didn't take long to confirm that his father wasn't there.

'What are you doing?' he heard Xavier ask Claire.

'Rooting out banned books.'

'You're doing what?'

Pierre returned to the counter, now thoroughly puzzled. 'Pierre's Major H was here earlier,' she said.

'He's not my Major H.'

'He gave me this list,' she said, holding a piece of paper, 'and said if I had any of these books I had to remove them from the shelves.'

Xavier scanned his eyes down the pile of books. 'Shakespeare? Dumas? Are they banned?'

'They are now.'

'They should ban that Proust; it could be used as a weapon, it's so heavy.'

'Are you all right, Pierre?'

'Have you seen my father? We saw him come in here – just a minute before us.'

'Your father?' She shook her head. 'No, he's not been in.'

'But–'

'I said no.'

'And Victor Hugo?' said Xavier. 'Why would *Les Miserables* be banned?'

'Ask Pierre.'

'What?'

'Yeah, come on, Pierre,' said Xavier. 'Why's your major banned Hugo?'

'He's not my–'

'And why have you got him up there?' asked Xavier, pointing to the portrait of Pétain.

'Why do you think?'

'Pierre's major.'

'Exactly.'

'I will not rise to the bait.'

Claire patted his arm.

Pierre decided to try again. 'So, my father – he didn't–'

She lowered her eyes. 'No.'

'No.'

The door swung open, and there, wielding a baton, was the major. On seeing the assembled, he stopped in his tracks. The four of them looked at each other while an undercurrent of surprise, mild embarrassment and awkwardness skirted from one to another. 'Hello again, Pierre, Xavier. Well, this is quite a little gathering.' Turning to Claire, he clicked his heels. 'Mademoiselle, how have you got on with the list?'

'I didn't think you'd be back so soon, Major.'

'I couldn't resist your charms too long. Anyway, I was passing.'

Pierre noticed Claire's face redden; her finger twirling a coil of hair. 'I've made a start. We haven't got all these books.'

'I see. Some excellent titles here, Mademoiselle.'

'Yes,' said Pierre. 'Xavier here was just wondering–'

'No, I wasn't.'

Claire laughed.

The major leant against the counter. 'And do you have any of these books behind the scenes? A basement perhaps?'

'No, no, not at all,' replied Claire.

'I see.'

'Can I offer you a coffee, Major?'

'A library that serves coffee? That's progress.'

'No but… In my office, if you like.'

'We never get offered coffee,' said Xavier.

'Very kind of you, Mademoiselle. As much as I could linger within these walls of literary merit all day, I have things to see to. I bid you good day.' With another click of the heels, he saluted and left, tapping his baton against his leg.

'Did you see that?' said Xavier.

'He clicked his heels.'

'Twice,' said Pierre.

'*I have things to see to. I bid you good day, Mademoiselle.*'

'At least he didn't say Heil Hitler.'

'Shut up,' said Claire. 'Both of you.'

'Do you have a basement?'

'No. Well, perhaps.'

*

They waited some distance away from the library on the other side of the road, behind a tree that stood alone on a square of grass. Lying on their fronts within the tree's shadow, they plucked at blades of grass. A few people passed but no one took any notice of a couple of teenagers lounging round on the green. Xavier lit a cigarette. Pierre took a few puffs and immediately began to feel sleepy. As he dozed off, he wondered what his father was doing in the library basement, especially as he was behind in his job of completing the headstone for the Algerian. Was that why he kept rushing off, pretending to be doing errands, when in fact he was meeting Kafka and the others?

But it was the way Claire and the major spoke to each other that really perturbed him. Perhaps Claire had been merely using her charms to distract the major from what was happening in the basement but Pierre feared it was more than that. They spoke as if they'd known each other for a while and Pierre didn't like it one little bit.

They'd been there for over half an hour when Xavier nudged Pierre hard in the ribs. 'That's Bouchette coming out,' he said. Monsieur Bouchette ran the local garage.

'We didn't see him go in,' said Pierre, rubbing his ribs.

'How do you know? You were asleep? A fine lookout you'd make. But you're right, we didn't. Look at him, looking left, right and everywhere. The idiot.'

'How not to draw attention to yourself.'

'He's got a book though. Let's hope it isn't *Les Miserables*. So where's your dad?'

'And who else is in there?'

Five minutes later, Monsieur Dubois emerged, wearing a blue beret, also carrying a book, heading in the direction of the town square.

'Bloody hell, he's carrying the Proust. He can hardly read a shopping list let alone something like that.'

'Wait, here's my father.'

They watched him hurry away from the library. The boys melted back behind the tree as Georges passed them, a book under his arm. 'He'd better be going home to work on the Algerian headstone; otherwise he'll have the mayor after him.'

'And look who it is…'

Standing at the library entrance, lighting his pipe, was Kafka. Throwing away the match, he looked up to the sun, smiled to himself, and walked off.

'The whole bloody town is up to something and we're not invited,' said Xavier.

'We'll just have to do our own thing then.'

'What – you and me? Our own two-man cell?'

'Exactly. I've got an idea. Meet me here at nine.'

'At nine? Kraut time? You've got to be joking. That's curfew.'

'All the better. Less people around.'

*

Sitting in the kitchen with his parents and the major, Pierre began regretting his haste. He pretended to read while wondering how he could extricate himself at this time of evening without arousing suspicion. His father and the major were talking music and books while his mother dried the plates. Despite saying otherwise, the major now seemed to be eating with the family most evenings. Not that they minded as he often returned from his work with something to eat – a cut of lamb, fresh vegetables, things that were harder to come by with each passing day. Pierre listened as his father extolled the delights of Beethoven and Brahms and German composers generally, while the major lauded Debussy and Ravel, and other great French composers. They seemed to be falling over each other in their praises. Lucienne, stacking the plates, winked at him.

'And you're reading Flaubert, I see, Monsieur Durand. You got that from the library?'

'Yes; this morning.'

'How strange. He was on my list.'

'List?'

'I'm going to bed,' said Pierre.

'Already?' said Lucienne. 'Are you feeling all right?'

'I've got a headache.'

'Well, wait there, I have some–'

'No, Maman, I'd rather just go to sleep. I'm tired anyway.'

'Tired?' said Georges. 'But you've not done anything today.'

'Nonetheless.'

'Pierre was also at the library this morning,' said the major. 'Weren't you, Pierre?'

'Were you?' said Georges.

'Not for long. Goodnight.'

Pierre took off his boots and placed them under his bed, putting on a pair of soft-soled running shoes. He sighed; this was a ludicrous idea. His door had no lock and he could hardly wedge it shut with the chair. He just hoped if his mother came in she would know enough not to say anything – at least not in front of the major. But he was committed now; he couldn't abandon his friend. He took some clothes out of his wardrobe, folded them over and put them on his bed, under the blanket. It was nowhere near enough. In the end, he had to use every item of clothing he had in order to create a human shape.

Earlier, Pierre had left a can of red paint together with a brush, a flat-headed screwdriver and a couple of pages from a newspaper behind the shed. Now, having put his tools of sabotage into his haversack, he slipped out of the yard and into the night. Still warm, the atmosphere outside was heavy with heat, and how silent the evening; not even the slightest wind to disturb the leaves. It was almost dark but, once his eyes had come accustomed, still plenty of light to see by. There were no street lamps – the Germans had seen to that. The people of the town certainly took the curfew seriously – not a soul in sight; all hidden away behind their shutters. The thought gave him courage – he and his friend were the only ones, out of all these people, prepared to make a stand against their occupiers. One day, maybe years ahead, he would be remembered and feted; for this, he decided, was but the start. They would tell no one for now and the whole town would wonder, as one, who was this hero in their midst; the mysterious fighter prepared to make a stand? Perhaps he would tell Claire. And she would fall in love with him. He visualised her yellow skirt, her soft legs. Calm down, Pierre, calm down, he told himself. He resisted the urge to run; after all, he was in no hurry. He heard the town hall clock chime nine o'clock. For a moment, he thought he saw movement up ahead. He stepped back into the shadows. Deciding it was nothing he moved cautiously on. He realised how much he was enjoying himself; every sense was on full alert, acutely aware of his surroundings, his heart pumping, and it felt great. He told himself he had to breathe deeply, to relax his muscles; he felt invincible yet, at the same time, knew he had to act with utmost trepidation.

He reached the tree where he had arranged to meet Xavier but there was no sign of him. A little bit of enthusiasm slipped away; he felt himself deflate. But it was only a couple minutes past nine. Xavier would show. He leant against the tree, facing away from the street, and waited. Nearby, an owl hooted. He counted the seconds in his head. Sixty seconds. Then another. The more he waited, the more he felt his courage draining away. He knew, if necessary, he could do this alone but he needed the reassurance of his friend's presence. On a more practical level, he needed a lookout. Bloody Xavier, where in the hell are you? He thought of home; thought of his bed, and wished now he was back there. What was he thinking of? Suddenly he saw his town, this place he'd known all his life, in a new light. It seemed bigger and in its utter silence a rather frightening place. A town of the dead, of the cowed. Sixty seconds more. He'd give him just one more minute while he tried to work out what to do. He would do it; damn him, he'd show him that he, Pierre Durand, had the bravery to act alone, a solitary act of defiance. It was better that way. He thought of Claire; he thought of his father, his mother. They'd be proud of him. The romantic within was coming back to the fore.

Leaving the safety of the tree, Pierre embarked on the walk up to the town square; his heart pumping furiously inside. Feeling a little sick, he tried to breathe away his nerves as each step took him closer to his fate. Constantly he looked round him, straining his eyes for even the smallest movement, checking for places he could hide in if need be. He was passing Monsieur Breton's, the undertaker's. The thought of the dead Algerian inside gave him renewed strength. If the Algerian could give his life for France, then the least Pierre could do was to make his small but symbolic stand for freedom.

The high-pitched noise made him jump. He squealed in fright as he fell back against the undertaker's wall, the can

of paint clanking against the brickwork. He saw the glint of
light in the eyes of the cat, a little black and white thing,
before it scurried away. Pierre leant against the wall,
catching his breath, and rolled his eyes heavenward.

He pushed himself on; his legs weakened by the fright.
He was nearing the bend in the road now, buildings on
either side and no doorways to hide in. Here he knew he
would be vulnerable. He feared he heard voices – German
voices. Peering round, the town square came into view –
Soldier Mike, the town hall with its huge swastika banners
hanging down, the square of grass, the decorative trees.
And there crowded round a bench beneath one of the
trees the silhouettes of about five German soldiers, talking,
smoking, occasionally laughing. He stepped back. Doubt
seeped through him again. What was he thinking; why was
he doing this? What if they caught him; what would they
do to him? He was only sixteen; they'd let him off, surely,
with no more than a verbal clip round the ear. The voices
– they'd stopped. Perhaps they were coming. He had to
run back but instead he glanced round the corner. He saw
them walking leisurely away in the opposite direction; their
rifles against their shoulders. Oh, the relief. He had to act
now – a moment's hesitation and he'd lose his nerve for
good. He waited until the soldiers had moved out of view,
then, holding his bag to his chest, sprinted across the
cobble-stoned road and to the nearest tree. He'd made it
this far. The bravado chased away the demons of doubt.
The clock showed nine fifteen. Was that all, he thought; he
felt as if he'd been out on his mission for hours. Checking
to see the coast was clear, he dashed for the next tree. He
plucked a leaf. From the tree, a quick run to the war
memorial. It was only now that the thought occurred to

him that the Germans might post a sentry at the doors of the town hall. But, as far as he could make out, they had not. He almost laughed. He'd got to the last tree, the last point of safety. The town hall door was just a few yards away, a little stretch of no man's land between him and it.

Checking again for movement, straining his ears, Pierre took a deep breath, thought of Claire's smiling face, and stepped out from behind the tree. Across the cobbled stones, he walked quickly, resisting the urge to run. Crouched down by the door, the entrance afforded him the comfort of darkness. Fumbling, he took out the can of paint and eased open the lid with the screwdriver. With paintbrush in hand, he suffered a moment of hesitation – the solid oak door seemed too good to deface. But seconds later he had painted an enormous red 'V'. He had done it. The rest came easily as he worked quickly. He thought of his mother; she'd be so proud, his dear maman. By the time he was painting the last 'e', he was giggling under his breath. Now he felt exultant; felt like screaming with joy. His work done, he wrapped the brush in newspaper and put everything back in his haversack, tying it shut, shaking with excitement.

Making sure again he was still alone, he stepped back and admired his handiwork. In glistening red paint, letters writ large, he had written *Vive La Framce*. He clenched his eyes shut as the realisation hit him. What a prized idiot; what a bloody fool. He thumped his thigh with frustration. He knew immediately how it had happened – it was the point he'd been thinking about his mother. The 'm' for *maman* had subconsciously gone where the 'n' should have been. Could he fix it? No, his nerves were frayed enough; he knew he'd used up his courage for the night, possibly a lifetime; he had to get home. His bed couldn't come soon enough.

He'd only made it as far as the second tree, the war memorial still ahead of him, Soldier Mike upon his plinth, when the stillness was shattered by the single shout: 'Halt!' Had he hesitated a single moment, he would have stopped. Instead, he ran. And ran. 'Halt!' came the voice again, this time even more urgent, more threatening. Gripping his bag to stop it clanking against him, he ran knowing his life depended on it, his vision blurred with tears. The sharp crack echoed through the air. He instinctively knew that it was a warning shot, fired high. The next one would be aimed at him. He sensed the German taking aim, closing an eye. Dead at sixteen; shot in the back. *Vive La Framce; Vive La fucking Framce.*

He felt himself trip; felt himself fall as if in slow motion, flying through the night air. He landed in a heap at the base of the tree – the very tree he had lain against with Xavier earlier in the day, so long ago; the tree where his friend was supposed to meet him. The side of his head had hit the trunk, the bark scrapping his ear, which now throbbed in pain. Panting heavily, lying on his front, he knew he was done for; finished. There were more panicked shouts in German – two or three of them, then several more, it seemed. He could hear the pounding of footsteps, boots on tarmac, a whole bloody battalion of them coming his way. In a rush of certainty, Pierre knew he had come to his last few moments. All he felt was a deep irritation that his final mark on the world should be a misspelt act of graffiti. Then came the unmistakeable rev of a German motorbike, more shouts, orders, rifles clicking, men ready for action. He almost laughed at the amount of effort they seemed to expending on his behalf. They came running – dozens of them. He closed his eyes, preparing for the bayonet in his back at any moment. But they were running past him; they'd missed him. Peering up from the grass, he felt as if they weren't making much effort to find him. He watched, bewildered, as they rushed by, making room for the motorbike and sidecar which roared through them and raced ahead. He lay on the grass, his ears pounding, and watched as perhaps a dozen soldiers disappeared into the distance, past the library and beyond, the sound of their boots fading away. His eyes remained rooted to the spot where they had disappeared from view. The burst of activity had left in its wake an eerie silence, an imagined echo of boots. Looking around he realised he was very much alone. Not a German in sight. Pierre's relief was tempered by a hint of anti-climax; a faint sense of disappointment that he hadn't been the focus of their attention. He told himself not to be so ridiculous. He wondered where they were going, what had seized them so utterly? There was nothing in that stretch of town apart from the railway line. Oh good God, he thought; someone was attacking the railway line. Someone had the gall to trump his graffiti. The swine.

The town hall clock struck half nine. It had been quite the longest half hour of his life. He rolled over and lay on his back, exhausted. But it wasn't over – a rustle of footsteps on grass had him scrambling to his feet, preparing for an attack.

'Pierre, Pierre,' came the familiar voice. 'It's me.'

Pierre breathed; realising he'd been holding his breath. 'Where the fuck have you been?' he said, sitting back down.

'Keep your hair on,' said Xavier, crouching. 'I'm bang on time. Half past nine.'

'I said nine.'

His friend was wearing his father's beret. Far too small for him, the fool; it made his ears stick out. 'You said half nine.'

'No, I said nine.'

'This could go on for a while.'

'You idiot.'

'What happened to your ear?'

'It's a long story.'

'Anyway, we've been beaten to it,' said Xavier, looking round. 'Someone had the same idea and painted all over the town hall door. But you never guess what?' He laughed as he said it, 'The suckers have gone and misspelled France. Put an 'm' instead of an 'n'. I mean, how stupid can you get? What bloody idiots.'

'Yeah,' said Pierre, feeling his whole body sag. 'What bloody idiots.'

*

Someone had locked his bedroom window. As well as meaning he couldn't get back in, it meant someone, probably his mother, had been in his room. Anything beyond a cursory glance and they would have realised that it was a pile of clothes in his bed. He deposited his bag in the shed, closed the door and wondered how on earth he was going to get back inside. He heard the chickens cluck within their pen. Leaning against the wall, the Algerian's headstone. His father had done more than he thought, even as far as half the wording. He laughed at the thought of his father engraving 'France' with an 'm'.

74

If his parents knew he'd gone, they'd be waiting up for him, however long it took. Circling round the house, he tried the front door. Locked. Creeping past the major's bedroom, he knocked on his parents' window. No answer. He hadn't expected one. He had no choice; he would have to knock on the kitchen door and hope to God the major didn't answer. He swore in frustration.

He tapped gently on the kitchen door. Not even a mouse would have heard that, he thought. Stealing himself, he knocked a little louder, then louder still.

'Who is it?' It was his mother. How lovely to hear her voice.

'It's me,' he whispered back.

The door opened and Lucienne almost pulled him into the darkened house, into the kitchen, lighted by just a couple of candles. 'Where in the blazes have you been?' she shouted, taking Pierre by surprise.

'Maman, keep your voice down!'

'Oh, don't worry – no one's here. I mean *no one*. First your father went out, then the major, someone called for him, and then I discover you'd gone too.'

'What? Where did they go?'

'You think they told me? No. You all leave me and I'm left alone worried sick.'

'Don't worry, Maman, I'm sure the major will be back soon.'

'Don't try to be funny. So where were you?'

'What?'

'You heard me. Where were you?'

'I can't tell you. I'm sorry. Business.'

'Funny that; that's exactly what your father said. It's not a game all this, Pierre, it's… What's happened to your ear?'

'I fell over,' said Pierre, rubbing it.

'On your ear? And what's that blood on your fingers?' She took his hand and turned it over. 'It's paint. Why have you got… OK, you're right; I don't want to know.' With a heavy sigh, she went to the sink to wash her hands. 'Did you see your father?'

'No.' She looked at him accusingly over her shoulder. 'No, really; I promise.' After a while, he asked, 'Is there a power cut?'

'No.'

'So why the candles?'

'Your father told me. Wants the world to think we're in bed.'

'The world? It's empty out there; no one will notice.'

'I'm only obeying orders. Anyway, it's not empty – out there somewhere is your father and the major, and I don't imagine for one minute they are together.'

Chapter 6

Pierre laid on his bed, the curtains open, a hint of sun shining through, motes of dust dancing in the air. He fancied a cigarette. It was still only seven. In the distance, he could hear the rumble of several trucks – he'd learnt that the Germans always went out on exercise at this time, always at seven. He dreamt of Claire, as he often did first thing in the morning. He was kissing her, always kissing her, only the location changed with each day. Today, he was kissing her at her work, in the library; next to them the pile of banned books, his hand on her breast. It seemed sacrilege to be fondling the librarian's breast in front of such greats – Flaubert, Shakespeare, Proust. He really could do with a cigarette. The sound of his parents talking filtered into his consciousness. So at least his father had made it back. The tone of their voices sounded normal; they weren't arguing. His father had already been forgiven. Back to Claire. He groaned. He dreamt of her nibbling on his ear – no, that hurt too much. 'Kiss me,' she whispered while pushing away Proust. She had such lovely lips. Pierre realised he had an erection.

'Pierre – breakfast time.' Claire vanished in an instant. 'Oh, dear. I do apologise.' His mother backed away from the door. 'I should've knocked,' she said, now knocking. 'I'm so sorry.'

He grunted.

'I'm sorry?' she said, still hovering outside the door. 'I didn't quite catch that.'

'Nothing, Maman. Nothing.'

'Can I come in?'

If you must, he thought. 'Yes,' he said, readjusting his blanket. 'OK.'

She slipped into his bedroom and, glancing surreptitiously behind her, closed the door. She was wearing an apron – a rarity these days, since the major moved in. She opened her mouth to say something but stopped as she registered the state of his room – the poster of Rita Hayworth which she always regarded as provocative; his bureau scattered with books and papers; the overflowing bin full of pieces of rolled-up paper; his dusty mirror, partially obscured by a French flag; the chest of drawers covered with statuettes, a chisel, and model aeroplane and goodness-knows-what and, leaning against it, a guitar he no longer played. She didn't have to say it, he needed to have a tidy-up.

'Pierre,' she said, sitting down gingerly on the edge of the bed. As soon as she sat, she shot up again. 'Oh, sorry; do you mind if I sit?'

He shuffled up against the wall. 'Yes, what is it, Maman?'

She checked the door. 'Listen, Pierre, about last night. I haven't told your father you went out; he doesn't know.'

'And you think we shouldn't tell him?'

'Yes, I think it'd be for the best. At least for now, for a while.'

'Fine. Is the major in?'

'Yes, he's having breakfast.'

'Good. Can I get up now?'

'Oh yes,' she said, getting to her feet. 'Sorry, I didn't mean to disturb your... I mean, your... well,' she added, cheerfully, 'breakfast is ready.'

*

Pierre ate his boiled egg in silence next to his mother at the table while his father and the major, opposite, discussed violin concertos. No one mentioned the railway. Pierre could tell that the major's musical knowledge was far superior but he was going to great lengths to play it down, not wanting to embarrass his host. Why, the major said, he had seen the great Furtwangler conduct. Pierre had never heard of Furtwangler but the name sounded grand and his father was certainly impressed.

'Sleep well?' his father asked him, spreading jam on his toast.

'All right,' he replied, wondering why, of all days, he'd ask a question he'd never asked before.

'What happened to your ear?'

'I fell.'

'When? It was all right when you went to bed last night.'

'I just fell.'

'Leave him be,' said Lucienne, quietly. Georges shrugged and bit into his toast.

'I passed through the square late last night,' said the

major, a coffee mug in his hand. 'Someone had painted a slogan over the big doors of the town hall.'

'Delinquents,' said Georges.

'Petty vandalism; it was nothing.'

'What did it say?' asked Lucienne.

'It said *Vive La France* in big red letters.'

Georges laughed. Pierre concentrated on his egg and soldiers aware that his mother had shot him a look.

'Silly thing,' continued the major, 'is that somehow they misspelled France.'

'What?' exclaimed Georges. 'How do you misspell France? Ha, it must've been the work of a German. No true Frenchman would have misspelled the name of his own country, for goodness sake.'

'Well, I'm afraid it will be a Frenchman who will have to scrape it off.'

Pierre grimaced as he swallowed down his spoonful of cod liver oil.

'Are you all right, Pierre?' asked Georges.

*

After breakfast, Pierre went to the yard and, having gathered his tools from the shed and donned his goggles, began work. The yard was still bathed in shadow; it would be another hour or so before it caught the sun. His father had already been out and unlocked the chicken pen. He watched them pecking at their seed, uncomfortably aware that news of his graffiti would be spreading through the town by now. He took no pleasure that everyone would be wondering who had done the deed. No one could ever know – the shame would be too much. He wanted to go and see it, see his work in the daylight but decided to wait;

thinking it best not to rush out. Instead, he would spend a little time with his White Venus.

He'd been chiselling away for ten minutes or more when the major appeared, as he knew he would. 'It's progressing, I see,' said the German. 'She's beginning to take shape.'

'Hmm.'

'It's lovely to see; a work of art being created before our very eyes.' He sat down on the rocking chair but then promptly got up again, disturbing the chickens from their pecking. 'I admire your dedication. When Joachim was young he used to paint. He wasn't bad. He doesn't paint any more; doesn't have the time, poor boy. I received a letter from him yesterday. The army's keeping him busy. He tells me they'll be on the move soon. Of course, he can't tell me where. Could be Poland, North Africa, Holland. Perhaps even France. I would love that. I miss him, you know. His mother is very proud of him, I'm sure. I know you are French and he German but you would like him, my Joachim. You're very similar in many ways.'

Pierre watched him from the corner of his eye. The man seemed on edge, pacing up and down, hands behind back, kicking little stones with the toe of his shiny boots.

'It does seem very young to put a boy in uniform. He's nineteen, but nonetheless. You'd have thought we would have learnt from the last war, but no. I know he couldn't wait to play his part, to fight for the Führer. But it's a cause of constant anxiety. I'm sure you understand.' He looked up at the sky. 'It's another fine day. Not a cloud in the sky. A fine day for the beach. Do you ever go to the beach here? I suppose it's quite a distance. When I was a boy... Listen to me. I talk too much. I ought to go.' He paused, deep in thought. 'It's times like these,' he said, eventually, 'that you think back to your childhood and it all seems such a long time ago. My father had a little shed like this. He used to sit at the door after dinner and smoke his pipe, staring up to the sky, looking at the stars. My mother, bless her, wouldn't let him smoke indoors.' He laughed, peering inside the shed.

Pierre wished he would go. He had enough to think about without this foreigner unburdening himself.

'What a lot of paint in here.' Pierre tried to focus on the work in hand. 'Red paint too, I see.' The major readjusted his cap. 'Well, Pierre, time I was leaving. It's been lovely talking to you. Keep up the good work.'

'Yeah.'

Pierre watched him leave, watched him as the major paused at the kitchen door. Without turning, the German said, 'Be careful, Pierre. It's a dangerous place out there. Just… just be careful.'

And with that he was gone.

*

A while later, Pierre was joined in the yard by his father, wearing his overalls, a pencil behind his ear, a damp cigarette between his lips. Without acknowledging his son, he pulled out his little stool from the shed and sat down in front of the headstone. He looked at it for a few minutes, checked the wording written for him on a sheet of paper by the mayor, and set to work on the headstone, delicately engraving the letters.

The two men, each with a chisel and hammer, worked in silence. After a while, the temptation to go see his graffiti became too much. Laying down his tools, Pierre removed his goggles and wiped the dust from his trousers. He left without saying anything. His mother was doing the washing, having pulled out the mangle, despite the warmth of the day outside. The kitchen smelt of damp linen. He washed his hands batting off questions from his mother asking whether he was feeling OK. 'You're very quiet this morning, Pierre,' she said, holding one of Georges's shirts, her head tilted to one side as if to emphasise her concern.

'I'm fine, Maman,' he snapped.

*

A small crowd had gathered in front of the town hall, sniggering at the slogan on the doors, shaking their heads as if in disbelief. Standing back, too afraid to mingle among them for fear they would sense his guilt, Pierre couldn't help but agree – it looked ridiculous. Nearby, a couple of soldiers watched them, little smiles on their faces. Pierre recognised Fritzes One and Two.

Vive la France. The letters were not as big as he thought. 'What must the Germans think of us,' he heard someone say. 'It's embarrassing,' said another. Pierre recognized Madame Picard, a baguette poking out of her basket. 'If I find out my son did this, I'll put him over my knee.' 'But he's nineteen.' 'I don't care; this is a disgrace.' The town hall doors opened. People stepped back. It was the major accompanied by a policeman, a Frenchman, with, thought Pierre, unusually long sideburns, a folder under his arm.

Pierre felt ridiculously pleased to see his German, pleased for the distraction. 'Hello, Major,' he said, brightly.

Striding past, the major saw him, looked straight at him with cold eyes, but made no acknowledgement. Pierre watched the two men go. Maybe, he thought, he had had the sun in his eyes. The major shouted something at Fritz One who saluted in return. Fritz One approached the gathering and said something in German. He repeated it, this time more loudly. 'I think he wants us to move on,' said Madame Picard. 'Let's hope they catch the little bugger who did this,' said someone. Slowly the crowd dispersed. Pierre watched the major and the policeman enter Café Bleu on the far side of the square, taking a table outside. A new sign had appeared above its door – *We welcome our German guests*.

'Hey, you.' Pierre heard the soldier shouting in German. 'Oi, are you deaf?' said Fritz One, poking Pierre in the arm.

Pierre turned to see the German holding out something in his hand. 'What?' It was a strip of sandpaper. Motioning with his head towards the door, the penny dropped. 'You… you want me to…?'

'Take,' said Fritz One in French, thrusting it at Pierre. Pierre looked round, hoping somehow to be saved. 'Take.'

'What now? Me?' Reluctantly, he took the sandpaper. '*Merde.*'

Fritz One strolled back to his colleagues who had formed a small semi-circle, their arms folded, their helmets pushed back on their heads.

And so Pierre began work, starting not at the beginning but at the 'm', the letter that had so mocked him. The sun beat down on his back and he soon broke out in a sweat. His hand ached as he rubbed and rubbed at the paint which, predictably, proved mightily hard to remove. Every now and then, the door would swing open, causing each passer-by to stop and look disdainfully at what he was doing. No one spoke to him. The soldiers giggled. One of them shouted at him. He turned to find the German taking a photo. Finally, they tired of the attraction and melted away. Only Fritz One remained, to ensure Pierre didn't slack. After half an hour, drenched in sweat and thoroughly miserable, he asked for a break. '*Nein*,' said Fritz One, motioning for him to carry on. Pierre hoped to God the major couldn't see him from the other side of the square, basking in the sun with his coffee. Indeed, he hoped no one would see him at this, his greatest humiliation. But, of course, at some point every person he had ever known, or so it felt, passed by and asked him what he was doing. 'You can give me a hand, if you want,' he'd said to Xavier. But no, Xavier had things to do, slapped him on the back, wished him good luck and, mounting his pushbike, buggered off on his merry way. The worst, of course, was the appearance of Claire, looking gorgeous in a lime-coloured blouse, her brassiere clearly visible beneath the fabric, and a rose-patterned skirt, the picture of gaiety. 'Poor Pierre,' she said. 'They should find the idiot who did this and get him to do it. It's not fair you should have to. Must go. Bye bye!'

Half an hour on, and Pierre was only half done. He needed a drink and both his hands throbbed. Fritz One kept guard still, pacing up and down. Pierre looked across at the café. The policeman had gone but sitting in his place, laughing and talking with the major, was Claire. How comfortable they looked together. Pierre groaned. Could the day get any worse?

*

Some thirty minutes later, exhausted and thoroughly

dejected, Pierre had finished. He had managed to scrape the red lettering off but the words were still visible as he had also removed much of the blue paint beneath. The doors would need re-painting. He was thirsty and hungry. For now, Fritz One seemed prepared to let him go. He sat down on a bench near the war memorial. Realising he had a few centimes in his pocket, he decided to treat himself to a coffee at Café Bleu.

Claire and the major were long gone but most tables were full of German soldiers leaning back on their chairs, helmets to the side. Many were singing, clapping their knees in time. An elderly French couple occupied the table nearest the door, trying their best to ignore the boisterous Germans near them. Having been outside for too long, Pierre was relieved to experience the cool and darkened interior. It was the town's smartest café – a two-toned red-and-white linoleum floor, a bookshelf full of ornamental books, framed pictures of cockerels hanging from the walls above the dado rail, a standard lamp, and a glass case full of crockery. The place smelt pleasantly of real coffee and cigarette smoke. In an annex on one side, a couple of soldiers played table tennis, while others watched and cheered, their shirtsleeves rolled up. The only thing that spoilt it was a framed portrait of Hitler with his silly moustache and icy stare. He wondered whether its placing, next to the door of the gents' toilet, was accidental. He hoped not. He sat at a table for two beneath Hitler, decorated with a long glass vase and a single flower, and ordered a black coffee and a single cigarette. A waiter in black and white returned with his coffee, cigarette and a clean ashtray. 'What's that awful song they're singing?' he asked the waiter.

'Keep your voice down. That's their *Horst Wessel* song. They're always singing it.'

'Their what?'

'Named after some dead Nazi martyr.'

Pierre leant back and allowed the rush of nicotine to pulse through his veins. The coffee, syrupy and strong, helped revive him. Things, he concluded, were not going well. His first act of sabotage had backfired in ways he would never have imagined and he had been chastened in front of the whole town and particularly in the eyes of Claire. He would finish his coffee and then seek out Kafka and demand he be allowed to join whatever he had formed.

A laugh erupted from a table of soldiers nearby. Much back-slapping ensued. In a peculiar sort of way, Pierre realised he rather envied them. They were men, doing men's work, united by their uniforms. Pierre had nothing – no sense of belonging. Just a vague feeling that the honour of France had to be salvaged, but this gave him no satisfaction – it was too big a concept, too nebulous, to mean anything on a practical level. He needed direction, to belong, to have a leader. He needed Kafka.

He was suddenly aware of a soldier standing over him, barking at him in an unpleasant tone. 'Out,' said the soldier in German. 'Get out of this seat.'

'I'm sorry?' The man, all six foot of him, was a lieutenant.

'I need this seat. I need to work,' said the lieutenant in heavily accented French, waving a file at Pierre.

'Yes, you can sit here, if you want,' said Pierre, motioning to the chair on the other side of the table.

The German considered the offer. With a shrug of the

shoulders, he sat down.

Pierre finished his cigarette, trying to hide his discomfort at sharing a table with a Boche. The German ordered a hot chocolate in bad French, then, pushing his peaked hat further up his head, opened his file and started to read. Pierre considered the man while trying not to. He wished he had something to read. The German seemed incredibly young – not more than a few years older than himself, but his face looked hard, his skin tight. He thought of the major's son.

The German looked up and caught Pierre staring at him. 'What are you looking at, little froggy?' he said in German.

'I'm sorry?'

'You speak German? No? Good.'

Pierre smiled.

'So, what's it like to drink your coffee beneath a picture of the Führer, eh? That's how it should be,' he said, nodding.

Pierre nodded back. 'Yes.'

'You're a fawning little shit, aren't you?'

'Yes.'

The German laughed and Pierre found himself laughing too. 'Are you a little Frenchie froggy, yes?'

'Yes, yes.'

'Ha! That's my boy.' The German glanced up worriedly at Hitler's portrait. 'We should not speak like this in front of the Führer, you scum.' Abruptly, he stood up and, facing the painting, saluted his leader, his arm outstretched. 'I'm sorry, *mein Führer*, forgive me my language.'

It was time, thought Pierre, to make a hasty exit. Rising to his feet, he quickly realised, was a mistake – the German thought that he too wanted to pay his respects to Hitler.

'Salute the Führer.'

'Yes.'

'Go on then,' said the German, elbowing Pierre hard in the arm.

'Ow. What?'

The waiter appeared at his side, carrying a tray with a number of dirty cups and saucers. 'Lieutenant Neumann wants you to do the Hitler salute.'

'What? Me?'

The lieutenant barked, 'Show some respect, Frenchie boy,' his arm still outstretched.

'He doesn't look too happy,' said the waiter. 'I'd do as he says, if I was you.'

'I can't,' said Pierre, his stomach caving in. 'Not that.'

The German turned to him, his eyes ablaze with anger. 'You salute the Führer, you little French frog.'

'Just get it over and done with,' said the waiter. A German customer called him over. 'I won't say anything,' he said as he left, balancing his tray.

And so Pierre found himself in Café Bleu standing next to a rabid Nazi who resembled a fury on the verge of tears, in front of a painting doing a Hitler salute. It was the final humiliation; he just hoped to God no one had seen him.

*

Pierre worked furiously, hacking away at the stone, sweating beneath his goggles. He changed them for his sunglasses. The yard at this time of day offered not an inch of shade. The hens had taken to their pen. Only Maurice the cockerel remained outside. He wasn't going to let a bit of heat keep him from his duty. The incident with the Nazi had proved to Pierre that all Germans were bastards; that he'd been a fool to allow himself to be charmed by the major. He was a German, serving Hitler, and by default no better than the bastard lieutenant. He would no longer listen to the major's whinging and waxing lyrical about his precious son. He was a Nazi too; they were all fucking Nazis. They had no right to be in his country and he would do whatever it took to play his part in kicking them out. He was relieved his father wasn't around; he needed to be alone, to think. His father was always out now. He, at least, had found a purpose, a cause. His mother popped her head round the kitchen door, asked him if he was hungry. Hungry? He felt weak with hunger. Even his mother had a cause, albeit one she didn't relish, the cause of finding food on a daily basis. And it could only get much worse. At the moment, only luxury things like cakes, butter and real coffee, seemed to have disappeared, almost overnight. Now, only the cafés frequented by the Krauts, had them.

As he was eating his bread and cheese, wishing it were so much more, his father returned, looking mildly perturbed. Although, mused Pierre, the emotional distance between perturbed and euphoric covered very little ground with his father. And he seemed continually entrenched in neutral, viewing a world that induced no feeling great or small, for the better or the worse. He remembered, before the war, his mother once returning with a brace of herring, a rarity, bought from a travelling fishmonger. She slapped the fish down on the kitchen table, remarking Georges was no longer the only cold fish residing in the house. A twitch of the moustache was probably the only response she got.

Georges sat down, stood up, paced up and down.

'Are you OK, Georges?' asked Lucienne.

'I'm fine, Lucienne.' He then did something that Pierre had never seen before – he reached out for his wife, took the bread knife she was holding and placed it on the table, then put his arms around his wife and hugged her. Why, wondered Pierre, did this unexpected and totally out of character show of affection worry him so?

*

Most of the population had never had a car. Georges once did, an old Daimler inherited from his brother, the tightrope walker, but even that had died a death a few years back. Now, all the family had was Pierre's bicycle. A few businesses owned a truck and that was about it. But they had mostly been requisitioned by the Germans – cars, lorries, motorbikes, the lot, together with the petrol. While the German staff drove round in their front-wheel drive Citroens, all that was left for the locals were the bikes. And whatever the farmers had – tractors mainly. The 'cemetery boys', as Pierre's father always called them, were allowed to keep their old wagon, and this battered four-stroke was now outside their bungalow, a small black monstrosity of a vehicle. The cemetery boys were, in fact, two bent old men, whose combined age, by Pierre's reckoning, must have been 120. Standing in the yard, hands on hips, soggy cigarettes on their lips, they admired Georges's handiwork, the Algerian headstone. Pierre made a half-hearted attempt at sweeping the yard, causing the hens to scatter in a cloud of dust and downy feathers. The two of them were mirror images of each other – both scrawny old men in dirty dungarees, skin as tough as leather, grey hair beneath their flat berets, thin moustaches, both smoking. 'Very nice,' said one, his voice gruff with age.

'It wasn't difficult,' said Georges.

'At least you spelt "France" proper.'

'And what have we got here, young Pierre?'

'It's my sculpture,' said Pierre, sweeping, wishing now he had left the tarpaulin over his work.

The man stroked his chin. 'Is it meant to be a woman?'

'Has she got any clothes on?' asked the other.

'It's classical.'

Both men laughed raucously. Even Georges guffawed while Pierre bristled.

'Classical, eh? Is that what you call it? And you feel qualified to carve the female form in all its glory, eh?'

Pierre blushed. 'I've – I've got a book on Renaissance art. It's Botticelli.'

'Botcha what?'

He was about to tell them its name but held back. He realised he hadn't even told his father its name, nor his mother. Only the major knew. He feared anyone else would only consider it pretentious, and mock him.

'Come on, boys,' said Georges. 'We need to press on.'

'In a hurry, are we, Georges?'

Georges didn't answer but it was enough to stir the men into action. They may have been ancient, mused Pierre, but they were strong. Between them, they hoisted up the headstone and, with Georges guiding them, urging them to be careful, carried it out through the yard door and round the front of the house, grunting, and onto the back of the truck. Pierre followed. The truck sagged with the weight of the headstone.

With the tailgate secured and with much wiping of hands, they were ready to leave. 'Where's your new family pet then, Georges?' asked the first chap, grinding his cigarette into the pavement with his boot.

'Our what?'

'I hear you've got your very own Kraut?'

'Oh, our family pet. Very funny. I don't know where he is. Have you seen him, Pierre?'

'Me? No. He's out.'

'Well, I worked that much out for myself.'

'So what's he like then?'

'I don't know; I have very little to do with him.'

Apart from long discussions about music, thought Pierre.

'You haven't poisoned his soup yet?'

'Leave him alone,' said the other as they climbed into their truck. 'They're not a bad lot, these Krauts. They'll sort out the commies for us, that's for sure. This country's gone soft. Not like your generation, eh, Georges?' He turned on the ignition and the old truck spluttered into life. 'Dig out your old bayonet, Georges; show them what we're made of.'

The truck bounced down the road, billows of black smoke in its wake. Emerging from the cloud of fumes, returning home with bulging shopping bags, was Pierre's mother.

'Do you still have your bayonet, Papa?'

'Don't be daft.'

'Hello, boys,' said Lucienne. 'Good news – plenty of marrows today.'

'Is that what you've got in those bags. Anything else?'

'No,' said Lucienne, lifting a bag as if in triumph. 'Just marrows. I've been to church as well.'

'Great. Well, I have to be off.'

'Where are you going?'

'Out.'

'Where?'

'To get my wages from the town hall – for the headstone.'

'Good, we could do with the money.' Lucienne went indoors, huffing. That, thought Pierre, was a hint that he should have carried her bags. Instead, he ran after his father, quickly catching him up. 'Papa, can I come with you?'

His father looked straight ahead. 'To the town hall?'

'No, I mean… I want to help.'

'With what?'

'With… whatever it is you do.'

His father laughed – heartily, a laugh that pierced Pierre.

'Go home, boy. Help your mother stuff a marrow. Have you slaughtered Madeleine yet?'

Pierre stopped and watched his father saunter down the lane, shaking his head. As he returned home, the White Venus beckoning, he remembered his father and Kafka remonstrating with Monsieur Breton, the undertaker, for wanting to claim payment for his work on the Algerian.

He passed through the kitchen where he found his mother stroking a marrow as if it were a cat. 'Are you OK, Pierre?' she asked.

'The world is full of hypocrisy, isn't it, Maman?'

'Yes, Pierre, I suppose it is.'

*

An hour later, Pierre was on his way to the library. His father's dismissive laugh was bothering him still, disrupting his concentration. Georges still hadn't come back and the longer he took the more agitated Pierre felt. Giving up on the White Venus, he covered it with the tarpaulin and decided to head for the library – to see if he could find his father there, plus, of course, the library always had the additional bonus of Claire's presence.

He slipped out of the house before his mother had chance to allot him an errand. He knew the library would probably be closed – it was often closed. No one in this town ever read. They'd probably read even less now, now that the major had stripped the shelves of all the interesting books. He thought of calling on Xavier but decided against it. He wondered whether fifty, sixty years hence, he and Xavier would resemble the cemetery boys. What a thought and not altogether an unpleasant one. Assuming of course they weren't all German citizens by then. He passed the baker's – the queue seemed to be longer with each passing day. He noticed Xavier's pushbike leant up against the wall. So his mother also got him to do the bread run. He resisted hiding his friend's bike, just to see the expression on his face.

He could see from a distance that the library doors were closed. He thought, nonetheless, he'd go investigate. Madame Picard was walking her dog, the little white terrier, on the grass, a small yappy little thing with a short tail. He saw it do a shit right near the tree he and Xavier had sat against.

Sure enough the library doors were locked. Yet one of the windows above him was slightly open. Disappointed, he walked round the building treading delicately on the gravel path but to what purpose he wasn't sure. He arrived back at the point he started from. He'd not seen or heard anything. He noticed a brick had fallen out from the sidewall. Without a second thought, Pierre had wedged his boot in the hole and clambered up the wall, grabbing the windowsill. It wasn't easy; he could feel his foot slipping. With some effort, he managed to lever himself up and was able to peer through the window. Inside it was dark but there at the counter he saw a figure, perhaps two. His foot slipped and he fell. He looked about. Madame Picard had gone; no one else was around. Someone was inside the library; he had to see who it was. He climbed up to the window a second time, pushing his boot into the hole as far as it could go. Holding onto the windowsill, he pressed the side of his face against the glass. He gasped. Something like a sledgehammer hit him on the chest. His legs turned to jelly. Unable to prevent himself, he fell, landing in a heap on the gravel path. His eyes blurred over. A pain gripped his heart.

'Are you all right there?' It was Madame Picard who had reappeared out of nowhere. Her dog sniffed at him. He scrambled to his feet, fighting back the urge to scream, fighting the urge to kick the sodding dog, the ugly mongrel. 'Are you... are you crying?' said Madame Picard, relishing the moment.

She stepped back on seeing the look of rage on his face.

He walked quickly, muttering the word 'bitch' over and over again, his fingers digging into his scalp. He could feel the bile at the back of his throat. He shook his head, as if trying to free his mind of the image. But it remained, imprinted, refusing to fade away. The image was of Claire – on the counter, her eyes closed, running her fingers through his hair; her skirt ruffled up, her legs around him as he fucked her, his trousers down at his knees. The bitch.

They'd kill her if they knew; they'd kill her for that; they'd bloody string her up for fucking a German, a fucking German, the fucking major.

Chapter 7

Pierre stared at his sculpture, wondering whether to carry on with his work. What held him back was the fear that the major would make his usual morning appearance before he went off to work, or to fuck Claire. Pierre couldn't bear the thought of seeing him. He'd spent the previous evening shut in his room, reading and sketching. He could hear his father and the major talking about art. He pricked up his ears whenever he heard his name mentioned – usually in the form of compliments from the major, about his artistic eye, his feel for sculpture. He waited for his father to say something of his own accord. But no. Nothing. Today for the first time in weeks, there was no sun. Overcast but still warm. His mother had been urging him to go to the town hall and ask if they had any jobs. So far, he'd resisted. His father's work, although well paid, was sporadic. It was, after all, a strange way of making a living – to wait for someone to die. Fortunately for Georges, his catchment area included the nearby town of Saint-Romain, five kilometres away. It was where the

Germans had set up their headquarters; they'd requisitioned a large office block next, apparently, to the dentist's. But she was right; he needed his own job.

The kitchen door opened. Pierre made to leave. He saw the major. 'No work today?' he asked.

'No,' said Pierre, barging passed.

'Pierre,' called his mother. 'If you're passing the baker's…'

And so he found himself, again, queuing up at the baker's. Outside, on the door window, the Germans had put up a notice announcing a blanket ban on anyone attending the funeral of the Algerian, due the following day. *Any citizen attempting to attend the funeral will face harsh consequences*, it read in bold red letters.

Inside the bakery, Pierre saw Xavier a few places ahead of him. They saluted each other. Monsieur Gide, the baker, was reading aloud from his newspaper. Marshal Pétain, apparently, had now been confirmed as president. 'He's too old,' said Madame Picard. 'He doesn't know what day of the week it is.' 'You don't know what you're talking about,' came a reply from further up. 'He's the right man for the job. At least he's here, unlike that de Gaulle man, spouting nonsense from his cosy London home.' 'You know, Pétain's found him guilty.' 'Who? De Gaulle? How can he? He's not even here.' 'You can try someone *in absentia*, it's called. And they've found him guilty of treason and he's to be shot.' 'In London? Will the English do that?' 'No, not the English. If he steps foot in France again he'll be arrested and then shot.' 'Shush, here come the Germans.' 'They've got Touvier.'

Pierre recognised the young lieutenant from Café Bleu, Lieutenant Neumann, walking ahead of two privates, his rifle over his shoulder, his belt buckle glinting in the sun. The soldiers were leading a dishevelled Monsieur Touvier, the blacksmith. Pierre slunk back behind Madame Picard; he didn't want the lieutenant to see him. Touvier, his overalls streaked with the dirt of his trade, was clasping his beret, his eyes looked wide with fright. But as they passed the bakery, Touvier shook himself free of his minders, and shouted at the queue. 'You have to resist, all of you; before it's too late, you have to—'

The lieutenant punched him hard in the stomach, bringing Touvier to his knees. He groaned, clutching his stomach while the queue gasped as one. One of the privates kicked him in the ribs. Touvier fell but was immediately scooped up by the other.

'Leave him alone,' shouted Monsieur Bouchette, stepping out of the baker's. Taking his revolver from its holster, the lieutenant strode up to the Frenchman who stood transfixed while those inside melted back. Without a word, the lieutenant pointed his revolver, pressing it against Bouchette's forehead. The two men glared at each other. Bouchette's courage took Pierre's breath away. The thought of that cold barrel against bare skin made him shiver. Slowly, Bouchette put his hands up. With quick movements, the lieutenant returned the gun to its holster and clicked shut the button, all the time keeping his eyes fixed on Bouchette.

He motioned at the privates to follow him. Now gripping the spluttering Touvier more firmly by his arms, they dragged the unfortunate blacksmith away.

The queue breathed a sigh of relief as Bouchette returned indoors. 'Are you OK, Monsieur Bouchette?' 'You're so brave.'

Pierre and Xavier acknowledged each other with raised eyebrows.

'Monsieur Touvier is right,' said Bouchette. 'We can't just let the Boches ride roughshod over us.'

'What did they want with Monsieur Touvier?'

'Perhaps it was to do with the other night. You know, on the railway.'

For his bravery, Monsieur Bouchette was allowed to jump the queue to be served ahead of everyone else. He left, with two baguettes under his arm, to a round of applause.

*

Xavier and Pierre walked home together, Xavier pushing his bike, a baguette each. 'You should do that,' said Xavier.

'What?'

'Stand up to the Boches like that.'

'What and get my head almost blown off?'

'Yeah, but just think how impressed Claire would be. Girls love that sort of thing.'

Pierre's stomach ached at the thought of Claire. 'So, you're an expert on girls now?'

'It's obvious, isn't it? What's the matter? You all right?'

'Yeah.'

'We could go out later, maybe–'

'No. Can't today.'

*

On returning home Pierre told his mother about the blacksmith. She called Georges in from the yard and made Pierre repeat the tale.

His father blanched. 'Shit. When did this happen?'

'About half an hour ago. Maybe more.'

'And you've only just come back?' He sprang over to the front door, turning the key and bolting it locked.

'I didn't want to lose my place in the queue.'

'You didn't want to… Oh Lord.' He began pacing up and down the kitchen. 'Someone's talked.'

'Georges, what's the matter? What are you talking about?'

He looked at his wife and Pierre, glancing from one to the other. 'Look, that night up at the railway.'

'Oh no, please, Georges, don't tell me you were involved.'

He nodded. He seemed to take no pleasure from confessing his involvement because, Pierre knew, Lucienne would be furious. He waited for the barrage of anger but instead his mother collapsed in tears. 'Georges, no, I begged you.'

'I had to. I've waited twenty-two years for this; I couldn't turn away – not now.'

'I don't understand – twenty-two years for what?'

'I can't explain; they could be here at any moment.' He started pacing again, running his fingers through his hair.

'Who? The Germans?'

'They've arrested Touvier. That means I'll be next. Maybe the others.'

'What others?' asked Lucienne, biting her nails.

'Don't ask. The less you know the better.' He stopped, as if an idea had just hit him. 'Listen, I need to go and lie low for a while.'

'Where would you go?'

'I don't know,' he screamed. 'That's the problem; I don't bloody know.'

'Why don't you stay at Monsieur Touvier's?' suggested Pierre. 'He lives alone, and they're hardly likely to return there, not now that they've taken him.'

'My word; that's not a bad idea. Lucienne, go pack me some clothes. Not too many. Thank you, son.' Georges briefly hugged him. He felt awkward but Pierre experienced a tremor of pleasure.

'It's OK, Papa. It's OK.'

'You're a good lad.'

Lucienne called through from the bedroom, 'Georges, will you want…'

The urgent rap on the door stopped her short. The three of them stood stock still as if frozen.

'Open up,' came the accented voice from outside, pushing at the door.

Georges's eyes darted left and right. 'I'll make a run for it.'

'Darling, no; they might shoot you.'

His body sagged. 'You're right. Pierre, let them in.'

It was strange, thought Pierre, how heavy his arm felt as he lifted his hand to turn the key in the door and undo the bolt.

The Germans barged past, pushing Pierre to one side, as a flurry of grey-green uniforms flooded into the living room. 'Georges Durand?' shouted the lieutenant, his revolver drawn. The two privates seized Georges's arms, twisting them behind his back. He made no resistance. 'You come with us.'

Lucienne screamed, her hands at her face, her wide eyes full of incomprehension. The soldiers pushed Georges towards the door.

'Where are you taking him?' screeched Lucienne.

'He come with us,' said the lieutenant, brandishing his revolver at Lucienne.

She stepped back, her eyes full of tears.

Georges managed to stop at the door, next to Pierre. 'Don't fight back, son, it's not…'

With a yank of his arm, the privates pushed him outside. The lieutenant pointed his gun at Pierre and, at that point, recognised him from the café. 'Heil Hitler,' shouted the lieutenant, his arm stretched out, before following his men out, laughing to himself.

Pierre caught his father's eye a second before the door slammed shut. He seemed calm, thought Pierre; resigned almost.

The sudden silence weighed heavily. Lucienne stood, her arm extended, as if seeking her husband's hand, her features drawn. She seemed to stagger through to the kitchen and plonked down on the armchair. Pierre knew he had to say something, to try and reassure his mother with empty words. Placing an awkward hand on her shoulder, he said, 'It'll turn out all right, Maman. Just wait and see.'

'Yes, Pierre; you're right. I know you are.'

*

Many hours later, near bedtime, Major Hurtzberger returned to the house. It had been an awful afternoon. Lucienne was beside herself with worry, frequently breaking down in tears, frequently washing her hands. The claustrophobia of her grief was too much for Pierre, who felt totally ill-equipped to handle the situation. He knew circumstances dictated he should hug his mother but having grown up in a less-than-tactile family, it was beyond him. Instead, he found himself agreeing with everything his mother said, even though she said the same things again and again, and making her so many cups of coffee, she complained of a headache. By early evening he was hungry. But how could he mention dinner on a day like this? Fortunately, around seven, his mother went for a lie down to help ease her head and Pierre attempted something he had never tried before – to cook. But the scrambled egg he cooked himself was burnt, littered with fragments of shell, and quite revolting. At least with his father gone, he was able to help himself to a larger portion of baguette than normally allowed. The pan proved almost impossible to clean but it provided a distraction. His mother had made him promise that he wouldn't go out. It was approaching curfew now, anyway.

He wondered where his father was at that moment. What would they do to him? Would they hurt him, torture him? He had heard such dreadful rumours. How long would they keep him? And what did he mean when he had said he'd waited twenty-two years? Waited for what? Twenty-two years – that made it 1918. The war.

An hour later, Lucienne re-emerged, her hair, usually so neat and carefully brushed, out of place; her eyes red. 'There is nothing to do except wait until the major returns,' she said, sitting at the kitchen table. And so they waited, in silence, for an age. When he went to put the light on, his mother asked him not to, she couldn't face the brightness of artificial light. So denied even the chance to read, Pierre sat in the armchair and, along with his mother, waited for the major's return. He still hadn't really spoken to their houseguest since he saw him with Claire. He realised that his anger with Claire, the all-encompassing hurt he had felt, had rapidly faded. Jealously had evaporated, leaving, in its place, a deep sense of disappointment and revulsion – disappointment with the major and revulsion at having caught him in the act. However much he tried, Pierre couldn't rid the revolting image from his brain. And the more he tried to purge his memory, the more ingrained the image implanted itself. The major had said he and his wife were separated, not divorced, thus he was still a married man. He would have thought that the major, so much older and so cultured, would have been above such baseness.

With the kitchen in total darkness, Pierre began to resent his mother for forcing him to endure this ridiculous situation. Had it not occurred to her that he might not want to sit in the dark for hours on end? When, at some point, he said he wanted to go to bed, Lucienne asked him not to; asked him to wait with her, her voice coming through the dark.

Sitting in the armchair, Pierre had drifted off into a light sleep when his mother said, 'He's here.' Sure enough, he could hear the major's now distinctive footsteps on the gravel outside, then on the wooden steps. Lucienne buttonholed the major the moment he stepped through the door, bombarding him with questions about her husband. 'Is there a power cut?' He flicked the switch. Pierre blinked as his eyes adjusted to the sudden light. 'Why were you sitting here in the dark?'

'Major, I asked you about my husband. Your colleagues… comrades, whatever you call them, came and took Georges away.'

'Oh dear, oh dear.'

'Oh dear? Is that all you have to say? They came in

106

here, just barged in, and pushed him out of the door and took him away. Did you know about it, Major; did you know he was about to be arrested?'

The major sat down at the table. 'Not really. I'm sorry to hear this.'

'Not really? Is that a yes or a no? Did you know, Major?'

He took off his hat. 'OK, I admit, I knew it was imminent.'

'Imminent? Did you order his arrest?'

'No, the order came through from Colonel Eisler.'

'The officer based in Saint-Romain?'

'Yes, the *Ortskommandantur*. Lucienne, you must understand – Georges, the blacksmith and a couple of others, tried to damage the railway line. They did not succeed but that doesn't diminish the gravity of what they did. We, as the German authorities, take this sort of thing very seriously. Georges knows that. Everyone does. Why, they even had a third party paint the door of the town hall as a sort of diversion. This third party was spotted – a young man but, lucky for him, he evaded capture.' The major glanced at Pierre. 'They were prepared to sacrifice a younger member of their community to obtain their objectives.'

'I heard about the paint. It caused some amusement.'

'Yes. Probably not the intended reaction.'

'This is beside the point, isn't it?' barked Pierre.

'I couldn't ask for a cup of your fine tea, could I, Lucienne?' Why did his mother's name always sound so odd when the major used it? He felt pleased that his mother was still calling him by his title.

'Major, I don't think you understand how worried I am,

and Pierre, both of us. What can I do?' The major remained silent. 'Apart from make you your blessed tea?'

'That would be nice.'

'Where are they keeping him?'

'Headquarters, Saint-Romain. It's where they take anyone wanted for questioning.' Pierre hoped it was just questioning.

Lucienne got up to make his tea when the major said, 'Lucienne, listen, I have a suggestion for you.'

Immediately, she sat down again. 'Yes? Yes, what is it?'

'It probably won't work but no one's tried it before, at least not to my knowledge. Colonel Eisler is a hard man; he has to be, it comes with the job. But he's not an unreasonable man.' Pierre could sense his mother's spirits lifting. 'Go and see him. Don't phone up first; you'll only be told no. So just go to Saint-Romain, both of you, and demand to see the colonel. Be prepared to wait; all day if need be. Be prepared to return the following day, the day after that. Eventually, Colonel Eisler will grant you an audience.'

'An audience? Is he the pope?'

'Tell him Georges is a soldier. Once a soldier, always a soldier. We all have respect for a man in uniform, even the enemy. Tell him you're all supporters of Pétain. Buy one of those postcards of him and have it in your purse and make sure the colonel sees it. Tell him Georges was led astray, that he hadn't been aware of what he was being told to do. Make him sound a little simple even. Simple but honest and honourable. It might help if you could borrow a small child; Pierre is too old. It probably won't make any difference but who knows? Colonel Eisler, I know, is a family man.'

'Thank you, Major. Should I take a present?'

'No, no. He will listen to a reasoned argument but a present could be misconstrued. The colonel is beyond bribery. Pierre, you'll go with your mother, yes?'

'Of course he will,' said Lucienne. 'We'll go tomorrow, straight after the funeral.'

'Funeral? The Algerian's? You know there are notices prohibiting attendance?'

'Major, I am prepared to listen to all your rules but not when they contradict the rules of God. That poor man is to be buried far from his home without his family present. It is our spiritual duty to pay our respects.'

'To a Muslim?'

'To a child of God, whoever that God may be.'

'Amen,' said Pierre. His mother and major looked at him. They'd quite forgotten he was there. Pierre had always found his mother's 'God first' approach to life suffocating and often tedious but right now, for the first time, he saw how profound her faith was.

'One more thing,' said the major.

'Yes?'

'I did not say a word of this. You understand? Not a word.'

'Yes, we understand. Thank you, Major. I'll make that tea now.'

Chapter 8

The Germans, as the major had pointed out, had banned the citizens of the town from attending the Algerian's funeral yet the ubiquitous notices only helped to spread the word. One person after another said they were planning on being there. If his mother was going then of course, thought Pierre, he had to go too. He had a neat shirt and a pair of dark trousers but had to borrow one of his father's jackets. It looked absurd – far too big. But there was nothing for it, he could not, insisted his mother, attend a funeral without a jacket. She too wore her only black outfit. She even had a hat with a black feather in it. 'You never know when a funeral hat will come in useful,' she said.

It felt as if the whole town was there, squeezed into the graveyard. Everyone he had ever recognized seemed to be here. He had noticed this, since the start of the occupation, a greater sense of community. Yes, people still argued over whether Pétain was a saviour or a traitor, but people talked as never before. He saw Claire. He wanted to look upon her and hate her. But in her black blouse with a pretty bow, and her knee-length skirt, and her hair tied back, she looked beautiful. He was too young for her; he knew that. If only he'd been a couple years older. If only he was a man; a part of the action, not, as he so often was, a spectator. But then, if he had been a couple years older, he'd probably be in a prisoner of war camp by now, somewhere deep in Germany. Either that or dead.

And for once, the Germans had been rendered impotent by this show of community togetherness. Not even they had the gall to break up such a large gathering under the eyes of God. Yet, still, they were making their presence felt. Dozens of them watched from the perimeter, making sure the mourners acted accordingly.

They were on the north side of the church. He felt at ease here. It was the southern side that he wanted to avoid. The little cross lost among all the other gravestones. Once a year, his mother dragged him and his father there where they would stand for ages, silently gazing down at the grave that took up so little space, and contemplate.

Father de Beaufort had insisted that the service within the church be limited to invitees only, in other words, the dignitaries of the town. Now, outside, under the intense early afternoon sun, he had to raise his voice in order to be heard.

'It is a sad gathering I see before me today...' Father de Beaufort liked to claim he was descended from Pierre Roger de Beaufort who, as Gregory XI, was France's last pope, back in the fourteenth century. No one ever contradicted the claim.

'We all know why we find ourselves in this situation; why we have been defeated. It is, without a shadow of doubt, a punishment inflicted on us from God Himself. We, as a nation, have become lazy, swayed by temptation. Too many are content to wallow in sin, materialism and pleasure-seeking. They have turned their backs on God. Liberation will only come when we heed this lesson, when we return to God and beg His forgiveness and seek His protection. Until then, we are not worthy of Him, and we deserve this penance of occupation.'

Many in the congregation shook their heads, disagreeing with the priest's version of events. If Father de Beaufort noticed their disagreement, he paid no heed. 'Now, dearest brothers and sisters, let us pray for our beloved brother, Mohammed El Harrachi, from faraway Algeria…' Pierre wondered what, at this precise moment, Georges would be doing. Pierre had never really thought of his father as an individual, a person with a history. He realized that Georges, while not a bad father, had never been a particularly good one either. He'd been brought up almost by a stranger, a man about whom he knew nothing – not where he was born, what his parents were like, where he had lived as a child. All he knew was that still, after all these years, he felt as if he belonged to an incomplete family; as if there was forever a place at the table, waiting for someone who would never return. And what would Georges be like when they let him out? Would he come home a different man? Perhaps, thought Pierre, he might see his life in a new light; come to treasure what he had around him; come to appreciate that he had a son, a son who loved his father very much.

'…whom the Lord has called forth from this world and whose body has been given to us this day for burial.' His mother sniffed next to him, clasping her rosary beads, twisting them around her fingers. He could recall no shows of affection from his father, or a raising of his voice. Perhaps if he had it would have been proof of a man who cared. Instead, he was man who drifted through life, happy to be on the sidelines, content to be left alone. He had no need for anything or anyone, the town, his associates, the church, his only son. So why had he been dragged into Kafka's net? What hold did Kafka have over him?

'May the Lord receive him into His peace, and, when the Day of Judgment comes…' He would go with his mother to see this Colonel Eisler; he would walk into the lion's den, and demand his father's release. Well, maybe not demand. Pierre knew well enough already that you could never demand anything of the Nazis. Was the major a Nazi? Was he a believer, like that brutish lieutenant, like Fritz One? Or was he just a man doing his job?

'… To raise our brother up to be gathered among the elect and numbered with all the saints at God's right hand. Amen.'

Father de Beaufort sprinkled a handful of soil on the coffin. 'We commit this body to the earth…'

Pierre wondered what Mohammed El Harrachi's parents were like. Was he their only son; did they shower him with affection; would they grieve for him for the rest of their lives? The word was that they would have been informed by now. That the town hall would have got his details from Paris; that they had written to them. It didn't seem right, somehow, that they were all attending the poor man's funeral while his mother and father, back in Algeria, had no idea that today, this day, their son was being buried in a Catholic churchyard, attended to by a Catholic priest.

Perhaps, thought Pierre, one day, when all this was over, they might travel across the sea from North Africa and across the length of France to this forgotten spot and kneel down here, in this graveyard and pray for their Muslim son. He hoped, one day, they might.

Chapter 9

Lucienne would have gone to Saint-Romain to see Colonel Eisler straightaway but the funeral meant they had missed the second and last bus for the day. The following day was a Sunday – and there were no buses on a Sunday. They knew no one who had a car, except the cemetery boys and their truck, and Sunday was their one day off. Pierre did wonder how a job in a graveyard could take up six days a week and guessed that, as very old men, they probably worked slowly and drank large quantities of tea throughout the day. Thus two days had passed. It was Monday. Lucienne, just back from church, was anxious, watering the garden, washing her hands frequently. Having worn her black dress for the funeral, she'd worn it each day since. 'I will wear black everyday now until they release your father,' she'd declared. 'Today we must go see this Colonel Eisler. Each day we leave it is another day Georges has to spend in that place.'

And so, it was at eleven o'clock that Lucienne and Pierre caught the bus the five kilometres to Saint-Romain, his mother carrying a parcel containing a clean shirt. Inside the breast pocket, on a slip of paper, she'd written Georges a note. What it said, she didn't say but Pierre could guess.

The bus was packed, stuffy and quiet, except for the noise of the engine and, strangely, the sound of turkeys. Every seat was taken, people standing, holding onto the bars, as the bus lurched from one stop to another. A young man with a walking stick offered Lucienne his seat. Politely, she declined. His need was greater than hers, her expression said. Pierre stood. Beneath him, on her mother's lap, sat a girl of about four sucking on her hair. Her mother, a well-to-do woman, using Lucienne's phrase, slapped her hand away. Next to them, was an old woman in black, at her feet three wicker baskets. Inside each was a turkey, making a dreadful din, their heads peering out. The smell wasn't pleasant either. The mother of the girl was clearly agitated by this. At each stop, more people got on but no one alighted. Those standing shuffled closer together. Considering the short distance, the journey was taking an age. Pierre had become separated from his mother, whom he could see, in black, fanning herself with her operatic fan. He heard the mother of the small girl ask the old woman, 'Can't you stop those birds from making that dreadful noise?' 'And how do you propose I do that?' snapped back the old woman. The girl began sucking her hair again.

Finally, the bus rolled into Saint-Romain, made its way to the centre and stopped. With a collective sigh of relief, everyone disembarked. Lucienne and Pierre and others were held up behind the old woman, also in black, as she struggled with her baskets and their heavy cargo. Lucienne nudged Pierre in the ribs, telling him to help her.

'Can I…?'

'I can manage. I've got muscles, you know.'

Lucienne shook her head as they got off the bus. 'Well, that is not something I would want to do everyday,' she said. 'Right, let's find the dentist's. The major said the office was next to it.'

'How are you feeling?'

'Oh, Pierre, I'm terrified. I'm trembling all over. Does it show?'

'No.'

'That's good then.'

Saint-Romain was so much larger and busier than their sleepy little town, thought Pierre, with its grander buildings, its shops and stores, the trams, advertising hoardings, ornate lampposts adorned with hanging baskets of flowers. Lucienne entered a tobacconist and bought a postcard of Marshal Pétain. She knew the way and soon they found themselves in a maze of narrower streets, with high buildings either side; balconies, many draped with laundry; little cafés, their outdoor tables brimming with smiling Germans; people on bicycles; a hotel with a swastika hanging above its front door.

'Do you know what you're going to say, Maman?'

'Yes. No. Whenever I try to rehearse it, I become too nervous and I can't think.'

'Do you want me to do the talking?'

'No, Pierre, you're just a boy.'

'Yeah. Thanks, Maman, just a boy.'

'Oh dear. Pierre, don't be so sensitive; I didn't mean… But this is serious.' She stopped. 'Oh my, here we are.'

They looked at the swastika-adorned building on the corner across the street. Lucienne clutched her handbag to her chest. It was an imposing work of neo-classicism: grey-bricked, three stories high, with a balcony at the top and adorned with large, elaborately decorated windows. A gravelled path surrounded it. A Nazi kept guard at the double doors at the top of a few steps, beside which hung another flag. On either side of the doors was a large pot of rhododendrons – a dash of colour, thought Pierre, in the drab grey.

'Oh, Pierre,' said Lucienne, her voice breathless. 'I don't think I can do this. It could make things worse. Those rhododendrons could do with a watering.'

'But it's what the major told us to do. We have to do it; we don't have a choice.'

She nodded, her jaw tightening. 'Come, let's go.'

The soldier at the door watched them as they crossed the road. As they approached, he slipped his rifle off his shoulder.

'Hello,' said Lucienne. 'We'd like to see Colonel Eisler please.'

'The *Ortskommandantur*? Do you have an appointment?'

'No.'

'But we're prepared to wait,' added Pierre.

'Why do you need to see him?'

'I – I can't tell you; it's very important I see the colonel. Most important.'

The soldier considered them for a moment. 'Wait here,' he said.

Pierre watched the cars pass on the street, pedestrians going about their business. He saw the woman from the bus, pulling her daughter by the hand, urging her to hurry up. The girl was sniffling, wiping her eyes.

The soldier returned. 'Your bag, please.' He rooted

inside Lucienne's handbag. 'Arms up.' He ran his hands up and down both of them, quickly but expertly. 'Follow me.'

Pierre held the door open for his mother and followed her in, wondering what on earth they were stepping into. The atmosphere inside was not dissimilar to the town hall back at home, thought Pierre – people in uniforms running round, carrying papers, folders, the click-clack of typewriters, muffled conversations, the echo of shoes on marbled floors, pillars painted white, a huge portrait of Hitler. Everything but the floor was white and polished, the floor consisting of black and green squares. A receptionist with pink nail varnish and startlingly bright red lipstick, introduced herself as Mademoiselle Dauphin and took their details. The soldier showed Lucienne and Pierre into a waiting area behind a glass screen, white-walled and high-ceilinged, and told them to wait. Sitting on the wooden bench were three elderly Frenchwomen, each wearing a headscarf. Lucienne asked them if she could take a seat. Reluctantly and wordlessly, they shuffled up and allowed Lucienne to perch on the end. Pierre leant against a pillar. He wished he could smoke. He wondered whether they were all here for the same reason, to plead on behalf of their husbands or sons. Another German kept watch over them. He could have been no older than nineteen, thought Pierre; the same age as the major's son. An hour passed before Mademoiselle Dauphin appeared to call the first woman through. No one said a word. Lucienne rested her handbag on her lap, playing with its catch. The German guard was relieved by another. Pierre would have sat down, but another woman came in, a dishevelled younger woman, and sat down on the bench. 'How long have you been here?' she asked the woman next to her.

'Hours,' came the quick reply. 'Oh.' She looked like a woman who wanted to talk but, sensing the atmosphere, held her tongue.

Finally, after over two hours, Mademoiselle Dauphin returned. 'Madame Durand?'

Lucienne and Pierre followed the woman across the hallway, up two flights of red-carpeted stairs and down a long corridor. She stopped to talk to a soldier standing guard outside a door, a strange looking man but for reasons Pierre couldn't work out. The man was, Pierre realised with a shudder, SS, wearing a black uniform with a swastika armband. The SS man knocked and they waited. A voice came from within. 'Wait,' the receptionist said to them, before entering, leaving the door ajar. 'Madame and Monsieur Durand, sir,' Pierre heard her say.

'Show them in.'

'You can go in,' said Mademoiselle Dauphin to Lucienne. Pierre nodded at the soldier who stepped in with them and closed the door. It was only then that he realised what was odd about him – his eyes were of different colour.

Pierre and his mother were greeted by the colonel, also wearing the uniform of the SS, sitting behind an expansive mahogany desk, his glasses perched on his head, his grey hair thin but neatly combed. His peaked hat sat on his desk, alongside a telephone, an ashtray, an empty vase, a bottle of water and a couple of glasses, piles of folders and a brass desk lamp with a hexagon-shaped shade. Behind him an opened window that reached the floor, its turquoise-coloured net curtain fluttering in the draft. The noise of traffic sounded in the distance. Next to the window, another portrait of Hitler. How often he had found pictures of Hitler ridiculous, with his stupid moustache. But here, in this office, behind the colonel, Pierre could feel the man's power, the intensity of his eyes, the aura of invincibility. He suddenly felt rather small.

'Take a seat,' said the colonel.

Lucienne thanked him nervously. There being only the one chair, Pierre stood behind his mother. He wished he could sit down; he was tired of being so long on his feet.

'Your name is Madame Durand, and you are Pierre Durand. Is that right? How old are you, boy?'

'Sixteen,' he croaked.

'What?'

'Sixteen, sir.' He found the unmoving eyes of the Führer staring down at him unnerving.

'And you've come presumably on account of your husband.' He checked the name against his paper. 'Georges Durand. Is that correct?'

'Yes, sir,' said Lucienne. 'You see, Colonel, Georges, my husband, is a good man.' She spoke quickly. 'He fought in the last war. I know that was against you but he fought honourably, like a proper soldier. He wore his uniform with pride, like all good soldiers, whether they are French or German. He was led astray. He is a good husband, a good father, and—'

She stopped midsentence; the colonel had raised his hand.

'This is all very well, Madame, but it is not his conduct in the last war that concerns me but his conduct now, during *this* war. Destruction of German property is a grave offence and an affront that I take very seriously. Now, do you really think that by simply telling me that your husband is a good man, as you call him, that I shall just

121

click my fingers and say, "OK, I'll have him released"? What sort of people do you take us for? I advise you not to answer that.'

'Colonel, we are great supporters of the marshal. I never go anywhere without a picture of him in my handbag.' She fished out the postcard and held it up for the colonel to see.

'What can I say?' he asked with a hint of an exasperated smile.

'Colonel, would I be allowed to give my husband a clean shirt? I've heard you permit such things.'

'Yes, that's perfectly acceptable. We may be severe sometimes but we're not savages. A man needs a clean shirt every now and then. If you want to pass it to me.'

Lucienne passed him her carefully wrapped parcel. The colonel undid the packaging and held the shirt aloft, inspecting it. He found Lucienne's message straightaway. Lucienne flushed red. He cast his eyes over the note, screwed it up and threw it in a bin at his feet.

'I'll make sure he gets it,' he said, handing it to the guard. 'You can put your postcard away, Madame Durand. Now, I shall tell you what happens next. We are investigating the attempted derailment of our train, and those found guilty will be retained here as punishment for up to six months. On release, they will be monitored. Any further transgressions would likely result in more severe punishment. I hope I've made myself clear?'

'Yes, thank you, Colonel.'

'You may, on occasion, like today, bring in provisions, small food parcels and such like. Do not ever attempt to smuggle in messages again otherwise your husband's stay here will automatically be extended.' Pierre made a conscious effort not to look at his mother. 'Now, if you don't mind, I have a lot of other business to see to.'

'Yes, of course.' Lucienne rose to her feet, her face flushed. 'Pierre...?'

'Before you go, however, I'd like a word with your son. In private.'

'Oh.' Lucienne looked at Pierre. 'In private?'

'Please.'

Lucienne looked flustered as she gathered her things. Pierre stood still, trying to maintain a look of impassivity, while wondering what on earth the colonel wanted.

The guard held the door open for Lucienne, who retreated with a final, worried look at her son.

'Right then,' said the colonel. 'Take a seat. Cigarette?' He pushed forward a pack towards Pierre.

Pierre looked at it. He was tempted but his mother would smell it on him. 'No, thanks.' The colonel took one and, finding a box of matches, lit it.

'So, when are you seventeen?' he asked, blowing out of column of smoke.

'Four months.'

'Old enough. Good.' He sat back in his chair and considered the young man opposite him.

Pierre felt as if he was being assessed and tried to hold the German's gaze. Failing, he glanced up at Hitler. A little jolt of apprehension ran down his back.

'What I am about to say is between you and me,' said the colonel. 'Is that understood? Not a word.' Pierre nodded. 'I wasn't being entirely honest with your mother. The fact is your father has been identified as being one of the ringleaders of this puerile attempt at sabotage. Now, if we show leniency, it would merely encourage others. This cannot be. Your father is due to be executed.'

'Shit, no.' The word tumbled out. His hand went to his mouth. Pierre looked aghast at the colonel, not totally sure he'd heard correctly.

'Tomorrow morning. Five o'clock.'

'No. Please. It wasn't that serious, no one–'

'It's not for you, young man, to tell us what we deem to be serious.' The colonel blew out another puff of smoke. Pierre felt a wave of nausea cloud his thoughts. 'But you can save him.'

'I'm sorry?'

'You heard me correctly. I said you can save your father from the firing squad tomorrow morning.'

'What can I do?' He tried to think but it was as if a thousand contradictory thoughts were rushing through his mind.

'Your father, I believe, was acting under orders. Someone else was the brains behind this little operation and I want to know who before he tries something else, something more adventurous, let's say.'

Immediately, Pierre thought of Kafka.

'Would you know who this man might be?'

Pierre tried to think of what his father would want him to say. 'No, I'm sorry.'

'Pity. We asked your father but he refused to name any names. I admire his stubbornness.'

'Did you–'

'We asked him. Let's leave at that, shall we?'

'Can I have some water?'

The colonel reached over and poured Pierre a glass. Sliding it over the table, he continued. 'I could ask you just to go home, find out the name and bring it to me. But that'd be too simple. I want more.'

Pierre gulped his water down. 'More?' He placed the glass on the desk and realised his hand was shaking.

'Yes, more. I want you to go to this man and offer yourself as your father's replacement. Become one of them, this merry band of resisters. Find out what they're doing; become party to their plans. Then report back to Major Hurtzberger.'

'The major?'

'Yes, he has been briefed. He'll be expecting good things from you. If you agree, I will guarantee no one save myself and the major will know, and I will order a stay of execution.'

'But I can't. I'm only sixteen; they won't let me in.'

'Who's they?'

'I don't know. Whoever they are.'

'Come, come, you're almost seventeen. You told me. Need I remind you what's at stake? By just having this conversation, you've kept your father alive for a further five days.'

'Five days?'

The colonel looked at his watch. 'Five days. That's how long you have to inform the major that you have infiltrated the group. Now, I've kept you long enough. You'd better not keep your mother waiting any longer. Off you go.'

The guard appeared at Pierre's side, casting a sinister shadow over him. 'Can I see my father?'

'No.'

'How do I go about—'

'That's for you to work out.'

The two of them locked eyes. Pierre felt the man's power invade his being.

'Five days, don't forget,' said the colonel.

'Can... can I take a cigarette for later?'

The colonel smiled an icy smile. 'Here, take the pack.' He threw it over.

As the guard escorted Pierre to the door, the colonel spoke. 'Remember, young man – not a word to anyone, including your mother. Especially your mother.'

*

With the colonel's cigarettes in his back pocket, Pierre descended the stairs, the guard behind him. He found his mother in the waiting room, now empty except for Lucienne and another guard.

'Pierre. Is everything OK?'

'Yes. Let's go home,' he said.

Outside, under the beating sun, they headed back towards the bus station, their shadows behind them. Everywhere were Germans, laughing, taking photos of each other, shopping for jewellery and souvenirs.

'Idiots,' growled Pierre under his breath.

Lucienne glanced behind her. Satisfied they were out of earshot, she asked Pierre why the colonel had wanted to see him.

'I can't say.' He hoped his voice was firm enough to dissuade her from pressing him.

She stopped suddenly. She reached out for his hand. He refused to give it. With her hand resting on his sleeve, she spoke quietly. 'Pierre, please, what did he want? You were in there for such a long time; I'm worried for you.'

'I'm not allowed to say and, anyway, you don't want to know.'

'He's asked you to do something. For the love of God, you're sixteen; you're a boy.' Her eyes narrowed, her shoulders flexed. 'How dare he.' She turned abruptly, and made to walk back.

'What are you doing?'

'If you're not going to tell me, the colonel can.'

He reached out for her. 'No, you can't do that.'

'We'll see about that.'

He had to jog to keep pace with her. 'What are you doing?' he repeated. He ran in front of her, then stopped her as she tried to sidestep past him. 'Maman, this is not one of my old teachers you're dealing with, it's a...' He stopped himself before saying something unflattering about the Germans.

'Tell me then.'

'Look at me. Yes, I am young, but I am no longer a boy. This war has made men of us all. You just have to trust me.'

She seemed to diminish in front of him, her verve draining away. 'They took my husband and now, somehow, they have you. Promise me, Pierre, whatever it is, you'll be careful.'

He tried to smile a reassuring smile. 'Yes, OK, I promise I'll be careful.'

Chapter 10

Pierre could only stare at his work. Chisel in hand, he had neither the strength nor the will to apply it. It was early; the yard was still mostly in shade. The hens pecked at the grain he had just scattered while Maurice, the cock, strutted around. The sculpture had broadly taken on the height and shape that he had been aiming for. One could see that it was a woman. But now came the part where more detail was needed – to separate her arms from her body, to slim down her neck, her ankles. Having come this far, he felt a strange responsibility for her. He had to give her characteristics, features. Her had to give life. She provided him the means to escape but he realised now, that she was as dependent on him as he was on her. He stroked her shoulder. 'Give me time,' he whispered. 'I'll get you out of there.' They had questioned him, the colonel had said; they had tortured him. 'Give me time.'

'And now you talk to her.'

Pierre screwed his eyes shut. He wanted to be left alone. He no longer enjoyed this routine – the major's daily intrusion into his thoughts. Pierre turned. The major stood there, in his uniform, his cap, coffee mug in hand. It annoyed him that his mother would have made him that coffee. Coffee was a fast disappearing product yet here they were – offering it to the fucking Germans. A wolf in sheep's clothing. The major's expression was not one of conviviality. His features had hardened, his eyes cold. Pierre knew their relationship had changed. He was one of them now. The major knew. They both knew. He had four and a half days. He remembered the colonel's icy smile, his aura of power. He saw it too now in the man who stood before him. He hated him. He hated him for being in his home, for being there when his father was not; for coming between him and his White Venus. He hated him for fucking Claire, for sullying his romantic boyish dreams.

The major sipped his drink, his eyes still fixed on Pierre. Pierre's fingers gripped the handle of the chisel. How easy it would be, he thought. And think of the satisfaction. The chest; he would aim for the chest. He felt every muscle tense, felt himself rocking on his feet, ready to pounce.

The major spun on his heels and left. Pierre stared at the kitchen door as it swung shut. The chisel slipped out of his hand.

＊

Standing outside, Pierre realised he had never been to Kafka's house before. He lived in a small grey-stoned bungalow on the outskirts of the town. Behind it, a vast expanse of woodland. The windows and shutters were open; everything quiet. To the side of the house, was a garage, its doors open. From the house to the garage, scattered everywhere, were bits of rusting machinery – old car engines, tyres big and small, a bashed-up car door propped up against the house, discarded boots, garden tools, an empty birdcage, a wooden chair without its seat. Gently, Pierre knocked on the door. Kafka's face appeared at a small window, pushing aside the net curtain. 'For fuck's sake.' A moment later, he was at the door. 'Jesus, you gave me a fright. What brings you here? You'd better come in.'

He found himself in the living room – an upright piano with brown keys, an Eiffel Tower on the dresser, a large stove, a collection of pipes in a rack.

'I heard about your father. Hard luck, that was. I sort of guessed I'd be next. Guess your father is tougher than I thought. Anyway, what brings you here?'

'I want to take my father's place.'

Kafka seemed taken aback by the boy's impertinence. 'You want to take your father's place,' he said slowly. 'In what exactly?'

'In your group.'

'In my…?' With two quick steps, he was on Pierre, clasping his shirt, pushing him back against the wall. 'What do you think you're saying? What group?'

Fighting for breath, Pierre gasped, 'I thought…'

Kafka released him. 'You thought wrong. You stupid little fool. Get the fuck out of here before I put you over my knee.'

Pierre felt the surge of humiliation but with it, came the anger, an outpouring of indignation. 'I am a patriot,' he said, his eyes prickling with tears. 'I watched them take my father away. I can't stand by and do nothing. I have to do something, anything. If you won't take me, then I'll find someone who will.'

'Oh, mighty words from one so young; so fine and dandy. And how do you propose this, eh? Go up to any fucker on the street and say, "I want to be in your gang"?'

'If need be.'

'Right. Easy as that. Go ahead and try it. Everyone is scared to death; no one will act. The Krauts have beaten them into submission. Collaborators – each and everyone of them. Active, tacit or horizontal – collaborators. So, you go and politely ask them. You'll be sharing a cell with your old man before you can say jackboot. Get out of here. Come back when you've become a man.'

Pierre tried to find a retort, his mind struggling with half-hearted insults. By the time he finally said, 'I'll show you, you stinking Kraut,' he was back at home.

*

Xavier knocked on the front door. 'Fancy coming out?' he asked.

'No, I bloody don't,' said Pierre.

He seemed taken aback by Pierre's abruptness.

Afterwards, as Pierre paced round the house, flitting from one room to another, he realised he'd been unfairly rude to his friend. His mother was out – where, he didn't know. He went into his parents' bedroom, rooting through their belongings. He had no idea what he was looking for, and he knew he was clutching at straws. The colonel's five days were already ticking by. His only idea had come to nothing. He didn't have a second option, no back-up plan. He hoped his father's belongings would provide some form of inspiration. There was nothing. A few letters, a couple of books, and that was it.

He tried to think of everyone he knew. Would Monsieur Bonnet be a secret resister? Hardly likely. And what about Clément? Perhaps. Who knows? Kafka was right – how does one go about asking the question?

He sat at the kitchen table, then stood up again. Finding a pack of playing cards, he sat back down again. Shuffling the cards, he tried to think. He kept glancing up at the clock. He laid out a card. The ten of spades. Spades. Without thinking, unconscious of where his feet were taking him, he went outside into the yard and to the shed. Yes, there were a couple of spades, a pick, an axe, a brush, the cans of paint, gardening gloves, secateurs, a jam jar full of screws, another of nails. He heard the front door. His mother was back. He found her in the kitchen, still wearing her headscarf despite the heat of the day. She had bought a few potatoes and a cabbage. 'Oh, Pierre. There you are. The major said he might be able to procure half a chicken for us tonight, save us having to kill one of ours, so I thought I'd get some veg. We might be eating like kings tonight.'

'Good.'

'But, my, it's so expensive. Prices are shooting up. I don't know how we'll manage. You must get yourself a job. You're the man of the family now, Pierre.'

'Funny that. I thought that was Major H.'

'We rely on his generosity. We have to be thankful for that.'

'Great. They take everything away; and give us back a little. And for that we have to thank them.'

Lucienne sat down with a heavy sigh, removing her headscarf. 'I hadn't thought of it in those terms. How quickly you're growing up.'

'Yeah, well, like you say, I'm the man of the family now.'

'Oh, and more coffee. The major said he could get more coffee. He likes his coffee in the morning, does the major. Poor Georges. I wonder how he is.'

'Nails.' Pierre slapped his forehead.

'I'm sorry?'

'That's it, the nails.'

*

The major did indeed bring back half a chicken. The smell of it cooking in the oven was both tortuous and wonderful. Lucienne ensured they had only small portions – enough for cold chicken tomorrow, she'd said. They ate in silence. Gone was the former joviality. OK, it may have been forced but at least it had been there. But since Georges's arrest, smiles had given way to fixed expressions, conversations on music to brief exchanges on the weather, the pretence of host and guest all but gone.

Afterwards, having eaten well, they sat in the living room and read. The major flipped through his papers, scanning each in turn before filing them neatly in his folder. Pierre picked up his book on renaissance art and scanned the pages for the umpteenth time. But, meanwhile, his mind tried to work out his plan of action. He had to be patient, had to hold his nerve.

'Are you tired, Pierre?' His mother's voice brought him back to the present.

'What? No.'

'It's just that you keep looking at the clock.'

'Am I? Oh. Sorry.'

'You don't have to apologise.'

'No.'

They all went to bed early. Night had still not fully fallen. Pierre lay, fully dressed, on his bed, the jar of nails in his haversack behind the door. It seemed weeks, months, since the night of the graffiti. But that was child's play compared to what lay at stake now. In some ways the task that lay ahead of him was easier. But it was more important. His mind raced through numerous scenarios and slowly he dozed off.

*

He awoke with a start. Finding the torch that he put beneath his pillow, he shone it on his alarm clock. Two o'clock. Quietly, he opened his bedroom door. He could hear the major snoring. Good. His mother, a heavy sleeper, would also be out for the count. The time was perfect. Outside, the night had retained the heat of the day. He slipped out of the yard, rounded the house and onto the street. He'd stuffed the jam jar full of socks and underpants to stifle the rattling of the nails. He looked left, right and around. Everything was inky black, no hint of a moon to illuminate the way. All the better for not being seen. Slowly, wearing his soft-soled shoes, he crept up the street, heading towards the town centre, his eyes adjusting to the blackness. The deep silence felt oppressive. There wasn't even the rustle of leaves. There was nothing. If only he could slow down the pounding in his chest. He wished he'd recruited Xavier but then, perhaps not. He had to do this alone. It wasn't difficult, he told himself repeatedly. It wasn't difficult.

Soon, he was on the bend of Rue de Courcelles, the road leading to the town hall, the road the prisoners of war had come down. This is where he wanted to be. He peered round the corner. Nothing; the road was clear. Ahead loomed the town square with Soldier Mike silhouetted in the foreground. He had to work quickly. Undoing the lid, he stuffed his underwear back into his bag. Gently, he poured out a handful of nails. Too worried to throw them, he almost placed them across the road, one handful at a time. His father wouldn't thank him for this – nails, like everything else, were now hard to come by, stupidly expensive for what they were. But, dear father, it's for a good cause. Within a couple of minutes, he had scattered the entire jar of nails on the tarmac, covering a good expanse of road. Satisfied, he returned the jar to his bag and crept quickly away.

Less than ten minutes later, he was back in his bed. Mission accomplished. He lay there, staring into the dark, his heart refusing to slow down. It was two twenty. The whole thing had taken only twenty minutes. The major was still snoring. He felt euphoric. In the grand scheme of things, this was a minor act of sabotage, but that didn't matter.

What mattered was the intent.

Chapter 11

Pierre woke early – soon after six. It was cloudy. This, Pierre concluded, was a good thing – less chance of the Germans seeing the nails glinting in the sun. Not so good was seeing the major, also up early, half dressed, lighting the gas flame on the cooker to heat up his precious coffee.

'You're up early,' said Pierre.

'Yes, early meeting.'

Pierre's chest tightened. The major's route took him up Rue de Courcelles. He would see the nails. The morning convoy of German trucks, taking the men out on their morning exercise, or manoeuvres, whatever they called it, always passed by at seven. Shit, he had to detain the major for almost an hour.

'What time is your meeting?'

'Seven.'

'Is it important?'

'What? The meeting? What an odd question to ask. Of course, it's important. Everything the German command does in the name of your country is important. Now, if you'll excuse me, I need to get dressed and shaved. Keep an eye on the coffee, would you?'

As soon as the major closed his bedroom door, Pierre turned off the gas, then switched the knob on again but without the flame. Taking the kitchen clock off the wall, he opened the glass and pushed the minute hand back ten minutes. He returned to his bedroom. Sitting on his bed, he tried to think. Nothing he said or did would keep the major from his meeting. Such a simple plan, puncturing a few German tyres, interrupting their routine, however briefly, seemed perfect for a solitary show of defiance. He hadn't counted on the major, of all people, upsetting his scheme. Minutes later, he heard the major come back to the kitchen and curse in German. The major called out his name.

'Pierre, what happened to the flame?'

'Why? Has it gone out? Oh, must have been a draft.'

The German looked round the room, as if seeking out a draft. He glanced up at the kitchen clock, then checked his wristwatch. 'Strange, your clock must have stopped – just in the last few minutes.' He re-lit the gas flame. 'Still time for a coffee, I think.'

At quarter to seven, the major pulled on his boots, put his cap on, checked his reflection and made to leave.

'Have you heard from your son?' asked Pierre.

'Yes, he's fine. Sorry, Pierre, I have to go.'

'I'll come with you.'

'What?'

'I feel like a walk.'

'Hurry up, then.'

They walked in silence. Pierre struggled to keep pace with the German. He could think of nothing to say and felt annoyed that his plan was about to go awry. As they turned onto the road, a hint of sun appeared behind the clouds. 'Could be a nice day again,' said Pierre.

The major ignored him. As they approached the bend, Pierre thought he heard the rumble of engines. He strained his ears – yes, the convoy was on the move, he could hear the trucks revving up in the distance, shouted orders. Yet, he and the major had almost come to the spot. He had to stop the German. He could only think of one thing. He screeched and started hopping.

'You all right?' asked the major.

'Ow, no. I think I've twisted my ankle.'

'How did you manage that?'

Pierre leant against the wall banking the road, holding up his left leg. 'It hurts.'

'Here, let me have a look.'

Pierre rolled up his trouser leg. The convoy was coming, the big German trucks rolling down the road, one by one. The major clasped his hands round Pierre's ankle. 'I can't feel anything,' he said.

The first truck was now at the bend. This was it. The noise was surprisingly loud – a screech of brakes, a skid, men yelling from within.

'What was that?' said the major. They looked up to see the first truck with a swastika painted on its side coming to a juddering halt as its tyres burst. A second truck crashed into it, forcing the first one off the road, tumbling down the ditch. The sound of many men shouting and swearing filled the air. Together, Pierre and the major ran up the road, Pierre forgetting his pretence of pain. 'It's an ambush,' shouted the major, drawing his revolver from its holster. 'Pierre, get back.' The scene was chaotic. Three trucks skewered across the road, their tyres rapidly deflating with a loud hiss; dozens of German soldiers pouring from the vehicles onto the road, their rifles at the ready, their eyes wide with fright and determination. They fell to their knees, the weapons trained on the surrounding area. The truck in the ditch had come to a halt, smashed up against a hefty tree trunk, a suspended wheel still spinning as men piled out. Then, everything stood still – dozens of Germans waiting for a burst of machine gun fire. Major Hurtzberger circled round, his every sense on full alert. Pierre, his back pressed against the wall, had to concede it was an impressive display. Satisfied that they hadn't been ambushed, the major asked the sergeant if everyone was all right.

'Look at all these nails,' said the sergeant.

'Swine,' said a corporal.

'We need to clear this up,' said the major. 'Rally up some locals. Where's Pierre?'

Pierre's heart sunk – not again. Instead, the major told him to go home. As he turned to leave, a number of villagers had already appeared, keen to know what had happened. Xavier slapped him on the back. 'Oh dear,' he said. 'What a mess, eh?'

'I wouldn't hang around, if I was you.'

'Fair point. Come round to mine, if you want.'

*

An hour later, having shared a measly boiled egg breakfast, Pierre and Xavier decided to venture back out. The sun had appeared, the day was already stiflingly hot. As they walked up Rue de Courcelles, they could hear a distant sound of crying.

'What's going on?' asked Pierre.

'I don't know but it doesn't sound good.'

Exchanging worried glances, they picked up speed, climbing up the hill. What they saw as they approached the bend made them both stop in their tracks. Lined up, either side of the road, were a number of German soldiers, rifles at the ready, screaming orders. Between them, on their hands and knees, were about a dozen villagers. They were being forced to pick up the nails, every last one of them. Some of the women were crying, snivelling.

'Have you noticed something?' whispered Xavier.

'They're all old.'

The Germans had selected the elderly and the fragile to do their work. Their trousers or skirts had shredded at the knees; many were bleeding.

'Faster, faster,' yelled a German.

Monsieur Roché was among them, his knees red with blood, his face covered in sweat. He made the mistake of protesting. 'We didn't do this. Why pick on us?' A German soldier swung his rifle round and with its butt hit him on the side of the head. Pierre grimaced at the sickening sound as the butt impacted the skull. People screamed as Monsieur Roché collapsed. 'Any more comments?' asked the German, his eyes gleaming with bloodlust.

'What do we do?' asked Xavier.

'We have to help.'

'How?'

'No idea.'

Together they strode up the hill. Pierre hoped to see the major – surely when he told them to round up some locals he hadn't meant this. It was barbaric. The villagers were at least eighty, thought Pierre, all of them. One of the old women looked up at him, her face soaked in sweat and tears.

He recognised the fanatical lieutenant leaning against one of the trucks, smoking. Three of its tyres had been replaced and a couple of soldiers were about to embark on the fourth. The other trucks, including the one in the ditch, had already gone. Monsieur Roché, Pierre noticed, hadn't moved, the side of his skull bleeding profusely.

'Hello. We want to help,' said Xavier, his voice cracking.

'*Was ist das?*' said the lieutenant.

Xavier pointed at Pierre and himself and at the old folk grappling for nails under the hot sun.

The German barked at a private, who came running towards the boys. 'What do you want?' he shouted in French.

'We want to help,' said Pierre, stepping back.

The private translated his request. The lieutenant laughed and responded in a quick, shrill voice.

The private snarled as he translated back. 'If you wimps aren't out of here in five seconds, you'll be spending the next six months with the Gestapo. Now fuck off.'

The boys scampered back down the hill, the moans and groans of the villagers and the abusive shouts in German ringing in their ears.

'Bastards,' said Pierre, once they were out of earshot.

'Whoever pulled that trick needs his head examined.'

'What an idiot.'

*

Later on, once Xavier had returned home, Pierre was relating the sorry saga to his mother, who listened with her hand over her mouth. 'Poor Monsieur Roché; he must be eighty-five if he's a day. Is he all right?'

'I don't know. He needed a doctor but the Krauts weren't about to call one.'

'What's happening to our world?'

A knock on the door interrupted his tale. It was Kafka, his pipe dangling from the corner of his mouth. 'You and I need words,' he said, on seeing Pierre.

'My mother's here.'

'Let's go for a little walk then, shall we?'

They traipsed in silence through the field behind the house, lifting their knees to navigate the long grass, and headed for the woods. Pierre wondered what Kafka had in store. Kafka glanced behind as they left the field. Sheltered from the blazing sun by the trees, they stopped to catch their breaths, leaning on a prostrate tree trunk. Pierre was pleased not to have to look at the man. Instead, he concentrated on the dappled spots of sunlight decorating the forest floor. Above them, sparrows and finches sang.

Kafka lit his pipe. 'Old Roché is dead,' he said, discarding the spent match.

Pierre screwed his eyes shut. 'Fuck,' he muttered. 'The sods.' He thumped his thigh in frustration.

'Who do you blame, eh? The Krauts or the person who laid the nails?'

'The Germans, of course. They killed him, not... whoever it was.'

'Still, I wonder who *that* person was.'

'I don't know.'

'But you blame the Germans?'

'Of course,' he said, stroking the bark.

'Well, you would say that.'

Pierre held his tongue. This is what he wanted, after all, but he wasn't sure how to proceed. What if he'd read the signals wrong? He wouldn't put it past Kafka to lure him into a trap.

Kafka stood up. Facing Pierre he leant towards him. Pierre recoiled from the stench of his tobacco breath. 'Whoever did this did so with the best intentions. Anything we do, however small, that shows the Germans that we don't accept their presence here is a step in the right direction. OK, Roché's death was unfortunate and unforeseen, but what's done is done. Now listen, take a book, any book, and meet me at the library at six this evening. The Krauts will be enjoying their dinner, scoffing our food and wine. Not a word to anyone. OK?'

Pierre nodded.

'I'm off. Wait here. Five minutes.' And with that, he was gone. Pierre watched as he strolled away, zigzagging through the trees, plucking at leaves as he went. The image of Roché lying on the asphalt, the side of his head congealed with blood, flooded his mind. 'What's done is done,' he said aloud. After all, he'd got what he wanted. He was a step closer to saving his father.

Surely, he thought, nothing else mattered.

*

Pierre's feet felt heavy as he made his way to the library. Under his arm, his father's copy of Voltaire's *Candide*. He had not been back to the library since he had spied the major and Claire having sex on the counter. The thought of it still made him feel sick. It was like an unmovable stain on his memory. Indeed, he still had not spoken to or even seen Claire since. But, unsurprisingly, it was Claire he saw first on entering the dark interior of the library, behind the counter, serving an elderly woman. His heart lurched on seeing her, pierced by a stab of anger mixed with jealousy. She looked gorgeous in a thin red cotton blouse, her hair tied back with a yellow bow. He could hear them, Claire and the old woman, discussing the wicked killing of Monsieur Roché and the pointless vandalism that led to it. His romantic imaginings were interrupted by the image of Monsieur Roché, his skull smashed in. If it hadn't been for him and his nails, Roché would be still alive.

Pierre flushed with shame. He browsed idly through the books, eying the counter, thinking of Claire's bare arse sitting on it. One day, he thought, when he was older, he would make Claire his. He would woo her, gradually breaking down her defences and winning her heart. He, Pierre, was far too good a man to simply seize her and rape her as the major had done.

With the old lady gone, he approached Claire. 'Follow me,' she said, darting out from behind her counter, her hair bouncing with her steps. She seemed to be expecting him. She led him across the library to a door at the far end, and, holding it open, pointed up the stairs. 'Second door on the left. Knock four times.'

'Not the basement this time?'

'No.' She left him to it, allowing the door to close on him. Pierre grimaced, annoyed that she hadn't said a pleasant word to him, not even an acknowledgement. He climbed the few steps slowly, wondering what on earth he was letting himself in for. He thought of his father, hoping the image of him would give him strength. It did no such thing. It'd been four days since they took him; and yes, he wouldn't want him to come to any harm, but, with aching guilt, he noticed how he was getting on with life without him.

He stopped outside the second door on the left – peeling green paint, a round, wooden door knob, a brass sign with the word 'Private'. Wouldn't this, he wondered, have been a better place to have sex? But then, with the library doors locked, one wouldn't anticipate anyone climbing up the outside wall to peer in.

He knocked. Four times. The door opened with a flourish and Pierre was surprised to see Monsieur Dubois with his blue beret and blue corduroy jacket glaring at him from behind his spectacles. A quizzical look passed between them until Kafka's voice came from behind. 'Let the boy in.'

Three men sat round an oval-shaped table in a dingy room, a small window high up let in minimal light, the brown painted walls were bare except for a large portrait of Marshal Pétain at the far end. The air hung heavy with cigarette smoke. 'Sit down, boy,' said Kafka.

'*Merde*, when you said you had a new young recruit, I didn't think he'd be still in his diapers.' This was Bouchette, whom Pierre recognised from his stand against the lieutenant at the baker's, thin-lipped, dressed in dungarees, twirling a penknife round his fingers.

'Leave him be; this is Georges Durand's boy.'

'That makes it OK, then, does it?'

'Is Durand still locked up?' This was Monsieur Dubois.

Bouchette began cleaning his fingernails with his penknife. 'We need men, more men, Kafka, not children,' he said.

'How old are you, son?' asked Dubois, drumming his fingers rhythmically on the table top.

'He's seventeen. Almost.'

'Well, Louis was only eighteen,' said Monsieur Bouchette. 'You knew Louis, didn't you, Pierre?'

Pierre nodded. Louis Bouchette, an obnoxious know-it-all, once pushed Pierre off his bicycle for no apparent reason except to get a laugh from his equally-obnoxious friends. But he'd been killed just a few weeks ago, caught up in the Nazi advance, and for that Pierre chastised himself for thinking ill of the dead, a hero of the Battle of France. Madame Bouchette, rumour had it, hadn't stop crying since.

Kafka held up his hand. 'OK, look; I know he's young but I reckon he's got fire in his belly. Think back to when you were seventeen, gentlemen. What if the previous generation of Krauts had taken your father? Isn't that motivation enough?'

Bouchette, still cleaning his fingernails, asked, 'And what exactly are your skills, boy? Any particular talents?'

'He's young. That in itself is good. He'll be able to get around easier than us lot. I can't step out of the front door without some sodding Boche asking me for my papers.'

'Yeah, but that's because you swear at them.'

'Not so much now. I keep my head down.'

'We can't talk while he's here,' said Bouchette, pursing his thin lips. 'We don't know whether we can trust him yet. Listen, son,' he said, turning to Pierre, 'one word to anyone that you've been here and...' He made an exaggerated throat-slitting gesture with his penknife.

'No need for that, Bouchette. Anyway, I have a job for him. A little mission with Claire. Nice and simple.'

'The leaflets?' asked Dubois.

'Exactly.'

'That's good.'

'Pierre, Claire knows what to do. Go speak to her.' Pierre nodded. 'Off you go, then, boy.'

Conscious of being watched, Pierre made his exit. It was only after he closed the door and was half way down the stairs that he realised he hadn't said a word.

Back in the library, Pierre saw that Claire had customers – two German privates leaning on the counter, their helmets pushed up their heads, grinning. The three of them spoke animatedly in German. Pierre headed straight out, still carrying his book.

*

Later that afternoon, Claire appeared at Pierre's house. Lucienne had been outside, watering the plants and flowers in front of the house, and showed Claire in.

'Claire,' she said, bringing her into the kitchen, 'what a lovely surprise. Can I get you a glass of water? It's so hot, don't you think? Is it Pierre you've come to see?'

'Yes. And thank you, a glass of water would be lovely.'

Lucienne grinned at Pierre, making no attempt to disguise her delight that her son had attracted such a pretty girl into the house. Pierre and Claire exchanged embarrassed glances, both aware that Lucienne had misread the reason for Claire's appearance.

'It is very hot still, isn't it?' said Pierre, feebly.

'Mm. What's the helmet?'

'Oh that. It's my father's. From the war. Well, the last one, that is.'

'I see.'

'Here's your water, Claire. That's a pretty outfit.'

Pierre groaned – his mother was trying too hard.

'Oh, yes. Thank you.'

'The red suits you. And that hat…'

'Maman, didn't you say…'

'I'm sorry? Oh, yes; you're quite right. If you'd excuse me, Claire, I have to pop out.'

'That's fine. Thank you for the water.'

Lucienne picked up her handbag and hovered at the door. 'How long should I pop out for?'

'Half an hour,' said Pierre.

'Five minutes,' said Claire at the same moment.

Lucienne raised her eyebrows. 'I'll be back in fifteen minutes then.' She gave Claire a self-conscious little wave. 'Yes. Well. Have fun,' she said, closing the door behind her.

Claire sipped her water, peering at Pierre over the rim.

Pierre shrugged his shoulders. 'Sorry about that.'

'Don't worry. Mothers are all alike.'

'Yes. Mine has been on edge since… you know.'

'Understandable.' She looked round the room, taking in her surroundings. 'How did your meeting go?'

'The meeting, yes. It went well, I think. I, er, made my case – you know, why they should trust me. I think they were impressed.'

'Really? Strange, it's usually impossible to know what Kafka's thinking.'

'No, no, he said I'd made a useful contribution.'

'To what?'

'I… I don't know. Anyway, he said I was to speak to you.' He tried desperately not to think of the major fucking Claire on the library counter. He tried to make the image disappear, shaking his head.

'You all right?"

148

'Yes. What? No, I'm fine.'

She looked at him as one might look at something peculiar. She placed her glass on the table. 'He's set us an assignment. We're to have a day out together.'

'Great!' Immediately, Pierre slunk back from his overenthusiasm.

She rolled her eyes. 'Yes,' she sighed. 'Together. As a couple. Even though I'm almost four years older than you.'

'That's not such–'

'Pierre, please. I think…'

Pierre felt himself sag. 'Go on.'

'Listen, you're a nice boy, but I'm twenty years old, and I have a….'

'What?' A boyfriend?'

She removed her hat, placing it on the kitchen table. 'Yes, if you like, a boyfriend.'

'What's he–'

'Pierre, we're got a job to do. It's important, and we have to do it properly.'

The image returned – the major's trousers down at his ankles. Pierre clenched his eyes shut, despite knowing he looked ridiculous.

'Please, don't get upset.'

'No, it's not that. What… what is it we have to do?'

'A day out – you and me, to the seaside. You have your papers, yes?' He nodded. 'All we have to do is take a single sheet of paper with us.'

'And it takes two of us to do that?'

'Normally, no. But Kafka's sees it as training. I'm there to watch you. Make sure you cope with it.'

149

'Doesn't sound that difficult. Have you got this piece of paper?'

'Not yet, no.'

'When do we go?'

'Tomorrow. Ten o'clock from Saint-Romain. So we need to catch the nine twenty bus. Is that OK with you?

'Yeah. Can't wait.'

'Good' She stood up. 'Bring some money – not much. And perhaps get your mother to do a sandwich or something. I'll see you tomorrow at the bus. Don't be late.'

Claire was at the door, adjusting her hat, when it opened. She gave out a little shriek, stepping backwards. It hadn't been fifteen minutes yet, thought Pierre. But it wasn't his mother returning – it was Major Hurtzberger.

The major stood at the door looking like a person who had walked into the wrong house. No one spoke. The three of them hovered awkwardly, unsure what to say. Eventually, it was the German who broke the silence, 'Am I interrupting something?'

'No,' said Claire breathlessly. 'I'd just popped by. I was worried about Monsieur Durand. Georges.'

Pierre watched them intently, determined to spot any tell-tale signs of affection in their body language.

The major looked slightly flustered, thought Pierre with a degree of satisfaction. 'Ah yes, poor Monsieur Durand. Well, don't go on my account,' he said. 'I've just returned for something I'd forgotten.'

'I was leaving anyway. Goodbye, Pierre. Send my regards to your father – if you should see him.'

The major clicked his heels as Claire squeezed passed him. '*Au revoir, Mademoiselle.*' He watched the door closing. Turning to Pierre, he said with a wink, 'Pretty girl.'

'She's only nineteen,' said Pierre, reducing her age to make his point.

'Ah. Nineteen? Bit old for you, then.'

Yes, and a bit young for you – how he wished he had the nerve to say it. The major disappeared into his room and returned, seconds later, with his buff-coloured folder.

'So, as we seem to be alone perhaps we should have a chat.'

'About girls?'

The major laughed. 'I'm flattered you should think of me as a man who can advise you on such things, but sadly, no.' In a flash, his face hardened. 'I think you know what I mean. I had a meeting with Colonel Eisler, and he informed me that you may have something to report to me.'

Pierre's insides tensed up. He swallowed, hoping his mother would choose this very moment to return. This was the conversation he had been dreading. He thought of his father, the reason why he was doing this. 'No,' he said, as firmly as he could muster. 'I have nothing to report.' He resisted the temptation of addressing the German as 'sir'.

The major looked at his wristwatch. 'The colonel mentioned five days. I think we've had some forty-eight hours already. Still – plenty of time. But, listen,' he added, lowering his voice, 'don't try to cross the colonel. He's not the sort of man you can play games with. He's a seasoned soldier who knows how to get what he wants. And he's ruthless. I won't ask what Claire was doing here, apart from enquiring about Georges, of course, but please, I beg you, be careful. You're a good boy and I like you, I think you know that, and I wouldn't want to see you – or your father – come to any harm. Anyway,' he said, returning to his normal tone, waving his folder, 'I must go.'

∗

Pierre stepped out into the yard. The White Venus looked pitifully incomplete. He sunk in the rocking chair and rubbed his eyes. *I have a boyfriend.* Her words rang through his head. Yes, you have a boyfriend. He so wanted to hate the major, felt that it was his duty to do so – he was a bloody Kraut and he was fucking the girl he loved, even if the girl had made her feelings perfectly clear. But what he really hated was the fact that he liked the man, despite everything, he admired him. There was something about him. He was authoritative, strong, at times intimidating but... but he was also kind. He thought of Joachim, somewhere faraway, proud to be his father's son, proud to be wearing his new uniform. He realised how envious he felt – how he would love to don a uniform, to play a proper part in defending his homeland, instead of embarking on trips to the seaside with a girl he loved but who viewed him below contempt. But, more than this, he envied Joachim having a father like the major. He looked skywards and watched a cloud the shape of Corsica drift by, briefing obscuring the sun. He gazed at the white stone, and her clumpy features – her bendy figure, ill-defined and rather awkward, unsure of her place in the world, dependent on others.

His mother had returned – he could hear her pottering round in the kitchen. He decided to ignore her. The Corsican cloud had passed; the sun returned. Lucienne came out to find him. 'Ah, there you are. How did it go with Claire?'

'Fine.'

'What was it she wanted?' she asked, shielding her eyes from the sun.

'Nothing really.'

'No? She's never called on you before. Are you OK? She's a lovely girl is Claire, so pretty, but… oh dear, how do I say this? Pierre, don't you think that perhaps she's a little old for you? After all, she is twenty-two, I believe, and you're only–'

'For the love of God, why does everyone talk about her age?'

'Pierre,' said Lucienne, straightening her back. 'Please don't use the Lord's name so–'

'It doesn't matter how old she is – she's not my girlfriend.'

'Oh.' Lucienne huffed, annoyed to have misread the situation.

'Maman, do you miss father?'

'What sort of question is that?' She began fanning herself with her hand. 'Of course–' A loud knock on the yard door interrupted her. 'Who could–'

'*Bonjour*? Madame Durand?' came a voice from the other side. Pierre recognised the voice – it was one of the cemetery boys.

Lucienne opened the door. 'Oh, hello. My, what–'

'It's heavy, Madame Durand, let us through.' Lucienne stood aside as the two old chaps carried in a rectangular slab of marble.

Pierre got to his feet. 'Is this for me?' he asked.

'Sure is, sunshine,' said the first. They placed the stone down on its edge leaning against the yard wall and straightened their backs. The first one removed his beret and wiped the perspiration from his brow. 'Good day, Madame Durand,' he said with a small bow.

'Good afternoon, gentlemen.'

'It's getting hotter every day, don't you think?' said the first.

'Must be German weather,' said the second.

'Is this for Monsieur Roché?' asked Pierre.

'Yes, indeed, God rest his soul.' Both men crossed themselves in unison.

'Poor man,' said Lucienne.

'Have you got the paper, Albert?'

'No, Hector, I gave it you to, remember?'

'Did you, my God?' Both men searched their pockets but found nothing. 'Wait, I may have left it in the truck. Excuse me.'

Lucienne, Pierre and Albert stood in the yard, Albert rocking on his feet. An embarrassed smile passed his lips. He eyed Pierre's sculpture. 'So, how's it going with your Botcha-whatsit?'

'Botticelli.'

'Do you approve, Madame Durand?'

'Of what, Albert?'

'Your son depicting the female nude.'

'He's learning his art, aren't you, Pierre?' she said. 'One day, he'll be a famous sculptor.'

Thankfully, Hector returned, waving the piece of paper. 'It's your instructions,' he said, passing it to Pierre. 'Monsieur Roché was a widower and had no next of kin, so the instructions and the text have been written up by the mayor.'

Pierre scanned his eye over the sheet of paper. 'He's kept it simple for you, lad,' added Albert. 'What with your father not…' He glanced worriedly at Lucienne, unable to finish the sentence.

'You'll be paid the full rate,' said Hector, 'so no worries on that score.'

'That's very good of the mayor,' said Lucienne.

'We'll tell him.'

'When's the funeral?' asked Pierre.

'Three days' time but don't worry, lad, it doesn't have to be done by then. Anytime, really. Right, we'll leave you to it.'

Lucienne thanked them and closed the yard gate behind them. 'Well, that's good, isn't it? We could do with a little money.'

'Yeah, great.' I caused his death, he thought, and now I get to earn some money from it. He folded the paper and slipped it into his back pocket.

'Is everything OK, Pierre?'

'Yeah, great,' he said again. 'I'll make a start on it later today.'

Chapter 12

Pierre and Claire waited in line, trying to board the front of the train at Saint-Romain. The time was a few minutes to ten. There were, it seemed, hundreds of Germans milling about, most of them very young, perhaps just a year or two older than Pierre. The train was huge – an old steam locomotive brought back into service, its pistons spitting hot water and steam, its funnels churning out dense clouds of smoke which swathed the platform. Most of the carriages were reserved for the Germans, large signs announcing *Für die Wehrmacht*, allowing only the first two for the locals. Pierre and Claire managed to squeeze on and found a pair of seats together in a compartment. Both had haversacks containing their homemade lunches, a flask, a book and a magazine each given to Claire by Kafka. Claire's magazine was called *Carrefour*, and Pierre's *Signal*. Both were pro-German, pro-Pétain and his collaborationist government. Folded into Pierre's book, alongside the mayor's instructions for Monsieur Roché's headstone, was the piece of paper. Monsieur Bouchette, arriving on his bicycle, had slipped it to him at the bus stop in the town. No words were exchanged. Pierre didn't dare look at it, thus he still had no clue what was written on it and why it was so important. Part of him fancied it wasn't important at all, and it was all part of his initiation test. What exactly he was to do with this piece of paper, he had no idea. But Claire did. She knew precisely.

The train compartment was stuffily full: Pierre, Claire and four others. Opposite Pierre sat a large, middle-aged couple with an Alsatian dog. 'Toby, sit,' roared the man, wearing an old jacket with elbow patches.

'Speak to him nicely, Claude,' said the woman.

Unseen to his wife, Claude dealt Toby a swift kick.

The woman asked Pierre to open the window. He was glad to oblige.

On the other side of Claire sat an older gentleman, dressed in a suit and tie, a newspaper on his lap, his frail-looking wife opposite him, her hair in a hairnet.

Pierre gazed outside and watched the comings and goings of more passengers, of soldiers, of the train guard in his black uniform and green flag, the grey smoke hovering under the rafters of the station roof. The time was now ten – time for departure. They had a ninety-minute journey ahead of them. They heard Germans shouting at one another, and the sound of train doors slamming shut. The guard, waving his flag, blew his whistle. Slowly, with more puffs of smoke, the train crept forward and edged out of the station into the morning light.

As soon as the train was out in the open country, picking up speed, the woman opposite brought out two hard-boiled eggs from her bag, passing one to her husband. They sat, peeling their eggs, with a sheet of greaseproof paper on her lap on which the woman had sprinkled salt. Pierre had his own hard-boiled egg in his bag but he hadn't thought of asking his mother for salt. He tried not to watch them as they dipped their eggs. Toby lay on the floor, licking his chops constantly.

Pierre had hoped to talk to Claire, to get to know her a little better, but he felt too self-conscious to strike up a conversation now. Anyhow, Claire, sitting next to him, was engrossed in her book, fanning herself. He wondered whether the fan was to keep herself cool or to flap away the stench of egg that, despite the open window, was now permeating the compartment.

Pierre noticed the man, Claude, wipe away his fragments of eggshell, half of which landed on the dog. He needed a shave, thought Pierre, specks of grey clearly visible in his stubble.

Pierre wanted to read but the heat of the compartment and the early start had made him feel drowsy.

He was woken up by the opening of the compartment door. A French ticket inspector leant in. 'The Boche are acting odd this morning,' he said quickly. 'They're searching everyone's bags, and being very thorough about it.' Pierre's heart punched him from within. The dog, Toby, growled. Then, looking down the corridor to make sure he wasn't overheard, the inspector added, 'Just as well they don't check the toilets. And mind that dog.' Then, just as quickly, he was gone, sliding open the door to the next compartment.

Claire looked at Pierre, her eyebrows knotted. But it was Claude, opposite, who spoke. 'I think I need the toilet,' he said.

Claire nodded. 'Yes,' said Pierre. 'So do I.'

'Let's go, then,' said Claude, picking up his haversack.

Together, with their bags, they headed to the toilet at the front of the train. Fortunately, no one had beaten them to it but there was only the one. 'After you,' said Claude.

Claude locked the door behind them. With the smell of the filthy toilet pan overwhelming them, they squeezed in together. 'Christ, open the window.' Pierre tried but it was stuck. 'What's your name?'

'Pierre.'

Claude offered his hand. As rough as sandpaper, thought Pierre. 'Claude. Nice to meet you.' His breath reeked of egg.

'And you.'

'Question is, should we trust the inspector. This might be a trap, you know.'

Pierre hadn't thought of this. His heartbeat quickened. Pulling on his bag strap, he asked, 'What should we do?'

They heard raised German voices at the far end of the corridor, doors opening. 'Too late now,' whispered Claude. 'We'll just have to sit it out.'

They waited, pressed into each other, Claude considerably taller, Pierre's eyes level with the man's mouth; the stench of stale smoke, drains and egg filling their nostrils. The floor was stained brown with years of piss, the tiny sink with its rusty tap marked with dark stains. Pierre could feel the sweat running down his back, like a thousand tiny insects creeping down his skin. The Germans were getting closer, more doors opening, barked orders, French protestations, doors sliding shut – all in quick succession. He wished he'd stayed now; the searches were quick. Claude jumped at the sound of his dog barking. He mouthed the word shit. More feet, more voices. How many of them were there? There seemed to be dozens. The dog didn't bark again.

Claude delved into his haversack, and pulled out a notebook. He began ripping out the pages from the binding, trying not to rip the paper in half. 'Let's hope the flush works,' he whispered.

Pierre found his single sheet of paper. Yes, there was writing on it, words leapt out – "We will not be defeated / Pétain has sold you out / Drive the Hun invader off our soil." He wondered whether it should say "*from* our soil". The footsteps were closer. Pierre realised what was happening – there were several parties of Germans, overlapping each other. Perhaps, after all, it was better to be here in this stifling toilet with eggy Claude. The man had his papers held above the toilet pan, ready to drop them in. It was too small a toilet, thought Pierre. Even if the flush did work, it would never get rid of all that paper in one go. With a sudden heaviness in his stomach, he knew they would never explain why the two of them were here together, in the toilet.

The door handle rattled. Sweat poured down his brow. A shrill, German voice. Claude's pupils dilated with fear, his mouth open, his dirty tongue lolling from his lips. Outside, the ticket inspector's voice – 'It's out of order.'

A pause. Silence except for the rumble of the train. Footsteps moving away. Claude's shoulders fell. More footsteps but no more rattling of the door handle. Claude let his head fall back, exhaling a deep breath. Pierre clutched his heart, felt his sodden shirt.

'Oh, mother of God,' muttered Claude. 'Come on, let's get out of here before we suffocate.'

Back in the compartment, Pierre almost fell into his seat. He sat there, breathing hard, unable to talk, Claude opposite, a mirror image of relief. Claude's wife had her hand clasped over Toby's mouth. The dog, though muffled, was still trying to growl.

Claire placed her hand on Pierre's thigh. 'Well done,' she said quietly. Pierre looked round at everyone. The elderly couple were smiling. The man winked at him. Claude's wife stroked her dog. Claude let out a little laugh. Everyone laughed quietly with him.

'Good work, young man,' he said to Pierre. Pierre beamed.

Claude's wife leant over, grinning. One of her front teeth was missing. 'Would you like an egg?'

'No. No, thank you. I'm fine. Just fine.'

*

Claire knew where to go. They headed towards the main street of the harbour town. Squinting his eyes against the sun, Pierre could see the sea in the distance. Seagulls flew above. Everywhere, the road signs were written in Gothic script. The street, fully in the shade, was lined with cafés, mostly full of Germans sitting outside under the parasols, enjoying rounds of coffee and cigarettes while playing cards. A couple of cafés had signs saying *Germans only*. Pierre shook his head. At one, he noticed a table full of German officers drinking champagne, the bottles resting in ice buckets. The atmosphere, as at home, was holiday-like with much laughing and soldiers taking photos of each other. Turning off the main street, Pierre followed as Claire wound down a couple of side streets full of boarded-up shops before coming to a stop outside a front door with a lion head brass knocker. Above it, a balcony with curved railings. 'This is it,' she said, pulling on the knocker. 'Don't say a word until I say.'

A man in a vest appeared on the balcony momentarily before disappearing again. Pierre could hear footsteps on the stairs and seconds later the same man was at the door.

'Sorry to bother you,' said Claire, 'but we're lost. We're looking for the Church of Our Saviour.'

'Where?' He wore shorts, was bronzed, solid muscles in his arms.

'Oh.' Claire stepped back. 'I think… it doesn't matter.'

'Hang on a minute.' He returned inside, shouting. 'Victor, there's a woman at the door, something about a church.'

A distant voice responded, 'Keep your voice down, you fool.' More quick footsteps on the stairs and another man appeared, older, taller, round glasses, and blond eyebrows despite his dark brown hair, wearing baggy trousers and a buttoned shirt with a frilly collar.

'Excuse my friend here.' The man eyed both of them but he had, thought Pierre, a kind expression. 'What were you saying, Mademoiselle?'

Claire repeated herself, word for word.

'Ah yes, as beautiful as anything you'll find in Florence. Come in.'

The man stepped aside to allow them through. 'This way; follow me.' The house seemed bigger inside – with a marbled floor, and an arched doorway to the side. He took them upstairs, a spiral staircase with an ornate iron bannister. Pierre noticed his well-polished shoes. 'Welcome, my name is Victor. That was Alain you saw just now.' Pierre turned round but Alain had gone. He realised the exchange about the church and Florence had been a pre-arranged code.

Victor led them into a room on the first floor, a large room with an array of settees and armchairs, a big fireplace, its bricks burnt black, a stone floor with a deep red rug. 'Take a seat. Can I get you both a coffee?'

Victor shouted for Alain, telling him to make a round of coffees. 'No sugar, I'm afraid. And the coffee is of inferior quality. But you know how it is,' he said with an exaggerated shrug of his shoulders. He asked them about their journey, about life in the town and what their Germans were like. Pierre told him about the major in his house, glancing at Claire who sat impassively.

'He doesn't sound too bad then. There's a big difference between your ordinary German and his Nazi colleague. You're lucky, but still – be careful. When push comes to shove, he's still a German. We're having an easy time of it here – relatively. I think they've all got heatstroke; they all seem rather lethargic, poor dears. I doubt it'll last long. So, while the lion sleeps, the deer will play.'

'Is that a saying?' asked Pierre.

Victor laughed. 'No, I've just made it up but I give you permission to use it as often as you wish and pass it off as your own. Well, thank you for coming to see us. I have to say I didn't expect two of you but still, it's lovely to see you both. So, are you two…'

'No,' snapped Claire.

'No. Right. OK.'

'So, erm,' Pierre tried to think of something to change the subject. 'Why are half the shops boarded up?'

'Lack of customers. We don't have any money to buy

anything any more. Only the shops that appeal to the Boche survive.'

'Souvenir shops.'

'Yes, that sort of thing.'

The door creaked open, and in came Alain carrying a tray bearing three steaming cups. 'Ah, here he is; that's what we like to see.'

'Messieurs, Mademoiselle, your coffee,' said Alain.

'If you can call it that. Thank you, Alain.' The two men exchanged furtive smiles. Victor watched as Alain exited, as if admiring him, thought Pierre.

'Cigarette? No?'

The coffee was fine, thought Pierre; he had become used to this ersatz stuff.

Victor screwed a cigarette into a holder and lit it with a large, silver lighter. 'So, what have you brought me?'

'We have the text for the flyer,' said Claire. 'Pierre, have you got it?'

Pierre fished out the piece of paper from his book and handed it over to Victor.

Adjusting his glasses, Victor unfolded the paper. 'Bernard Roché, fourth June 1861 to… I don't understand.'

'Sorry, that's the wrong paper.'

'Thank God for that.' He drew on his cigarette, producing a cloud of purple smoke. 'For a horrible moment I thought you wanted me to print a death notice. Oh, he died yesterday.'

'This is the text.'

Claire cleared her throat. 'Kafka, my boss, of sorts, said you could print a thousand of them.'

They waited while the man read. 'Yep,' he said, pushing

his glasses back up. 'Shouldn't be a problem. It reads well. Perhaps a couple small grammatical errors but I can fix that. You can reassure your boss that I've got the transport heading your way at the end of the week. You'll have five boxes – two hundred in each.'

'Thank you.'

'Now, a bit early perhaps, but how about a spot of lunch?'

*

An hour later, Claire and Pierre sat on the sea wall, watching the sea lapping on the beach, the sun beating down on their backs. Not too far away, a group of Germans were drying themselves off after a dip in the sea. 'They really think they're on holiday, don't they?' said Claire, watching the men with, thought Pierre, a little too much interest. 'Drinking our best coffee, shopping, sunbathing. It's sickening.'

'At least we're doing something about it now.'

'Yes, it all helps.'

'Excuse me.' A German-accented voice made them jump. They turned to see another fresh-faced German struggling with a town plan. 'Sorry to be startling you.' He spoke slowly, each word separated by a space. 'Do you know the way to *Le Café de la Mer*?'

'Yes,' said Claire. Pointing the way, she gave him a complicated set of instructions.

The young soldier bowed and thanked her.

'I didn't know you knew this place so well,' said Pierre.

'I don't. I just made it up.'

'Oh.'

'Did you see those café signs earlier – Germans only?

Well, I'm damned if I'm going to tell him where a café is that I'm not even allowed to go into.'

'It shouldn't be that difficult – with all those Gothic signs everywhere. Poor chap; he'll still be walking round in circles for hours to come.'

Claire winked at him.

'The men in the house – they were nice, weren't they? Especially Victor.'

'I thought he was a bit creepy. Nice lunch though.'

'Yeah, saved me from having to eat my mother's hardboiled egg.'

Claire laughed. 'I think we've had enough stinky eggs for one day.'

'You should have been in the toilet with him. No escape.'

'I can imagine.'

'So, did they search you?' he asked.

'They searched my bags. Took everything out and went through it. Even my lunch. So I was happy not to have eat my sandwiches that had been manhandled by a German with dirty fingernails. In fact…' She retrieved the sandwich, unwrapped it from its greaseproof paper, and left it on the sea wall a few feet away. Sure enough, within seconds a seagull swooped down and snatched it. They watched it as it flew round before disappearing, other seagulls in its wake. 'That poor woman had to restrain the dog, Toby. I thought for a moment they might shoot it.'

The Germans had dressed and strolled by in their bare feet, trouser legs rolled up, squinting in the sun. Each one stole a look at Claire. A young mother passed them, holding a toddler by his hand, a bucket and spade in her other hand. The boy, with his pudgy knees, wore a wide-brimmed straw hat. 'Look at all the birdies, Patrick. Look, there's one over there with a sandwich. Can you see? Oh, it's gone.'

This, thought Pierre, would be a good time to broach the subject of the major but however he tried to start the conversation, he couldn't think of the words.

'Come,' she said, after a few minutes of awkward silence, 'let's have a paddle.'

'What?'

'In the sea.'

'I… I'd rather not.'

'Why on earth not? Come, I'll beat you, last one in is a rotten egg.' Hurriedly, removing her shoes, she raced towards the water, giggling.

Pierre followed, slowly; his shoes scrunching on the sand and pebbles. He watched as Claire hiked up her skirt and waded through the gentle waves. 'It's cold,' she screeched, holding out her hand.

Pierre shuddered. All that water. Yes, it looked inviting in its calmness yet it still repulsed him.

'Ow, the stones are sharp. Come on, what's the matter for goodness sake?'

'I don't like water,' he said, knowing how feeble it sounded.

'There's nothing to be scared of,' she said, splashing

Reluctantly, he took off his shoes and socks and gingerly stepped forward, allowing the water to reach his ankles. Yes, it was cold, but it wasn't that that made him shiver. The teddy bear with its yellow waistcoat and green trousers flashed through his mind again.

'I can't,' he said, spinning round. 'I just can't.'

*

Ten minutes later, they were back on the sea wall, Claire with her bare legs stretched out, allowing her feet to dry off in the sun.

'So, what was that about, then?' she asked.

The mother and toddler sat nearby, building a sandcastle, the little boy slapping the sand with joy. Claire smiled, pushing tendrils of wet hair from her face, while Pierre tried to distract himself from her sodden blouse.

'I have a thing about water.'

'Why, you can't drown if you only go up to your legs.'

'I know.'

'Can't you swim?'

'No,' he said quietly.

'But it's more than that, isn't it?'

Almost imperceptibly, he nodded.

'Well? You can tell me, if you like.'

He shook his head, ashamed that, after all this time, water still had the same effect on him. 'I can't tell you. I'm sorry.'

*

They caught the train home, again sharing a compartment with others. This time they were left undisturbed. Much to Pierre's delight, back home, Claire accepted his offer to walk her back.

'Well,' said Claire, 'that was a really entertaining day; I enjoyed your company. Thank you, Pierre.'

'Pleasure. We must do it again one day. Soon.'

'We'll have to see what else Kafka has in store for us.' They'd reached her bungalow, an old white-stoned house with small windows, a weather vane in the shape of a cockerel on its chimney, a gravelled front garden with a set of iron table and chairs. 'Here we are,' she declared. 'I'd invite you in but I'm exhausted. All that sea air. And my feet are killing me.'

'It's fine. I'm tired too.'

She hesitated, as if changing her mind. 'Another time then.'

'Yes, another time.'

Chapter 13

'The thing is people are getting soft.' Pierre had been instructed to have a walk with Kafka. They walked briskly through the woods, Kafka in front, a large bag round his shoulder, following a narrow path. The sun slanted through the branches, and the ground, after weeks without rain, was hard. The birds were in full song. 'People seem to have accepted this invasion as if it was a good thing.'

'People say the Germans will deal with the communists. And the Jews.' Pierre regretted his afterthought.

'We can deal with them ourselves. We don't need foreigners coming in sorting out our affairs. People see the Germans as a sort of deliverance; they forget they invaded our country and for what? On the whim of a madman. Take your houseguest, for example. The villagers like him; he's a cultured man, he holds the door open for the ladies. Your mother seems to have grown used to his presence. I know all this; I keep my eyes and ears open. They forget, he's not here as our friend; he's here as an invader, a bloody invader.' They jumped over a stream. 'It's up to people like you and me to keep the flame of resistance alive. How will history remember us? You have to ask yourself that. In years to come will your children thank you for having been a collaborator?'

They walked in silence for a while. Pierre picked up a stick and beat at the long grass bordering the path.

'Keep up,' said Kafka over his shoulder. 'So, your trip went well?'

'Yes.'

'Yeah, Claire told me all about it. You did well. Victor prints newspapers. The Krauts have got him printing their rubbish but by night he supplies the whole region with flyers and "subversive literature", as our German friends call it. He's rich; he can afford to do it for free. He's got quite a network already.'

They'd been walking for over half an hour when Kafka declared, 'Here we are.'

At first, Pierre couldn't see what Kafka was referring to – but there, under the shade of a large cedar tree, was a small wooden hut. Its walls were made up of huge logs, it had a window covered in tarpaulin. Kafka undid the padlock and beckoned Pierre in. Inside, daylight permeated the gaps between the logs and through the roof. There was a bed covered in a brown blanket, a table and chair, a shelf half full of food tins, and, on the wall, a large framed portrait of Marshal Pétain peppered with holes. 'Welcome to my second home,' said Kafka. Reaching into his bag, he placed more tins on the shelf. 'Emergency supplies.'

Pierre watched, wide-eyed, as Kafka produced a rifle from under his bed. 'Yeah, I know, I didn't hand it in. I'd be shot for having this around. It's an old M16 carbine. Old but still effective. I stole it from the army in eighteen.

I used to be a sniper, you know. In my day, I could hit a centime from seventy metres. My eyesight's not what it used to be, but, though I say so myself, I've still got an eye for a target. This,' he said, lifting the rifle as if testing its weight, 'is the only rifle we have but one day we'll have more. I'm working on it. So, as you're now officially one of us, I thought you need to be prepared.'

'You want me to fire it?'

'Not the rifle, no, but this... another souvenir from the army.' From his pocket, he produced a revolver. 'That's why I've brought you out here. I wasn't taking you on a walk for the good of your health.'

Pierre watched as Kafka took a tobacco tin also from under his bed and fished out a handful of bullets. 'Let's go outside. Take the photo with you,' he said motioning at Pétain.

Pierre followed Kafka out, the picture under his arm. 'Right, there's a hook on that tree there. See it? Hang the photo up on it.' Pierre did as told, then re-joined Kafka, standing behind him.

Kafka loaded the revolver, took aim at the portrait and fired. The shot cracked through the trees, causing a cacophony of noise as thousands of birds, or so it seemed, took flight, squawking and flapping. 'Did you see that? Right in the old git's forehead. Dead. If only it was that easy. Right, your turn. Take the gun.' He passed Pierre the revolver. 'Always keep it pointing downwards until you're ready.' Pierre did as told. 'It holds five rounds. I can only spare a few, so listen. Hold it solidly, keep your arms straight. The recoil on these things isn't too bad.' Pierre concentrated as Kafka went through his instructions. Finally, Kafka declared that Pierre was ready to have a shot. 'Aim above your target and slowly lower it, then, just at the right moment, pull the trigger.'

Pierre held his breath and did as instructed. But he was unable to fire. Sighing, he tried again.

'Steady now,' said Kafka just behind him.

This time, Pierre pulled the trigger. The revolver jumped back in his hand, despite Kafka's reassurance. What he hit, if anything, he had no idea.

'Not bad. Try again,' said Kafka.

The second attempt hit the tree above the portrait with a satisfying dull thud. 'Hey, you're a natural,' exclaimed Kafka. 'We'll make a sniper out of you yet.'

Pierre grinned, felt his chest expand.

'Come on, let's head back and I'll tell you what's next.'

They returned to the hut. Pierre waited outside while Kafka went in, re-emerging a few seconds later, padlocking the door. 'Even if the Krauts managed to discover this place and ransacked it, they'd never know who it belonged to.'

'They're not likely to come out this far on foot.'

'No, exactly.'

Pierre followed Kafka back, back over the stream and down the zigzag path; this time trying to familiarise himself with the landscape, in case he ever needed to return alone. He noted a tree engraved with the initials 'RJ', and another fallen, its trunk blocking the pathway. With the town in view, nestled in the valley, they trudged back across the fields. As they drew closer, Kafka said, 'If anyone asks, we'll say we just went for a walk for a man-to-man talk. I'm looking after you now, we'll say; now that your father's gone.'

'I miss him.'

'I dare say. But they won't keep him long. I've heard they've got limited room, and they can't shoot all of them. Well, they could, I suppose, but I doubt it.' He stopped, gazing at the houses nearby. 'We'll go our own ways here. Listen, you've passed your first test but there'll be much harder, sterner ones to come. You still in?'

'Yes,' replied Pierre, despite wanting to scream no.

'Good man. Come to the library tomorrow morning at eleven. Make sure you're carrying a book – just in case, you know.'

Pierre nodded.

'See you tomorrow. *Au revoir.*'

*

Returning home, Pierre decided to make a start on Monsieur Roché's headstone. He slipped out the instructions from his pocket and re-read them. He did think the wording was rather brief – just the basics. And no hint about how Roché had met his end – clubbed to death like a baby seal by a German. It contained just the text – no clue as to what sort of lettering, whether it was to be big or small, straight or sloping. He realised he felt daunted by the task. It wasn't difficult but it was a responsibility and he had to get it right. It was the least he could do for Monsieur Roché. He wished his father was here to advise him. He fed the chickens some corn and watched as they fell onto their food. He poured fresh water into their trough, swept the yard, tidied the tools in the shed. Anything to delay actually starting his work. It was always the most daunting part – just starting; making that first engraving onto the pure, virgin surface of the marble. Taking his tape measure, he measured out the width of the stone, and how much space he needed for the first line, then the second, and so on. He wrote out the words lightly in crayon. Dissatisfied with the spacing, he rubbed out the crayon with a rag dabbed in white spirit, and tried again. This time, he decided, he had it right.

Poised with his chisel and hammer, he heard the front door open and clattering in the kitchen. It had to be his mother. Seconds later, she emerged at the kitchen door, her headscarf still on. 'Oh, Pierre, there you are. Where have you been?'

'Oh, nowhere really. I needed a walk to think about how to do this stone.'

'That's OK then. I do worry when I don't know where you are. You are being careful, aren't you, Pierre?'

'Yes, Maman.'

'I can see you're busy, so I'll let you get on. I'm going to Saint-Romain later today to take your father some fresh clothes and a bit of food.'

'Don't put a message in anywhere.'

'Of course not,' she huffed.

'I'll walk you to the bus stop.'

'No need but if you want to, that'd be nice.' She paused. 'Your father – he'd be very proud to see you doing this work.'

'I know.'

She smiled a maternal smile, and returned indoors.

'Right then,' said Pierre to himself. '"In Loving Memory of..."'

*

An hour later, and Pierre had finished. His mother, ready to go to Saint-Romain, joined him outside.

'So, how's it going?' she asked.

'All done, I think.'

Together, they admired his handiwork. 'You've done an excellent job. Simple but dignified. And there's not much of that around any more – dignity.'

Pierre tried not to think of Roché's undignified end. 'Yeah, I'm pleased. Poor old Monsieur Roché. I'll take you to your bus now, if you're ready.'

It was early afternoon. The streets were deserted, the shops closed; not a French person in sight. 'It's like a ghost town,' remarked Pierre.

'Things have changed so quickly. Only the cafés and restaurants seem to thrive nowadays. They're busier now than they ever have been.'

They passed through the town centre and, sure enough, the cafés were open for business and, as usual, doing a roaring trade with their German customers.

'Oh, isn't that our major?' said Lucienne, pointing ahead.

'*Our* major?'

'With that pretty girl. Claire.'

'Oh. Yes. So it is.'

'Pierre, I know what you're thinking but she is a little old for you. Can't you find someone your own age?'

'Where, Maman? They all left, didn't they, during the fighting.'

'They'll be back one day.'

Now, they passed through the square and onto the road on the other side that led to the bus stop.

'I don't think Claire should be cavorting quite so openly with the Germans,' said Lucienne. 'Especially our major.'

'Maman, stop calling him "our" major. He may be nice and all that, but he's still a German.' Pierre remembered Kafka's words. 'He may be cultured and hold doors open for you but don't forget, he's still part of the people who invaded us on the whim of a madman.'

'Invaded. You make him sound like a barbarian, like a Viking, raping and pillaging.'

'But that's exactly what he is.'

'What? Has the major raped someone? I should hope not. And I would have noticed if he had stolen anything from our pantry. There's little enough as it is.'

'No, I don't mean... It doesn't matter. Look, here's your bus. You don't want to miss it.'

'No. Thank you, Pierre. I'll be back in time to do some dinner. Major Hurtzberger brought us some sausages today. That'll make a nice change, won't it?'

*

'Claire told me more Germans are coming in to borrow books, at least the ones who can read French.' Kafka was at the head of the table, addressing the meeting which, this time, numbered six of them.

'I'm surprised they can read at all – French or German,' said Bouchette, idly playing with his penknife.

'She reckons they're bored.'

'Oh dear. Maybe we should lay on some entertainment for them.'

'Right. Yes. What did you have in mind? No, don't answer that. I'm worried in case you take me seriously and we start doing Punch and Judy shows for them.'

A polite tittle of laughter circled round the room.

'Anyway,' said Kafka, 'my point is that I reckon it's too dangerous to meet here any more. Pétain's portrait up there is a good cover but it's not enough. We need somewhere else. Any suggestions?'

Pierre put his hand up. 'What about–'

'Shut up, Pierre.'

'Sorry,' he muttered. Obviously, Kafka didn't want anyone knowing about his hut.

'What about the crypt?' said Dubois, wiping his spectacles.

'Yes, not bad.'

'The Germans are so atheist they never go in the church. We can go in, one-by-one, and sit at the front to say our prayers–'

'Or pretend to.'

'Or pretend to, and once we feel it's safe, we can pop down. Lots of exits too. Not out of the crypt but out of the church. And I'm sure Father de Beaufort won't mind.'

'Good idea. That's what we'll do. Can you speak to Father de Beaufort, Dubois? He's more likely to listen to you.'

Dubois nodded.

'Right, to the main business. No doubt you'll have noticed all the trains passing through at night from Nantes on their way to the Reich, filled to the brim with French goods. We need to do something about it, to hold them up for a few days.'

'Not again?' said Bouchette. 'Look what happened last time. Pierre's father was arrested.'

'And Touvier,' added Dubois.

'So what? They're stealing from us, stealing the fruits of French labour.'

'He's quite right,' said a man nicknamed Lincoln, a gaunt man with long, black sideburns who, people felt, resembled the American president. No one seemed to remember his real name. 'As patriots, we have a duty.'

'But the whole line is guarded, especially round here, after our last attempt,' said Dubois.

'Yeah, but only by collaborators, bloody traitors.'

'Have you a plan, Kafka?' asked Lincoln.

'What do you think? Of course I bloody have. It doesn't involve all seven of us–'

'There's only six,' said the other new man, Gide, the baker.

'Plus we can always call on Claire.'

'A girl?'

'She's keen, and that's what counts.'

'For God's sake, man, what have we come to?' said Bouchette, stabbing his penknife into the table top. 'Children and girls. Next, Kafka, you'll be recruiting from the nunnery.'

'If I thought it would make a difference, I would.'

'And what if one of the nuns turned traitor?' asked Gide.

'I would deal with her. No hesitation. A traitor is a traitor. I'd shoot my own mother if I thought she was sleeping with a Kraut.'

'Isn't she dead?'

'That's not the point.'

'We don't have a nunnery,' said Dubois.

Kafka shook his head. 'Jesus, it's like a chimp's tea party.'

Bouchette whispered to Dubois, who laughed.

'Right,' said Kafka, 'here's the plan. We go tomorrow night, two hours after curfew. Memorise all of this, if you're capable of that. Don't write a single word of this down.'

*

The sausages, Pierre had to concede, were delicious. With a large helping of potatoes and French beans, the three of them retired to their armchairs, relaxed and opened their books or knitting. An hour before, the major had returned from his work with a framed watercolour – an Alpine scene portraying long-horned cattle on rolling lush grass with snow-peaked mountains behind. He said he'd bought it in Saint-Romain and was giving it to Lucienne as a present for all her hospitality. Lucienne oozed gratitude; said she loved it.

'I'll hang it up for you,' said the major. 'Perhaps after dinner.'

'Well, that would be lovely. Thank you.'

Now, after dinner, Pierre found himself alone with the major, or Thomas, as he seemed to have become. Pierre dreaded what he knew was coming next. It didn't take long.

'So,' said the major, quietly, drawing out the word. 'The colonel is expecting a response tomorrow, Pierre.' He didn't look up, keeping his eyes fixed on his book.

Pierre tried to picture his father, tried to remember why he was doing this. He had plenty to tell; enough to save his father and secure his release.

'I don't know anything.'

'And you think the colonel will accept this? I don't.'

'But I do know someone who is working against you – nothing big or dangerous, just leaflets, that sort of thing.'

'Oh?'

This was difficult, thought Pierre but, after all, he had to save his father. It didn't make it any easier.

'Pierre – you have to tell me. Remember what's at stake.'

'I know. It's… I met a couple of men – in a town on the coast.'

'Go on.'

Bracing himself, Pierre told the major about Victor and Alain and their printing press. The major, having placed his book on the floor, listened intently, nodding his head.

'Leaflets, you say?'

'Yes.' Pierre felt himself go red.

'And where are these leaflets? I haven't seen any?'

'They haven't arrived yet.'

'When are they due?'

'I don't know. I think within the next few days.'

He paced up and down. 'This is good.'

'What will happen to them?'

'Don't worry about that.' He slunk back into his armchair and reached down for his book. Reclining, he rested it on his lap, and closed his eyes.

Pierre sighed. He seemed strangely aware of his own naivety, aware of how ill-equipped he was in dealing with this. He felt as if he'd walked into a minefield and had no idea how to extricate himself.

Chapter 14

'It's Monsieur Roché's funeral today, isn't it, Pierre?'

'Yes.' Pierre was eating scrambled egg on toast for his breakfast – he was beginning to hate eggs. He had no appetite, too worried for Victor and his friend and what might happen to them. His mother hovered over him; the major was at the mirror, adjusting his tie.

'Thomas, are you about to go to work?'

'Soon.'

'Would you have time to put that lovely picture up?'

He glanced at his watch. 'Yes, of course. Shouldn't take long.'

'Pierre, you've got nails in the shed, haven't you?'

'Yes – in a jam jar.'

It was only when the major went out into the yard that Pierre remembered.

Within a minute or two, the major had returned, holding the jam jar in his hand. 'It's empty.'

'Oh yes, I forgot, I lent them all to Xavier.'

'You *lent* them?'

'Gave.'

'All of them?' asked his mother.

'Yes, his father needed them for… for something.'

'But it was full before,' said the major holding up the jar, peering into it as if he might have missed one. 'There must've been a hundred nails in here.'

'It was a big job.'

'Let me have a look in the shed,' said Lucienne. 'There must be one lying around. It does seem strange though, Pierre. All those nails.'

The major waited for her to leave. Turning to Pierre, he said, 'It was you.'

'What?'

'Don't play games with me.'

'I… I had to do something – to get into the resistance.'

'An old man died as a result.'

'That wasn't my fault.'

'Wasn't it?' he snapped. 'Every action has a consequence. You're old enough to realise that.'

'I didn't want that to happen.'

'But it did. As a direct result of what you did. I should tell Colonel Eisler.'

Pierre's heart caved in at the sound of the name.

Lucienne returned. 'Couldn't find any. I don't understand, Pierre – why did you have to give them all to Xavier's father?'

'Well,' said the major, re-adjusting his tie, 'if Pierre could ask Xavier's father if he could give us one back, I'll put the picture up tonight.' He put on his cap. 'I'd better go.'

*

It was the afternoon of Monsieur Roché's funeral. Pierre and Xavier were slowly making their way to the church, surprised at how empty the streets were. Lucienne had left earlier. Xavier had elected to wear his father's tight beret.

'Why do you wear that thing? It makes your ears stick out.'

'Your ears stick out by themselves.'

'No they bloody don't.'

'Anyway, you're telling me that you want one nail. Just. One. Nail. Don't you have any left? None at all?'

'No.'

'One nail?'

'Yes.'

'OK. I'll bring round one, solitary nail a bit later. So, why you're so keen on going to this funeral?' he asked.

'I told you. It's because I'm doing his headstone, so I feel I should attend and pay my respects.' He could never admit the real reason, the sense of responsibility that hung so heavily on his conscience.

'Should we be wearing black?'

'Yes. No. I don't know. We hardly knew him.'

'I didn't know him at all. I'm only going to keep you company – remember?'

'Let's go and see. We can always rush back.'

They heard the church clock chime two. As they approached, they could see a strong German presence and, in front of them, remonstrating, a few villagers. 'This doesn't look good,' said Xavier, slowing down.

'The church doors are open.'

'There's the coffin.'

Pierre narrowed his eyes. The coffin, on a trolley, was just inside the church doors. Draped over it was a French flag. The next moment, a German soldier passed by, whipping off the flag. 'Arse.'

'Look out, here comes your mother.'

'Pierre.' Lucienne emerged from the throng. 'They won't let us through.'

'Why not?'

'Hello, Xavier. I don't know. They say only family can attend the funeral.'

'But he doesn't, I mean, didn't have any family,' said Xavier.

Pierre could see the German lieutenant leaning against a jeep to one side while his men stood in front of the church gate, their rifles held across their chests.

Bouchette and Dubois were among the villagers. 'This is outrageous,' shouted Dubois, dressed in a black suit, approaching Lucienne. 'They're saying we can't even pay our respects now?'

'They don't want a repeat of the Algerian funeral,' said Pierre.

'Buggers. Oh, sorry, Madame Durand.'

The villagers began dispersing, intimidated by the German presence. 'Let me try. I'm doing the headstone; they'll let me through.' said Pierre. He approached the soldiers at the gate as everyone else left, Bouchette and Dubois among them. Beyond the gate, Pierre could see Father de Beaufort arguing with a German soldier who was smoking, sitting on the grass next to the gravelled path, with his back propped up against a headstone. The soldier threw away his cigarette and rose, slovenly, to his feet.

'Hello,' said Pierre to two German privates, adapting a deep tone. 'I am preparing the headstone for the deceased.

I'm supposed to be here. Can I come through, please?'

The soldiers stared blankly beyond him, resolutely gripping their guns. Behind them, Father de Beaufort had stubbed out the fizzing cigarette end with his shoe, and was walking back into the church, his robes flapping behind him.

In his side vision, Pierre saw the lieutenant spit. 'It's you again, Frenchie,' he said in German.

'I want to go to the funeral.'

The lieutenant idly produced his revolver, clicked the hammer back and, without warning, fired at Pierre's feet, hitting the gravel path with a sharp ping. A cloud of dust exploded around his shoes as Pierre jumped back. 'OK, OK,' shouted Pierre, scurrying back to join Xavier and Lucienne.

He found his friend almost doubled-up in laughter.

'Are you all right, Pierre?' said his mother, reaching out for him.

'I'm fine, thanks,' he said, jutting out his jaw.

'Well, they sure listened to you,' said Xavier, guffawing.

'Yeah, very funny.'

Lucienne shook her head. 'Come on, I think we should go home.'

*

The night was eerily still, broken only by the distant hoot of an owl. Pierre looked up as the slither of moon disappeared behind a cloud. Kafka had told him to meet up at eleven in the ditch beneath a small junction box on the railway line. He was told to keep an eye out for the French guards the Germans had posted as patrols along the track. The railway was a good couple of kilometres' walk away. He glanced at his watch. It was quarter to. He walked slowly, continually checking behind him, pausing at corners, conscious of the sound of his footsteps on the road. He knew that if caught out this long after curfew, he would never be able to explain it. He'd reached the point where he had to leave the road and follow a path with a field on one side and the woods on the other. Here, at least, he felt more secure – the trees providing him ample cover. He realised how heavily he was breathing – not from the excursion but from the tension. Glancing behind, beyond the field with its corn swaying gently in the breeze, he could make out the outline of the town, the church spire looming in the dark sky. How peaceful the world seemed. A bat flew by. Pierre wanted to smile, wanted to console himself with the thought that nature had no truck with the misdeeds of man. But the thought provided no consolation. He pressed on, his feet as heavy as clay.

Beneath the trees he could no longer make out the time on his watch. He could see the junction box ahead of him, up on the embankment. No sign of a patrol. The last stretch, from the edge of the woods to the line, was across an expanse of barren grass. He ran across, stooping, half expecting to hear a shot ring through the air. As he approached, he saw the figures of others crouching against the bank. They weren't Germans – that was all he needed to know for now.

'Good boy.' It was Kafka. Someone shook his shoulder in a paternal sort of way – it was Monsieur Dubois, wearing his blue corduroy jacket with a wide leather collar. Next to him, Monsieur Gide. Pierre felt relieved to see them all. Safety in numbers, he thought. But no Lincoln or Claire. Pity, he thought, she'd be missing out. Behind

Dubois, crouching, was Monsieur Bouchette. The man gave Pierre a wave. They were lying in a ditch at the bottom of the bank – above them, the junction box.

'Right,' said Kafka. 'Everyone ready?' He spoke in a whisper yet it still sounded too loud. 'Good. Let's go.'

As previously instructed, Pierre and Dubois edged about fifty metres to the right, while Bouchette and Gide covered a similar distance to the left – leaving only Kafka, with his explosives, in the middle. Dubois led the way. A thin veil of rain began to fall. Continually crouching, Pierre's back began to ache. After a while, Dubois told Pierre to stay put while he went further along. Kafka had devised this system of lookouts – an outer one and an inner one, each armed with a white handkerchief and, if that failed, a whistle. The whistles, Kafka had told them, had been provided by a sympathetic school teacher in Saint-Romain, while the explosives had been commandeered from a quarry left to waste since the Germans' arrival. Dubois and Bouchette, as the further lookouts were each armed with a cosh. Kafka held onto the only firearm they possessed – his wartime revolver.

Pierre watched as Dubois made his way along the ditch. With a start, he realised someone was on the track; two men heading their way. Dubois, too far down, hadn't seen them. The men, strolling along, had rifles slung behind their backs, their silhouettes made hazy by the rain. Pierre had his handkerchief at the ready but he couldn't use it – Dubois had his back to him and it would only attract the patrol. The whistle was just as useless. He looked back, hoping to see Kafka but the man was out of view. His mouth felt dry. Creeping forward on the damp grass, he kept the two men in sight. They had stopped. Holding his breath, Pierre stopped also. Dubois, at last, had seen them too. He also halted, waiting, Pierre guessed, for him to catch up. One of the men was patting his pockets, as if looking for something. Pierre crawled forward on his knees, using his hand on the grass to help him keep balance. The patrolmen were lighting cigarettes, talking quietly but loud enough for Pierre to hear what they were saying. They were talking about the war memorial, Soldier Mike. The Germans had ordered its destruction. Why, wondered Pierre, would they want to do that?

With a wave of the hand, Dubois urged Pierre forward but he felt unable to move any further. The two patrolmen moved slowly on – they were now half way between Pierre and Dubois, Dubois behind them, making hand signals which Pierre tried to decipher while not wanting to take his eyes off the men on the line. Dubois was creeping up the embankment. Pierre felt at a disadvantage – the men were in front of him; if he moved now, they would see him. Dubois had reached the train track. One of the men turned. Dubois screamed as he sprinted with, thought Pierre, surprising speed for a man in his forties. Both men reached for their rifles. Pierre tried to climb the bank but his legs, shaking uncontrollably, gave way beneath him and he slipped down the wet grass. 'Shit,' he muttered, trying to maintain his balance. With frightening clarity, he suddenly realised he would rather be shot than be found simpering at the bottom of a ditch. With renewed determination, he ran up the bank, knowing that any moment could be his last. Clambering to the top, his mouth gaped open at what he saw. The three men were sharing a cigarette.

'Pierre,' whispered Dubois, beckoning him over. 'Come

here. Come meet my brother-in-law.'

His knees gave way as the relief flooded through him. With a stab of shame, he realised he had tears in his eyes. Surreptitiously wiping them away, he hoped Dubois and the patrolmen wouldn't notice in the dark and the rain.

'Don't worry,' said Dubois. 'We're safe here.'

But, thought Pierre, are we not exposed up here on the track?

'Hello,' said the two patrolmen, shaking Pierre's wet hand.

'You gave us a fright there,' said Dubois's brother-in-law.

'Likewise,' said Dubois.

Pierre couldn't see their faces. He hoped they couldn't see him. 'I don't understand.'

'Gustave and François are, how shall we say it, unwilling collaborators.'

Gustave sniffed. 'I'd rather we didn't use that word, unwilling or not.'

'We didn't ask to do this,' said François.

'Don't worry about Pierre,' said Dubois, wiping the rain off his spectacles. 'He's just a kid.'

Just a kid? thought Pierre. I'm out here, aren't I?

Footfalls on the track made them step back. 'It's only Kafka,' said Dubois.

'What's going on?' asked Kafka, his revolver at the ready.

'Put that away, you fool. We're among friends here.'

'No man doing Germans' work is a friend of mine.'

Dubois flung his cigarette away. 'Oh, do shut up.'

Bouchette and Gide had joined them. The seven of them climbed back down the bank.

'Have you chaps heard?' said Gustave on reaching the bottom. 'The Germans are planning to pull down Soldier Mike.'

'What on earth for?' screeched Bouchette.

'I don't know.'

'It's obvious, isn't it?' said François. 'It's a memorial to the 1870 war – against them.'

'Yeah, but they beat us that time.'

'And that will be the only time,' said Kafka.

'You're going to have to hit us, you know,' said François.

'My sister won't thank me for it,' said Dubois.

'Oh, I don't know.'

'Why do we have to hit them?' asked Pierre.

'Come on, boy, think about it. So they can say to the Krauts that we overpowered them.'

Kafka put his revolver back into his jacket pocket. 'I'll happily oblige. I'll take you,' he said, pointing at François. 'Pierre, you can hit the other one.'

'Me?' The idea of hitting someone without the benefit of a fight seemed preposterous.

'It'll be good for you. So, how shall we do this?' he said, stepping up to François.

'I don't know but…' The man fell back as Kafka's fist caught him on the jaw. He remained on his feet until a second punch floored him. He landed on the grass. After a while, he sat up, puffing his cheeks, and holding the side of his face. 'Whoa. Hopefully that'll do it.'

'Your turn, Pierre.'

Pierre considered Gustave. The man raised an eyebrow. 'Get it over and done with,' he said.

Clenching his fist, clenching his jaw, Pierre stared at

him, trying to summon a feeling of hatred. But it wasn't working; he felt himself go slack. 'I can't do it.'

'You have to,' said Dubois.

'You'll be doing me a favour,' added Gustave softly. 'Believe me, I'd rather be hit by you than a Nazi.'

Not wanting to give himself time to think about it, Pierre swung his fist. It caught the man on the side of the nose. He shook his knuckles, surprised at how much it hurt. Gustave, meanwhile, did not move. With a groan, Pierre realised that his punch had barely registered.

'Come on, boy; you can do it,' said Kafka behind him. 'Imagine he's a Kraut, imagine he's just raped your mother; no, not your mother. Claire. Yes, Claire. This bastard in his Nazi uniform who has no right to be in our country has just forced himself onto Claire. Poor Claire; defiled by a…'

Gustave staggered back. Having hit him, Pierre held his fist under his armpit. Gustave laughed. 'That's better,' he said, dabbing his lip.

Kafka stepped up to him just as he was recovering his balance and struck him again. 'Just for good measure,' he said.

Gustave flew back, landing heavily. This time he didn't move. Dubois went to him, bending over his stricken friend. 'Jesus, Kafka; you've knocked him out cold.'

Kafka winked at Pierre. 'You'll learn,' he said. 'Right, back to work. Our little homemade device is in place. Now, just a gentle little explosion. Oh…' He took the patrolmen's rifles, handing one each to Dubois and Bouchette. 'We'll take these, thank you very much.'

Chapter 15

Pierre lay in bed, watching the second hand of his bedroom clock go round. It was almost eight. He knew he had to get up; he had work to do – now that Monsieur Roché's headstone was finished, he wanted to get on with his Venus. He replayed the events of the previous evening through his mind. They'd left François dozing in the rain next to his unconscious friend. The story for their German employers was that both had been taken by surprise and knocked out. By the time they came to, it was almost morning; too late to check the rail track. Kafka had cursed the lack of rope to tie them up with. The first German train, which would have left Saint-Romain at six, should have been derailed. Pierre hoped their battered faces looked convincing enough.

*

Hair is a difficult thing to fashion on stone. Success is in the detail. But not too much. Too much and it detracts from the rest of the work; too little and it begins to resemble so much rope. Consulting his book containing Botticelli's masterpiece, Pierre saw the amount of work that lay ahead of him. The hair of Venus ran down her back, round to her front, finishing at her pubic mound. It amounted to hundreds, no, thousands, of strands. It was easy for Botticelli, he concluded – he had only to work on the front. For him, Pierre, it was far more daunting a task, because it had to look right front and back. The more he pondered, the greater his sense of unease. Best, he thought, to make a start, to allow the chisel to do its work, and to see where it took him. He'd propped Monsieur Roché's headstone up against the yard wall. His mother said she would call on the cemetery boys to ask them to come pick it up. Then, he could make his way to the town hall and pick up his wages. The thought pleased him no end – a man's wage for man's work. His father would be proud.

It had been over a week now since Georges's arrest. It disturbed Pierre how quickly he had become accustomed to his absence. He reasoned that it was not necessarily due to a lack of concern. It was just that he could not imagine what ordeals he would have had to endure; what indignities may have been heaped on him. And he, Pierre, had been given to the chance to save him and he knew, following the railway sabotage, that he was already failing him. He only hoped his information on Victor and his friend made a difference.

The kitchen door burst open. It was the major, already returning from work, and Pierre knew straightaway that he wasn't pleased.

'Did you know about last night?' snapped the major.

'Last night?'

The major considered him for a few moments, as if trying to see whether a lie hid behind his idle tone.

'I've just found out. I came back because I thought you might, perhaps, know something.'

'No.'

'I believe you do. The railway line has been sabotaged. Two guards beaten up.'

'I didn't know.'

The major's eyes scanned the yard as if looking for evidence. He stiffened, his eyes momentarily narrowing. 'OK; you can lie to me if you want to but I warn you, you cannot lie to the colonel. And it is to the colonel you have to report.'

The major was right – it was easy lying to him, but he baulked at the thought of being confronted by Colonel Eisler. 'I have to go see him?' he asked, aware of the quiver in his voice.

The major heard it too. His eyes beamed, pleased to have caught Pierre out so easily. 'He wants a word with you right away.' He looked at his watch. 'You'd better go now. Take your bike.'

Pierre gazed at Venus. Her hair would have to wait a little longer. He wondered whether he ought to change, to dress up for the occasion. No, he decided, it wouldn't make any difference. 'I'd rather take the bus.'

'You'll have to wait too long. No, cycle. It'll be quicker.'

Well, it wasn't far, he thought, and the ride might help calm his nerves. He ought to tell his mother. He made for the kitchen.

The major called out to him.

'Yes?'

'Don't even attempt to conceal the truth; don't play games with him. His eyes will see into you.'

*

Colonel Eisler eyed Pierre menacingly from across the mahogany desk, his fingers intertwining a fountain pen. On the desk stood a vase of flowers; many of its petals had fallen, forming a circle of colour round its base. The brass desk lamp with its hexagon-shaped shade was lit despite the light pouring through the huge French windows. 'I think you know why you're here,' said the colonel in a gentle tone.

'I didn't know anything about it,' said Pierre, trying to maintain the colonel's gaze.

The colonel raised an eyebrow. 'You didn't know anything about it,' he repeated slowly. 'Not good enough. You had your instructions and you have failed me.'

Pierre had to stop himself from shrugging his shoulders.

The colonel continued. 'As it is, the saboteurs caused minimal damage. We are dealing with amateurs here. The railway line will be fixed in no time but my point is your failure to keep the major and me informed. I thought you knew what was expected of you. Well? What have you got to say for yourself?'

'I'm sorry.'

'You're sorry. Is that it?'

'I tried but I can't find out who is part of this group.'

He slammed the table with his palm causing Pierre to jump. 'You have to try harder. What you do think this is? A friendly chat with your headmaster? First we have the incident with the nails and now this. Major Hurtzberger told me about the printing press and the flyers. You'll be pleased to know that their little operation has been broken up, and both men are now in the custody of my seaside colleagues. So, that was good; enough to save your father from the firing squad for a while longer but it's not enough. It didn't tell me anything I didn't already know. Have you forgotten we have your father within these walls? I have come to admire him; he is a stubborn man. Foolish but stubborn. He is our hostage but he is only useful to us if, in return, we have a grasp of what's going on in your town. If not, as I told you before, he will be executed. We, the might of Germany, have conquered huge swathes of Europe. Do you think I will allow this little community of ne'er-do-wells to derail my work here?'

'No.'

'What?'

'No, sir.'

The telephone on his desk rang. He looked at his watch, snapped it up, grunted something in German, and slammed it down again.

'Right,' he said, returning his attention to Pierre, 'it's time.' He rose from his chair and squared his cap. He clicked his fingers. 'Follow me.'

Pierre felt a wave of fear; he hadn't expected this. A soldier, standing guard outside the colonel's office, closed the door behind them, then followed the colonel and Pierre down the corridor. Together, they descended one flight of stairs in silence, and along another corridor where they came to a halt next to a window half way along. The soldier opened the window, pushing up the top half, then stepped back. Peering out over the balcony, Pierre saw beneath him the courtyard, the floor made up of red bricks, the occasional potted plant dotted round, along one side a laurel hedge, at the far end a stone wall partially covered by creeping stands of ivy. In itself, it was a pleasing view yet for reasons he couldn't fathom, Pierre's blood ran cold. Something, he knew, was wrong.

They waited but for what, Pierre had no idea. The colonel stood, his arms behind his back, watching him, his face stern. Pierre felt himself wilt. The whole building seemed to hum but despite so many people within its walls there were no voices to be heard. A flock of swallows flew by overhead; somewhere, on the street, a lorry sounded its horn. The soldier behind him cleared his throat. And still the colonel remained motionless. Then came the noise from beneath him, of a bolt being pulled back, of a heavy door being pushed open. Craning his neck over the balcony, Pierre saw a number of German soldiers appear, one after the other, their rifles against their shoulders. Six, seven, eight of them. They drew up in one line, facing the ivy wall, a few feet away. Then, more slowly, a man accompanied by a priest, his hands behind his back, followed by an officer and two more soldiers. It took a few seconds for it to register. 'No,' Pierre yelped as his knees buckled. The colonel stepped forward to hike him back up. Pierre reached for the windowsill to steady himself. The man was his father and he was being led to his execution. The priest, a Frenchman, walked alongside him in his black robes, his bible open, reading quietly in a soothing voice. Whether Georges was listening, whether he found it any comfort, Pierre could not tell.

'Do not to say a word,' said the colonel. The soldier was directly behind him. Pierre felt a nudge in his back, a revolver.

He tried to control his breathing; clutching at his heart. Feeling lightheaded, he feared he was about to fall.

His father was placed against the wall. His hands had been tied behind his back. Pierre's mouth gaped open at his appearance – his father looked ten years older, his skin taut and grey, heavy bags beneath his eyes. His clothes, streaked with dirt, hung off him. He hadn't said a word; not a flicker of emotion had crossed his face. He seemed almost not to care. 'Look at me,' thought Pierre. 'Look up, look up at me.'

The officer stepped forward and, from a sheet of paper, read a few words aloud at Georges. The firing squad took their positions, rifles drawn, at the ready.

'I'm sorry,' muttered Pierre, aware he was crying. He spun away, unable to look. The guard jerked his revolver up, aiming at Pierre's forehead. 'Turn around,' ordered the colonel.

'No, please, no.'

The guard clicked off the safety catch.

Feeling unable to stand, Pierre turned back to see the priest cross Georges. He placed his hand on Georges's head, muttered a final few words, then stepped back.

The officer's voice echoed across the courtyard as he ordered his men to take aim. Pierre swayed on his feet. He heard the round of rifle fire just as he blanked out.

*

Pierre opened his eyes and realised he'd fallen against the colonel who now had his arms round him, propping him up. The sound of gunshot still reverberated through his head. His limbs felt heavy, his heart more so.

He felt the colonel's hand resting on his head. 'It's OK

now, Pierre. There is but a hyphen that separates life and death. Look outside.'

Pierre wanted to pull himself away but found he had not the strength.

'Go on; look outside,' repeated Colonel Eisler. 'Tell me what you see.' The German helped Pierre find his feet and most gently pushed him back towards the open window.

Pierre wanted to protest but his voice could not be found. He felt nothing; his mind devoid of thought, his heart laden with so much weight. Even the smallest movement felt as if he was struggling through the heaviness of nothingness. It took him a few seconds to register as he tried to focus his eyes. Yet, there, standing in the courtyard, as if nothing had happened, was his father. He still wore the same dulled expression as if he was unaware of his surroundings; of what was happening around him. But yes, he was standing, he was breathing. He was alive.

Behind him, with head bowed, stood the priest, his bible, held in both hands, closed. Pierre noticed the officer glance up at the balcony and from the corner of his eye, he saw Colonel Eisler nod. A soldier prodded Georges from behind with his rifle and slowly he stepped forward. Pierre watched, numb, unable to understand, as his father was led back the way he came. A few seconds later, he heard the door close, the bolt pushed back into place. The courtyard was empty. Yet Pierre continued to stare, unsure now whether the drama had been a figment of his imagination. One of the potted plants had been kicked over.

*

Pierre sat in the colonel's office, unaware of having been

led back. Colonel Eisler sat opposite him, staring, his head cocked to one side, a look of concern in his face, his hands on the armrests of his chair. The French windows had been opened, the heavy turquoise-coloured curtains swaying slightly in the wind. The desk lamp had been switched off. Sunk in the chair, Pierre felt tired, exhausted even. He concentrated his gaze on the vase of flowers, on the petals around it. The vase, also turquoise, was embedded with the shape of a woman with a long flowing dress that disappeared into the glass. Pierre studied her hair, following its contours as it circled round the vase.

'Pierre.' He looked up. The colonel had removed his cap. He looked younger for it; less severe. 'You've had a shock, I understand. Forgive me but it was necessary.' He paused perhaps waiting for Pierre to respond. 'You were not taking me seriously. I believe you saw it as a game of some sort. I had to make you realise that war is not a game and that I am serious. Go home now. Find out who is in this town gang of yours and report back to me via Major Hurtzberger before they manage to do some real damage.'

Pierre tried to speak but could only manage a nod of the head.

'Next time, your father's execution will be for real.'

*

Riding home on his bike was an effort; he could hardly concentrate. He had stumbled out of the building and had to return to sign out with the receptionist with pink nail varnish. Wherever he could, he freewheeled, zigzagging down the streets of Saint-Romain, passing a parked convoy of German trucks, and out into the countryside. The clouds hung low but it was still warm. He wondered whether his father was aware that the execution would be fake. Somehow he thought not. His father had stood up to them; and even at the supposed moment of death, he refused to break. His courage was admirable. Should he tell his mother? Tell her what a brave husband she had? No, he couldn't. Not yet. So why did Kafka mock his father so? He'd like to see Kafka withstand a week in Nazi custody with such dignity.

Some three kilometres from home he faced a steep incline. Any other day, he knew he'd be able to cycle up without too much effort but this was far from any other day. Half way up, short of breath, he dismounted. In his trouser pocket was the packet of cigarettes the colonel had given him on the first visit. Dropping his bike on the grass verge, he sat down and leant against a tree. He lit a cigarette and closed his eyes. The thought of his father remaining in that place, at the mercy of the colonel, was too much to bear. The colonel had made his point – he would, from now on, do whatever he could to save his father. Sod France, sod patriotism; his father was his father, his flesh and blood. Nothing else mattered any more.

Having smoked his cigarette and cleared his mind, Pierre re-mounted his bike and cycled up the rest of the hill. Having reached the top, a nice downhill road led to home. He paused and looked upon his town in the valley with the church tower at its centre. From here, from this vantage point, it seemed as if God had casually dropped the whole place from on high. He never felt so pleased to see it. He raced down, pedalling hard, joyous with the wind blowing through his hair. He felt like screaming but couldn't find it within himself to let go of his emotions to such an extent. Having reached the bottom of the hill, the road flattened out as it snaked into the town itself. This was the road the PoWs came through, he remembered. Would he ever forget? He slowed down as the road plateaued. Then, from seemingly nowhere, he felt a terrific smash against his right side. He screeched as he fell and landed heavily on his left arm, his bicycle skidding on its side away from him. A man in a cap appeared from behind him, running. Pierre sprung to his feet, the pain in his arm vanishing in an instant. 'What are you doing?' he shouted as the man grabbed his bike. The thief tried to make off but, losing his balance, had to try again. Pierre was on him, barging into him, pushing the man off. He pulled the bike from him, its pedals hitting the man in the shins. Now, he feared the man would turn on him.

Instead, he remained on the ground, his cap lying next to him. 'I'm sorry,' he said. Slowly, he got to his feet. He was tall with black hair, shaved at the back but long at the front, his fringe covering one eye. He tossed his hair back to reveal strange eyes. His black trousers were covered in dust, a jacket pocket torn. 'I'm sorry,' he repeated. 'I shouldn't have done that.' He offered his hand.

Pierre, sensing a trick, ignored it. He didn't recognise the man's accent – he wasn't a local. 'Where are you going to?'

The man eyed him, perhaps, thought Pierre, wondering whether to trust him. He didn't look much older than himself – perhaps eighteen or nineteen. Eventually, he answered. 'I need to get to the Free Zone,' he said, looking round as if they might be overheard. But there was no one around – just large expanses of fields flushed with corn, grass verges adorned with wild flowers, the sound of bees.

'The Free Zone? That's miles away.'

He shrugged. 'That's why I need a bike.'

'Well... I suppose you could take mine.'

The man smiled. 'That's awfully generous of you but I feel bad enough as it is; I couldn't now. Are you hurt?'

'No.' Pierre looked down at his left arm. His sleeve was ripped, the skin beneath grazed. 'Who are you?' he asked.

'I can't tell you that.'

'You're not French.'

'No. Belgian. Listen...' The man ran his fingers through his hair. 'I need... I need your help. They're looking for me. You could turn me in; you'd probably get a decent bounty.'

'I wouldn't do that.'

'No, I guessed that. You offered me your bike after I tried to steal it from you.'

Pierre thought of Kafka. How much he would relish this. 'I know a man who could help.'

'You do?'

'The town wouldn't be safe now. If you stay here, I'll come and fetch you about six o'clock. That's the time the Krauts eat their dinner. It's the best time. Do you have a watch?'

The man nodded. 'I'll find somewhere to hide in those woods.' He scooped down to retrieve his cap. 'I couldn't ask you to bring me some food, could I? I've a bottle of water but that's it. And this man of yours... I don't have any money on me.'

'It'll be fine.'

The Belgian smiled. 'I'm lucky to have found you.'

'If you can't tell me your name, I'll call you Tintin – he's Belgian, isn't he?'

'Tintin's a great name. You're a good man. So, what's your name?'

'I can't tell you that.'

*

Pierre cycled straight to Kafka's and found him wearing overalls, painting his porch. The old car door propped up against the house was still there, along with the empty birdcage and discarded boots.

'Ah, young Durand. What brings you here? You can give me a hand if you want.'

'I found a Belgian,' said Pierre, propping his bike against a tree.

'A Belgian bun?'

'No, a…' He hated it when Kafka mocked him. 'A Belgian on the run.'

'Ha, it rhymes. Have you indeed? Good for you.' Kafka stepped back to admire his work.

'He needs our help.'

'Does he? In what way?'

Pierre stood next to him. The new green paint reflected the sun. 'He's on the run from the Germans. He's trying to cross the demarcation line.'

'He's got a long way to go.'

'That's what I said. He needs somewhere to stay until things quieten down.'

Kafka placed his paintbrush on the upturned paint tin lid. 'OK, tell me everything.'

The two men sat on the porch as Pierre related his tale, of how the Belgian, Tintin, had tried to steal his bike, of how he said he would return at six. Kafka picked up a bamboo stick and jabbed at the ground, making little holes in the dry soil. Pierre could tell Kafka was excited by the prospect of doing something.

'And how do you know he's trustworthy?'

'I don't; not really. Although when I knocked him off my bike he could have fought back – he's bigger than me. And desperate.'

'True. I'm impressed; you've done well.'

Pierre smiled.

'I'll speak to Bouchette and Dubois. You can leave it to me now.'

'But you'll need my help. He might not trust you if you all turn up looking for him.'

'Hmm. All right. Meet us at a half past five at Bouchette's garage. We'll be within striking distance of him from there.' He threw away the bamboo stick. 'Meanwhile, I'll work out what to do with this Belgian.'

*

Pierre returned home, waving to Xavier as he passed.

'Pierre, where have you been?' Lucienne was outside the house watering the flowers as Pierre jumped off his bicycle.

'Nowhere. Just things to do.'

'Your sleeve – it's ripped. What happened?'

'I fell off.'

'Is that all? Does it hurt? You're up to something. Tell me, what is it?'

'Nothing, Maman. I need to get on.'

Having escaped his mother, Pierre paced up and down the yard disturbing the chickens. Already, the certainty he felt cycling home had drained out of him. This was the sort of thing he should report to the major but he'd taken an immediate liking to the Belgian with his strange eyes. How could he deliver him into the hands of the Nazis? God knows what they would do with him. He remembered enough from Sunday school to know that he'd been assigned, albeit unwittingly, the role of the Good Samaritan.

*

'We have to be careful. After the railway attack, the Boche are more nervy.' Kafka, Bouchette, Dubois, Claire and Pierre had gathered in Bouchette's kitchen. Monsieur Gide, apparently, had declined to have anything else to do with Kafka's group, finding the derailment episode too traumatic. On the kitchen table, a fishing rod and a small bucket of maggots. It was half five.

'How's the coffee?' asked Bouchette. His wife had made them each a cup. Every time one of them took a sip they couldn't help but grimace.

'Disgusting,' said Dubois.

'It's made of beetroot and chicory.'

'What happened to all your wine? Did the Germans take it?'

'Ha, no! The idiots. I buried it in the garden.'

'All of it?'

'Every last bottle.'

'What do you think of the coffee, Pierre?' asked Claire.

'It's… it's fine.'

'Not like the coffee your friendly Hun supplies, eh?'

'Leave him alone,' said Kafka. 'The boy's done good work today.' Pierre noticed Kafka's fingers were stained with green paint. How did Claire know the major gave his mother coffee? The answer, he guessed, was obvious.

'So how do we know if he's genuine, this Belgian?' asked Claire.

'We'll interrogate him tonight.'

'And if he's not?'

'Then we'll deal with it,' said Kafka, patting the revolver in his jacket pocket. Dubois and Bouchette exchanged glances, raising their eyebrows.

'Do you always carry that thing with you?' asked Dubois.

'Only on special occasions.'

The Bouchettes' Alsatian dog wandered in. It made for Pierre's bag and sniffed it, pushing his nose against it. 'Oi, Daisy, leave it alone,' said Bouchette. 'What have you got in there?'

'Two chicken legs. For the Belgian.' He placed the bag out of reach on the kitchen table.

'I'd like to see you explain away chicken legs if the Germans stop and search you.'

'So, what's the plan, boys?' asked Dubois.

'Hide him in the crypt,' said Claire. 'Father de Beaufort wouldn't mind.'

'Are you mad?' exclaimed Kafka. 'That means bringing him into town. Too dangerous. No, what we'll do is take him to Lincoln's farm. I've already spoken to him. He said we could hide him in his barn. It has a loft.'

'Perfect,' said Dubois. 'Then what?'

'We need to find someone in Sainte-Hélène to take him.'

Bouchette slapped his dog. 'That will take him four kilometres closer to the demarcation line.'

'It all helps,' said Kafka. 'Right, we'd better go. Pierre and I'll pick him up now, take him to Lincoln's. Claire, you can come with us. A woman's presence might help calm him down. We'll all meet here tomorrow at ten.'

Dubois and Bouchette nodded.

'Not at the crypt, then?' asked Pierre.

'No, we got short shrift from the father,' said Dubois. 'He went all strange when I mentioned Kafka's name.'

'Idiot,' said Kafka.

Madame Bouchette reappeared, a rotund woman wearing a bulging floral dress. 'Any more coffee, gentlemen?'

'No, no, no.'

*

Bouchette's garage lay on the outskirts of the town on the road to Saint-Romain. There was always a chance of a German convoy returning but Pierre knew they'd be able to hear that in advance. The chances of a German patrol, this far out, was, he hoped, slim, and, as he'd said to Tintin, they'd be having their dinner now. The three of them walked quickly, keeping to the side of the road. Kafka carried the fishing rod, Pierre the bucket of maggots. This was to be their alibi if stopped. Less than a kilometre on, they'd come to the place where Pierre had had his encounter with the Belgian.

'Let's hope he appears soon,' said Kafka.

'I told him six. Five minutes.'

'I know.'

Sitting on the verge, they waited, their shadows on the road in front of them. Ahead of them, a field of corn, bordered on the far side by the woods. Pierre stared into the bucket and watched the constant movement of the maggots, with their slimy yellow and green bodies.

'Revolting things,' said Claire. 'Any news on your father?'

'No.'

The church bells rang six o'clock. They waited, the silence broken only by the sound of bees and the squawk of a blackbird. Two white butterflies danced before them.

'Good God, is that him?'

Pierre looked up – coming towards them, across the field, was the Belgian, his cap pushed down over his eyes. 'Yes, that's him.'

The three of them stood up. Pierre waved. The Belgian waved back.

'He doesn't look like a man in a hurry,' said Kafka.

'Hello,' said the Belgian, his hand outstretched. Shaking hands, Pierre introduced Tintin to 'his friends who can help'.

'Nice to make your acquaintance,' Tintin said to Claire, removing his cap. He offered his hand to Kafka but Kafka, like Pierre earlier in the day, refused to take it.

'So who are you?' asked Kafka.

'My name, as christened by your young friend here, is Tintin. I was fighting with the 35th Infantry Regiment.'

'What happened?'

'We were totally overrun.' He shook his head at the memory. 'We suffered badly. Many killed. It was horrible. Truly horrible. I was lucky; I was taken prisoner. Then I escaped.'

'How?'

'On a march. A week ago. We were being transported. I don't know where. Three of us made a dash for it. The others were gunned down, shot in the back, but, as you can see, I got away. I've been on the run since, stealing food, sleeping in forests. I stole these clothes. From a washing line.'

'A good fit.'

'I was lucky.'

'I'm told you're a Belgian.'

'Yes but I've lived in France since I was ten. Look, I know it must be difficult for you, but can you help me? I thought of getting to the Free Zone.'

'And then what?'

'To get to Spain eventually, then perhaps from there, to England. I'm a captain; I have a lot of experience. I want to offer my services to the English army. Anything to fight these pigs.'

Kafka eyed the man, looking at him up and down, considering what to do. 'OK, this is the plan. We'll take you to a farm a couple of kilometres from here, belonging to a friend of ours. You can sleep in his barn for a night or two while I arrange transportation to the next town.'

'Thank you; that'd be…' Unable to finish his sentence, Tintin bowed.

'Come on,' said Kafka. 'We ought to get going. We'll need to go back through the field. It's on the other side of the woods, nice and isolated. If we should get stopped, we've been out fishing. You lead the way,' he said to Pierre.

Claire walked alongside him. 'Is it just me, or does this feel wrong somehow?' she whispered.

'He seems genuine to me.'

'I suppose. Ignore me, I'm being paranoid.' After a pause, she added, 'He's got very clean fingernails.'

*

Ninety minutes later, Pierre was back at home. They'd taken Tintin to Lincoln's farm. It was obvious that Kafka had browbeaten Lincoln into taking the Belgian. Reluctantly, Lincoln had led them to the barn. Inside was a loft, reachable by ladder. Having settled Tintin there, and left him with Pierre's chicken legs and half a bottle of red wine and a hunk of cheese, courtesy of Monsieur Lincoln, they descended back down the ladder and removed it. Kafka told them all to meet again at Bouchette's garage the following morning at ten. It had all gone well. Almost too well.

Pierre lay on his bed and tried to read his biography of Botticelli but something was troubling him. His mother came in, asking whether he'd taken the chicken legs she'd been saving. Pierre confessed and apologised. He heard the major return, heard him and his mother talking. He knew he had the power now to save his father; he merely had to tell Major Hurtzberger that they were hiding a fugitive in Lincoln's barn. But he knew he wouldn't.

That night, Pierre slept fitfully. When, finally, he managed to doze off, he dreamt vivid dreams that involved maggots and bicycles and eyes and dogs. The maggots, millions of them, were everywhere, climbing up his legs, wriggling on his stomach, crawling across his neck. He sat up, his hands frantically flapping them away, his body quivering with revulsion. Realising he'd been dreaming, he breathed a sigh of relief. He felt thirsty. Turning on his bedside lamp, he swivelled his legs out of bed, nodded at his Rita Hayworth poster and made for the kitchen. He waited for the tap water to run cold as he took a glass from the draining board. He drank the water down, relieved to feel the cold water cascading through him. Returning to bed more relaxed, he fluffed up his pillow and lay back, switching off the light. He lay there with his hands behind his back, hoping sleep would soon return. As, slowly, he drifted off, the Belgian's strange eyes came into view. One was blue, the other green. He saw them, appearing in the dark, peering intently at him from beneath the Belgian's cap. They seemed to be mocking him. The cap transformed into a helmet – a German helmet. Two different-coloured eyes beneath a German helmet.

The realisation hit him with the force of a hammer. He screeched, sitting up in bed. He had seen the Belgian before – in an SS uniform.

Chapter 16

Pierre woke up with a start but it took him a few seconds to work out why. The memory came flooding back. He remembered all too well – the guard with his different-coloured eyes beneath his helmet opening the door to Colonel Eisler's office; his mother and he entering. He jumped out of bed and swiftly pulled on his clothes. He had to warn Kafka and the others. They were to meet at ten but were due to arrive in ten-minute intervals. Too many men arriving at the same time could raise suspicions. It was Kafka's new idea. Pierre had been instructed to arrive last at ten thirty. He realised as he was getting dressed that mixed in with the dread was a sense of excitement. The gang would be pleased with him, pleased that Pierre, through his sharp observation, had spotted a trap.

He managed to escape the house without his mother noticing. The major had left earlier. A steady drizzle fell. The meeting in Bouchette's kitchen was already well under way when Pierre arrived a few minutes before ten thirty.

Kafka was, as usual, holding forth. 'We'll have to search him, of course.' He looked up as Madame Bouchette showed Pierre in. 'You're wet. Were you seen?' he asked.

In his haste to get there, Pierre hadn't thought to check. 'No,' he said firmly, as he took his place opposite Claire. She winked at him.

'What were you saying?' said Kafka to Bouchette.

'What? Ah yes.' Bouchette twiddled his penknife between his fingers. 'I have a mate in Sainte-Hélène. Owns a garage like me. And like me he has bugger all to do nowadays. Bloody Germans, how they expect us to survive when they close down our businesses, I don't know. I'll go over and see him today; see if he can help us move our Belgian friend.'

'Good; that'll get him off our hands,' said Dubois.

'He'll still have a long way to go,' said Claire.

'We can only help so far,' said Kafka.

Madame Bouchette appeared carrying a tray laden with steaming coffees. 'Here were are, gents; I know how much you enjoyed it last night.'

A round of muttered thanks circled the table.

Pierre cleared his throat. 'Ahem, erm, the Belgian; he's not who he says he is.'

'What?' screamed Kafka. Claire choked on her coffee.

'He's German.'

'Good God.'

'Are you mad?' said Dubois, his face red. 'How do you know?'

'You said he was a Belgian,' said Bouchette.

Pierre hadn't seen Kafka come over to him until he felt himself being hoisted out of his chair by his lapels. 'You assured us; how do you know he's German?'

Claire rose from her chair. 'Kafka, leave him be, let him speak.'

Kafka thrust Pierre back down.

'I'm sorry, I didn't realise. It was only last night when I was asleep. I woke up and I remembered I'd seen him in…' He stopped. He couldn't tell them where he'd seen the Belgian.

'In what?' asked Dubois, his face redder still.

'In a German uniform, SS. It's his eyes.'

'SS?' shrieked Bouchette. 'Oh shit.'

'Yes,' said Claire. 'His eyes are odd.'

'Couldn't you have remembered this earlier, you idiot?' Pierre slunk down, fearful that Kafka was about to strike him.

'There, there,' said Bouchette. 'Let's not get upset. It's not Pierre's fault he didn't recognise him at once. Indeed, we should be grateful he remembered at all.'

'Exactly,' echoed Claire.

'But are you sure, Pierre?' asked Dubois. 'It's important you get this right.'

'I've never seen eyes like his. One of them is green and the other is blue.'

'It would also explain why he was so clean-shaven,' said Claire.

'Yes, you're right,' said Kafka. 'He's got thick black hair; and he said he'd been on the run for a week. He'd have a full-blown beard by now. That man has had a shave within the last day or two.'

'And it would explain how he miraculously managed to find perfectly-fitting clothes to change into, and why, for a man living off the land, his fingernails were so clean.'

'Yes, good girl, Claire; you'd make a great detective.'

The five drank their coffee in silence. Daisy, Bouchette's dog, entered, pushing open the kitchen door. Claire stroked it. 'She's got very thick fur for this weather.'

It was Dubois who broached the subject that was on all their minds. 'So, what do we do with him? We can hardly return him to the Germans.'

Kafka took another sip of his coffee. 'There's only one thing we can do.'

'Exactly,' said Bouchette. 'So I suggest we get it over and done with as quickly as possible.'

'Claire and Pierre should go home,' said Dubois. 'This is no job for women or boys.'

'No,' said Claire. 'I want to be there. I'm part of this group; I need to be there.'

Kafka nodded. 'She's right. And Pierre, you're almost a man now.'

Pierre nodded, unable to speak.

*

Again, Pierre was obliged to arrive last at Lincoln's farm. He waited in Bouchette's kitchen while, one by one, starting with Kafka and Claire, the others went ahead. Politely, he turned down Madame Bouchette's offer of more ersatz coffee.

She sat down with a sigh in a squashy armchair in the corner of the kitchen. Balancing two dirty cups on her hefty bosom, she said, 'I was sorry to hear 'bout your father.' It sounded as if he'd died. 'It's a nasty business all this, mark my words. I don't like it one bit. Do you mind if I smoke? Don't tell my old man, though. He'd have my guts for garters.' She lit a handmade cigarette and blew a billow of smoke through her nostrils.

'Won't he smell it?'

'He won't be back in here until he wants his lunch. Anyhow, the windows are open. You won't tell, will you?'

'No.'

'Our secret.' Daisy wandered in and nuzzled her mistress. Placing the cups on the floor, she beckoned the dog onto her lap. Pierre couldn't help but think she looked ridiculous sitting in an armchair with a huge Alsatian dog on her. She shook her head. 'First they take your father, God rest his soul–'

'Madame Bouchette, he's not–'

'Then that poor Monsieur Touvier.' She tapped her ash directly on the dog where it rested on its fur. 'It's probably best we don't have no horses left for there'd be no one to mend their shoes. And they killed my Louis. I hate them.'

Pierre nodded sympathetically. 'Madame Bouchette, I have to go now.'

'Yes, yes, you go. Don't let me hold you up.'

She ruffled Daisy's ears.

*

Pierre made his way to Lincoln's farm. The drizzle of earlier had turned into steady rain. The clouds moved quickly across the sky. The road was empty, the rain keeping everyone inside.

Leaving the road, he followed the path alongside the cornfield to the farm, relieved to reach the shelter of the trees. Lincoln's farm lay in a little dip and walking down the path towards it, the sight of it, cloaked in mist, depressed him.

He skirted past the farmhouse, across the yard, watched by a black and white goat, and made straight for the barn.

The barn had two double doors, both painted black, one big, one small. The drain, he noticed, was blocked; rainwater was pooling beneath the drainpipe. It was only now that the thought occurred to him that he might be walking into a trap. Trying not to make too much noise, he eased open the smaller door and peered in. Inside, he saw the ladder lying on the floor, undisturbed since the previous evening. He crept in. Shafts of light broke through the doors. Bales of straw were stacked high to the far end. Nearer by was an assortment of crates, boxes and bins. A cat slept in a wheelbarrow; various tools were propped up against the barn wall – a couple of brooms, a hoe and an axe. A coat hung on a hook. The cat lifted its head as Pierre crept by but wasn't perturbed enough to give up its place of comfort. The door behind him opened. Quickly, he looked round for somewhere to hide. But then he saw Claire's silhouette. He breathed a sigh of relief. Lincoln, Dubois, Bouchette and lastly Kafka followed her in.

'Is he still up there?' asked Dubois, wiping the rain off his spectacles.

'I don't know,' said Pierre. 'I've only just arrived. Where were you?'

'In the kitchen.'

Tintin's head appeared at the square gap above them. 'Good morning, friends,' he called down.

'Keep your voice down,' said Lincoln, who was wearing a long raincoat that reached his ankles. 'Here, boy, help me with the ladder.' Together, Pierre and Lincoln hoisted the ladder up to the loft. Tintin skated down, jumping off the last few rungs.

'Here,' said Lincoln, 'breakfast.'

'Lovely. Thank you. Wine?'

'No coffee. Sorry.'

'That's fine.' He bit into the baguette. 'Mm, bread and wine. Anyone would think it was my last supper. Most welcome.'

Pierre and Claire exchanged glances. Pierre noticed that Tintin's stubble had noticeably grown overnight. Kafka was right – if it could grow this fast, how come he'd been so clean-shaven the day before?

'Nice wine. And this sandwich – delicious. Listen,' he said, his mouth full of bread, 'I was thinking – perhaps you chaps could do with some help. Rather than going south or to England, I'd happily stay here and volunteer my services.'

Kafka cleared his throat. 'That's good of you. We'll certainly consider it. Look, we'll need to search you,' he said.

'What?' His hand, gripping the baguette, stopped half way to his mouth.

'I'm sure you understand.'

'I assure you I'm who I say I am.'

'You haven't told us your name,' said Bouchette.

'I just thought the less we know of each other the better. I told you, I'm a captain in the 35th Infantry Regiment, I fought–'

'You're very young to be a captain,' said Dubois.

'I'm twenty-three.'

'Come on,' said Kafka. 'Arms up.'

The Belgian glanced at each of them. Placing his wine on the ground and passing his baguette to Claire, he stretched out his arms. Bouchette and Dubois stood with their arms folded while Lincoln hung back near the barn door. Kafka delved his hands into the Belgian's jacket pockets. He pulled out a penknife, a box of matches and, from the inside pocket, a photograph. 'My mother,' said the Belgian.

'Pull out your trouser pockets.'

'Is this really nec–'

'Do as I say.'

The Belgian pulled his trouser pockets inside out – empty but for a trail of dust and crumbs.

Reaching behind him, Kafka checked his back pockets. 'What's this then?' he said, retrieving a folded piece of card.

Kafka was standing too close to the Belgian to notice the fist. He doubled up as the punch caught him in the stomach.

'Stop him,' yelled Bouchette.

Dubois fell as he tried to seize the man. Pushing Claire aside, the Belgian reached for the axe leaning against the barn wall. The cat leapt from its wheelbarrow.

'Hey, steady with that,' said Lincoln.

The Belgian swung the axe in front of him. 'OK, let me go, and no one will get hurt.'

'No,' said Kafka, his revolver trained on the Belgian. 'Put that down or I'll shoot you.' He clicked off the safety catch.

The Belgian seemed to consider his options for a moment before dropping his axe.

Pierre tiptoed across and retrieved it.

Without taking his eyes off the Belgian, Kafka passed the card to Claire. 'Here, read this.'

Claire's eyes widened as she scanned the writing. 'It's an SS identification card.'

'Is it indeed?' said Kafka, a note of triumph in his voice.

'Oskar Spitzweg, born ninth November 1920. It's got a Nazi stamp on it.'

'You rat,' said Lincoln, spitting. 'To think I gave shelter to a fucking Nazi. SS at that.'

'You're only nineteen, not twenty-three,' said Claire.

'So what do we do with him now?' asked Dubois.

'We let him go,' said Bouchette. 'So that he can report us to his superiors who'll come and arrest us and then execute the lot of us.'

'Exactly,' said Kafka. 'That's what will happen if we let him go.'

Dubois ran his fingers through his hair. 'That means only one thing…'

'You don't have to,' said Tintin, stepping forward. Kafka lifted his revolver. The SS man paused and lifted his arms higher. 'Look, I won't say a word. Please, you have to trust me.'

'Huh,' snorted Bouchette. 'Trust a German?'

'Not just a German,' said Lincoln. 'SS. Remember? Let's see that card.' He scanned it, shaking his head. 'Just looking at it gives me the willies. You look like one evil sod.'

'But I'm not. Not really.' He was sweating now, his face red. 'You saw the picture of my mother.'

The men laughed. 'I imagine even Hitler loved his mum,' said Claire.

'Please, you can't kill me like this – in cold blood.'

'Oh the irony,' said Dubois.

'Here, Pierre, take this,' said Kafka, handing his revolver over. 'If he should so much as blink – shoot him.

Got it?'

Pierre nodded and tried to control his trembling hand.

The four men moved to the centre of the barn where they fell into a heated discussion. Pierre gripped the gun, feeling vulnerable. Claire stood next to him; their eyes fixed on the German. His eyes looked left and right. 'So I know your name now as you know mine. Tell me, Pierre, what would you do if I made a run for it?'

'He'd shoot you dead,' said Claire.

'I doubt it. Ever handled a gun before, Pierre? I thought not. It's not as easy as it looks, is it?' He took a step forward.

'Get back. Get back, I say.'

'What, and wait for those fools to kill me? They wouldn't have the balls.'

'Those fools fought in the last war,' said Claire. In the corner of his eye Pierre swore he spotted them playing rock, paper, scissors.

A sudden flurry of movement to his side took Pierre's attention. The cat. A mouse. The German sprang, leaping through the air. Pierre fell back, the German fell over him. The gun fired. Claire screamed. The men came running, shouting. Pierre still had the gun. The German tried to release his grip, slamming Pierre's hand against the barn floor, before slumping on top of him. Pushing him off, Pierre staggered to his feet. The German stirred, rubbing the back of his head. 'Good work, Claire,' said Dubois. Claire stood, panting, grinning, the spade in her hand. Behind her the cat dragged its victim away, its tail twitching.

Bouchette patted her shoulder. 'That was one hell of a swipe, girl.'

'Get up,' ordered Kafka. The German straightened his back. 'Are you listening?' The German nodded. 'We may be enemies but we are not monsters. However, we have decided we have no option but to execute you. Monsieur Lincoln owns a rifle and has volunteered to carry out this unpleasant duty.'

Lincoln had gone; presumably, thought Pierre, to fetch his gun.

The German stood hunched. The man was crying. 'I had so many plans,' he said. 'After the war, I was planning to resume my studies in Bremen. Architecture. I never wanted to be a soldier. I had dreams of designing lovely buildings, meeting a pretty girl and settling down. Nice house, children, you know.' His eyes widened as Lincoln returned, carrying his rifle. His legs buckled. Kafka helped him stay on his feet. 'I am as helpless in the face of death as that mouse was with the cat.'

'It's a bit old,' said Lincoln apologetically as he approached them. 'It's a Berthier from the war. My brother gave it to me.'

'Oh God,' said the Belgian. He began muttering in German, crossing himself.

'I think it'd be best if you stand next to the wall,' said Kafka to the German. 'Come on.'

'Yes, thank you. Thank you.'

Pierre tried to swallow. He couldn't believe he was about to witness a man being killed. It seemed unreal. Lincoln looked as if he might be sick. He too was muttering, talking about his brother. No one was listening. Bouchette and Dubois had stepped back. Dubois was shaking, Bouchette covered his mouth with his hand.

Claire wiped her eyes. 'We should have a priest,' she

said. 'Look at him; he needs a priest.'

'I know but what can we do?' said Kafka. 'I'm sorry,' he said to the German, who, gulping, tried to speak. 'Lincoln, you ready?'

'Here, hold this a minute, boy,' said Lincoln to Pierre, handing him the rifle. Lincoln approached the German, now standing with his back against the wooden slats of the barn wall. He offered the German his hand. 'I'm sorry I have to do this.'

'You have no choice,' said Oskar. 'I see that now.'

After a moment's hesitation, the two men embraced. The German sobbed into Lincoln's shoulder as the Frenchman patted his back, repeating, 'Forgive me, forgive me...'

'Please, do it now. Get it over and done with.'

Pierre handed Lincoln back his rifle. The German hung his head, reciting a prayer in German. Lincoln lifted the gun, took aim. Everyone took a further step back. Lincoln, Pierre noticed, was shaking terribly. 'Go on, do it,' whispered Claire.

The crack of the rifle shot sounded. Oskar screamed. He fell to his knees, clutching his shoulder and grunting. Blood seeped through his fingers. Lincoln spun away; his eyes clenched shut.

Claire patted her pockets and found a handkerchief. 'Here, let me,' she said to Oskar. The man fell on his back. Claire scooped up his head and rested it on her lap. He removed his hand and allowed Claire to press the handkerchief against his wound trying to stem the flow of blood.

Lincoln let the rifle fall to the ground where it landed blowing up a cloud of straw dust. 'I can't do it again.'

Oskar screwed up his face. 'Please, Mademoiselle, post the handkerchief to my mother.' Claire glanced at the others. Kafka was removing his revolver from his inside jacket pocket. 'I want her to have this handkerchief with my blood on it. The street is Winter Strausse in Bremen, number fourteen. It hurts. Will you remember that?'

'Yes, yes, I'll remember.'

Quietly, Kafka walked up to Oskar.

'Tell her I died for Germany; tell her I died with her name on my lips.' He looked up at her. He had no idea Kafka was next to him, slightly behind.

Kafka lifted his arm.

'I'll tell her; I'll write to her. I promise.'

'Thank you, Mademoiselle.'

Pierre closed his eyes. The shot rang out. Claire screamed. Somewhere birds squawked. Pierre forced himself to look. Claire, her jaw quivering, her hands against the sides of her head, was sprayed with the German's blood, her coat splattered with fragments of brain and tissue. Frantically, she tried to wipe it off.

Kafka strode back to his friends. Pierre was sure he was grinning. The nausea rose in his throat. They each patted him on the back; Lincoln, with great solemnity, shook his hand.

Pierre turned round and vomited.

*

Kafka allowed Pierre and Claire to return to the town immediately. He, and the others, would stay behind and bury Oskar Spitzweg in the grounds of Lincoln's farm. 'Should we not get Father de Beaufort?' asked Bouchette.

'No,' said Dubois. 'It could complicate matters.'

'Perhaps after the war?' suggested Claire.

Pierre pushed the small barn door open. He saw Lincoln's wife at a distance throwing grain for the chickens while stroking the head of the goat. 'She must have heard,' said Pierre.

'Yes, but it's easier to pretend it's not happening.'

The rain had stopped, the dark clouds dispersing revealing islands of blue sky. Pierre walked with his head down, his hands in his pockets; Claire alongside him, her coat filthy with blood.

'I hope never to have to come back here,' said Pierre. 'That was horrible.'

'But necessary.'

'Do you think so?'

'Of course. It would have been us at the end of the rifle barrel had we let him go.'

They walked in silence until they were back on the road leading down to the town. The day didn't feel real somehow, as if time had suspended itself. Outside, everything looked normal, the sky, the fields, the woods, the town ahead. Yet the world looked uglier; it felt different, and Pierre felt older, his feet heavier.

Claire muttered something to herself.

'What did you say?'

'I was just repeating the address. Number forty, Winter Strausse in Bremen.'

'Number fourteen not forty.'

'Is it? Are you sure?'

'I couldn't forget it if I tried. One day, after the war, in years to come, I might go visit it.'

'And what would you say?'

'I don't know. Perhaps I won't even knock. I'd just

stand outside and watch.'

'You're being sentimental. The man would have had us shot in a blink of an eye.'

'Different-coloured eyes.'

'That's what made you remember, wasn't it?'

'Yes.'

'You know the Germans are pulling down the war memorial the day after tomorrow. It's been announced. The barbarians.'

'It won't look the same without Soldier Mike.'

'Listen.'

'What?'

'I can hear boots.' It sounded like a group of German soldiers running, just round the bend in the road, their heavy boots slamming against the tarmac.

'They might ask for our papers,' said Pierre. 'They might ask where we've been.'

'They'll see the mess on my coat.'

'Get rid of it.'

'Too late. Quick, kiss me.'

'What?' Before he had time to prepare himself, Pierre felt Claire's arms around him, her lips on his. He closed his eyes. He felt quite lightheaded with the mixture of emotions – the tension of German soldiers about to pass them, the execution and the unexpected delight of kissing Claire. He felt her hand on the nape of his neck. His back muscles relaxed at her touch while the sound of the thumping boots became louder, pounding in his brain. Opening his eyes a fraction, he saw them pass, about eight of them, exercising in full uniform, with heavy packs on their backs. They waved and cheered as they ran by. One of them whistled, another put his thumbs up. Pierre waved back but made sure to keep his lips to Claire's. The sound of their boots receded but he held Claire tightly, not wanting the moment to end. But it did. Claire pulled back. 'That did the trick,' she said.

'Perhaps we should carry on in case they come back.'

'Come on, this is no time to be flippant. Oh, you've got blood on your coat as well now.'

'It's stopped raining so we can take them off.'

He walked with a lighter step, wanting to take her hand, holding his coat over his shoulder. He knew the kiss had been meaningless but still, he felt marvellous.

He hadn't realised that Claire had stopped. He turned. She had her hand on her forehead. 'You OK?' he asked.

'Those soldiers – they may talk. They might tell their comrades.'

'About what?'

'About you and me just now. *Merde.*'

'I don't understand. What would it matter?'

But of course he understood only too well.

*

Having said goodbye to Claire outside her house, Pierre ambled home, in no hurry to return. He wondered about her life in Paris, how different it must have been from her life here. He wondered whether she wanted to return there; whether, indeed, she might take him one day.

Taking a detour via the library green, he leant against the tree he and Xavier often used to sit under. The grass was wet. He hadn't seen his friend for a while. He rather missed him, yet when he thought of the games and antics they used to get up to, he realised none of it appealed any more.

A truck full of soldiers rumbled past behind him. So Tintin the Belgian had been Oskar Spitzweg the German SS. And now he was dead. It must have all been planned. Yes, of course it was – he remembered the major insisting on him cycling to the colonel's office. So, Spitzweg, on duty there, would have known he would be cycling by on that road around that particular time, tipped off by Major Hurtzberger, and had enough time to set up his little ambush. After Pierre had been pushed off his bike, he was too stunned to react that quickly, and his left arm throbbed in pain. The man had plenty of time to make his getaway on the bike, but no, he purposely got the pedals stuck, allowing Pierre time to get up and seize him. But why? The man had offered his services to them. Perhaps that was it – simply to infiltrate and report back to the colonel.

Bremen. He wondered what sort of town it was, whether it was big, a city, or small like Saint-Romain. Did he drink coffee in its cafés, did it have a cinema, did he have lots of friends there? A girlfriend? One day, soon, Oskar Spitzweg's mother would receive a letter from northern France enclosed with a handkerchief stained with her son's blood. How does one cope with that? Did he have brothers in uniform? Sisters? What would Claire say in her letter? Would she say he'd been captured and executed with tears in his eyes, regretting the life that had eluded him, his plans to study, to become an architect? Would she say he was buried in unconsecrated ground on a bleak farm without the attendance of a priest? Nineteen years old, almost twenty, born after the last war, born in a time of peace. What an age to die.

He flung himself down on the armchair in the living room. The major had put up the painting of the Alpine scene. Pierre wasn't sure that he liked it. He saw, hung up on the coat rack, the major's cap. Normally, at this time, he would be still at work in the town hall. Something felt strange, an odd atmosphere in the house. As soon as he stepped through to the kitchen, Pierre knew something was wrong. He found his mother and the major in an embrace. Involuntarily, he let out a sound of surprise. He stepped back, hoping to escape back out but his mother heard him.

'Pierre, come in,' she said quietly, disentangling herself from the German. There was nothing unusual in her expression, no sign of shame. Pierre realised their embrace was not improper. Something was wrong. 'Thomas has had a letter.'

The major's eyes were red. He looked older, his face drained, his hair dishevelled.

Pierre sat down at the kitchen table. The major withdrew and disappeared into his bedroom, gently closing the door behind him.

'What's… what's happened?'

Lucienne sat on the bench next to him. 'It's the major's son, Joachim. He's been killed.'

'Oh.'

'Yes.'

*

Pierre spent the rest of the morning working on his sculpture, trying not to think about the major's son or the executed SS man. He found comfort from the familiar presence of the chickens near him. Madeline, Marlene, Monique… The work was going well, he chiselled away feverishly, keen to distance himself from the real world.

He remembered that the major had promised to have the finished sculpture displayed at the town hall. He hadn't mentioned it since. Perhaps, when the opportunity presented itself, he would remind him. He imagined the sign next to it – 'The White Venus by Pierre Durand, 1940.' His father would burst with pride. His mother would tell everyone in the town. If only things were so easy.

Concentrating as he was, Pierre hadn't realised the major had come out into the yard and was standing behind him.

'You made me jump.'

'My apologies.' He lit a cigarette, closing his eyes as the smoke filled his lungs. 'It's coming along nicely, I see,' he said nodding at the sculpture.

'Yes. I'm doing the hair. It'll take a while.' Pierre wondered if he should mention his son; he had no idea what the etiquette was concerning a bereavement.

'Yes. It looks like a lot of work. I admire your patience.'

'Thank you.'

'My son, Joachim, he had too little patience. Always in a hurry, wanting to do whatever came next in life.'

'Yes.'

'Always in such a damned hurry. Too keen to do the Führer's dirty work. Your mother told you?'

'Yes. I'm sorry.'

'Hmm.' He sat down in the rocking chair. 'North Africa. Killed in action. "I regret to inform you…" Fighting for the Führer. At least that's what the telegram said. It makes it sound as if it was a worthy death. Nineteen years old. No death is worthy at that age. Goodness knows how his mother is coping. I ought to…

Never mind.' He stood up again, struggling to extricate himself from the rocking chair. 'I need to go back to work. It's just another day; a day like any other.' He threw away his cigarette, half smoked. The hens jumped and squawked. 'Pierre, I have… There's something else.'

'Yes?'

'I've been told… I mean, they, my superiors, have told me…' He looked to one side. 'I'm being transferred. They'll give me a few days leave, but when I return to France, I'll be heading for another garrison, one in Paris, I think.'

'Oh.' A heavy silence settled on Pierre's heart; a form of guilt that he should be pleased, pleased to ridding his home of this invader, but, instead, a blanket of sadness wrapped over him. He stared at the sculpture, his hand, holding the chisel, poised; his mouth hung open. 'Oh,' he said again. The news, so sudden, had taken him unawares; he'd never considered the possibility. Of course, it was obvious but still… 'I…' Summoning the courage, he turned to face the major. 'I'd be sad to see you go.'

The major smiled a smile filled with painful regret. His eyes turned heavenward, running his fingers through his hair, clenching at strands so tightly to have hurt. He shook his head and was gone.

Pierre leant over and scooped up the major's half smoked cigarette.

Chapter 17

Kafka slammed the table. 'What idiots we were; we should have kept him alive.'

'No – the only good German is a dead German,' said Bouchette, his hand beneath the kitchen table, stroking Daisy.

'Don't you see, you fool; if we'd kept him alive, we would have had a bargaining tool. One German SS for our boys holed up in Saint-Romain.'

'No, you're the fool here. If you can think you can outfox the Germans at games like that, you're mad. Can you imagine the swap? Off you go then, Oskar, go join your mates over there while our lads come back to us. Can you imagine? They'd slaughter us; they'd shoot us down in an instant.'

'He's right,' said Dubois. 'If there's one thing their madman of a leader has taught them, it's that you don't win wars by gentlemanly agreements.'

'That's your problem, Kafka,' barked Bouchette. 'You think only of the here and now; no thought to the repercussions.'

Kafka sprung out of his chair. 'And your problem is that you're cowards.' With his knuckles on the table, he spoke quickly. 'All we've done so far is down to me. The railway sabotage, the capture and killing of that Kraut.'

'Right, yes, the railway sabotage that they fixed within a couple of hours, and the killing of one solitary boss-eyed Kraut hardly dismantles a regime, does it?'

'He wasn't boss-eyed,' said Pierre. 'It was just that his—'

'Yes, whatever, it doesn't make much difference,' said Bouchette.

Claire winked at Pierre.

'And now, Lincoln's bowed out.'

'Another coward,' said Kafka.

'We need more men,' said Dubois.

'And we will have more men,' said Kafka, sitting down. 'I've been sounding people out; we have a lot of support.'

'Is that so?' shouted Bouchette. 'So where are they, these mythical men?'

'They'll be ready when I tell them, don't you worry.'

'Oh but I am; I'm very worried.'

'Let's be honest,' said Dubois, 'we're out of our depth. The Krauts think we're simple hillbillies and frankly I reckon they've got a point.'

'Speak for yourself,' said Claire.

'Yes, sorry, Mademoiselle.'

'Any coffee, gentlemen?' asked Madame Bouchette, popping into the kitchen.

'No.'

Daisy barked. 'Shush, girl,' said Bouchette, slapping the dog.

'Hey, what's happened to those leaflets?' asked Dubois.

'Claire said we'd have them by now.'

Kafka shrugged. 'That's a point. Do you know, Claire?'

She shook her head. 'They must've got held up.'

'Not good.'

Pierre tried to hide his grimace as he thought of Victor and Alain hauled away by the Gestapo on his say so.

'So, what's next?' asked Dubois.

Kafka grinned. 'Our next hit.'

Bouchette threw his hands up in the air. 'I'm not risking my neck for another pointless—'

'No, this will be big,' said Kafka sharply. 'This will show we mean business.'

'Oh, so that's all right, then,' said Dubois. 'And what did you have in mind?'

'A bomb. Right at the heart of their operations.'

'What?' screeched Bouchette. 'That's preposterous.'

'Hear me out. We quietly leave a bomb in a briefcase at the town hall reception. You know I used to work in the quarries. The Krauts may have closed it down but they didn't empty it. Never even bothered to look. I know for fact there's still a mass of explosives down there. You know how busy it gets in the town hall and tomorrow they're tearing down Soldier Mike so no one will notice. But, just in case, we'll create a diversion or two.'

'Tomorrow? You're mad,' said Dubois. 'Quite mad. Have you thought of the consequences? For every Kraut we kill; they'll kill ten of us – at random. I've heard it done, not far from here—'

'This is war, for pity's sake. Yes, there'll be casualties but we can't lie back and let the bastards trample over us. This is just a small outpost for them. By our actions they'll think it's not worth the candle and move on. Christ,

Bouchette, they killed your son. We have to fight back.'

'If you want to go down in history as a martyr, Kafka, that's your lookout.' Bouchette's face had turned quite red. 'Shed your own blood, not the blood of innocents.' He looked round the table, seeking support. 'I can't be party to this; I'm going home.'

'This is your home, you idiot,' said Dubois.

'Yes, yes, I know that; I meant hypothetically.'

'What about you two? Claire? Pierre?'

'There is a risk, yes,' said Claire. 'But it's war. I'm prepared to help. As a woman, they'd suspect me less.'

'Good girl. Pierre?'

He would have said no, but following Claire's show of hand, he felt he had no choice. 'I'm prepared to help in any way,' he said quietly.

'Ha! So you see, Bouchette, even the kid and the girl you've so dismissed in the past are prepared to play their part.'

Bouchette slapped his dog in frustration. 'OK, OK, tell me the plan – in detail; then I'll decide.'

*

Pierre felt sick. He accompanied Claire in silence to the library. Despite hints of sunshine coming through the high windows, the place still felt dank and dark. A thin layer of dust had settled on the books. 'Yes, I know,' said Claire. 'The place needs a thorough clean.'

'Do many people come inside?'

'Not often. The odd German. People are too busy trying to survive to worry about reading. Especially now that your major forced me to remove all the good books.'

Once, recently, Pierre would have resented Major

Hurtzberger being referred to as *his* major; now, the thought struck him, he felt rather pleased with the association.

'I have a few minutes before I need to unlock the front door. I'm going to write that letter today – to Bremen.' She jumped up onto the counter and crossed her legs. Pierre tried not to look at those legs. If only he had the excuse to kiss her again. 'So, Pierre, what do you think of Kafka's grand plan?'

'Bouchette is right – it's a mad idea. The notion of walking into the town hall, nonchalantly leaving a bomb and making our escape seems absurd.' Would it cow the Germans, he wondered? No, of course not. Since their arrival, the Germans and the French had settled into a state of acceptance. They weren't the barbarians people feared they would be; they had, in fact, gone out of their way to be polite and accommodating. Life was harder, that couldn't be denied; the lack of petrol, radios and the rising prices, the introduction of coupons to purchase items, these things ground people down. Yes, one knew who had the power and that the Germans, at any time, could turn nasty but for those who chose to accept their presence or simply ignore them, and that counted almost everyone, then life was bearable.

'Kafka seems more unhinged with each passing day,' she said, filing her nails. 'He has to be stopped. How many innocent people, French people, would be caught by the blast?'

'So why did you agree to it?'

'I could ask the same. I wanted to hear his plan.'

'Me too.'

'We have to stop him; you need to tell your major.'

Now, Pierre had the perfect reason for approaching the major; something that, hopefully, would secure the release of his father. This time, he knew he wouldn't hesitate.

'Well, time to open the doors. Brace yourself for the rush…'

*

Back at home, Pierre found his mother at the kitchen table, her head in her hands, a glass of water next to her. More worryingly, on the table, in front of her, were his father's war medals, unclipped from their frame.

'Mama, what's the matter?'

'Oh, Pierre. I'm sorry, I didn't want you to see me like this.'

'It's fine.'

'It's just got on top of me today. Your father. I need him back.' Pierre had to fight the temptation of telling her that it would soon be over, that Georges would soon be home, that he had the means to make it happen, but he knew he couldn't say it. 'I think it's seeing the major in his sadness; it brought it all home for me. Do you think your father's OK in there? You hear of such dreadful things.'

'I'm sure they'll let him go soon.'

'Oh, I so hope you're right. And the major, Thomas, why do I feel for him so? He's lost his son, a German soldier, one of them. Yet I see only a father grieving. A friend. It feels terrible saying that.'

'I know; I feel the same.'

'He's our enemy, isn't he? Goodness knows how many Frenchmen he's killed.'

'Perhaps none.'

'We don't know, though, do we?' She took a sip of

water. 'Well, this is no good. They may have taken my husband but I still have to prepare something to eat. I'd better put these medals away. Your father never looks at them. He would have thrown them away by now if I hadn't stopped him.'

While his mother clattered around in the kitchen, tidying things that didn't need tidying, sweeping the spotless floor tiles, Pierre stepped outside into the yard and turned his attention to his sculpture, trying to blank everything from his mind. It would be a few hours yet before the major returned. In some ways, he was pleased to have seen his mother in such a state. Without realising it, it had bothered him how calm she'd seemed; as if her husband's arrest had not affected her. What he took as indifference was, in fact, strength. But now, at least, he knew she cared.

It was almost seven in the evening before the major returned. Lucienne was knitting and Pierre reading in the living room. A standard lamp standing on the fireplace hearth shone despite the day still being light; above the fireplace was a framed print of a Renoir painting – *Young Girls at the Piano*. A large bookshelf contained only a map of the area and a few books, a few French classics that no one read but Lucienne insisted on keeping, if only for appearance's sake – Guy de Maupassant, Jules Verne, Flaubert and others Pierre knew nothing about. A pair of binoculars hung from the back of the door.

The major came in, unfastened his belt buckle, removed his cap and plonked himself in an armchair with a heavy sigh. 'I'm sorry I'm late. I hope dinner's not ruined. I do apologise, Lucienne. A lot of work on at the moment. I'm expected back in two hours as well. More manoeuvres.'

'I do understand, Thomas.'

'It's a good thing, really. It acts as a distraction from... you know.'

'Yes, of course. Wait there, I'll get your dinner. Nothing's ruined.'

'Thank you, Lucienne. I'll go have a wash.' He turned to Pierre, removing his boots. 'And how are you, Pierre?'

'Fine. I guess.'

'I shall miss this place, this house. After a day's work, it's like coming home.' He smiled. 'I shall miss you all.'

'Major, I need to speak to you.'

Lucienne, wearing her apron, appeared at the doorway. 'Would you like to eat here or in the kitchen, Thomas?'

'I think perhaps in here for a change.'

The major went to have his wash and returned as Lucienne came into the living room with his dinner and a small glass of red wine on a tray. 'There you are,' she said, 'chicken stew.'

'The chicken I brought yesterday?'

'We wouldn't eat nearly as well if it wasn't for you. What shall we do after you've gone, Thomas? Anyway, I'll leave you two to it.'

'Give me a minute, Pierre,' said the major as he tucked into his dinner. 'Delicious.' After a few minutes, he asked Pierre what he wanted to speak about.

'Well... you know Colonel Eisler said I had to speak to you if I heard anything. I've heard something.'

'This sounds serious.'

'Yes, there're some men who plan to bomb the town hall.'

'Good God.' He gulped down his wine. 'Are you sure?

How do you know this?'

'I was… I was approached.'

The major placed his glass carefully on the table. 'To do what exactly?'

Pierre glanced at the Renoir painting. He had never liked it. It reminded him of his own failure to learn the piano. Eventually, his parents, disillusioned with their son's lack of musical aptitude, had sold it, replacing it, instead, with something easier – a guitar. That hadn't worked either. They just had to accept their son had no musical ability whatsoever. The little girls in this picture looked too pleased with themselves, irritatingly self-assured with their pretty dresses and their concentrated expressions.

'Pierre – I asked a question. To do what exactly?'

'To work with Claire to create a diversion.'

'Claire? How did she get involved?' He played with the stem of his glass. 'When? What time?'

'Tomorrow. Eleven o'clock.'

'You've done right in telling me. And who are these men?'

'Do I have to tell you everything?'

'You either tell me everything or you tell it to the colonel.'

'Will it…'

'Yes?'

'Will it be enough to get my father released?'

'I can't promise, but I'll speak to the colonel. He usually listens to me. And after all, you've done as he asked. Now…' He took another mouthful of wine. 'You'd better tell me everything.'

Chapter 18

Kafka was right. The town square was packed with soldiers and civilians. Even the mayor was present, standing outside the town hall wearing his robes, a tricolour sash across his chest, his face as red as the colour in his sash. The mayor had made his protestations, he had tried, at least everyone believed so, but he had failed. To remove the statue would be sacrilege, a violation to those who had fought in the war seventy years ago. There were still village elders who were alive and could remember, as children, the calamitous events of 1870 and 1871. Word went round that the official response from Colonel Eisler was that the steel within the statue would be better used as German bullets.

At the town hall doors stood two German guards, searching a woman's handbag. Kafka had planned two diversions; the first, involving himself and Bouchette, aimed to divert these guards. The sun, although shining, was cool. A pleasant wind filtered through the square. Pierre, who had joined the crowd of spectators, watching with Xavier, felt the tension in his head and his shoulders. The town hall clock showed ten to eleven, German time. Ten minutes. With plenty of shouting and bellowed instructions, the Germans had thrown ropes round the statue's neck, torso, knees and ankles. 'Shame on you,' came a shout from the crowd of French onlookers. 'Leave him alone.' 'Monsieur le Maire,' came another voice, 'can't you do anything? Can't you stop them?'

'My dear people, don't you think I've tried?'

A few Germans approached the crowd, their hands on their rifles, and eyed them while, behind them, their colleagues were busy securing the ropes to a truck. Murmurs of discontent circled the crowd, a constant hum of disgruntled voices.

'Can you imagine what the square will look without our statue?' said Xavier quietly. 'I never really appreciated him before.'

'I know; he was just – there.'

'Exactly. I shall miss him. So, how have you been? Haven't seen you for ages.'

'Oh, you know. Busy.'

'Have you heard – some of the Krauts are being transferred to Paris. What about your major? Is he one of them?'

'I don't know. Maybe. He's not my major.'

'Whatever, it will mean fewer for us to contend with. Oh shit, look, they're bringing out the blowtorches.'

A fresh chorus of complaint rose from the villagers. But it wasn't the Fritzes lighting up their blowtorches that caught Pierre's eye but the sight of Dubois appearing in the square, carrying a small, brown-coloured briefcase, his glasses perched at the end of his nose. Kafka had decided to entrust the placing of the bomb to Dubois, not Claire as originally decided. Claire reckoned Kafka didn't trust her sufficiently enough to carry out such a task. 'After all,' she'd said, 'I'm only a woman.' He watched as Dubois mingled with the crowd, bumping into someone he knew, shaking hands and shaking his head. That means, thought Pierre, that Kafka wouldn't be far away. He craned his neck, trying to find him. A different truck, one with a broken windscreen passed by, a swastika painted on its side, full of soldiers going somewhere, its exhaust clattering loudly, leaving a dense cloud of fumes in its wake.

'Hello, boys.' Claire had appeared, squeezing in between them. 'Not a day we'll want to remember, is it?' She looked lovely, thought Pierre, very Parisian, wearing a polka dot skirt with a frilly white blouse, her hair tied back with a blue bow, carrying a petite red handbag with a shiny, silver clasp.

'We'll hardly forget it, though,' said Xavier. 'Not with the base left behind as a constant reminder.'

'Plinth,' said Pierre. 'Not base.'

'Ah, thank you. I stand corrected.'

Two of the Germans, wearing goggles beneath their helmets, were now working at the statue's ankles, weakening them with their blowtorches. The crowd edged forward. The Germans guarding them pushed people back, making sure they were aware of their rifles. 'Heathens,' shouted someone from the back. 'Barbarians,' came another.

The mayor, still within the sanctuary of the town hall, had been joined by Father de Beaufort. The priest, in full regalia, shouted over, 'Citizens, citizens, these men are under orders. Don't persist in abusing them. No good will come of it.'

Claire nudged Pierre and motioned with her head that it was time to go. The clock read three minutes to eleven. His heartbeat quickened. 'OK,' he mouthed.

He slapped Xavier on the shoulder. 'We have to go. We'll be back later.'

'Eh? Where you going?'

'We've just got to see the town hall reception about something.'

'Don't you want to see them pull the statue down?'

'We won't be long.'

'Well, all right. Mind how you go.'

'Yeah. Thanks.'

'Cheer up, my friend, it can't be that bad.'

'No.'

The ankles of the statue had taken on an orange glow as the flame did its work. 'You OK?' whispered Claire.

'No.'

'No, nor am I.'

His mouth felt dry; he felt the need to be sick. There were so many people around. Kafka thought this would be a good thing; lots of activity. But Pierre knew that among all the Germans many would be waiting for them, ready to pounce. Somewhere, among all these uniforms, was the major. He wished he could see him; wished he had the reassurance of his presence. He knew he had done the right thing but the thought that Kafka and the others would be captured, perhaps killed, weighed heavily, a weight on his back, his crooked back.

A soldier, sitting in the truck, was revving the engine while his colleagues, with much yelling, checked the tension and positioning of the ropes. The crowd hissed as one, a sinister sound that soon gathered momentum and volume. As Pierre and Claire approached the town hall, circling round the hissing protestors and the animated German soldiers, they caught sight of Bouchette wearing, despite the sun, a heavy overcoat, torn on one pocket. Not far from him, wearing expressions of weary resignation, were the priest and mayor, church and state unified in their disgust of the symbolic rape of their town which they had been powerless to prevent. Pierre and Claire had been told by Kafka not to turn round, not to appear as if they were looking for someone. But Pierre did turn round. Not far behind him, he saw Dubois with his briefcase taking an interest in the proceedings as the German driver slowly eased his truck forward, picking up the slack on the ropes. 'Go on, forward,' shouted a German. 'Put your foot down, slowly. Slowly, mind,' yelled another above the continuous hiss.

Claire took Pierre's hand. This meant Kafka had appeared. Yes, there he was – approaching Bouchette, hands in pockets, hoping not to be noticed. Kafka would strike up a conversation with Bouchette, which would soon descend into an argument and a fight. Claire and Pierre headed for the town hall entrance. They were to keep the receptionist busy while Dubois slipped in with the briefcase containing the bomb.

Pierre and Claire sidled up the town hall steps, avoiding the mayor and the priest who, watching the truck straining with the ropes, were in deep discussion, and up to the large open doors. Both doors still bore the scar of Pierre's graffiti, *Vive La Framce*. How long ago that seemed now. 'Halt,' said the first guard, a plump man, his eyes obscured by his helmet. 'Your business?'

'Hello,' purred Claire. 'I need to apply for my clothing coupons. I was told I could do it here.' In the corner of his eye, Pierre could see Kafka and Bouchette talking.

'And you?' said the guard to Pierre in a thick German accent.

'I'm her boyfriend.' Even in his state of nervousness, it felt great saying that. Claire suppressed a grin.

'Your handbag.' Pierre could sense Claire wince as the German delved his fat fingers in. The conversation between Kafka and Bouchette had increased in volume, catching the attention of Father de Beaufort. A burst of laughter erupted behind Pierre. One of the ropes had snapped. The soldier statue, although at an angle, wasn't prepared to be pulled down quite yet. The mayor clapped then, abruptly, stopped.

'OK, you can go in,' said the guard stepping aside. Pierre followed but the man held up his hand. 'Not you.'

'Can't I–'

'No. You wait here.'

Claire, the other side of the guards, looked back at him. With a shrug of the shoulders, she disappeared into the darkness of the town hall.

Pierre trudged back down to the bottom step.

Kafka and Bouchette were now pushing each other. 'You're a son of a bitch,' yelled Bouchette.

'And you expect her to stick by a useless old git like you?'

The truck engine revved again.

Bouchette pushed Kafka back into the road. Regaining his balance, Kafka leapt forward and struck Bouchette. Bouchette staggered back, his hand on his lip.

The guards, thought Pierre. The guards should have reacted by now, allowing Dubois the chance to slip into the building. Instead, a number of soldiers stepped away from their colleagues and ran towards the quarrelling Frenchmen, rifles at the ready. Kafka had seen them too. He drew his revolver from his jacket pocket. A shot rang out through the square. People screamed and ducked. A soldier fell, clutching his stomach. Others drew their rifles, ready to fire. The German truck with the broken windscreen, now empty of soldiers, chose that moment to make its return journey. It passed between the Germans and Kafka and Bouchette. The two men ran down the side of the town hall. The Germans screamed at the driver who, on misunderstanding them, stopped. The soldiers had to run round the truck, losing valuable seconds. Pierre heard a scuffle to his left. Three soldiers had bundled Dubois to the ground. Dubois bawled as one of them put him in an arm lock. Another hit him in the stomach. His shrieking stopped. The third took the briefcase. The crowd gasped. The soldiers chasing Kafka and Bouchette fired round after round, then resumed running. A couple of others ran to their stricken colleague. The mayor and the priest had backed against the wall. The priest crossed himself.

Two soldiers emerged from the town hall, between them, with her hands held above her head, was Claire.

Pierre jumped as he felt a hand slap against his shoulder. Fritz One, the German with boxer's nose, was arresting him.

The tremendous sound of metal on gravel made everyone stop. A cloud of exhaust fumes floated up. The Germans cheered; the crowd booed, the mayor and the priest shook their heads. Soldier Mike had fallen.

*

The room was small. Pierre sat at a table. Opposite him sat a German major – not *his* major but an SS major wearing a black uniform, who introduced himself as Hauff. The table was bare except for a table lamp, a dirty glass ashtray and the major's papers. Above them a bare light bulb emitted a feeble glow. There were no windows. On a long table adjacent to the wall were various jars and trays containing instruments that made Pierre shudder – knives, pincers, hammers. Had his father sat in this very chair? Had those instruments been used against him? In the corner, a broom and a mop and bucket. Major Hauff puffed on a pipe, producing a sickly sweet smell. Next to the door, stood a private, his hands behind his back.

'So, let's go through this again.' The man had a gaunt face, heavily lined. A pair of metal-rimmed spectacles merely added to his gauntness. 'You say after Colonel Eisler made his offer, you tried to enlist in this group run by Albert Foucault, who goes by the name of Kafka. Why does he call himself that? Does he have literary pretensions?'

'I don't know.' Pierre pulled at his collar. The room, airless and claustrophobic, was hot.

'Speak up.'

Pierre cleared his throat. 'I said I don't know.'

His lips, Pierre noticed, were chapped, while his nose had a pronounced bump half way down. 'You say after his refusal, this Kafka, you tried to prove yourself by sabotaging a convoy of German vehicles with a jarful of nails.'

'Yes.'

'Hmm.' He scribbled something on his paper. 'Most enterprising. It was lucky for you that no one was hurt.' Pierre thought of Monsieur Roché, beaten to death, but thought it best not to say anything. 'Very lucky.' Carefully, the major placed his pen on the table and straightened his back.

'So, where is this Kafka?'

Pierre glanced at the private in the corner. 'I don't know.'

'Do you want to know about your friends? Albert Bouchette is dead. He was shot as he tried to make his escape.' Pierre caught his breath. Poor old Madame Bouchette, her son killed and now her husband. Major Hauff continued, 'And Albert Dubois – perhaps your Kafka would have accepted you sooner had you changed your name to Albert.' He guffawed at his own joke. 'Where was I? Yes, Albert Dubois is in custody. He's been most helpful – to a point. He told us Foucault has a little hideaway in the wood outside your little town. He's escorting Major Hurtzberger and a couple of privates to this hut. Let's hope they leave a trail of breadcrumbs, eh? Major Hurtzberger, I believe, is billeted in your home? And then we have your girlfriend, Claire Bouchez–'

'She's not my girlfriend.'

'No? She should be. She speaks very fondly of you. Mademoiselle Bouchez told us much the same as Dubois. You'll be pleased to know we have released her. Dubois, however, will be executed.'

'Oh.' The image of his father's mock execution haunted his subconscious, the courtyard, the priest, all those guns. 'Even if he helps you find Kafka?'

'Yes, I'm afraid so. What did you expect? If it wasn't for you, he would've blown the town hall to smithereens. Well, maybe not smithereens; it was quite a small bomb; the damage would have been minimal. The work of an amateur. But that, and I'm sure you'll agree, is not the point.' He tapped his pipe against the ashtray. 'I will say, Colonel Eisler is most grateful for your co-operation. Indeed, we all are.'

Pierre would have said thank you but the words caught in his throat. Instead, he mumbled, 'Can I have some water?'

'No.' The major ran his fingers over his chapped lips and grimaced. 'Now, let me ask you again, and think carefully – where is Albert Foucault?'

Pierre shook his head. 'I promise you I have no idea. I would have said his hut in the woods but…'

'Yes, exactly. And there's nowhere else he might have escaped to?'

He thought of Lincoln's barn. 'No,' he said firmly.

'If anything comes to mind, you'll let us know.' The major re-read his notes. 'On a separate note, did your little gang, this gang of Alberts, run across a comrade of ours, a lieutenant by the name of Spitzweg, Oskar Spitzweg?'

'No.'

'Pity. A good fellow, young. Good-looking chap. Odd eyes though. He was sent on a mission to follow you. Yes, you, Durand. He went out and we haven't seen him since. So your paths didn't cross?'

'No, sir.'

'Interesting.' Pierre saw the major write a large 'X' on his paper. 'Right, the colonel has instructed me to inform you that your father will be released today.'

Pierre sat up in his chair. 'Really?'

'He is a man of his word, is our colonel.'

'Can I see him?'

'You want to thank the colonel?'

'No, I meant my father.'

'Your father? No. But you'll see him later today no doubt. Now…' He scanned his paper, adjusting his glasses. 'I think that is all. You may go, Monsieur Durand. Private Dassler here will see you out.' The private stepped forward.

'I can go? You mean… just like that?'

'Unless you want to stay?'

'No, no.'

The major picked up his pipe. 'No, I thought not.'

*

'He's here! Pierre, he's here; your father's back!' Lucienne, still wearing black, her hands clasped as if in prayer, welcomed Pierre back. 'Isn't it marvellous?'

Pierre stepped into the living room, his heart beating wildly. The curtains were drawn, the lampshade, with its weak light, on. 'Papa?'

Georges was standing next to the fireplace, circling his cap in his hands, a slight smile on his lips. 'Hello, Pierre.'

'Papa.' How small his father seemed, so diminished, his hair greyer, his eyes dulled. He'd lost so much weight, his clothes, like rags, hung off him. His skin, it seemed so thin, so fragile, as if it might tear. There were no obvious signs he'd been tortured but he tried not to look too hard. It was the smell that hit him, a stench of dirt and sweat. But Pierre cared not a hoot. It was his father; he had returned from the dead, from the hands of the Gestapo; his brave father, this man he had never really thought about, had never appreciated, the man who had fought against the Germans as a young man, who had, no doubt, seen horrors that Pierre couldn't begin to imagine, and, in the process, had his faith in God destroyed; and who now, in his middle age, was still fighting them. The Germans had bowed him, had killed a part of him, this much was already obvious, but they hadn't finished him. For he was back, at home, where he belonged, with his wife, his son, and even the son he had lost. He was back in his home with its years of memories, of routine, of comfort, with his little knick-knacks, his mementoes of times past, his books, his photographs, even his armchair. 'Papa.' He felt himself move as in slow motion, a step towards his father, Georges's arms outstretched, ready to embrace his older son, tears smearing the dirt on his haggard face, tears of joy, yes, and tears of relief. They fell into each other, Georges's hand against the back of Pierre's head, his whole body now convulsed in sobs, great, giant sobs. His father's grip weakened. Quietly, he slipped away from his son and, with awkward steps, manoeuvred himself to his armchair and fell upon it, exhausted, faint. He put his head into a hand and with his eyes clenched shut, continued sobbing, his delicate frame shaking.

Pierre felt his mother's hand in his. 'Come,' she whispered. 'Let's leave him be for a while.'

Pierre nodded and, following his mother, retired to the kitchen.

*

Georges was having a bath, a very long bath. He'd eaten a whole baguette with ham and cucumber, and had been sick soon afterwards. 'It's to be expected,' he'd said. 'Even ham and bread is too rich after the water soup they give you in that place.' Pierre had fallen asleep on the sofa while his mother fussed about in the kitchen, humming to herself. She'd changed out of her black dress and was now wearing a light green outfit. She'd applied lipstick and painted her nails. 'I want to look nice for my husband,' she'd explained to Pierre. 'Isn't it just so wonderful to have him back?'

'Oh, that's better.' Pierre opened his eyes and smiled. His father had re-emerged from the bathroom in a fresh set of clothes that Lucienne had laid out for him, his hair was washed, his skin free of the prison grime. 'I feel half human again.'

'Sit down, Papa.' The clothes that once appeared a little tight now dwarfed him.

'I don't mind if I do. What's that hideous painting?'

'What? Oh that. It's, erm… a present from the major.'

Georges considered it for a while. 'Is it, indeed? Oh well. Something smells good.'

Lucienne appeared from the kitchen. 'Oh, Georges, you look so much better.'

He laughed. 'I feel it.'

'I've got my old husband back.' She sat on the armrest and pecked him on the cheek. 'Welcome home, my love.'

He patted her hand. 'It's good to be back.'

'Now, dinner won't be long. Mutton chops, mashed potatoes and runner beans. Oh dear, it won't be too rich for you?'

'I should be OK. I'll just have a small bit.'

'It's thanks to Thomas we've got the chops.'

'Thomas? Oh yes, the major. Food, paintings, whatever next? Still here, is he then?'

'Yes, I'm afraid so. But tonight's dinner, as so often, is courtesy of our Major Thomas. He should be home by now.'

'Home?'

'Well, his... home from home. He said he'd bring back a nice bottle of red; said we should have a little celebration for you, Georges.'

'I don't want a fuss.'

'Perhaps but we have much to thank him for – your release was entirely down to him. Isn't that what you said, Pierre? That Thomas had a word with that colonel and secured father's release?'

'Yes, Maman.' One day, he thought, one day, when he was much, much older, he may tell her the full story.

But not yet.

They waited a while for the major until Georges, understandably famished, could bear it no more. And so they ate dinner, their mutton chops, mashed potatoes and runner beans, without the major and without his wine. Georges did indeed have a small portion, and felt quite emotional, only to be followed by another small portion and a third. At ten o'clock, tired after an exacting day, they retired to bed. Pierre felt more content than he had in a long time. His brush with the Gestapo was over; he had no need to worry about Kafka again; and he had survived. It was only now, now that it was all over, that he realised quite how frightened he had been of Kafka. His was not a fight for France against the invaders; it was a personal crusade, a vendetta carried from the previous war against all things German; and in his desire for vengeance, he had no qualms about using others. Bouchette, Lincoln, Dubois, Claire and he, Pierre, had been all sucked in. They had been expendable to Kafka's wishes. Bouchette and Dubois had been unlucky. But it was over now. Kafka was in the past and his father was home. For the first time in ages, Pierre could go to sleep and not worry, and dream of pleasant things.

The only concern, the only slight niggle in his thoughts, was why had the major not returned home.

Chapter 19

Pierre woke up thinking of Monsieur Dubois. He wondered whether he'd been executed yet. Poor old Dubois; a decent man, trying to do his best but led down the wrong path by Kafka.

After breakfast, he went out into the yard and started work. His father had gone to report himself at the town hall. He was obliged to do so every morning, he'd said. A while later, he returned and stepped outside to see Pierre.

He circled round the sculpture, his shadow long in the morning sun, but much to Pierre's disappointment, said not one word about it. Instead, he enquired about the blessed chickens. 'You're feeding them?' he asked. 'Their water looks a little dirty.'

'I changed it yesterday.' In fact, it'd been three days.

'Your mother told me the major's son's been killed.'

'Yes, out in Africa somewhere.'

'Hmm. I wonder where the major is. Thomas, as your mother calls him.'

'I don't know. Did you sleep well then?'

Georges's shoulders dropped. 'Did I sleep well? Ah, I slept like a king; it was heaven. A proper bed. Although I still feel tired. And a proper breakfast. I feel human again. The food at Hotel du Gestapo leaves a lot to be desired. I dread to think what Monsieur Michelin would make of it.' He sniggered to himself as he stepped inside one of the sheds.

Pierre changed the chickens' water, slightly irked that his father had found him out.

The knock on the front door was alarmingly loud. 'Blimey, someone's in a hurry,' said Georges, popping his head out of the shed.

'Perhaps it's the major,' said Pierre, surprised by how much he hoped it was.

Pierre followed his father back into the house. The living room felt crowded as Georges and Pierre were confronted by three Germans. Their presence seemed to take all the space. Lucienne, wearing her headscarf and outdoor jacket, ready to go out, had already let the visitors in. Pierre recognised the officer, Lieutenant Neumann. Lucienne, fidgeting with her ring, said, 'These gentleman want a word with you, Pierre.'

'Where is he then?' barked the lieutenant. 'Has he been back?'

Pierre found himself stepping back. 'Who? The major? No.'

'Have a look round,' said the lieutenant to the two privates. While they searched the house, the lieutenant eyed Pierre with narrowing eyes. 'My French – it's good now, no?'

'Very good.'

'We were expecting the major back last night for

dinner,' said Lucienne. 'Weren't we, Georges?'

'Where is your friend, Foucault?'

'Kafka?' said Georges. 'I haven't seen him for weeks.'

'And you?' he said to Pierre.

'Nor me, not since the…'

'Shoot-out?'

'Yes.'

The two privates returned to the living room, shaking their heads.

'If you hear anything, you tell us straightaway. You understand, yes?'

'Yes, of course, Lieutenant,' said Lucienne. 'Straightaway.'

The lieutenant nodded and left; the two privates following in his wake.

Pierre and his parents watched them leave, then turned to each other. 'Oh dear,' said Lucienne. 'This sounds serious. Where could they be?'

'I don't know,' said Georges, 'but something tells me they're together somewhere.'

'You mean Kafka has kidnapped Thomas?'

'Seems mad, I know, but then Kafka *is* mad. Always has been. You can never know what idiotic scheme he'll come up with next. Doing nothing has never been his way; he'd rather do anything, however stupid, than do nothing.'

'I don't like this one bit,' said Lucienne. 'Oh well. I was about to go the bakery and a few other chores. You two need anything? No?' She kissed both her men. 'I'll be back soon.'

*

His father went off to have another bath, 'purely for the indulgence,' he'd said. Taking his bicycle, Pierre decided to visit Claire. After all, they were accomplices now. He found her coming out of the chemist. 'Look,' she said. 'Shampoo. Quite a rarity these days. Come, let's talk.'

They walked towards her home, Pierre pushing his bicycle. 'So, how are you, Pierre? How did you get on with the Gestapo?'

He shrugged his shoulders. 'They were fine. Just asked me a few questions.'

'Me too. We must be the only people in France who have walked straight out of a Gestapo interview intact. They asked me where Kafka's disappeared to. And your major. They actually believed me when I said I didn't know.'

'The same.'

'Do you think it's a coincidence – both of them disappearing at the same time?'

'I don't know. Probably.'

Madame Clément passed by, her shopping bag full of vegetables. They waved at each other. 'They knew about the bomb,' said Claire. 'Someone told them.'

'Yes, someone must've talked.'

She smiled. 'Well, it couldn't have been Bouchette or Dubois, and it certainly wasn't Kafka, and it wasn't me. So…,' she said, drawing out the word. 'That only leaves you, Pierre.'

'Does it?'

'Come on; don't play games with me.' She stopped and placed her hand on his sleeve. 'I approve, you know, you did the right thing.'

He leant his bike beside the wall of a house that backed onto the street. 'Monsieur Bouchette was killed. I didn't want that to happen, and now they're going to execute

Dubois.'

'It was their choice, Pierre. Remember what we said in Bouchette's kitchen? "Shed your own blood, not the blood of innocents." Those were Bouchette's very words. No one but me realises it, but think of the people you saved, the innocents.'

'Apparently the bomb was small and would have done minimal damage.'

'Yes, but think of the reprisals.'

'I suppose.'

'You suppose nothing. Come here, you... you brave man.' She pulled him in by the lapels of his jacket and gently, very gently, kissed him on the lips. Pierre felt a warmth cascade through him. His fingertips tingled, his heart burned with a feeling he'd forgotten – the feeling of joy. She wrapped her arms round him. Emboldened, he followed suit. Her kiss became more urgent. This, he realised, was the real thing, the real Claire, so unlike the kiss on the roadside leading into the town. She pulled away and lowered her eyes, momentarily abashed.

He tried to suppress a grin. 'I thought I was too young for you.'

'Not any more, you're not,' she said quietly, looking up at him through her fringe.

*

Back at home, Pierre found his father sitting in his armchair, deep in thought. 'Oh, Pierre, I was miles away. You OK? Good. Listen, Pierre... Sit down. I need to tell you something.' Pierre took a chair opposite him. 'I never thought I'd tell anyone this tale; I'd promised myself never to mention it, but I think you need to know what sort of man Kafka really is.'

'Are you sure?'

'I've never told your mother this.' He paused, his eyes drifting away. 'It was night time, the first of January 1918. New Year's Day. Kafka and I had been in a patrol with some boys from our battalion. Kafka's main job was to be a sniper. I have to give it to him, I've never met a man who can fire a rifle as accurately as that man. Something to behold. Well, on the way back from this patrol, we became the subject of a German attack. Shells, machine guns, the lot. We fought back. A few of ours were killed. Kafka saw his mate have his head blown clean off. It upset him terribly; made him determined to fight back in any way he could. His mother had recently died, and he was close to her. So he was already churned up. Then the bombardment stopped as suddenly as it had started. When the smoke cleared, Kafka and I found ourselves alone. The others, if they hadn't been killed, had gone on without us. We didn't know where we were. The attack had disorientated us. We didn't know which way was forward, which way was back. It was pitch black, and bucketing down. We were utterly lost and, I don't mind admitting it, Pierre, we were scared…'

'What happened?'

'We tried to find our way back, naturally. We must've gone the wrong direction because we found ourselves in an area that had seen a lot of shelling. German dead lay everywhere and bits of German, an arm here, a leg there. We'd already been fighting for a year or more so we took it in our stride. But when I think about it, as I do everyday, it was enough to turn your stomach. At the time, though, I was just impressed that our artillery had done such an effective job. Kafka and I knew we had to turn tail and make our escape before we were seen. And that's when we came across him – this German boy, lying wounded in a ditch. His hand hung off by the tendons; he was barely conscious and had lost a lot of blood. He could have been no more than nineteen, maybe twenty. Not much older then you, Pierre. Fair hair, clean-shaven, bright blue eyes. He had a ring on the hand hanging off. His other hand clutched a crucifix. I read his name on his dog tag – Otto Zeiss, a corporal. He didn't have long but at the time, I thought we could save him. I wanted us to carry him back to our lines. I thought our medic boys would simply amputate the hand, cart him off as a prisoner and he'd be fine. I was already thinking, you see, of the future. I wanted to be able to live with my conscience after the war, and to be able to say "yes, I saved a man, the enemy; my place in heaven is assured". Kafka was having none of it. He wanted to kill him off there and then. He could only think of the here and now; angry that his friend had met such a horrible end at the hands of the Hun. We argued; we pushed each other. I said, you cannot kill him in cold blood. He said the man had killed his friend and many others besides; he deserved to die like a dog, without mercy. I knew then that the boy was as good as dead because there was no way I could carry him by myself. So I begged Kafka to make it quick; to allow him, at least, a merciful death. He called me a German-lover, a secret enthusiast of all things German, and said, "He'll have the death he deserves". Oh, Pierre, I'll never forget it. I was powerless to stop him. He stuffed a handkerchief or a rag in the boy's mouth and then went at him with his bayonet – in the legs, his knees, the testicles. I tried to stop him, to pull him off. The tortures that poor boy endured. Only when he had lost consciousness, did Kafka administer the fatal blow. He pocketed the boy's ring and that crucifix, and ripped off his dog tag, and threw it into the darkness. It was the final humiliation – his parents would never know; only that he was missing, and would have to endure the agony of waiting and not knowing.'

Georges fell silent, his head in his hands. Fishing a handkerchief from his inside pocket, he blew his nose.

'The war unhinged Kafka. It was me who gave him that name by the way. He was reading *Metamorphosis* when I first met him. He must have read it a dozen times during the time I was with him in the trenches. I hadn't known him beforehand. He lived a few towns away. But getting to know him in the army during the autumn of sixteen, he was your usual happy-go-lucky chap.'

'I… I don't understand. Did he want to torture him?'

'Just killing him wasn't enough. He'd wanted to hurt this German boy; he wanted to take revenge for all the misfortunes that had fallen on him. I remember, a few months before, we were behind the lines, enjoying a few days off. We were exercising in some woods. Kafka caught a rabbit. Rather than kill it, he stunned the creature and took it back to our lodgings where he put it in a crate or a cage the farmers use for their dogs. Then, he took a serrated knife to it and hacked off one of its feet. The poor thing screeched to heaven come. I remember him saying, "A rabbit's foot is meant to be lucky, isn't it?" Then, the next day, he hacked off another foot. By the following day, someone had killed the poor creature out of mercy. Kafka was livid; someone had spoilt his fun.'

'Do you think he's kidnapped the major?'

Georges rose to his feet. 'Either that or perhaps the major's captured Kafka a long way from home and is on his way back through the woods.'

'Perhaps one of them is wounded.'

'I don't know, but I intend to find out.'

'What? How?'

'I know his hideaways. Come help me get some food from the kitchen.'

They'd moved into the kitchen. Pierre watched as his father filled a small haversack with a baguette and a sausage. 'But why, Papa? Why do you need to get involved?'

Georges stopped. 'You're right – I don't have to. But I need to. I could have saved that German. I could have informed his parents. What I did that night, Pierre, was cowardly and I've never been able to forgive myself. Not a day has passed when, at some point, I haven't thought of Otto Zeiss. Every night now, for twenty-two years, I've gone to bed with his face in my mind, the memory of that horrible day. I should've saved him from that monster who lives in our midst. I cannot let him do the same to the man who saved my skin from the Gestapo. I know this sounds dramatic, but it's time to atone for my sins.'

'It wasn't…'

'Yes?'

'No, nothing.' It wasn't just the major who saved you, father; it was me, forced to turn on my countrymen, forced to work for the enemy; it was me who saved you. But he couldn't say it.

Georges sighed. 'Your mother, she thinks I'm a godless person. She has no idea. I have great faith; I just never show it. I don't allow myself. I believe God looks over us, takes note of our actions and our… inactions. It's just that I am still, even now, too ashamed to step into His house; too ashamed to let Him into my heart. He knows. He knows I could have stopped Kafka from killing that man.'

'But, Papa, it was war–'

'Murder is murder, Pierre. The circumstances excuse nothing. Kafka is a murderer and I, by my complicity, am no better.'

'No, Papa, you can't say that, you can't mean that.' He remembered the expression on Kafka's face after he'd shot Tintin, a look of diabolical pleasure.

'Oh but, my son, my dear son, you have suffered too. What sort of father have I been to you? What sort of example have I set you over the years? I've ignored you, haven't I? I've been no father to you, just a presence. I didn't want children; I admit that. I didn't want to pass on my genes. But of course your mother… She wanted children, lots of children. Of course, we had the two.' He found a bottle from under the sink and filled it with water. 'He'll be waiting for me; I know that. He'll see it as a game. And if I don't get there in time, he'll cut his fingers off one by one.' He bounced his haversack by its strap. 'That's everything, I think.'

'Can I come with you?'

'No.'

'But what if you don't come back?'

'Pierre…' he placed his hand on his son's shoulder. 'If I don't come back it's because the fates have decreed it. It'll be my own fault.'

'What do I tell mama?'

'Tell her… tell her the truth, that I've gone to look for Major Thomas. Tell her I've gone to look for Corporal

Zeiss.'

With that, he was gone.

*

Pierre spent the next few hours trying to kill time. He was tempted to go see Claire again but, somehow, after their kiss, he feared he wouldn't know what to say to her any more. Instead, he visited Xavier and together they went for a cycle ride round the outskirts of the town. They lay in a field, leaning against an elm tree and idled away the time. Pierre found he had little in common with his old friend now. 'I'll give you a race,' said Xavier.

'What?'

'To that rock over there. And back.'

'Don't be so childish.'

He returned home in the late afternoon. His mother had been back and gone out again. A pan of chicken stew simmered on the stove. Taking a wooden spoon, he helped himself to a sip, burning his lips in the process. Rather watery, he thought. He went out into the yard and sat in the rocking chair and considered his sculpture. He wasn't sure he even liked it any more. Her arms seemed too big, her legs too bulky. It lacked finesse. His amateurism stared back at him. Why did adults, proper adults, always say what they thought he wanted to hear? Why did they always hide behind deceit dressed up as kindness? Who did it benefit? Picking up a stick, he jabbed at the ground. Otto Zeiss. He would probably have been the same age as his father. He would have had a family by now, living a comfortable life somewhere in Germany. Perhaps Bremen. It had already been several hours since his father left. With each passing hour, his unease intensified. And now, hearing the front open, he would have to tell his mother.

'Pierre, Pierre,' she rushed into the yard, untying her headscarf. 'Where's your father?'

'He… he went out. Earlier.'

'Where on earth to?'

'I don't know.' He ran his finger along the tip of the stick.

'Pierre, you do know. I can tell. Where is he?'

'He's gone to find the major.'

Her hand went to her mouth. 'Oh no. No, no, no.' Rubbing her eyes, she asked. 'How long will he be?'

'Well, I wouldn't know, would I?'

'Oh dear, oh dear. Why does my heart feel so heavy? If the Germans can't find him, then what makes your father think he can?'

'He does know the area better than any German.'

'Pierre, if that's meant to reassure me, I'm afraid it doesn't.'

*

Georges still hadn't returned by bedtime. Lucienne had been unable to keep still all evening. 'This is so hard to bear.' She pulled back the curtain, looking up and down the street. 'It's long past curfew. I had my husband back with me for one night and now he's gone again. It seems so unfair. If anything, this is worse. At least, before, I knew where he was. It's the not knowing that is so trying.'

'I know.'

'Could you not have stopped him?'

'How? I didn't know he'd be gone for so long.'

She sat down on the sofa and immediately sprung up

again. 'No, I suppose not. I wished I smoked, or drank. Anything. You go to bed if you want.'

'What about you?'

'I'll wait up a while longer. He must be back soon.'

'It is strange. First Kafka, then the major and now–'

'Yes, thank you, Pierre.' She re-arranged the vase within the living room niche. 'I don't care about Kafka; I don't care so much now about the major. I just want your father home.'

Chapter 20

Pierre ate his boiled egg breakfast in silence. His mother, wearing black again, maintained a silence borne out of worry. She busied herself in the kitchen, continually washing her hands. When, earlier, Pierre had tried to suggest Georges would surely be back today, she snapped back at him. How on earth could he know? Deciding that saying nothing was the best option he concentrated on his egg. Once this war was over, he thought, once everything was back to normal, he would never eat another egg in his lifetime. Nor the cod liver oil.

He decided he would venture out to Kafka's hut as soon as he was done with breakfast. Best not tell his mother. If they weren't there, he thought, surely it would provide a clue as to where they were. Problem was finding it. If only he'd paid more attention that time.

Lucienne snatched away his plate and eggcup before he had chance to finish. He thought it best not to complain and, instead, gulped down his cod liver oil.

An urgent knock on the door stopped them in their tracks.

'Oh dear,' said Lucienne. 'Not again.'

'I'll get it,' said Pierre. Taking a deep breath, he opened the door. He barely had time to register, when the lieutenant barged into the living room. This time, at least, he was alone. 'Where's your father?' he snapped.

'I – I don't k-know.'

Lucienne came in from the kitchen, gripping a tea towel. 'We – we both don't know.'

The lieutenant eyed them both, his eyes narrowing. With quick strides, he marched into the kitchen, the bedrooms, the yard. Moments later, he was back. 'Where is your father?' he repeated, screaming.

'We really don't know, Lieutenant,' said Lucienne, her nervousness dripping from her voice.

'He's not reported in. He has kidnapped Major Hurtzberger. We will find him. He will be shot for this.'

'He hasn't kidnapped the major,' said Pierre quickly. 'He wouldn't–'

The slap took Pierre by surprise. Lucienne screamed. Falling back, he was more shocked than hurt.

'We will find him, we will hurt him, then we will shoot him dead. *Sie verstehen?* You understand?'

Both of them nodded, too fearful to say anything more. The lieutenant clicked his heels and left as abruptly as he'd appeared.

'Pierre, are you OK, my love? Does it hurt?'

Yes, he thought, it bloody did hurt. 'No, not at all. I'm fine, Maman.'

They sat in the living room, neither able to talk. Every now and then Lucienne would mutter an 'oh dear, oh dear.' He had to find his father before the Germans did, thought Pierre; that much was obvious. But where? Where could he have gone?

A distant voice seized their attention. Both of them cocked their heads.

'What is that?' whispered Lucienne.

'I don't know. Wait...' He went to the living room window pushing aside the net curtain. The sun shone weakly, failing to melt away the clouds drifting across the sky. Straining his neck, he saw, coming slowly up the road, a German motorbike and sidecar mounted with a machine gun. The driver looked slightly ridiculous – wearing goggles despite driving at walking pace. His companion, in the sidecar, was standing up, shouting through a loudhailer. People passing in the street had stopped to listen. Lucienne joined Pierre at the window.

'What's he saying?'

'...*At twelve o'clock. Attention, attention! By orders of the Ortskommandantur, all citizens without exception are ordered to congregate in the town square at twelve o'clock. Twelve o'clock. Any citizen not accounted for will face harsh penalties. Attention, attention! By orders of the Ortskommandantur, all citizens...*'

'Oh dear,' said Lucienne. 'I don't like the sound of this.'

'It must be something about the disappearance of the major.'

'And your father.'

'Maybe about Kafka too.'

Lucienne sat at the kitchen table, pulling at a thread in her tea towel. 'Oh dear, oh dear; I don't like this one bit.'

It was nine o'clock. Pierre wondered whether he had time to hunt out Kafka's hut and make it back in time. No, he decided; it'd be too risky; he could easily get lost. He would simply have to postpone it until the afternoon.

*

At five minutes to twelve, Xavier appeared. 'Hello Madame Durand. Hi Pierre. Do you mind if I join you?'

'Don't you want to go with your parents, Xavier?' asked Lucienne.

'They've gone ahead. They wanted a seat at the front.'

'That's brave of them,' said Pierre.

'Are they providing seats?' asked Lucienne.

'Huh, that's what I said.'

'We'd better go,' said Pierre. 'See what they've got cooking now.'

They joined a procession of villagers making their way to the town square. People raised eyebrows at each other in the form of acknowledgement but no one spoke. Everyone could sense the anxiety in the air. Shops were closed for the hour. As they turned the corner coming into the square, Xavier nudged Pierre in the arm. 'Look,' he said, pointing. There, on a tree, were two posters. Both posters bore the word, printed large, "Missing". The top one had two pictures – of the SS man, Oskar Spitzweg, and Major Hurtzberger; the second had the names of Pierre's father and Kafka – Albert Foucault. Beneath the names, also in large writing, was an offer of an unspecified reward. Peering closer, both posters warned of severe penalties to anyone withholding information or harbouring the four men. Every tree, Pierre noticed, every shop front, every lamp post, had these posters.

People had already gathered, milling round the square but no one pushed. Mothers held onto the hands of their children. A few chairs were provided for the elderly, including Albert and Hector, the cemetery boys. German soldiers lined the perimeter. At the front, Pierre spotted the mayor and the staff from the town hall. This time there was no stage, no decking, no microphone. He spotted Claire, looking gorgeous in her polka dot red dress, speaking to a couple of friends. The town hall clock chimed twelve. As the last peal faded away, Colonel Eisler, flanked by two privates, appeared from the town hall. A hush descended on the crowd. The colonel scanned the audience, his expression hard and resolute, emotionless. Lucienne reached for Pierre's hand. As subtly as he could, Pierre ignored it.

One of the privates handed the colonel a loudhailer. 'Monsieurs, mesdames.' He held in his other hand a sheet of paper. Behind him, standing to attention, were another group of soldiers, their steely expressions fixed on the villagers in front of them. 'I do not intend to keep you long. You will have seen the posters concerning the sudden disappearance of two of our men and two of yours. I am deeply concerned for the welfare of my men. I believe their vanishing is no coincidence. I also have reason to believe that these bandits, Foucault and Durand, are responsible for the disappearance of Major Hurtzberger and Lieutenant Spitzweg.' Pierre winced at hearing his father being described as a bandit. 'If my men are indeed being kept against their will, the consequences for their captors, and for you, will be severe. I will not tolerate such actions. If you have any information or suspicions, you must inform the town hall staff straightaway. Your information will be treated with the utmost confidentiality. If the provided information bears fruit in any way, you will be heartily compensated. You have until midday tomorrow. If our men are not located by this time tomorrow, there will be consequences.' He paused. Not a sound. 'I would like to call on the following citizens to step forward.' Putting on his glasses, he unfolded his sheet of paper. He read out the names of six villagers, three men, including Monsieurs Picard and Gide, and three women. The last name was that of Claire. What was this, thought Pierre? Why Claire; what did they want with her? The six of them shuffled forward and made their way to the front, Claire glanced behind, anxiety etched all over her face. On making themselves known, two German privates herded them together, pushing Monsieur Gide, the baker, roughly in the back. Gide put his hands up.

The colonel removed his glasses. 'Unless we can account for all these missing men within the next twenty-four hours, these six citizens will be shot.'

A shocked gasp passed through the crowd. Madame Picard screamed her husband's name. Another fainted and had to be caught. Someone behind Pierre muttered, beasts. Resting the loudhailer against his side, the colonel turned to the hostages. 'You,' he said, pointing at Claire. 'Come here.' His voice was still audible.

Pierre held his breath. Cautiously, Claire approached the colonel, her eyes downcast. Even from here, thought Pierre, one could she was trembling.

'I need a seventh person. Choose someone.'

She looked up at him, her mouth open, shocked. Slowly, as if death had already half claimed her, she turned and gazed at the crowd. Instinctively, it drew back, frightened of her. Colonel Eisler had transformed her into the Grim Reaper. She had come amongst them to dispense death. So many people, but not a single sound save for the gentle mewling of a baby in its mother's arms. Many were shaking their heads, beseeching Claire not to choose them. And Pierre was one of them. If you choose me, he thought, we're as good as dead; I'm the only one capable of finding them. Claire stepped into the crowd splitting it into two as people backed away, like Moses and the waves. She cast her eyes left and right; her skin ghostly white, as if she was looking for someone specifically. His stomach caved in as the realisation hit in – she was looking for him. If he begged her she would only see it as cowardice and he would be damned in her memory for eternity – she wouldn't realise. He had to remain free to save her, to save them all. Xavier glimpsed at him, his eyes filled with terror; a look reflected everywhere. And still she came, closer and closer. People were crying while shuffling away. Mothers hid their children; some of the men stepped in front of their wives, while most did not. Monsieur Bonnet, Pierre noticed, furtively stepped behind his wife. Claire ignored them all, looking for Pierre. And she found him.

'No, not Pierre,' said Lucienne, pressing herself into him, trying to ward death off.

She stood so close to him, he could smell her breath. Her eyes were dry, it was almost as if her brain had stopped functioning, as if her soul had already departed her physical presence. 'Help me,' she whispered. 'Tell me… Tell me what to do.'

Aware of every pair of eyes fixed on him, he whispered back, trying not to move his lips, 'I don't know but I can save you. Give me time, I'll save you.'

It registered. Her eyes widened a fraction. She stepped away. Pierre felt his knees give way. Three paces on, she lifted her hand and pointed a finger.

'Nooo,' screamed Monsieur Clément, shattering the unearthly silence. 'No, I don't deserve to die.'

'I'm sorry,' said Claire quietly.

'You chose him,' shouted Madame Clément, pointing at Pierre. He felt the eyes of everyone bore into him. They knew she was right; he felt their raw hatred. Lucienne took his hand. He gripped it. 'You chose him. I saw him – he asked you not to.' She began crying while her husband, next to her, started shaking. 'You – you can't do that,' she spluttered between sobs.

Two German privates approached, their boots resounding on the stones.

'No, please, I beg you,' said Clément, his knees buckling beneath him. 'I beg you, Claire. There must be someone else. Please, I thought we got on.' Claire took a step back, her work done. Clément knew it. 'You bitch, you fucking bitch.'

'You can't take him,' yelled Madame Clément at the soldiers as they almost picked her husband up by the elbows. 'This is not fair; it's not fair.' She began thumping the back of one of the soldiers as they dragged her husband, still cursing Claire, through the crowd. 'It should be him, that boy,' cried Madame Clément. 'That boy. Please.'

The soldier spun round and, without warning, punched her. Her body jerked back as if the life had snapped out of her. 'Chrissy,' yelled her husband. 'Chrissy…' His voice deteriorated into sobs. He tried to wrestle his arms free but stood no chance against the bulky Germans. Madame Clément lay in a heap on the ground, not moving. Those nearest to her seemed too frightened to help her, as if she was the carrier of a disease.

The soldiers deposited Monsieur Clément at Colonel Eisler's side, where he fell, and took their places a few yards behind. Without being told to, Claire obediently followed them, her head bowed, and took up her place beside her fellow hostages. The crowd re-converged, a mixture of terror and relief sweeping through it.

'Get up,' shouted the colonel. If Clément heard through his sobs, fear had stripped him of the ability to move. The colonel unclipped his holster. 'Get up,' he repeated, brandishing his Luger in his right hand.

This time, Monsieur Clément heard. Looking up, he saw the revolver pointing down at him. With great effort, he clambered onto his knees and up.

The colonel clicked his fingers. A soldier passed him back the loudhailer. Holding it in his left hand, he switched it on. 'I need these missing men here at precisely twelve o'clock tomorrow in this very place, otherwise these six men and women will be shot.' Monsieur Clément's weeping had been amplified by his close proximity to the loudhailer, sniffling in the background as the colonel spoke. 'All citizens will be required to attend the executions.'

Why had he said six? thought Pierre. There were seven hostages now.

'Be warned,' said the colonel. 'We are not playing games here.' Then, sweeping his right arm straight, he fired his Luger. The sound of the shot rebounded throughout the square. People screamed. Like a collapsing puppet, Monsieur Clément fell at the colonel's feet, dead, a crimson hole in his forehead.

Colonel Eisler cast his eyes over his audience. 'I hope I have made myself understood.' And with that, he handed the loudhailer back to his attendant, and returned to the town hall, the mayor in his wake. Monsieur Clément lay on the ground, his dead eyes open, a pool of blood forming beneath his head.

'Claire… Claire,' muttered Pierre. He watched, open-mouthed, as, together with the others, she was led away, German soldiers surrounding them.

He wanted to rush over, to save her now. He felt Xavier's hand on his shoulder but there was nothing he could say.

Nearby, Monsieur Gide's wife began crying. 'This is not fair,' she screamed. Her companions tried to calm her. 'Bertrand! Why pick on my Bertrand?'

'This is too awful,' said Lucienne, her face etched with anxiety. 'What can we do?'

'Hope something happens,' said Xavier. 'Something will turn up,' he said to Pierre.

'You think so?'

'Well…'

Someone pushed towards them – Madame Picard. 'Did you see that?' she shouted at Lucienne, her hand pointing at the Germans behind her. 'They took my Gerard. This is your husband's fault, isn't it?'

'No.'

Her son, a man in his late twenties, as wide as he was tall, tried to pull her back. 'Where is he?' hissed Madame Picard. 'Where is he, you bitch? Him and that stupid friend of his.'

Pierre could tell his mother was on the verge of tears. 'Madame Picard,' he said, stepping forward. 'This won't help–'

'Proud of your father, are you? Well, let me tell you,' she said, turning to Lucienne, 'if they murder my Gerard, I won't rest until I find your husband and rip him to pieces.' She spat at Lucienne, catching her fully on the cheek.

Taking her brusquely by her arm, Madame Picard's son yanked her away. Delivering her into the arms of another, he turned back. Squaring up to Pierre, he growled, 'She's right. Your father's as good as dead.' Pierre watched as he disappeared, with his mother, into the crowd. He realised he was shaking.

Lucienne, also trembling, searched her pockets for a handkerchief. Xavier offered her his. She took it without thanks. 'Pierre, take me home please.'

Chapter 21

Back at home Lucienne took to her bed. She had a headache, she'd said. Pierre, on the other hand, knew he had to find his father. The Germans were assuming Georges was in cahoots with Kafka; that, between them, they had somehow kidnapped the major and Lieutenant Spitzweg. It was vital he found Kafka's woodland hut as soon as possible. He decided against leaving his mother a note. Taking his bicycle, he'd cycled through the town, past the shops and through the town square. The crowds had melted away, gone home, like his mother, to lie down, to hope, to pray. Soldier Mike's plinth remained in place, fragments of bronze scattered around its base. The cafés had reopened. There were no locals, only Germans, filling every outdoor table, playing cards or dominoes, laughing. It was as if nothing had changed.

He visualised Claire's face as she was led away, her eyes wide with fright. The thought made him speed up. It was down to him, and him only. To save them all. He had to find that hut. But why? They wouldn't be there. He remembered Major Hauff, at the Gestapo headquarters in

Saint-Romain, saying that Monsieur Dubois was leading the major and a couple of privates to Kafka's hideout. Dubois would be dead by now, that was for sure, executed by a German firing squad. He thought of his father's mock execution. He tried to remember everything his father had said about Kafka: *The monster who lives in our midst. Kafka is a murderer and I, by my complicity, am no better.* He thought about Kafka and the rabbit, hacking off one foot at a time. Was it possible that Kafka had taken Major Hurtzberger as a hostage? But why would he do that? To what end? Did he really think he could outwit the might and ruthlessness of the Germans? *The war unhinged him*, his father had said. So much to remember. Yet, he pressed on, pedalling hard, knowing that he had to do something; that doing nothing would be unbearable.

He'd come out of the town now, and had begun cycling up the hill, on the other side of which was where Oskar Spitzweg had knocked him off his bike. *I know his hideaways.* He braked abruptly to a halt, almost falling off. Letting out a cry, he could hear his father saying it: *I know his hideaways.* He'd said hideaways in the plural; that must mean he had more than one.

His breath came in short bursts, but whether from cycling hard or the realisation, he didn't know. *Hideaways.* The lake. He'd heard it some point, a lake hideaway. Yes, it was that first day, when the whole town, like today, had gathered to 'welcome' their invaders. Kafka had been hit to the ground by Fritz One when the major had stepped in. Afterwards, as they wound their way home, his father had mentioned it – *Take a few days off, Kafka. Go to your island on the lake, have a rest.* An island on the lake. Good God, yes; that was it. But no, he couldn't go there; he couldn't face seeing the lake. He'd never been back; not since that day, had sworn he would never go back. He didn't even know where it was; he'd blanked it out. He knew that it was kilometres away, a good ten, twelve kilometres. He could hardly breathe. The thought of it was too much to bear. All that water; that deep, dark water. Yet, he knew he had no choice; he had to face it; he had to go. There was a map back at home, on the bookshelf in the living room.

*

He laid the map out on the kitchen table. His mother was still in bed, fast asleep. Yes, there it was – the lake. Too small to have a name but still, large enough to be quite clear on the map. There was no sign of Kafka's island but, thought Pierre, it was probably too tiny to show. Taking a piece of string he found in a table drawer, he measured the distance as the crow flies – six kilometres. Half on the road, half through the woods. With all the bends and curves in the road and through the forest, it was likely to be twice that distance. It'd take, what, two hours?

He never thought he would have to return to the lake. Not wanting to, he cast his mind back six years, entering a dark place he'd spent his whole youth trying to blot out. He realised he could remember every last detail of it. He walked over to the photograph of the young boy in the flat cap. Taking it off the wall, he sat back down. Rubbing the dust off with his sleeve, he ran his finger across the glass. He'd never done this before, had never wanted to look at him. The boy was smiling, acting up for the camera. He looked so happy, so full of cheekiness, yet Pierre saw his vulnerability. 'I'm sorry, Michel. I'm sorry.'

* * *

I remember every last moment of that day. I wish I could forget the details, but no, they are part of me, ingrained. I tell myself we had a nice day that day. But we hadn't. Not from the moment Papa called us over from the house and asked whether we wanted to go fishing with him. He often went out fishing but always on his own. He'd never asked us before, so I suppose we felt it was a special treat.

The day started off well. I remember. Like I said, I remember every last moment. Michel and I are playing in the field behind the house. On the other side of the field, the edge of the woods, a dark, forbidden place Michel is frightened of. He is only six, after all. I'm not afraid – but then, I am ten. Double figures. It's about nine on a chilly February morning. The grass is wet; the whole world smells damp. The clouds move quickly in the wind. I have an idea. I fetch a kite from the house, a kite as purple as the foxglows that grow in the hedgerows nearby. Michel is desperate to have a go by himself, but, I tell him, it's easier when there are two of you. Papa says it's a good kite-flying day – a 'medium wind', he calls it, enough of a wind but not too much. Michel, in his funny shorts that fall below the knees and the clunky shoes he always insists on wearing, whatever the weather, runs around in circles, his arms outstretched, pretending to be an aeroplane. He's skinny, my brother, dark hair, almost black, like mine, but a little longer, curls at the front. Maman says it's a cowlick which always makes him laugh. *Aeroplanes don't sound like that*, I tell him.

How do you know?

Come on, do you want to hold the kite?

He leaps over, his cardigan flapping. *Here*, I say to him, *hold the kite while I unroll the string.*

With my back to the wind, I tell him to walk with the kite. After about twenty metres I shout stop.

Right, throw the kite.

Now?

Yes, now, go on.

He throws it up. Quickly, I pull on the string, hoping the tension will help it launch. It doesn't. It falls.

Michel stamps his feet. *That's rubbish*, he shouts.

We'll try again.

After twenty minutes or more, Michel and I have had little joy with the kite. Once, we managed to get it air bound. Michel leapt with excitement, clapped his hands. The next moment it plummeted faster than a stick thrown from a bridge. It is a relief when we spy Papa at the yard gate, waving at us. We run over. Michel, with his heavy shoes, falls over in the long grass. He doesn't hurt himself. Pity.

You boys want to come fishing with me today?

Oo, yes please, we both reply.

If only we had said no.

*

Papa takes us in the car. We have everything we need – the rods, a tin with an extra line and hooks, the bobbers and sinkers, a horrible box of worms, our coats, boots, gloves and rain hats, and, most importantly, a packed lunch each. Maman had packed it all, a haversack for Papa and a smaller satchel each for Michel and me. But I was cross. I had wanted to sit in the front and, as I'm the oldest, felt it was only right. Michel put on his trembling lip act and Papa fell for it, as always, and allowed him to sit in the front, while I sat crossly in the back, arms folded. We hardly ever get to go in the car. Maman doesn't drive because ladies don't, and Papa only uses it for work and things. But he loves his car, as we all do – it's a 1928 Daimler, C class, he says. He inherited it from my Uncle Jacques, the tightrope walker, who was killed by a car. I don't remember him.

It's a fair walk, though, boys.

But we're driving there, says Michel.

Papa laughs. *No, I mean from where I park the car.*

It's not through the woods, is it?

Yes but don't worry, my little cabbage. I'll look after you. Papa slaps Michel's knee.

Oo, I say from the back. *Think of those dark woods, Michel, anything could be–*

Stop it, Pierre. Leave your brother be.

After a few minutes, Papa takes a turning off the main road, and down a smaller one and finally comes to a stop. *Here we are,* he says, rubbing his hands excitedly. *Let the day begin.*

Papa, it's raining.

Come now, Michel, you're not going to allow a little rain get between us and our lovely fish.

And it's cold.

Leaning forward from the back, I make a suggestion. *We could wait in the car until it stops.*

Not you as well. Nope, come on, the rain's good for you, and you'll soon warm up.

And so, reluctantly, we leave the warmth of the car, both my brother and I regretting our earlier show of enthusiasm.

We follow my father through the woods. Michel is trying not to show that he's frightened. At first, I laugh at him, jeering him. But now I feel sorry for him. *You can take my hand if you want,* I say, offering it to him.

Thank you, he says in a little, quiet voice. He takes my gloved hand.

Papa races ahead. *Papa, wait for us; we can't keep up.*

He stops, waits for us. *Come on, boys,* he says. *By the time we get there, the fish will have gone to bed.*

Do fish have beds? asks Michel.

Of course.

How much further, Papa?

Oh, not so far now.

I can tell he is lying. We carry on. I can also tell Papa is regretting bringing us.

Who's got the worms? asks Michel.

Papa.

Good.

Do you want me to take your bag?

Yes, please.

We walk in silence for a while getting further and further behind again. Eventually, Papa stops and waits for us. *For goodness sake, Michel, pick up your feet. You can walk faster than this; a girl could walk faster than this.* He stomps ahead.

You OK, Mickey?

He looks up at me and smiles. He likes it when I call him Mickey, like Mickey Mouse. It cheers him up for a few moments.

Papa, I shout. *Are we lost?*

No, I've done this hundreds of times. We're almost there now.

Almost there, I repeat for Michel's sake.

I want to go home.

I know. So do I.

* * *

Pierre placed his elbows on the table and rubbed his eyes. For so long now, he'd managed to file away the memory in a locked compartment in his brain labelled 'Do not open'. But now, like Pandora's Box, the lid had opened and it all came flooding back in all its dreadful, sickening detail. But he had to close it again, had to think of the present, of how to save his father – from Kafka, from the Germans. He remembered more of his father's words: *I believe God looks over us, takes note of our actions and our inactions.* Yes, thought Pierre, God will look over me; He'll look after me.

*

This time, Pierre decided to take some provisions – the map, a bottle of water, a hunk of cheese and an apple. And this time, he did leave a note for his mother: *Just popping out. Back soon.* He heard her stir; she was waking up. Quickly, he slipped out of the house, quietly closing the front door behind him. He didn't want to see her.

Ten minutes later, cycling hard, he'd reached the top of the hill, outside the town. He stopped and looked back on it. How peaceful it looked from up here, just a normal, rather quaint French town with its comings and goings. People lived here all their lives. He hoped he wouldn't be one of them; there had to be more to life. For them, a trip to Saint-Romain constituted the height of cosmopolitanism. He'd heard someone say that, now, without cars, the kilometre had returned to what it had been in the nineteenth century – a fair distance. How lovely it would be, he thought, to escape this place, to stroll through the streets of Paris, hand in hand with Claire; to sunbathe together on the beaches in the south. He had to tear himself away from his daydreams. A part of him felt as if he was saying goodbye to his town, goodbye to his life as he had known it; something told him he would return a changed person.

Remounting, he pushed on. It was two o'clock. Twenty-two hours left. A while later, he took a left fork, onto a smaller road, no more, really, than a dirt track, uneven and potholed. The sun was strong now, his shadow on the track in front of him. On the bend, up ahead, he spied a vehicle. He slowed down. It was parked up on the verge. Approaching it, he realised he recognised it – it was the truck used by the cemetery boys. He peered inside – nothing untoward, nothing to give an indication why it was here, seemingly abandoned. He tried the door handle. Unlocked. The keys had gone. The glove compartment contained various bits of paper and rubbish. Had the cemetery boys given the major a lift to this point? But then, why hadn't they taken it back to town? Why leave it here, abandoned? He'd seen them, two hours earlier, in the town square. Its presence here meant something. The back of the truck was empty save for a tarpaulin, a couple of spades and a plank of wood. He took a sip of water. It was time to move on.

* * *

And here we are! bellows Papa from far ahead. *We've made it; plant the flag.*

Why do we have to plant a flag? Michel asks me.

It's just Papa being funny.

Oh.

Yes, we've come to a lake. I thought we were getting close, by the way the trees were thinning out. We catch Papa up standing on a stretch of sand, gazing across the water. Now, out from the trees, the rain comes down harder.

It's lovely, don't you think?

No, says Michel.

What's the matter with you two? I always used to go out fishing with my old man. Loved it.

Is this a beach? I ask.

Looks like it, doesn't it? We could come back with your mother during summer and sunbathe. She'd like that. Come on, we can't fish from here. We need to get to a bank just over there, he says, pointing vaguely to his left.

Not more walking, says Michel.

It's not far. Just a bit further.

That's what he said last time, I say quietly to Michel.

And the time before that.

I heard that, says Papa.

We seem to go be going back into the woods. But now, we re-emerge next to the lake a bit further on. There's a wall, like a harbour wall. Grey stones. It's not long, perhaps twenty metres or so, and wide.

This is it, boys! says Papa, swinging off his haversack.

I peer over the edge. There are bunches of reeds. The water comes up high. It looks deep and dark. I don't like it. Michel joins me. *Get back, Mickey, it's dangerous.* He does as he's told.

Right, let's get started, says Papa.

Can't we have lunch first? asks Michel.

Papa spins around in a way that makes us step back. *Look, you little nincompoops, stop complaining. I've had enough, got it? One more moan and I'll throw you in the lake.*

He is angry now. He unties the top of his haversack and throws out everything from inside, muttering things Michel and I can't hear but don't like. Michel's chin disappears into his collar.

Papa calms down a bit and gets everything ready – the rods and lines and the rest of it. We empty our satchels too and put our lunchboxes to one side.

You've brought Munchie?

Hmm.

Munchie is Michel's old teddy. He wears a yellow waistcoat and green trousers. Michel likes to take it on expeditions. *Why did you do that? He's all scrunched up now.*

He shrugs his shoulders. *I don't know.*

Let's put him back in your bag. He'll keep dry there.

It's strange, I think; most of the time Michel gets on my nerves and I get annoyed that I have to play with him so much. It's not playing; it's looking after. But out here, with this horrible lake, and the dark skies and the rain, and that scary wood, he looks so small. I feel sorry for him.

*

We sit with Papa for ages, our feet dangling over the wall, the wind blowing round our heads, the rain in a steady drizzle. Papa casts the line and lets us have go at holding the rod. He tries explaining things to us, like how much worm we should use, how to attach the sinkers and things, but it's too complicated for Michel and I am too cold to concentrate. We've had our lunches; ham sandwiches and cheese, so we don't even have that to look forward to any more.

We've been here, sitting on this wall, for a while now, and my bottom is starting to get cold. I'm too frightened to ask if we could get up and move around. I hope Michel will ask – being younger he'll be more likely to get away with it.

Michel sits there stirring the worms round with a stick. Papa won't like that, I think, but Papa hasn't noticed it yet.

Oh, I think we've got something.

We sit up, peering across the lake, trying to find where the line meets the water. I can't see it.

Papa, Papa, squeaks Michel. *Can I hold the line; can I hold it? Please.*

Papa hesitates. I know what he's thinking – he wants to encourage him but knows if he does, we will certainly lose the fish, I mean, the catch. *We'll hold it together. There, put your hands over mine. That's it. Now, all we have to do is... Wait a minute. Oh, no, I don't believe it. Shit. We've lost it.*

Papa.

Yes, Michel? he snaps.

You said...

Yes, I'm sorry. I shouldn't use words like that.

Thank you, Michel. Look, why don't you two go and have a wander. See if you can find any wolves.

Wolves? cries Michel.

He's joking, I say.

Are there wolves in the woods?

I'm on my feet. What a relief. *No, there are no wolves around here. It's too cold for them.* Actually, I have no idea if that's true. Maybe they like cold weather but it sounds good and Michel believes me.

I don't want to go into the woods without Papa.

Don't be silly. Come on, we might find a unicorn, and unicorns are nice. I head the opposite way from the one we came.

Unicorns don't exist, silly.

Go on, Michel, says Papa. *Follow Pierre. He'll look after you and by the time you get back, I'll have caught a fish so big it could be a whale.*

He's joking again, isn't he?

Yes, Papa's always joking.

Don't go too far, boys.

Come on then, Mickey Mouse; let's find ourselves a unicorn.

He could give us a ride.

Good idea. Where would you like to go?

He thinks about this for a while. *The moon,* he says.

Yeah, the moon. That's a good idea.

* * *

The road petered out and soon came to an end at a hedge and a gate. Beyond it, the woods lay ahead. Pierre dismounted and left the bike against the hedge. How daunting the woods looked, the hider of so many secrets.

He followed a path, either side of which lay a carpet of bright purple woodland flowers. He followed the path into the forest where, to begin with, the trees were few and far between. A couple of dragonflies whizzed by. The woods soon became denser, more foreboding. But at least it was cooler.

He followed the path until it split into two. Consulting the map, he decided to take the right fork, heading due north. It was only now, now that he began to feel confident that he would find the lake, that he realised he had no idea what to expect and no idea what to do once he got there. Surely, with Claire and the others due to be shot, Kafka would listen to reason. But part of him knew that Kafka was probably beyond reason.

After a further twenty minutes of walking, Pierre came across another fork in the path. This one, however, he recognised – the tree with the engraved initials, 'RJ', next to the fallen tree blocking the pathway. The map showed that he should continue north but he knew if he took a brief detour on the left fork, heading northwest, he would soon come across Kafka's hut. The temptation was too much. Having taken another swig of water, he followed the path that he knew would end at the hut.

It was a steep descent. The sudden appearance of a magpie made him jump. Looking ahead, he saw a dark plume of smoke drifting up into the air. This, he thought, was not a good sign. Picking up pace, he strode forward, his chest fizzing with anticipation. Approaching the clearing, he heard voices. German voices. He stopped, wondered whether to continue. The sensible part of his brain told him to walk away, that he would gain nothing by venturing forward. But he did. He crept forward, his eyes and ears fully alert for danger. Creeping closer, he came across a scene of devastation. He saw that Kafka's hut had been set on fire, the wood audibly crackling as the flames did their work. On the patch of ground in front, where Pierre had done his target practice, a number of German soldiers, wielding spades, were digging. Nearby, lay two German corpses plus another. With a jolt, Pierre recognised the corduroy jacket, now heavily stained with dried blood, with its leather collar, the spectacles glinting in the sun – it was Monsieur Dubois, still wearing his blue beret. From their uniforms, it was obvious that the German dead were privates. Pierre looked round, hoping to see the major. But no, the most senior man here was a corporal. The men under his charge were digging graves while he, the corporal, kept an eye on the fire, smoking a cigarette. The diggers, stripped to the waist, did their work in fine spirits, flicking clods of mud at each other. How could they be so light-hearted in such a grim scene? Gravediggers from hell. The corporal flicked his cigarette into the fire and turned, his eyes scanning the woods. Pierre ducked behind a tree. Surely, he was too far away to be seen. Inching his head from behind the trunk, he saw the corporal urging his men to hurry. Pierre had seen enough; it was time to go.

He made it back up the hill, glancing back frequently, making sure he wasn't being followed. He made it to the fork with the fallen tree, his mind whirling as he tried to imagine what had happened there. Did Kafka shoot them all? He had, after all, served in the war as a sniper. But surely, Kafka wouldn't have shot Dubois? And what happened to the major? Had his father been there? A dreadful thought struck him. Once the corporal had reported back to the colonel, then Claire's situation, perilous enough already, would be made worse. He had to find that lake.

He headed north for another twenty minutes, then, following the map, veered east. Tired, his calf muscles aching, he stopped for a rest and ate his cheese. The apple, he decided, would be best kept for later. His water was already half gone. As he swung his bag over his shoulder, he spied a kingfisher swooping low at great speed. He thought of his mother's brooch. With a lurch, he realised that meant only one thing – the lake was nearby. Eagerly, despite the surging apprehension, he pushed on. And yes, the trees thinned out and behind them lay the lake. He halted, allowing his bag to slide off his shoulder. So this was it, the lake. Slowly, he stepped forward, mesmerized, dragging his bag by its strap. He reached a stretch of sand, a small beach. How blue the water; the gentle ripples, the sun reflecting on its surface, the freshness of the air, the utter quiet of it all, a silence broken only by the sounds of the woods – insects humming, birds singing. This was it; this was the lake he remembered; the place that had haunted him through the years. Yet, there was no island. He could see the far side; the lake was not that big. He let go of the strap. But it could not be Kafka's lake. Consulting his map again, there were no other lakes in the vicinity, this was the only one. Unfolding the map, there was another, much bigger lake, much further north; some fifty kilometres or more. No, this had to be it.

He so wished now he'd brought his father's binoculars. He could see them hanging up on the back of the living room door. He wondered whether his mother had seen his note. She'd be beside herself by now. So be it, he thought;

he had a job to do and he wasn't turning back now.

* * *

If Michel and I had hoped to be cheered up by wandering through the woods, we were soon disappointed. Still, we carry on, picking our way along a little zigzag path. At least it's stopped raining now but we still get caught by big raindrops falling off the leaves. *I spy with my little eye something beginning with 't'.*

Tree.

Yes. Well, that's that game done with.

That was too easy.

I know.

He picks up a stick and smacks it against the trunk of a tree, bringing down a little shower of rain. He squeals and throws away his stick. *I wish we were still playing with our kite. We could have it flying by now. Can we try again later?*

Maybe tomorrow, eh? Hopefully it won't be raining. Listen, if tomorrow Papa says "would you boys like to go fishing?", what do we say?

He giggles at my impersonation of Papa's voice. *We say no!*

No! Never again.

We laugh together. *Have you remembered to bring Munchie?*

Yes, he's in my bag. Where's your satchel?

I left it with Papa. Have you got any lunch left?

No, I ate it all.

Yes, so did I. Oh, look, Mickey, another place for fishing. Maybe Papa would have better luck here. It's almost the same – a stone wall, more like a platform really. This one's smaller, lots of puddles on it. To one side, hanging from a branch just beyond the platform, I see something red. *Look, Michel, what's that?*

We run over. It's a scarf; a child's scarf, all wet.

What's it doing here?

I don't know. Maybe some kid dropped it. Someone's tied it round the branch in case they ever come back, I guess.

We leave it where it is and return to the wall. Creeping up to the edge, I look to the right to see if I can see Papa. I can. I wave but he doesn't see me.

Who are you waving at?

Look, it's Papa.

Considering we'd only left him four or five minutes ago, Michel is excited to see him from here. He calls out but Papa doesn't hear.

He's probably singing to himself, I say.

I wish we could catch a fish for him.

I laugh. *Yes, that would surprise him. I don't know whether they swim up so close to the wall. Step back, Michel.* I yank him back, perhaps a little too hard because he looks shocked, upset even. *Sorry, Mickey, but you had me worried there. Not so close, OK? You could slip.*

I won't slip.

Still. Don't go so near.

A thought occurs to me. *Stay here a minute,* I tell him. If it's a kid's scarf, it might have a nametape stitched into it. I wander over to have a look. And that's what I'm doing when my life changes forever – twisting a wet scarf round in my hands, looking for a nametape.

There was no sound from him. Just a mighty

splash. I know at once, I can feel it as if someone's punched me in the stomach. I run across faster than I've ever run before. I can hear him screaming my name. I stop at the edge and see him in the lake; his arms thumping the water, making huge waves, his satchel round his neck. *Mickey, no.* Quickly, I lie on my front and reach my arm out, stretching out my fingers. It's too far, just too far. He's fighting the water, choking. The water – it's like a beast, an evil thing and I'm frightened of it.

On my feet again, I look round, desperate to find something to throw to him. There is nothing, nothing at all. My satchel? No, I haven't got it. I think about running back into the woods to find a long stick but that'll take too long. I know he can't swim but then – neither can I. He screams my name, screams help again and again. I feel sick. *Hold on, Mickey, hold on,* I shout. I scream for Papa louder than I've ever shouted before, jumping up and down, waving both my arms. This time he hears. We waves at me, grinning, holding up a fish he's caught. But then he realises something's wrong. He stands up slowly, looking over at me. He looks worried. Then, suddenly, he throws down the fish and his fishing rod and runs into the woods. *Michel, Michel, Papa's coming. Try to swim, try to...* But there's no answer; why doesn't he answer me? His arms are still flapping, his body bobbing up and down; he's gagging. Why did he have to wear those heavy shoes?

The scarf; I remember the scarf. I run over to the branch and untie it.

Mickey, take this, I scream. But I can't see him any more. Still, I throw the scarf into the water. It flops just a metre or so out; it's useless.

Michel, just swim, can't you? I'm crying; I don't know what to do. Oh, God, please help me.

I pull off my coat, struggling to get my arms out, and then my shoes, yanking them off. Michel's head comes out again; he tries to scream but there's too much water spewing from his mouth. I have to do this, I have to try and save him; even if it means I drown, I have to do this.

I stand on the precipice of the wall, willing myself to jump. Michel is gurgling, choking. He disappears again, the water claiming him. I can't do it; I'm too frightened. The nausea rises up my throat. He's drowning, I know this for sure; my brother is drowning, and there's nothing I can do. I don't know what that noise is. I look for Papa. Where is he? Please let him come. That noise – it's me; I'm crying; no, more than that; I'm wailing.

Michel, screams Papa, breathlessly arriving next to me, terror written all over his face.

He's there, I yell, pointing vaguely to where I last saw Michel just a few moments before.

He looks at me a second, shooting me a look I don't understand, throws off his coat, before jumping into the water with a huge splash. He swims out, his arms thrashing through that water, but I know it's already too late. Papa swims round frantically in circles. *I can't see him, I can't see him,* I hear him shout.

I can't stand up any more; I feel faint. *Find him, Papa; please find him.*

He does! He's got him. He's pulling him back. One arm round Michel's neck; the other splashing through the water. I pace up and down the wall, crying, begging God to let him be alive.

Help me, Pierre, Papa shouts up at me as he approaches the wall. I lean down but I don't know what he wants me to do. Papa pushes Michel up. I grab him from under the armpits but I can't move him; he's too heavy for me. Papa climbs out of the water, then, pushing me off, pulls Michel up. He lays him on his back. Michel looks like a ghost, his face horribly white, his lips blue. Papa pinches open his mouth and breathes into him. He thumps him on his chest. He repeats it over and over again.

I don't know what do with myself. I grab fistfuls of my hair. And still Papa carries on, sobbing, getting more frantic. Michel doesn't move. I will his chest to go up and down but nothing moves.

Michel, Michel, screams Papa so loud I think the forest will fall round our ears. *Michel, my son, my son...*

He staggers to his feet, his knees bent like an old man in a nursery rhyme. Next to him, like a rag doll, Michel lies still, utterly, utterly still.

Why didn't you save him? Papa cries. *Why couldn't you have...* His words trail off into great, giant sobs.

I tried, I weep. But Papa, collapsed next to Mickey, doesn't hear me. *I tried.*

I see something yellow and green nearby. It's Munchie. I pick him up and hug him as tightly as I can while, all around me, darkness descends.

Chapter 22

'I'm sorry, Michel; I'm sorry.' Retrieving his bag, now covered in dry dust, Pierre walked along the sand. It soon came to an end, and he was faced with a bank teaming with vegetation. Pulling himself up by a root, he realised what a task laid ahead of him. Each step now involved concentration, pushing back bushes, stepping over roots, ducking under low-lying branches. The sound of the lapping water, to his left, never far away, made him more anxious by the minute. He thought back to the stories he read as a child, of famous French explorers battling through the unknown jungles of the Dark Continent. He tried to remember them, tried to keep his mind busy.

He slipped. Trying to retain his balance on the wet bank, he only slewed further. Skidding down the bank, he grabbed clusters of grass and managed to stop himself slipping into the lake. Regaining his balance he stood and eyed the water lapping at his feet.

They buried him three days later – on the southern side of the church. Father de Beaufort had led the service.

Pierre had never seen a coffin before but he was surprised by how small it was. He tried not to think of his brother within. Pierre had only a vague memory of the day; his mother convulsed in sobs, his father speechless with grief. People shook their hands, offered their condolences, but not to him, not to Pierre. No one spoke to him; no one looked at him. It was as if he wasn't there. His father blamed him; he never said it again, he didn't have to, once was enough – *Why didn't you save him?* Pierre knew that how ever long he lived, he'd never be able to erase those words from his memory. It took weeks before Lucienne stopped laying a place for Michel at the kitchen table. She would sit for hours at a time in Michel's bedroom, burying her face into his clothes, breathing in his aroma. Each day she'd go to church but she never came back any happier. Pierre had given her Munchie. She washed it under the tap, then, to remove the dirt from her fingers, she washed her hands – again and again. And ever since, she'd been obsessed about washing her hands, and whenever she felt under strain, it was to the sink she'd go. His father spent his time in the yard building a second shed though they had no need for another. Pierre went to school everyday and returned in the afternoons with no recollection of anything the teachers had said. They never upbraided him for failing to do his homework, for failing to listen. His friends avoided him, not wanting to be contaminated by his grief. His parents never asked him how he was, how his day had been. They lived in silence, unable to speak to one another. All the time, he longed for his mother to hug him, to reassure him that everything was OK. But, more than anything, he longed for his father to say that it wasn't his fault. He never did.

Once he heard children playing outside the house. His heart caved in, thinking for a moment he'd heard Michel's shrill voice.

Weeks later, they erected a little cross at Michel's grave with his name. Pierre and his father never visited it except once a year, the anniversary of his death, when Lucienne took Georges and Pierre there to stand and remember. Lucienne still went almost every day.

He gazed across the water. How calm it looked now. He wondered whether Michel's spirit was still out there. Could he have done more; could he have saved him? He felt lightheaded, dizzy almost. He placed one foot into the water, then the other, the water seeping through his shoes. He never did learn to swim. He'd swim now though; he'd find Michel. Removing his jacket, he threw it behind him onto the bank. The icy shards of water bit into his ankles, into his calves, but still he placed one foot in front of the other. He had to save him; he couldn't fail him a second time; not this time. He realised he was crying, his tears clouding his vision. 'Michel?' he screamed. 'Michel, where are you?' The water now reached the belt of his trousers, lapping around him. His hands skimmed the surface, causing ripples. Wiping away the tears, he scanned the lake, looking for movement. 'Mickey,' he yelled. 'I'm sorry.'

A voice, faraway, it seemed, echoed his screams. 'Michel, Michel, is that you?'

Someone was behind him, splashing. Turning, he saw his father wading through the water. He stopped. 'Oh my dear Lord, I thought...' Throwing his head back, his eyes clenched shut, his mouth opened but there was no sound.

'It wasn't my fault, Papa; I didn't mean to...'

Another voice filtered through. 'Georges, no. Who is

Michel?' That voice – it was the major, Major H. 'It's Pierre,' said the voice, the major. 'Your son, Pierre, not Michel.'

What was that sound, that clawing, frightening sound? He wished it would stop; that screaming; he didn't like it. 'Nooo, no, it's Michel; it's my son; the Lord has delivered him back. My son…'

*

Pierre opened his eyes. He found himself inside a shack of some sort, walls made up of wooden planks. To his right, lying on the wooden floor, the major, soaked through, shivering. On his left, hunched up on a child's wooden chair, also wet, his father. Opposite, perched up on a stool with a rifle on his lap was Kafka.

'He's awake,' he heard Kafka say.

'Pierre, are you OK, son? How are you feeling?'

Someone, presumably his father, had covered him with a blanket. 'Fine, I guess.'

'Here, Foucault, give him some water,' said the major.

'*Monsieur* Foucault to you,' said Kafka. 'Georges, give him that bottle.'

Pierre took the water while taking in his surroundings. Against one wall was a stove with its black flue rising half way up the wall, a bucket of coal beside it; in the corner a bed, next to it, an upturned crate for a bedside table, a paraffin lamp on top. A simple table showed remnants of a meal, metal plates piled on top of each other, a couple of tin mugs, an empty beer bottle. Next to the table, a couple of sturdy-looking chairs. A coil of rope, along with a number of coats and jackets, hung from a large brass hook on the back of the door. On the wall, above a low-lying sink, a portrait of Joan of Arc and a calendar displaying the month of April 1939. Next to them, a crucifix. Somehow, Pierre knew it was the one Kafka had taken from the dead German on New Year's Day in 1918. He looked round for his bag but it was nowhere to be seen.

'What happened?' asked Pierre.

'You fainted in the water,' said Georges, his voice distant. 'We'd heard your screams from here, calling out his name. I'm sorry if…'

'It's OK,' he said, knowing it was far from OK. 'I don't understand, what are you all doing here?'

'Ask him,' said the major.

'And I will tell you,' said Kafka. 'It's simple – your father and I have taken your major as hostage.'

'I'm not part of this,' said Georges.

Kafka laughed again. 'Think the Krauts will believe that? Come on, Georges. All for one, one for all.'

'Trust me with the gun then.'

'Yeah, like I did in 1918. I think not. The Krauts sent your major and a couple of lackeys to find me. That traitor, Dubois, was their guide. I shot the fucking lot of them.'

'As well as the soldier in the square,' added the major. 'You'll never get away with this.'

'Shut up. Your, not totally unexpected, appearance is fortuitous, boy.'

'How did you get away from the town hall?'

'They killed Bouchette; shot him in the back, the murderers. I got away thanks to that truck getting in the way, and got to my *getaway car*.' He said the words in an ironic tone. 'OK, it was the slowest thing on Earth but it brought me enough distance.'

'Hector and Albert's truck.'

'I was going to send your father, but it'd be better if you act as our messenger.' He spoke quickly. 'Go to Colonel Eisler and tell him – release the prisoners from his jail and he can have his major back.'

Kafka's words and the hopelessness of his situation galvanised Pierre. Throwing off the blanket, he leapt to his feet.

'But that's just stupid – as soon as you hand the major back, he'll re-arrest them and have them shot.'

'He does that and your friend here will be a dead man, you mark my words, there'd be no hiding. They won't want to lose a major – far too senior. A private, yes, they're two a penny, but a major with all those years of training and experience, no.'

'The Germans, they killed Monsieur Clément – in the square, in front of everyone.'

'Monsieur Clément? No,' said Georges.

'It was horrible. And they've taken hostages.'

'What?'

'Six hostages, including Claire.' The mention of Claire brought both the major and Georges to their feet. 'If you don't return the major by midday tomorrow, they'll be shot also.'

'You must give yourself up,' shouted the major.

Kafka slid off his stool, gripping his rifle, his face screwed with hatred. 'All the more reason for the boy to get back there and tell them our terms.'

'How do you know I won't just lead them back here?'

The gunshot took them all by surprise. Instinctively, they ducked. A black hole smouldered in the wooden wall just above Georges's head. 'You try it, and it won't just be the major with a hole in his head. You understand? OK, so a few people get shot. Such is war. They'll die in the name of sacrifice.'

'Steady, Kafka,' said Georges. 'The boy said they had Claire.'

'Good, she deserves to be shot, the slut. It was she who denounced us, told the Germans our plans.'

'No,' said Pierre. 'It wasn't Claire; it was never Claire.'

'What? What are you saying?'

'Was it you, Pierre?' asked his father. 'Did you tell the Germans?'

Kafka shook his head in disbelief. 'You're weak. Sucking up to the Krauts. Like father, like son.'

Georges stepped forward. 'I've had twenty-two years of this. Murder is murder, you pig. The rules of war—'

'The rules of war! There are no rules in war. Get back, all of you, get back.' The veins throbbed in his neck, his bestial eyes glared.

But Georges didn't step back, inching towards Kafka, his eyes red with pain. 'You killed that boy in cold blood. I've lived with his memory all these years.'

'Proves my point – you're weak, sentimental. Get back or I'll shoot you now.'

'Papa, get back, please,' screamed Pierre.

Kafka, so concentrated on Georges, didn't see it coming. In a flash, the major was on him, seizing him by the waist. The two men fell but Kafka, holding onto his rifle, was too fast for the German, pushing the major down. He punched him in the chest. Nimbly, rising to his feet, he lifted his rifle and smashed it into the major's face. The major fell onto his back, blood streaming from his cheek. Kafka spun his rifle round, taking aim at him. The major covered his face.

'No,' cried Pierre, leaping onto the major, trying to smother him.

'Pierre, stop,' screamed Georges.

Kafka, with the rifle ready to shoot, shouted at Pierre, 'Stand aside, boy, now.'

'Get off me, Pierre,' groaned the major. 'Don't do it. Just get off.'

'You harm my son…' Kafka turned to face Georges, just as Georges's fist caught him on the chin; just at the moment the gun went off. This time, Kafka fell back. Georges leapt on him before Kafka had chance to right himself. Both men fought for the rifle, grunting, trading ineffectual blows. Pierre stood up, wanting to help but, with a jolt, realised he was afraid. He looked to the major for support. The German staggered to his feet only to fall again, his eyes glazing over, blood pouring from his shoulder. The stray bullet had caught him. Pierre looked round, searching for something, anything, to help. The chair. Get the chair. Georges and Kafka screamed at each other, the rifle spinning loose, sliding across the floor. Both men leapt for it, each preventing the other from reaching it. Calmly now, Pierre picked it up, nestled the butt against his shoulder and pointed it at Kafka.

'OK, OK,' said Kafka, extricating himself from Georges. Puffing his cheeks, he rose to his feet, raising his hands. 'What now, eh?' He stood, hands in the air, his chest heaving. 'Durand and son; turncoats, each as fucking useless as the other.'

Georges, too, got up, dabbing the blood from his lips, stepping to one side.

'Shut up, Kafka.'

Kafka laughed. 'So, are you going to do the Germans'

work for them again and shoot me then, Pierre, like I taught you? Remember?'

'No, I'll do it; nothing I wouldn't like better.' It was the major, panting, leaning against the chair, his face white, accentuated by the deep red hole in his left shoulder.

'Let the boy, do it,' said Kafka, slowly putting his arms down. 'Let's see if he's man enough.'

'Put your hands back up,' ordered Georges. 'Pierre, give me the gun.'

'Man enough? People always want me to be a man.' He was speaking in a whisper, to himself. *'Pierre, you're just a boy. We need men, not children. Come back when you've become a man. He's only a kid.* If this is being a man, I'd rather stay a child.' He tried to focus but realised his tears were obscuring his vision.

'Here, Major, tie him up.' Georges threw the German the coil of rope.

Distracted momentarily by the rope, they didn't see Kafka's hand as it went to his back pocket. Backing against the wall, he pointed his revolver at Pierre, clicking off its safety catch. The two of them faced each other, their guns trained on the other, Georges and the major either side, the German holding the rope. Transfixed by the black hole of the revolver's barrel, Pierre's vision blurred. He knew he could never pull the trigger, even to save his life; the rifle was as useless in his hands as a stick. 'Don't do it,' said the major. 'Like you say, he's still only a boy.'

Kafka's eyes darted from one to the other, his revolver still trained on Pierre, snorting like a bull.

'Please, Kafka, I beg you. I've lost one son, don't take the other.'

It took but a second. The barrel in his mouth, the shot;

Kafka on the wooden floor, the splatter of blood and brain on the wall behind him

The three of them stood in silence, gaping at the fallen figure, the revolver still in his hand.

'Pierre? Pierre, you can put the gun down now.'

But Pierre didn't hear his father. Images flashed through his mind – Claire's ashen face as she was led away, Tintin at the moment he knew death was about to come, Monsieur Roché with his skull caved in, the exhausted Algerian killed like a dog. *Vive la Framce*. Michel. Poor Michel, at the bottom of the lake, dead at six. The rifle felt heavy now, his arms weak. Gently, a pair of hands circled round the barrel, taking its weight. He saw the glint of the signet ring.

'It's OK, Pierre,' came the reassuring German accent. 'It's over now. It's over.'

Chapter 23

There were perhaps two dozen or more of them, crammed into the waiting area at Gestapo headquarters in Saint-Romain. Parents, spouses, children, siblings. A soldier stood guard at the door kept open on a latch. The atmosphere inside, although tense and full of anticipation, was jovial. They had all believed they would never see their loved ones again yet, here they were, within minutes of being reunited. Everyone seemed to have dressed up for the occasion, the men in suits and ties, the women in their best frocks. Pierre too had worn his father's smart jacket with a blue-collared shirt and matching tie; his mother having helped tie it while he tried to flap her hands away. At least he had managed to persuade her that he didn't need her to accompany him to Saint-Romain. They had gathered earlier in the town square to catch the bus. They greeted each other with hugs and tears. People slapped Pierre's back and shook his hand; the women kissed him – congratulating him on having such a brave father. Pierre, like many of the others, bore a bunch of flowers, wild flowers plucked from the village hedgerows. The mayor would have disapproved having issued a ban on such activities. But nothing mattered – their loved ones had been spared the bullet, the sun was shining and the world seemed a better place. Major Hurtzberger, Georges and Pierre had left Kafka's body in his lakeside shack. Later in the day, four privates were sent to retrieve it. What happened to it after that, no one knew and no one cared. On receiving back his major, Colonel Eisler called off the town gathering and declared that the six hostages would be released from Saint-Romain at midday.

There had been similar outpouring of emotion when Georges, Pierre and the major returned home. On seeing them, Lucienne cried. And then carried on crying for hours, thanking God, unable to speak coherently, hugging all three of them in turn. It was, she said between sobs, the happiest day of her life. A bottle of red wine was opened, toasts made. Retiring to her bedroom, Lucienne returned a couple minutes later, in her yellow dress, having stuffed, she said, the black dress to the back of the wardrobe. 'I hope not to see that hideous garment again until the day I have to bury Georges.'

'Lovely,' said Georges.

'And let's hope,' said the major, lifting his glass, 'that's not for many, many years to come.'

'Absolutely,' she purred, planting a kiss on her husband's cheek.

Pierre smiled at the memory. The mood in the waiting room became almost hysterical with good cheer. The men swapped jokes, the mothers reminisced about their children growing up, husbands recounted their first dates, wives their wedding days. Even the guard was unable to keep a straight face. Pierre had no history with Claire, and providing an account of boyhood lust and a solitary kiss didn't seem appropriate somehow. A sudden hush descended over the room at the sight of the receptionist, Mademoiselle Dauphin, with her tight skirt, pink nails and bright red lipstick, approaching them. 'Monsieurs, mesdames,' she said, enjoying the moment. 'If you would care to follow me.'

After numerous rounds of 'after you'; 'no please, after *you*', the gathering tumbled past the grinning guard and followed Mademoiselle Dauphin into the courtyard. Despite the jovial mood, a chill ran through Pierre, remembering all too well the last time he'd seen this place with its red brick flooring, its laurel hedge. Along the far wall of creeping ivy, standing to attention under the shade, eight German soldiers, with their rifles against their shoulders. He felt weak all of a sudden, dizzy almost.

'You all right, Pierre?' said Madame Bonnet.

'Something's wrong,' he muttered.

'Wrong? What on earth could go wrong now?'

An arrow of terror struck Pierre's being – this was their shooting range; it was a trick; they were going to shoot the hostages after all. They weren't here to welcome back their loved ones, but as witnesses to their deaths.

'Oh, Lord, no.'

Madame Bonnet had already disappeared, her arms round a friend, giggling with excitement. There was nothing he could do; no way out; they were trapped. With every sense on full alert, he heard the click of the door latch open. They all turned to see the hostages file out, under German escort, one after the other. Screams of delight ensued as they were engulfed by their loved ones.

Claire was last to appear, in her polka dot red dress, now crumpled, her face pale. She waved on seeing Pierre, an embarrassed little gesture, and came towards him, almost stumbling. Pierre pushed his flowers at her but couldn't bear to look at her; too fearful of the soldiers against the wall, distracted by their hateful expressions.

'I can't take these,' she said handing them back to him. 'Everyone despises me. I killed Clément.'

'You had no choice.'

'No, but… Pierre, are you OK?'

He looked up to the balcony, to where he had been, to see if he could spot Colonel Eisler looking down on proceedings. He dropped the flowers.

'What's the matter?' she asked, her expression streaked with concern.

Around him, people embraced, laughing, crying with such gaiety, such joy.

'Claire…' He didn't know what to say. Taking her hand, he pulled her to one side, yet knowing that these four walls offered no escape.

'Pierre, you're worrying me now.'

'When I say get down, lie down and I'll lie on top of you. I'm sorry; it's all I can do. I'm so sorry.'

'For what, Pierre? Tell me, for what?

'Attention!' The word rang out across the yard, bringing with it immediate silence. It was Colonel Eisler. Pierre's hand tightened on Claire's. 'It's lovely to see such celebrations, but we have work to do. So I ask you kindly to make your way out now please. Mademoiselle Dauphin will escort you. Good day.'

With a wave and a kindly smile, Mademoiselle Dauphin beckoned everyone to follow her. The soldiers next to the wall remained static, their expressions unchanged. Still laughing, the gathered trotted back inside, and along the ground floor corridor. Last in line were Claire and Pierre, Pierre continually glancing behind but slowly daring to hope that they were free.

He wandered slowly down the corridor, falling behind the others, Claire looking at him with a puzzled expression.

'I think we're OK now,' he said, hardly able to breathe.

'I don't understand. Did you... did you think they were...?'

He nodded.

'You said you would have lain on top of me. You...' Pierre felt Claire's hand. 'Come on, let's get out of here.'

The others had disappeared.

'Pierre, I have to leave.'

'Leave what?'

'This town. I'll go back to Paris.'

'Oh, there you are.' It was Mademoiselle Dauphin, holding a clipboard to her chest. 'I thought I'd lost you for a moment. Unless you particularly want to extend your stay, Mademoiselle Bouchez, I'd recommend you and your friend follow me.'

'With pleasure,' said Pierre.

They stood outside, alone, exposed to a shower. Pierre looked back at the grey, foreboding building, a guard standing at the door, oblivious to the rain. He hoped never to see the place, or Colonel Eisler, again.

'Do you have to leave?' he asked.

'You should have heard them in there. The names they called me.' She shook her head. 'I can't stay. They'll never forgive me for what I did; they'll never forget.'

'Take me with you.'

Chapter 24

Perched high above them on a branch, a pigeon cooed. Madame Picard passed by, walking her little terrier, stopping to allow the dog to sniff. She waved on seeing Pierre and Xavier resting against the tree across the green, opposite the library. They waved back.

'How long now?' asked Xavier.

'About five minutes, I think.'

'She must love her work to want to go back straightaway.'

'She's not going back. She just wanted to collect her things.'

'Must have been difficult, thinking, you know, this could be my last night on earth.'

'Yeah.'

'But you, eh? You got the girl in the end?'

Pierre tried to smile. 'I guess.'

'Well, you're one lucky chap, Pierre Durand. Horrible business, though, wasn't it? Everyone was worried about your papa. Has he spoken to you about it?'

'Papa? Speak to me about anything? Hardly.'

'People are saying all sorts of things. How he singlehandedly found Kafka out on that lake, and the wounded major, and killed him. Claire and the others, how do they express their thanks for something like that? I mean, hell, if it wasn't for your papa, they'd be…'

'Yeah, I know.'

'How is he?'

'He's at home at the moment, doing a stone for Monsieur Clément.'

'Oh yeah. Poor old sod.' Xavier pulled up a few blades of grass. 'Fancy a fag?'

'Not really.'

Xavier took a blade of grass and, holding it between the tips of his thumbs, blew on it, producing a high-pitched whistle sound. 'How's that thing of yours?' he asked between whistles. 'What do you call it? The Black Maria thing?'

'Oh that. I don't know if I can be bothered with it any more.'

'You should. It's good.'

'I'm not sure. I think I should have started on something… I don't know.'

'A little bit less ambitious?'

'Yes, that's it. Something a little bit less ambitious.'

'Come on, she should be coming out now.'

'Hopefully.'

They got to their feet and stretched.

'I know,' said Xavier, 'let's have a race. To the library wall and back. Oh no, I'm sorry, I forgot, it's too childish for you now.'

'No, it's not that.'

'What is it then?'

'I wouldn't want to embarrass you. I'd beat you too easily.'

'You… What? Right, that's it.'

'Get ready then. On your marks, get set… go!'

'Hey, I wasn't ready. That's unfair!'

Thus, almost tripping over with laughter, the two boys sprinted across the soft grass of the green, with the wind in their hair, the sun on their backs. Claire appeared, her yellow dress flapping slightly. She stood with her back to the library wall and watched, smiling, as the two boys sprinted towards her. She squealed as Pierre, on seeing her, ran straight at her. Slamming his hands against the wall either side of her, he leant forward, planted a kiss on her lips, before racing back to the tree. And there, bending over, catching their breaths, hands on each other's shoulders, Pierre and Xavier laughed, at nothing really, just the pure delight of being there, of being young and alive.

*

Major Hurtzberger stood in the centre of the living room in full uniform, his suitcase and a shoulder bag at his feet, scanning the room, knowing he would probably never see it again. Georges, Lucienne and Pierre were with him, also on their feet, making the room seem rather small. 'Well, this is it,' he said, with a sigh.

'We shall miss you,' said Lucienne, her hands clasped as if in prayer.

'Yes, well. I shall miss you too.' He cleared his throat. 'I know it hasn't always been easy; I am your enemy, after all. My presence here could not be under more unfavourable conditions. Yet… yet, I could never have asked for kinder, more generous hosts. And for that, I thank you all.'

'You've done a lot for us, though, Major,' said Georges. He had changed into his corduroy jacket and canvas trousers, as if to mark the occasion.

'Perhaps.'

'You will come to visit us, won't you, Major? I mean, after all this is over.'

'Oh, Lucienne, there would be nothing on earth that I would like better.'

Pierre frowned, trying to work out whether that was, essentially, a 'yes'.

'Oh, would you mind?' The major rummaged in his bag. 'I've been given this,' he said, holding up a camera. 'A gift from the men, a going away present. Could I…'

'Yes, by all means,' said Lucienne. 'Where would you like us to stand?'

'Just here, next to the fireplace. Now, which button is it? Ah, here we are.'

The three of them hunched together in front of the fireplace, Pierre in the middle, his father's hand resting awkwardly on his shoulder. 'I haven't had my photograph taken in years,' he muttered. Lucienne fluffed up her hair and grimaced in her attempt to smile.

'Ready?'

'*Ready.*'

Click.

'Perhaps one more – just in case. Keep still…' Click. 'Lovely.'

'Thank you, Thomas.'

'And now, I ought to go.'

'You sure you don't want us to come with you?'

'It's very kind of you, Georges, but no, I think best not.

It wouldn't do to be seen waving off the enemy, would it?'

'No, I guess not.'

The major patted his pockets. 'Oh, before I go, I wonder if I could have a final look at your White Venus, Pierre?'

'Really? OK.'

'White Venus?' said Georges. 'Is that what you call that thing out there?'

'Leave him be, Georges. If it amuses him…'

'Come,' said the major. 'Come with me, Pierre.'

Late afternoon, and the yard was half in the shade, the chickens sticking to the cooler side. The major inspected the sculpture as if seeing it for the first time, circling it, considering it. 'Very good,' he said, rubbing his chin. 'May I take a picture of it?'

Pierre shuffled on his feet. 'If you want. I don't…'

'Yes?'

'I don't really like it any more. It's nothing like the painting.'

'Rubbish, it's an excellent piece of work; you should be proud. Do you think Botticelli managed it in one go?' He took his photograph. 'No, he probably worked on it for months, years even. I'm sorry the town hall said no. I think it would have graced the reception area very nicely. Here, let me take another with you next to it. Go on; don't be shy. That's it. Smile, Pierre, give us a smile. That's it. Good lad.' He turned the camera round in his hands. 'Am I meant to switch this thing off, I wonder? You know, Kafka has been buried.'

'No.'

'This morning. In an unmarked grave'

'Oh.' Bouchette, Dubois and Kafka – all dead.

'Why are all your tools here?'

Pierre hadn't noticed but the various shovels, brooms, sledgehammer and hoe were all lined up neatly against the shed wall. 'Perhaps Papa's having a sort out now that's he's started working again.'

'I see that you've become close to Claire.'

Pierre nodded, not sure how to respond.

'That's good. I'm sorry that I…'

'It's… it's fine.'

'You know, don't you? It wasn't her fault. I knew she was under orders and I took advantage of that. If I'd know you were…'

'It's fine,' he repeated.

The major covered his embarrassment with a smile. 'She's a charming girl. You'll make a lovely couple. I'll be expecting an invite now.'

'Sorry?'

'To the wedding.'

Pierre laughed politely, hoping the conversation would end.

'Pierre, listen. I want to give you something.' Placing the camera on the rocking chair, he slid his ring off his finger and held it out in his palm.

'Me? You want me to…?'

'It would have been for Joachim, as you know, but…'

'I… I'm not sure.'

'Please, it would be an honour. You are very much alike my Joachim; you remind me of him in so many ways, I'm sure I've told you. It would make me happy to know you wore his ring.'

Pierre took it.

'Try it on.'

'It fits. Different finger to yours but it fits.'

'Perfect.'

'I'll… Thank you. I shall wear it always.'

The major glanced up at the sky. 'And now, I really ought to be going.'

*

The major had gone, handshakes all round, an embrace and a peck on the cheek with Lucienne, closing the door gently behind him. Georges, Lucienne and Pierre sat in the living room, an air of gloom hanging over them, unable to find anything to say. Pierre had slid the ring off and secreted it in his pocket. He couldn't face telling them why he had it. Not yet.

Eventually, Georges broke the silence. 'I wonder whether they'll send us another guest.'

'I hope not,' said Lucienne. 'Despite the extra food, it's somebody else's turn. I want Michel to have his room back to himself now.'

'Hmm.' He patted his knees. 'Well, this is no good. Did you say you were going out shopping?' Lucienne nodded. 'I think I'll come with you. It'll give me something to do. Did he take his camera?'

Immediately, Pierre could see it in his mind's eye. 'Oh no,' he yelped, springing to his feet. Dashing out in the yard, he saw it where the major had left it, on the rocking chair.

Georges had followed him out. 'Is it there?'

'Yes. What do we do?'

'Well, run after him, of course. He wouldn't have got far with that suitcase. Hurry up, then!'

Pierre rushed out the house, slipping the ring back on.

The major had said a car was taking him from the town hall to the train station at Saint-Romain. He ran up the hill, round the bend and towards the town square. As he approached the square, he could see the car with its swastika pennant, a private, doubling up as a chauffeur, lifting the major's suitcase into the boot. The major, next to the car, was shaking hands with another officer. The two men parted with a Hitler salute. Pierre waved. The major hadn't seen him. The major strode stepped away from the car, as if preparing himself for the journey ahead, pulling the creases out of his tunic.

'Major! Major Hurtzberger.'

This time, the major saw him. Walking quickly towards him, he shouted, 'Pierre, is everything OK? What's wrong?'

Pierre caught him up, slightly abashed to be so out of breath. 'Your camera. You forgot your camera.'

'Oh, thank you!' He took it. 'Silly me. Thank you so much.' The two of them stood facing each other, not sure what to say. 'That's my car.'

'Yes. Your driver's waving at you.'

The major glanced back, acknowledging the summons. 'Yes, I'd better go.'

'Yes.'

'This is it then, Pierre. I hope, one day... You're a good boy.'

'Goodbye, Major H.'

'Major H, yes.'

Pierre offered his hand, another handshake. The major ignored it and, stepping closer, flung his arms round him. Pierre, unable to reciprocate, stood with his arms hanging at his side. The major smelt clean – aftershave and soap.

'Goodbye, my boy. I shall miss you.'

Pierre watched him as he marched quickly back to the car, clutching his camera. The driver, waiting at the wheel, started the engine. The major got into the back, closed the door behind him, and wound down the window, looking straight ahead. The driver eased the car off, round the green, round where once had stood the statue of Soldier Mike, and onto the road to Saint-Romain, its pennant flapping gently in the breeze. With his breaths coming in short gasps, Pierre watched the car disappear into the heat rays of the late afternoon. The major didn't look back.

*

Pierre returned home almost in a daze, feeling like a drunk man. Images, uninvited, sprung into his consciousness, of playing with Michel in the fields behind the house, flying a kite, of his father pulling his brother out of the lake, his fist beating Michel's chest, giving him the kiss of life – *Why didn't you save him?* The words, the accusation, had always haunted him. *Why didn't you save him?* He thought of Joachim, killed at nineteen; of the major's last words, calling him 'my boy'.

He stopped, his head pounding. Someone passed by, a woman with a walking stick, a breezy greeting. He wiped his forehead with the back of his hand, felt the unfamiliar gold of the ring scrape his brow. *Generations of my family were cavalrymen.*

He staggered home. The sculpture. He'd only done it for his father, a means by which to finally supplant Michel from the forefront of his affections. It hadn't worked; nothing would work. He knew that now. The major would never see it again, would never see the final work. His mother had never shown any interest, and his father… he was more interested in the chickens. It was Michel he was saving from the water yesterday; Michel, not he, not Pierre. The wrong son. A memory – that of Georges playing with Michel, running round the house, playing hide and seek, Michel almost falling over with such laughter. His brain was full of such memories – Georges and Michel. Michel and Georges. But never him. Not a single one. He kissed the ring.

He burst into the house and found it empty. They'd gone shopping. He raged from room to room, pent up energy threatening to overcome him. He wanted to hurt him, to hurt his father. He gripped his hair, told himself to calm down. Yes, Michel had been the favourite but only by the virtue of his death. It was natural. But why then, this pain, this stabbing of his heart?

He went through the kitchen and out into the yard. The chickens fled upon his arrival. There she stood, the White Venus, her face still without features, mere hollows where her eyes should be. The White Venus – *is that what you call that thing out there?* She was still anonymous, still just a block of sandstone. And how he hated her. She'd known all along that it had been a pointless exercise. *I am not a work of art*, she seemed to be saying, jibing him. *I am a work of desperation. You can't manipulate me, just as you can't manipulate your father. You're weak. Like father and son. Weak.*

'Yes, I am weak,' he said through clenched jaws. 'I let him drown, and no one's listened to me since.' With rapid movements, he scooped up the sledgehammer, taking its weight and bracing himself. With a mighty sideways swing, he smashed it against her head. A cloud of splinters burst; a crack appeared, running from her ear to her throat. A second blow, the head flew off, crashing against the yard wall with a satisfying thud. The chickens squawked. 'I am not weak,' he screamed as he delivered a third blow, a fourth, a fifth. His chest heaving, his hands dry with dust, he carried on and on until like a snowman melted to its core, only a stump of the White Venus remained. Finally, panting, unable to see with dust and sweat in his eyes, he dropped the sledgehammer. He felt sick; he felt evil; he felt triumphant. Wiping away the sweat, he viewed the chaos he'd created, white dust everywhere, the fragments, the shards and bits of sandstone, scattered across the ground. Tears came to his eyes. The White Venus was no more; he'd killed her, and much more besides. He had no need for her any more; he had Claire, his very own White Venus.

He heard the front door open. His parents were home.

THE END

For a list of all fiction and non-fiction by Rupert Colley, visit **rupertcolley.com**.

Printed in Poland
by Amazon Fulfillment
Poland Sp. z o.o., Wrocław